GALLANT MATCH

JENNIFER BLAKE

GALLANT MATCH

MIRA®

MIRA®

Recycling programs
for this product may
not exist in your area.

ISBN-13: 978-0-7783-2619-9
ISBN-10:   0-7783-2619-5

GALLANT MATCH

Copyright © 2009 by Patricia Maxwell.

www.MIRABooks.com

Printed in U.S.A.

For my gorgeous and talented daughters,
Delinda Corbin and Katharine Faucheux,
merci beaucoup for all the seagoing memories.

One

The rain fell with the dreary persistence of a widow's tears. Sonia Bonneval stared through the silver streams that poured from the barrel-tile roof, splattering over the tough leaves of a palmetto and into the courtyard below, joining the small river that swirled along the open stone drain leading to the porte cochere. The droplets slanting down made a copper haze around the pitch-pine torch at that dark, tunnellike entrance to the courtyard. From her concealment behind a tangle of wisteria growing up the gallery post of the *garçonnière*, Sonia searched the opening. At any moment, her father's secret visitor would appear from the blackness like some demon from Hades.

Just moments ago, the dangling bell beside the wicket gate had rung its summons. Eugene, her father's majordomo, spare, precise in his movements and with features older than his thirty years, descended the outside staircase in answer. She could hear him speaking now in deferential greeting, hear a deep voice in response that resonated with strength and purpose. The footsteps of the pair grated on the stone paving, one set a shuffle in slippers designed for quiet, the other a steady, booted stride.

Shadows shifted in the dim mouth of the entrance. They elongated as the two men passed the flaring torchlight and emerged under the arcade that edged the courtyard.

Sonia drew a sharp, silent breath of alarm.

The newcomer was enormous, an impression increased by the long, caped greatcoat that billowed around his ankles. Raindrops glistened upon wool-clad shoulders so wide they seemed to fill the archway. His bell-crowned beaver hat came close to scraping the brick ceiling, and he wore it set straight across his forehead, without the least tilt to give it style. It was impossible to see his features from where she stood above him, but he gripped the cane he carried as if it were a weapon.

Formidable, the man was formidable.

Abruptly, he turned his head, his gaze fastening on the shadows where she stood. He could not see her—surely it was impossible—yet some animal instinct seemed to guide him. She felt nailed in place, as if she might never move again. Her breath stopped in her throat while her heart throbbed against her breastbone with frantic haste. Her skin prickled as at some primitive warning of hazard. The night seemed to grow still, waiting.

Eugene reached the stairs that led to the interior

gallery of the town house. He paused, the dim light from the rooms above sliding over his walnut-colored skin as he looked back at the visitor. "This way, *monsieur*."

The man glanced toward the majordomo. He hesitated a moment longer, then followed after him.

Sonia put a hand to her chest. Her breath rasped in her throat as if she was running, fleeing instead of standing there watching the stranger's unhurried ascent to the second-floor living section of her home.

She should not be here, was not meant to know about the arrival of this midnight guest. How very like Papa to keep it from her, as if she had no say in the matter that brought him. He expected to present the gentleman as a fait accompli, no doubt, relying on good manners to overcome any objection she might make when he was finally introduced.

That was her father's mistake, not that it was surprising. He had never understood her, never had the time to make the effort.

It was always possible the latest applicant for the position her father had in mind would fail to gain favor, that he would be questioned and sent away like all the others. She prayed it transpired that way, but could not depend upon it.

This one was clearly different. He had no look of the vagabond adventurer, Captain Sharp or gambler in need of passage to a more salubrious port. He moved like a man of purpose, one more than capable of fulfilling the duty that might be entrusted to him. He was the very essence of masculine danger.

Sonia drew her India-woven shawl more closely around her shoulders as a sudden chill moved down her spine. That someone suited to the task would appear had always been inevitable, but she had thought to have more time. Her plans must be set in motion at once. She could delay no longer.

The steam packet that traveled between Mobile and New Orleans would make port in a day or two. Pray God an answer from her grandmother was on it, for she knew not what she would do otherwise.

Or was that strictly true? She paused as an idea flickered to life in her mind.

Suppose the gentleman could be dissuaded from accepting the position? That might happen if he took an aversion to his charge, she thought with a frown of concentration. Few gentlemen appreciated a harridan, still less would they care to be cooped up with one for days on end. She could be such a one if necessary. Yes, indeed.

Fortitude and daring might gain her another week, possibly two, though her father's wrath would be difficult to face. She shivered a little at the thought of his cold withdrawal, so much more deadly than simple anger.

She had always dreaded it as a child, the feeling that she had disappointed him and embarrassed herself. She would have done anything to gain his smiles again. It had ceased to hurt so much once she realized his whole purpose was to insure her abject obedience, making her malleable and dependent, but it troubled her all the same.

Dwelling on it served no purpose. By the time he discovered the full extent of her deception, she would be far away. Besides, some things were worth the risk.

On the gallery across the courtyard, Eugene and the visitor paused outside the door of her father's study and smoking room. Eugene relieved him of his outerwear along with his cane, and then opened the study door so he might enter. The gentleman raked a hand through his hair, set his shoulders and walked into the lamp-lighted chamber.

The glimpse Sonia had of his face made her throat close. It was arresting, almost harsh under a thick cap of hair the rich brown color of oak leaves in autumn. His eyes were deep-set, appearing cavernous in the uncertain light, though with a flashing sheen of silver. She recognized in the angular planes of his face and determined jut of his chin a harsh and powerful, almost primitive, form of male beauty that was beyond her experience. And she was appalled at the immediate clench deep in her abdomen in response.

He was American, she thought, most likely a *Kaintuck,* as the French Creoles called those from the wild mountain country of Kentucky and Tennessee. They were a breed apart, so it was said, less mannerly, less gallant in their approach to females than their counterparts in the Vieux Carré. Some were outright ruffians who piloted their keelboats laden with hogs, corn and corn liquor downriver. They used the money they made to carouse through the more squalid sections of the city, drinking, fighting with fists, feet and teeth, indulging in the most disgusting debauchery.

Others of their ilk, Americans from the North and East, might have more polish but still lacked social grace, wit or civilized conversation, seemed to care for nothing except adding to their wealth. Priggish and puritanical, they looked down their long noses at what they considered to be the ungodly habits of French-Creole society. And why, pray? Merely because the gentlemen of the Vieux Carré amused themselves rather than chasing after every *piastre,* because their ladies were fond of fashions *à la Parisienne* and aiding nature by the delicate application of cosmetics.

They also objected to the practice of theaters and gaming houses remaining open on Sundays, these Americans, and to the genteel habit of hostesses providing music for dancing when they arranged a Sabbath soiree. What arrogance, to assume that sitting and staring at each other with plain, solemn faces while buttoned up in unfashionable clothing was more virtuous than dressing well and seeking amusement after one had made one's peace with *le bon Dieu.*

It would be just like her father to select this man for his background alone. Papa would be certain nothing in the man's mien or manner could attract her. He was exactly correct in this instance.

Mère de Dieu, but she must do her utmost to prevent the *Kaintuck* from being chosen.

Stepping back into her bedchamber, which lay behind her, Sonia moved to the fireplace and lit a paper spill at the glowing coals in the grate. She took the flame to the candles in girandoles on either side of her dressing-table mirror, setting them alight. In their bright glow, she appeared pale in contrast to the auburn gleam of her hair. Her eyes were like burning blue holes in her face, circled by lavender shadows. The cause of the strain of the past weeks, she knew, for they had not been easy ones.

Disposing of the spill, she returned to the dressing table. She considered her father's guest a moment longer, her lips set in a thin line. What would he think, she wondered, of a painted harridan?

With sudden resolution, she dropped her shawl and caught the edges of her bodice with both hands, tugging it lower to expose more of the white curves of her breasts. The effect was almost wicked, she thought, which was all to the good. Next, she reached for the small packet of red Spanish papers that lay on the tabletop. She pulled one free, brushing it across her cheekbones with heavy, deliberate strokes and moistening her lips with a quick flick of her tongue before pressing it to their damp surfaces. Still it was not enough. Greatly daring, she brushed the paper across her eyelids, down the curve of her neck and into the cleft shadow between her breasts. There, that was better.

She was using an artist's brush and a little oil to paint the line of her lashes with lampblack when the door opened behind her. She flinched, almost dropping the brush.

"*Chère!* What are you about? You look the very image of a wanton!"

Sonia directed a defiant look at the reflection of the soigné older lady in the doorway. "My exact intention, Tante Lily."

"What can you mean? Your papa will be scandalized."

"It will be worth it if the gentleman with him is the same. Besides, you will know just how to charm Papa and smooth over the situation."

Her aunt and duenna of many years stepped inside and closed the door. "But, no, *chère,*" she said, her features puckered with concern. "Subtlety is everything with such aids to beauty, as I've told you time and time..." She paused in midlecture. "Gentleman? What gentleman is this? I know of no gentleman."

"An American, a *Kaintuck* by his looks. They prefer their women wan and frail, I believe, and covered to their throats like nuns. Painting one's face is frowned upon as the devil's handiwork."

"You wish to give this American a disgust of you? In the name of all the saints, why?"

"So he will refuse the position Papa is offering as we speak. Why else?"

Her aunt put a hand to her temple. "*Tiens,* another candidate as your guard? Perhaps this one will be sent away like all the others."

"I fear not. He is...different."

"But a man all the same, or so one supposes. Should he find favor with your papa, I suspect he will accept the post *tout suite* in hope you may be the loose female you appear. No, truly, *chère,* this will not do."

Sonia gave her handiwork a doubtful look before meeting her aunt's gaze again. "You think I've gone too far?"

"Most assuredly."

Tante Lily was better acquainted with such matters than she. Her aunt had been married twice, widowed twice and was still a fine-looking woman with a number of older gentlemen in regular attendance. These suitors vied for the honor of holding her fan or dance card, offered their arms for assistance with stairs and curb-stones, appeared on her visiting days and entertained her with charming discourse.

They received little encouragement in return. Inde-pendent of nature and means, Tante Lily merely enjoyed being courted, Sonia thought. She might have married a third time except she had given up her household to act as chaperone to Sonia, only child of her sister who had been dead these many years. Her figure was superb due to the efforts of her *corsetière* and dressmaker. Her lustrous hair gave no sign of the strong black coffee used to maintain its golden-brown color and the dark-ness added to her lashes rivaled nature. It was Sonia's dearest ambition to be just like her at the same age. Though she would, if possible, avoid a first marriage, much less a second.

"The effort must suffice," she said now, "for I have no idea how else to discourage the man." Leaving the mirror, she scooped up her shawl from the floor. "With any luck, he will be as moralizing and disapproving as the rest of his kind. Wish me *bonne chance?*"

Her aunt might scold but made little effort to actually curb her charge. "With all my heart," she said, a worried look in her fine brown eyes, "though I still think you're making a mistake."

"If he won't be put off by this display, then I shall have to arrange something else, yes?" Sonia's smile was satirical as she looked back over her shoulder at her aunt. Drawing a deep, sustaining breath, she sailed out the door.

Two

Kerr Wallace rose to his feet as a whirlwind of silk, lace and tantalizing perfume swept into the room. It was polite homage to a lady, his gesture, but also a move of purest alarm. This was surely not the daughter who required an escort to her wedding? Not this creature of fiery hair, flashing eyes and tender white breasts warmed to a pink satin sheen by candlelight?

If so, he'd have his work cut out for him.

Why in God's name couldn't she have been dowdy and meek, with a flat chest and a squint in one eye? He could have dealt with such a female.

He should have known better. A man like Jean Pierre Rouillard would have nothing to do with a plain bride. He'd have the most beautiful, most refined to be found; his pride would demand it if not his conceit.

Monsieur Bonneval, his host, was also on his feet, though a frown sat on his face like disapproval carved in marble. "Sonia, *ma chère,* you interrupt a matter of business. Leave us, if you please."

It was an order; Kerr recognized that easily enough. The lady seemed unimpressed. Coming forward, she held out her hand. "But we have a guest, Papa," she said with only the briefest of glances over her shoulder. "He must be made welcome. Will you not present me?"

"Sonia!"

She paled a little under the hectic color that flushed her cheeks, Kerr noticed. He was sorry to be the cause, saw no reason that it should continue. Besides, he rather resented the implication that he was not a person to be introduced to Bonneval's daughter until well and truly hired for the post under discussion.

"Kerr Wallace, at your service, *mademoiselle*." He bowed over her hand, holding it with light and rather awkward pressure since hers was bare and he had left his own gloves with the butler who had admitted him.

"Enchanted, Monsieur Wallace, and I am Sonia Blanche Amalie Bonneval. I believe you and my father, between you, are arranging my wedding voyage, yes?"

"That's so."

Her fingers were cool and not quite steady in his, as if she held to composure by a thread. He kept his gaze impassive but couldn't help wondering at the cause of it, yes, and at the strain between father and daughter as well. Not that it was any of his affair. He was here for one purpose only. The people involved mattered not at all. No, not even if the lady's touch did send a numbing flash up his arm like a bolt of lightning.

He would have released her but she would not allow it. She clung to his hand while searching his face with wide eyes fringed by lashes that glinted auburn near her eyelids but were oddly black at the tips. They were the blue-gray of a storm sky, he saw, veiled with an illusive tint of periwinkle like the mountain asters of autumn. And like a storm sky, they promised sore problems ahead.

"I am afraid it may be a perilous passage with this terrible threat of war hanging over us," she went on, her hand sliding deeper into his, her skin warming against his callused palm. "You do not shrink from it?"

"Nonsense," Monsieur Bonneval said with the rasp of irritation in his voice. "A few border skirmishes do not make a war. There is nothing whatever to fear."

The lady paid scant attention to her father, which led Kerr to discount much of the man's sternness as bombast. Her concentration was on him. "What of it, *monsieur?* You are in agreement?"

It was all Kerr could do to concentrate on the words falling from her lips with their tender curves and lush, berry-stain surfaces. He could feel his mouth water with the need to taste their sweetness. Staring at them was not the most intelligent thing he'd ever done, but seemed better than allowing his gaze to settle upon the enticing décolletage such a short distance below. Amazingly, he could feel his body responding, stirring as hot blood surged in his veins.

He was also aware of a prickling at the back of his neck, a warning he had learned not to ignore these past few years. It came, he thought, from the tension in her grasp, the intent appraisal he saw in the depths of her eyes.

"Oh, there'll be war," he allowed, his tone even, though a little gruffer than he had intended.

"A dangerous situation then."

"Could be."

"Papa thinks it will not matter, that civilians, particularly females, will be safe enough regardless of what may happen. What think you? Will I be safe?"

Kerr's private opinion was that Bonneval was overconfident about Mexican gallantry. Either that or he had no particular care for his daughter's safety. Such details were no more his business than the discord between the pair. All he required from Bonneval was the job of escorting the future bride. He needed that as his ticket to Mexico and entrée into Rouillard's household, and that was all he needed.

"I doubt your father would deliberately put you at risk," he answered with self-conscious diplomacy.

"You are certain you wish to venture the journey yourself?"

"Always planned on making it. This seems as good a way as any." Plain words, those. Kerr winced away from them in his mind. A lady like this one would be accustomed to more polished phrases, to graceful compliments and assurances of her safety tacked onto every reply like lace around the edges of a Valentine. They weren't in him. He said what he meant and meant what he said. Most of the time, he never gave it a second thought.

"It's unlikely Monsieur Wallace will feel concern, my dear Sonia," her father said with a trace of derision. "He is a *maître d'armes,* after all."

The lady snatched her hand away as if she touched hot coals. "What?"

"A teacher of fencing with his salon on the Passage de la Bourse which runs from rue Saint Louis to—"

"I know where it is! But you can't mean this."

"Come, *ma chère,* you didn't think I would trust your protection to just anyone. You should be delighted to know you will have an expert at swordplay accompanying you, a gentleman intimately acquainted with danger, since you are so certain it awaits you."

"Don't mock me, Papa! How can you think such a one will be acceptable? But you did not think it. You know he will not do."

The lady appeared rigid with distress, her hands clenched into fists at her sides and her color so high her cheeks seemed to flame with it. Her eyes were hot enough to shoot blue lightning and her red lips compressed into a firm line. It was quite a show, particularly the way her breasts strained at the silk that confined them, barely, at her bodice.

Kerr stepped back and crossed his arms over his chest as he waited to see how matters would settle out. If he was pained by her rejection, and he was in some peculiar fashion, he refused to allow it to matter.

Her father leaned over his desk, resting his fingertips on the polished surface. "He is a gentleman who comes with references of the most impeccable, including the personal recommendation of the Condé de Lérida."

"Who was once a sword master himself so has sympathy for their kind. No, and no again! Monsieur

Wallace is obviously a boorish *Kaintuck* without proper
manners or deportment. An hour spent in his company
would be insupportable, much less days on end."

"Control yourself, Sonia. The gentleman is a guest
in this house."

"Not of my choosing. I did not invite him, cannot bear
the thought of having such a one near me on the voyage
to Vera Cruz. Jean Pierre would be as aghast as I am."

"And this war you prattle about, what of it? Think you
a mere dandy who waltzes well and sings praises to
your fair face will be of use if it comes to pass? We must
be practical, your fiancé and I, where you cannot be."

"Surely there is someone of more address, more
grace, or at least less gawky, muscle-bound clumsiness."

"I repeat, the looks and manners of your escort are
not of importance. I need not remind you, I feel sure,
that he is not accompanying you for your pleasure."

There was more, but Kerr barely heard it. *Her
pleasure.* The images conjured up in his mind by the
thought—soft sighs and moans, pale, open thighs,
reaching arms—should be banned by the church, and
probably were. They made his collar feel tight and his
brain hot in his skull. He drew a deep breath in an
attempt to regain command of what were undoubtedly
improper reactions to the woman and the situation.

"But his French, Papa! *C'est atroce!* Truly terrible!
I should go mad if I had to listen to it for so long. And
what of the embarrassment of having him at my side,
obviously attached to me as escort? I cannot tell you
how uncomfortable it would be."

For a moment, there at the beginning, Kerr had almost felt sorry for the lady. Being married off to a man like Rouillard and sent away from her family to a strange country couldn't be easy. As far as he could tell, the match had been arranged by her father who expected her to go along with it. But maybe there was a reason she was still unwed. Could be such a virago was a fine match for a lowlife like Rouillard.

"Then do not tell me. In fact, tell me nothing more." Monsieur Bonneval frowned upon his daughter while leaning over his desk, his face red with anger. "Since you cannot conduct yourself in a becoming manner, you will leave us at once."

"But, Papa!"

"Now, Sonia."

It was an outright command. The lady pressed her lips together while her chest heaved with angry breaths. She divided a last glance of fulminating wrath between her father and Kerr, then whirled in a silken whisper of skirts and swept from the study. The door banged shut behind her.

The silence she left behind her lasted long seconds. Bonneval pinched the skin at the bridge of his nose and closed his eyes, looking suddenly a decade older. Then he shook his head with a dismissive gesture.

"You must forgive my daughter, Monsieur Wallace. She has been without the calming hand of a mother these fifteen years and more. I fear she has been allowed too much her own way by her aunt who took the place of my dear wife as her chaperone. Marriage to Monsieur

Rouillard will cure this ridiculous self-will, yet another reason for proceeding without delay."

The remedy was excessive in Kerr's view, and in spite of his slighted feelings. Not that it was any of his business. "She does seem set against me as her escort."

"She has been set against every man who might be suitable. Pay no attention. Your job will be to see her delivered safely to her future husband. That is all."

"I'd not thought differently."

Bonneval pursed his lips. "My daughter's comments may have led you to believe there could be a social aspect to the position. It's good to see you are aware of the limitations."

In other words, Kerr thought somewhat sourly, he was not to get too cozy with Mademoiselle Sonia Bonneval while aboard the ship. Her father need have no fear. He'd as soon start a flirtation with a she-bear. "Does that mean I'm offered the job?"

"If you care for it," Monsieur Bonneval answered with a grave dip of his head.

"I'll take it." Kerr got to his feet, reaching across the mahogany desk that separated him from his host for the handshake that would seal the agreement.

"Excellent." Bonneval followed suit, though after an instant of hesitation, as if unused to such a gesture or perhaps the instant decision. These aristocratic Creoles, Kerr had discovered, liked to take their time about things.

"When do I start?"

"At once, if you please. The *Lime Rock* out of Vera Cruz docked at the levee this morning. You will make whatever preparation you require then hold yourself ready to depart on its return run."

The time allowed him was limited, only the few days necessary to off-load cargo and take on more. Kerr would make certain it sufficed since another such opportunity was unlikely to come his way. He'd spent years kicking his heels in New Orleans with no word of Rouillard. It had come at last, falling into his lap like a ripe plum in the form of this deal as escort for the man's bride. He had feared he would be too late with his application for the post. Seemed the lady's contrariness had kept it open for him. He was much obliged to her, no matter how she cut up about it. Nothing was going to keep him from boarding that steamer with Mademoiselle Bonneval.

Kerr took his leave with the formality that so gladdened the hearts of these Frenchmen he'd been living among for four years. The majordomo returned his belongings, including his sword cane, and let him out of the wicket gate set into the larger wrought-iron gate of the carriageway. Kerr strode away into the wet night, a frown between his eyes as he gave thought to the arrangements he'd need to make, from checking that he had adequate linen for the sea voyage to shutting down his fencing salon. He had almost reached the corner where the gaslight of a street-lamp on an ornate bracket wavered behind thick glass, when he heard the scuff of footsteps behind him.

He spun with the lithe contraction of hard muscles and wide swing of his unbuttoned greatcoat. The sword hidden in his cane hissed as he drew it in the same swift movement.

"Monsieur!"

Angry astonishment held Kerr transfixed for an interminable instant. He eased from his instinctive swordsman's crouch then. Snapping his sword cane together again, he removed his beaver hat and held the two together against the long skirt of his coat.

"That's a dangerous trick, Mademoiselle Bonneval, coming up behind a man this time of night. You could get yourself killed."

"So I see."

She was pale, her eyes wide in the piquant, diamond shape of her face. She didn't shrink from him, however. She'd thrown a cape over her gown, drawing the hood up to shield her face from the falling rain and view of passersby, but made no real attempt to hide within it. A valiant lady, Mademoiselle Sonia Bonneval, if not a particularly cautious one.

"You wanted a word? Best make it quick, since it can't do your good name any good to be seen on the street with me."

"I am aware." Her voice dropped a degree or two closer to freezing at the irony in his tone. "I wanted… that is, I would ask that you refuse the position offered by my father. I'm sure it's a great inconvenience to you, this journey, and truly, Mexico is not a place for Americans just now."

"Kaintucks, you mean."

"I apologize for the insult of calling you so, and will a thousand times if it may persuade you to what I ask."

He allowed himself a sardonic smile, even as the

raindrops landing on his hair began to slide down his temples. "No insult taken as I happen to be from Kentucky. But this request of yours must be mighty important to you."

"You have no idea. My every hope depends upon it. Please, I beg you, decline this position."

"Tell me why I should."

She searched his face for a long moment, her eyes shadowed with doubt even as the streetlamp picked up flashes of blue-violet fire from their depths. For an instant, Kerr was painfully aware of the rain that pattered around them, the creaking of a shoemaker's sign above a shop down the street, the moist night air that swirled past with its smells of mud, freshly brewed coffee and rain-wet sweet olive blossoms. Her scent was in his nostrils, too, a powdery essence of fine-milled soap, violets and warm, damp woman. His stomach muscles contracted, pulling at his groin with a force that made his eyes water at the corners.

Finally she spoke, as if the words were being dragged from her. "I don't care to be wed. I especially have no desire to become the wife of Monsieur Rouillard."

"You know him, maybe." Kerr refused to be sympathetic, would not allow it to make a difference.

"We were children together. He had spots on his face and bad breath, was the kind of young man who tormented kittens and snapped off the tails from chameleons just to see them break."

"A telling bill of indictment," he said dryly. "Could be he's changed."

"Unlikely." She closed her lips tightly on the word in apparent token of her unwillingness to say more. Her gaze appeared to track the raindrops that trickled along his jawline, plopping onto the wilted collar of his shirt inside his greatcoat.

"But you don't know."

"I know he failed to address himself to me concerning the proposal that I become his wife. He simply told my father he wished it and set a date for my arrival."

"High-handed." Kerr clenched his gloved hand on his sword cane as memories slid through his mind of acts by the gentleman that were even more arrogantly self-serving. Things like lying, cheating, stealing and leaving his friends to die.

"Overconfidence personified, not that I am surprised. He always—" She stopped, drew a deep breath, met Kerr's gaze an instant before looking away again. "But that's not what I meant to say. I won't go to Mexico, won't marry him, so will have no need of an escort, protector, guardian or whatever you may call yourself. There will be no position to be filled. You may as well save yourself the trouble of making ready only to learn your services aren't required."

"Your father seems to believe otherwise."

"He is mistaken."

Kerr was silent a moment while the rain beat down harder upon them, splattering in the gutter, then ran beside the banquette, falling from a balcony into the street, pelting out of the night sky in endless barrage. It dampened the front of her cape so it draped over her breasts in soft fidelity, chilling her so that their tips made small, hard beads beneath the rich purple silk. It would be ruined, that fine cloth, though she seemed not to care.

At least he supposed it was the cold and wet that caused the reaction. It seemed unlikely to be anything that could be chalked up to his presence.

Voice reflective yet a little strained, he said, "Most daughters among your kind have little say in these arrangements, so I've noticed."

"My kind?" She lifted her chin as she stared at him.

"The French, the high-class Creoles of this fair city, the— What is it you call yourselves? Oh, yes. The crème de la crème. Or maybe that other description, *sorti de la cuisse de Jupiter,* those taken from the thigh of old Jupiter himself so descended from the gods."

"You despise us. You think, in your ignorance, that you are better."

"Equal, at any rate."

She flung back her head, a movement that dislodged the hood of her cape so it fell to her shoulders, allowing the rain to bejewel her hair. "It's as well that you won't be traveling anywhere with me."

She was magnificent in her disdain, glorious in her contempt. He wanted nothing in that moment so much as to take her in his arms and wipe both from her mouth, her eyes, her heart. He ached to reach for her, feel her melt against him, to respond to him as she might, and no doubt would, respond to the gentleman she was to marry. He wanted to be worthy, to be seen as valiant in her eyes, to be raised up to reside among the gods and goddesses himself.

And horses might fly.

His attention was caught by black streaks sliding over her cheeks, tracking down her face. He blinked and reached to brush at one with his thumb, watched as its darkness pooled against the callused edge. Her skin, ah, her skin was cool and firm yet so soft that his mouth drew with the need to lick it, taste it, brush his eyelids against its fine grain.

"You're crying black tears," he said, an unaccustomed huskiness threading his voice.

"I'm not crying!"

She dashed a hand at her face, knocking his hand away and smearing the dark color across her cheekbones. He stared, intrigued, as he realized she used face paint that was melting in the rain. He'd heard French-Creole ladies painted, but only noticed it among the actresses and operatic divas at the theater. She had no need of such tricks that he could see, none at all. The ruin of it was funny yet touching in some peculiar fashion, like a mournful clown.

"Look, I'm sorry you're so dead set against being married off," he told her in his most reasonable tone, "but there's nothing I can do. I've been hired for a job. That's all there is to it."

"You're sorry," she repeated, her wet eyes blazing. "I spit on sorrow without heart, sorrow you will not even try to help change!"

Oh, he'd help her all right. He'd see her to her wedding, and afterward…

Afterward was nothing he could promise, not with any certainty.

"You do what you must, Mademoiselle Bonneval, but I'll let your father be the one to dismiss me." He replaced his hat, giving it a firm tug before making her a truncated bow. "Until then, I'll look forward to our journey."

He turned on his booted heel and walked away, leaving her standing there in the rain. The temptation to look back was like a rope halter tied to his head, drawing tighter, pulling at his stiff neck with every step he made.

He didn't do it.

He kept walking, and every stride he took added to his determination. He would see the lady to Mexico and into the arms of Jean Pierre Rouillard if it was the last thing he did.

When that was done…

Well, when that was done, he would finally be his own man. Matters would be different. The lady might well be glad of the aid of an ignorant Kentuckian with an atrocious accent.

Three

Sonia passed through the columned entrance of the Hotel Saint Louis and paused beneath the soaring, stained-glass dome of its famed rotunda. Moonlight, shining down from the massive skylight more than sixty feet above, dappled the marble floor in dazzling patterns in spite of the gas lighting. Dozens of people milled about. The majority were men, though some few were accompanied by ladies gowned for the evening. Their voices echoed against the marble-covered walls of the vaulted space, mingling with the strains of music heard from a string quartet in the second-floor ballroom to create such a din it was almost impossible to be heard. Sonia's Tante Lily whispered while clutching her arm, but though her breath tickled Sonia's earlobe, she could not tell what she was saying.

Ahead of them lay the broad, circular staircase that led to the ballroom, one of the most beautiful in the city. They moved toward it, being mindful of their crinoline-supported skirts that required a wide avenue of progress.

The lingering smells of cigar smoke and perspiration were a reminder that the spacious lobby area was usually the domain of business concerns, the so-called exchange area where auctions were held on alternate Saturdays for everything from stocks and bonds, land and property, to ships' cargoes and slaves. Sonia wrinkled her nose a little as she lifted her skirt to put her foot in its silk slipper on the first stair tread.

"There, you see?" Tante Lily gave her arm a sharp tug as she spoke in more urgent tones. "Don't look now, but I'm sure it's your *Kaintuck.*"

The urge to glance around was almost overpowering. Sonia continued up the stairs in stringent resolve, however, waiting until its graceful sweep allowed her to look out over the open lobby in the direction her aunt indicated.

Monsieur Kerr Wallace was not difficult to locate. He stood head and shoulders above most of those around him, a mountain of a man not unlike those that must be his home. His evening dress was adequate; his hair had the gleam of polished leather in the gaslight. And his eyes, as he followed her progress, were like rain-wet slate, dark as the night outside.

Sonia's heart stuttered in her chest. The heat rising into the rotunda was suddenly suffocating, leaving her breathless. A confusion of anger, despair and fascination boiled up from somewhere inside her.

She had not realized she had halted until her aunt stumbled against her. It was a good thing her hand was clamped on the railing or they might both have fallen. That would have been embarrassing beyond anything.

"Take care, *ma petite*," her aunt exclaimed as she steadied herself. "But I have it right, yes? It is he? I wonder what he does here."

"It's a public hotel. I suppose he may visit whomever he pleases."

"It occurs to me the street of the sword masters is mere steps away. No doubt they make good use of the hotel dining room." Her aunt leaned closer. "It's a marvelous figure of a man, I must say. Yes, and regard the gentleman at his side. *Magnifique*, in a savage fashion."

Her aunt was inclined to think most men magnificent in one way or another, but the gentleman speaking to Monsieur Wallace was certainly unusual. His skin had copper shadings quite unlike the olive tones of the gentlemen of Sonia's acquaintance, certainly unlike the outdoor bronze of the Kentuckian's features that could be likened to parquet flooring. This man's brows were thick and expressive, his nose like a blade, his chin uncompromisingly square, and his hair so black it had a bluish sheen. Of a size with Wallace, the two of them stood out in the milling crowd like two stalwart oaks caught in a flood.

Frowning a little, Sonia said, "He appears to be…"

"But, yes. They say the blood of the Great Suns, once rulers of the Natchez tribe, runs in his veins though he was baptized by the priests as a child. Christien Lenoir, they christened him. He is called Faucon Nuit, Nighthawk, at times, as that was the meaning of his name in his own language."

"You seem to know a great deal about him."

Her aunt's smile was a shade conscious. "I made inquiries yesterday morning, having a sudden interest in anything and anyone connected with Monsieur Wallace. Fonts of information, the ladies of my embroidery group."

"I'm sure." Sonia would have liked to ask precisely what had been said of Monsieur Wallace, but that could wait. For now, she refused to stand gawking and whispering like some country *mademoiselle*. Nor would she allow the Kentucky gentleman the satisfaction of thinking his presence mattered to her. Collecting the ends of her shawl and her fan in one hand, lifting her skirts of pale aqua silk with the other, she turned her back on him.

The movements of Monsieur Wallace made no difference to her in all truth, she thought as she continued up the stairs. She had no intention of being escorted anywhere by the man. She had made her plans, and nothing would stand in her way, particularly not a lout of an American, be he ever so daunting.

The hard planes of his face as he watched her had revealed what could almost be termed a proprietary expression. It was most annoying. Where she went and what she did was none of his concern. Her father might have given her welfare into his keeping, but she had not accepted his guardianship.

Brave thoughts, yet her nerves felt unstrung and a hollow dread lingered under her breastbone, as if she stood on the edge of a precipice. She could not recall when she had ever been so unsettled.

The ball this evening seemed much like any other,

with the string quartet playing on a dais, the perfume of roses scenting the air from their pedestal vases, gentlemen in somber evening garb and ladies in a pastel kaleidoscope of silk gowns. Dozens of such entertainments had been held during the *saison des visites* that was now winding down, some here, some at other hotel ballrooms here in the Vieux Carré and the American area uptown becoming known as the Garden District. A group of gentlemen each subscribed a set amount to hire the ballroom, have it decorated, provide refreshments and engage attendants to manage the carriage traffic and see to the comfort and security of attendees. The guests were chosen at their discretion, with close family members first on the list, followed by friends and their ladies then other members of their particular set. Such an invitation was seldom declined as all of New Orleans was mad for dancing, particularly the dizzying whirl of waltzes arriving weekly from the ballrooms of Paris and Vienna.

One met, in the main, the same people at every ball, those who belonged to the *haut ton*. Sonia, glancing around, saw hardly anyone of close acquaintance. It was curious, but perhaps understandable. Mardi Gras and Lent had come and gone, and the palm fronds of Easter, blessed by the priest and tucked carefully behind mirrors and picture frames, had begun to shatter to the floor. A few cases of fever had been reported as the days grew warmer. Many had begun to pack for the return to country plantations, or else for travel to watering places such as Saratoga and White Sulphur Springs or the pleasures of Paris, Rome or Wiesbaden. Even her father was planning a business journey to Memphis.

Yet no one came forward to greet Sonia and her aunt, no familiar faces appeared in the crowd. Most of the guests in her range of vision belonged to the far fringes of the French-Creole society. She recognized a noted divorcée seldom received in respectable households, a planter who had spent much of his youth in exile in Havana due to a taste for purple silk shirts and handsome young boys, and a dowager rumored to have buried her second husband an embarrassingly short time after the nuptials. Present, too, was the famous sword master and duelist Pépé Llulla, Spanish-dark, debonair and deadly, and his Italian counterpart, Gilbert Rosière. Wherever the pair walked, a clear lane appeared miraculously before them, closing behind them when they were well past.

Hardly had the true situation begun to make itself known to her when Monsieur Wallace and his copper-skinned friend appeared in the ballroom entrance. They presented invitations, were relieved of their hats and sword canes and ambled forward as if they belonged.

"Tante Lily," Sonia began, "I do believe…"

"I know, *chère*. Not our usual circle at all. Exciting, is it not?" Her aunt's eyes sparkled as she swept a fan of black lace back and forth with languid waves.

"Papa will be livid."

"Now how can that be? You have your protector in attendance. If your papa will hire such a one for your wedding voyage, he can hardly object to you being in his company this evening."

"I doubt he will be so reasonable. But you don't seem surprised."

"Let us say I guessed how the affair would turn out," her aunt agreed in roguish tones. "The sponsors are four former sword masters of note, after all, the Condé de Lérida and Messieurs Pasquale, O'Neill and Blackford. These gentlemen have all become respectable in the past few years through marriages to French-Creole ladies. That's ever been the way of it, you comprehend. Even the Spaniards who came to conquer decades ago were accepted only after they married among us."

"I didn't realize… I mean, who reads the list of sponsors?" She recognized those mentioned, now that they had been brought to her attention, striking men who stood with their ladies in an informal receiving line near the fireplace that formed a focal point for the ballroom. The group laughed and talked among themselves with great camaraderie, one source of amusement being, so it appeared, the cunningly fashioned gowns of at least two of the ladies who were obviously *enceinte.*

Some would say they should have remained at home in such a condition. It appeared they flouted opinion in this as well as in their choice of husbands and guests.

Her aunt lifted a brow as she surveyed Sonia's set features. "You have been complaining this entire season about how bored you are with the usual balls and other entertainments. I thought this one might pique your interest. Besides, you will soon be married so must broaden your horizons, *chère.* I very much doubt Jean Pierre will be as nice in his associations as your papa."

Sonia was forced to admit the point. Not that her betrothed's choice of acquaintances was a concern, since she would not be at his side to receive them.

"How did we come to receive an invitation, do you suppose?"

"I have no idea." Her aunt lifted a well-rounded shoulder. "Perhaps one of the hosts is aware of your connection to Monsieur Wallace."

"You don't think we should leave?"

"No, no. The evening promises to be something out of the ordinary. I would not miss it for worlds. As for propriety, I am here at your side, am I not? And you will not desert me."

"Naturally not," Sonia said in staunch acquiescence. In truth, it was rather exciting to be among this more dashing set; she had often wondered at the difference between it and the more staid circle she frequented. Her concern was primarily for her father's disapproval, which might cause curtailment of the little freedom she was allowed. That would not be at all convenient just now.

As for the man from Kentucky, she would pretend he did not exist. That should be no great effort.

It was more difficult than she imagined. He seemed to hover on the edge of her vision no matter where she looked. The rumble of his voice drifted over the crowd. It was maddening.

Still, the evening promised little variation from the dozens of others she had attended that winter. The music was just as sprightly, the decorations as lavish and the food and drink as bountiful. She was not left to sit and make tapestry, as the saying went, in spite of the strange company. Hardly had she disposed herself on a chair with her skirts spread around her before she was besieged by a number of gentlemen. Denys Vallier, brother-in-law to the Condé de Lérida and a gentleman most *comme il faut,* was in their forefront. With him were his particular friends, Albert Lollain and Hippolyte Ducolet. The two dances they each begged made a fine showing on the dance card she had been handed at the door, though she became more selective after they were recorded. The filling of such a card required great care. A lady needed to avoid blank spaces but might wish to leave a dance or two free in case some particularly agreeable gentleman should be tardy in approaching her.

Monsieur Wallace took the floor once or twice, so she noticed, waltzing with the wives of friends. He was not as clumsy as she expected. More, he seemed to enjoy the exercise, particularly making the skirts of his partners fly in the turns, though his great strength prevented them from losing their feet. Sonia almost wished that he would petition her for a dance, but naturally only for the pleasure of refusing him.

It was while she was dancing for the second time with Hippolyte, a sportsman, noted wag and bon vivant only an inch or two taller than she and already taking on the rounded contours of his esteemed father, that she noted a gentleman approaching Monsieur Wallace. She would have paid no attention except that elderly roué with sparse locks but sparkling charm had been chatting with her aunt just moments before. It appeared now that Tante Lily might have sent the gentleman on a mission. He gestured toward where that lady stood in an alcove, an expression on her features that could only be called imploring.

The exclamation Sonia made under her breath was so sharp that her partner pulled back a little to gaze into her face. "A thousand apologies if I stepped on your toes."

"No, no, I only— That is, I saw something that surprised me."

"I'm relieved. A clumsy oaf I may be, but I usually notice when I crush a lady's slippers." He turned in the waltz to follow her line of sight, watching as the sword master began to stroll beside the envoy, heading toward Tante Lily. "*Sacre,* but your aunt is setting up a flirtation with Wallace. She knows who he is?"

"You may be sure of it, at least by reputation."

"She enjoys new people, your tante Lily," her partner said gallantly.

It was true enough, particularly when they were male. "She also likes tweaking my father's nose."

"Your mother's sister, I believe."

"As you say." Sonia's smile had a wry curl to it.

There had been a time when she had thought her father and Tante Lily might marry. It was not uncommon when a deceased wife's sister joined a household to care for children left without a mother. Not only did it satisfy the conventions that frowned upon an unrelated female living under the same roof as the widower, but it was assumed she would have natural affection for her charges. It hadn't happened. Tante Lily considered her brother-in-law remote and undemonstrative, which was to say he was not attracted to her. Her father, for his part, thought her aunt lamentably outré in her ideas about child rearing and the place of women in the world, but tolerated her for Sonia's sake. Both disregarded the impropriety of the arrangement from a stubborn refusal to be bound by such nonsense.

Hippolyte sent another quick look toward the alcove. "If annoying your papa is what she's after, making Wallace free of his town house should do it."

"I doubt she will go that far," Sonia answered. "Most likely, she's curious. But you know the gentleman?" It didn't seem necessary to say immediately that she had already made the acquaintance of Monsieur Wallace.

"I've marched with him in the Louisiana Legion, even faced him on the fencing strip at his salon once or twice."

The last was telling information since only the most promising swordsmen dared face a *maître d'armes,* or were allowed the privilege, for that matter. Hippolyte must be an accomplished fencer himself. "Your impression was favorable?"

"Oh, assuredly. He has the strength of a bear, the cunning of a wolf, and his great height makes his reach with blade in hand the very essence of terror."

Her smile was wry. "An edifying description, I'm sure, but I meant as a person."

"Ah." Color rose from under Hippolyte's collar to make his cheeks ruddier than they had been before. "I wouldn't mind having him at my side when walking the streets on a dark night."

"Praise indeed."

His shrug was offhand, or pretended to be. "He's a straight one. All agree on that."

"You don't find him a little uncouth?" She allowed her gaze to rest a bare instant, no more, on the Kentucky sword master who was now bowing over her aunt's hand.

"Pardon?"

"Because of his birth."

Hippolyte shrugged. "He's not exactly a barbarian, seems to feel just as he ought about most things. A man of affairs, Monsieur Wallace. Though he held off opening a fencing salon until a mere two years ago, he has all the clients he can handle. And I saw him just this morning at Hewlett's Exchange, changing notes. That's the bourse preferred by the Americans, you know."

"Did you indeed?" she said encouragingly. She might not care for what she was hearing, but it could benefit her to learn as much as possible about the gentleman in question. Not that she was curious in the same way as her aunt. No, far from it.

"They are saying he's resigned from the Legion, and after serving the best part of his four years in the city. Just when things are heating up and war may be declared any day, he's off to Vera Cruz."

"Is that so strange?"

"It's odd to say the least, as he's always seemed determined to put his sword arm to use in a good cause. A man may be forgiven for suspecting the decision was brought on by some matter of importance."

"Such as a need to leave New Orleans?" She kept her tone light, impersonal, as they spun gently in the dance.

"Or perhaps to reach Mexico. Since hearing of it, I've been racking my brains for something someone said to me about Wallace. Seems he came to the city on the trail of some scoundrel, a matter of a score to be settled."

"Most peculiar."

Hippolyte lifted a shoulder. "Of course, I could have it wrong."

It seemed best to change the subject for the moment, else her interest might begin to appear too personal. "We have been hearing of war with Mexico forever. Some say it's inevitable. Do you believe it will actually come to pass?"

"Bound to. I mean, only look at what's happened since Texas was added to the Union last fall. First the Mexicans refused to acknowledge Louisiana's own John Slidell as the American envoy, threw his offer of forty million for California and New Mexico back in his face. Now their General Ampudia has invaded the strip between the Rio Grande and Rio Nueces with more than five thousand men, facing off against General Taylor and his battalions after their forced march from Fort Jessup to stop his advance. If they don't get into a scuffle, I'll eat my cravat. Once it starts, Congress will have to come down in favor of war."

"And the Legion will be in the fight."

"*Naturellement.* There's to be a rally at Hewlett's to enlist more volunteers and orders to march are expected to come down at any moment. Texas is entirely too near Louisiana, you comprehend. If we don't stop them there, next thing we know we'll be fighting on our own doorstep."

"Papa says the skirmishing at the Texas border is mere heroics with both sides flourishing swords and rifles at each other. Nothing will come of it, just as nothing has come of all the talk since Texas won its independence a decade ago."

Hippolyte shook his head. "It's different this time."

"But you will have to fight without the *Kaintuck* sword master." Tante Lily, she saw, was fluttering her lashes at the gentleman as they exchanged greetings. The approval that lay behind that small flirtation brought the sting of betrayal.

"Just so." Hippolyte paused, then went on with some diffidence. "I am curious, Mademoiselle Sonia. Is it the war that interests you, or is it Monsieur Wallace?"

Her smile was wan. "You have caught me out, I fear. What the gentleman might be like has some small bearing as he has been engaged to provide protection during my wedding journey."

"*Quel dommage!* You are to be married?"

"But, yes, to Jean Pierre Rouillard, by the arrangement of my father. He is presently at Vera Cruz. Our vows will be spoken immediately upon my arrival with Tante Lily."

"Your father doesn't travel with you then? I mean, as you have need of other escort."

"Business affairs prevent him unfortunately." She forced another smile. "No doubt it's this threat of war which makes him think Monsieur Wallace acceptable as an escort."

"So his resignation from the Legion is explained. Who would not prefer such pleasant duty?"

"You are too kind. I'm sure his application for the position has nothing to do with me."

Her partner made no reply as a pensive expression rose in his brown eyes. "Rouillard," he mused aloud. "You know, I do believe…"

"Yes?"

"Nothing. It can't signify, I'm sure." He gave her a dolorous smile as the music came to an end. "Permit me to extend my felicitations on your marriage and my prayers for your safety during the voyage to Mexico. I should be wary of allowing a lady of my family to embark for Vera Cruz just now, but I'm sure you will be well protected by Monsieur Wallace. And I trust I've said nothing to offend concerning the gentleman."

An impossibility, Sonia thought; Kerr Wallace offended her to the greatest extent imaginable simply by being alive. She did not say so, however, but only accepted the congratulations and turned toward where her aunt stood with the sword master and his friend. But she was thoughtful, most thoughtful, as her footsteps carried her in that direction.

"Truly, it's a sad thing to be married against your will, Monsieur Wallace," her aunt was saying as Sonia drew closer. "I speak from experience, you must understand. My own papa was so certain he knew best—but there, we won't speak of that. *Ma chère* Sonia has conceived a hatred of the idea beyond anything you may imagine. I blame myself, for it was I who introduced her to the romances of Monsieur Scott and his ilk. She will become resigned to the match in time, as most of us do. Meanwhile, she can hardly be blamed for kicking against it, or for sighing over the dream of true love. A little headstrong she may be, but she has the kindest of hearts."

The Kentuckian's answer was a deep and oddly musical murmur of politeness, far less audible than her aunt's carrying tones. Sonia made no attempt to understand it. "I fear you are wasting your time explaining my feelings to Monsieur Wallace. He can have scant interest in them, and none whatsoever in my heart."

"Oh, I'm sure you are mistaken," her aunt said, reaching out to take Sonia's arm and draw her close beside her. "He seems a quite reasonable gentleman."

"For a *Kaintuck,*" Kerr said with a flashing smile.

Sonia stared, disconcerted by the teasing light in his eyes that gave them a silvery sheen, the brightness of white teeth against the sun-burnished hue of his face, the sudden appearance of a slash in the lean plane of his face that just missed being a dimple. The transformation was startling when she had thought him stern and forbidding.

"Just so," her aunt replied to his sally, twinkling up at him in blatant flirtation. Nodding toward his companion, she said to Sonia, "*Ma chère,* permit me to make known to you the friend of Monsieur Wallace, Monsieur Christien Lenoir. His salon is next door to that of Monsieur Wallace in the Passage de la Bourse, if I have that correctly."

"Perfectly, *madame.*"

The dark-haired sword master took the hand Sonia

offered, his bow as brief as her curtsy. The look he turned on her as he stepped back was searching, though his expression gave away nothing of his conclusions. His brows were dark slashes above deep-set black eyes, his features harsh yet noble in some ancient fashion, and his hair, innocent of the pomade that controlled the locks of most gentlemen, had the sheen of black satin. The curl of his well-formed mouth as he glanced at his friend at the end of his perusal seemed to have an element of pity in it.

The Kentuckian was not attending. His gaze was on Sonia, she saw, his lips parted as if he would speak. She thought he meant to ask her to dance. The sensation that entered her chest, like the dry fluttering of butterfly wings, was so disquieting that she swung, abruptly, toward her previous partner who had followed to stand just behind her.

"You know these gentlemen, I believe, Monsieur Ducolet."

Tante Lily gave a small laugh. "*Mon Dieu, chère,* such an introduction. Monsieur Wallace, Monsieur Lenoir, this is Monsieur Hippolyte Ducolet."

During the exchange of bows and acknowledgments of past fencing bouts, the next waltz began and the moment passed for joining the dancers. The Kentuckian seemed to forget the impulse, though his gaze that traveled over Sonia was dark before he turned back to Tante Lily. "Call me Kerr, if you please, *madame*. To stand on ceremony seems foolish when we will be thrown together in close quarters within mere hours."

"I fear my friend considers any formality absurd," Christien Lenoir said in dry tones.

"And so it is. People might as well not have first names here. A man and woman may share a bed for forty years, have a dozen children together, comfort each other in sickness and grief, and still call each other *monsieur* and *madame* when one of them lies at death's door. What could be more ridiculous?"

"Monsieur!"

Kerr looked at Tante Lily with a raised brow. "What did I say? Oh, the part about a bed and children. You'll forgive me, I hope, but surely that's the most telling point of all. Only consider if in the throes of—"

"We will not consider it, if you please!" Tante Lily tapped him on the arm, the words censorious though her eyes sparkled. "This politeness you so despise makes possible a pleasant life, *n'est-ce pas,* particularly in marriage. Where would we be if everyone said exactly what they thought and felt with no manners, no reserve or regard for the consequences? Why, men and women could never live together without quarreling. If they were not at each other's throats a week after the wedding, I should be very surprised."

Kerr's bow was courteous, but lacked the depth of true humility. "I stand corrected, *madame.* I'm sure your experience in such matters goes beyond mine."

"Impudent scoundrel." She gave him a darkling look. "But you mentioned imminent close quarters just now. Pray, what did you mean?"

That was a question Sonia wanted very much to hear answered herself.

"Nothing scandalous, I promise. I only intended to convey that the steamer for Vera Cruz has completed her unloading, taken on new cargo and now awaits only her orders for departure."

"Oh, dear."

"You're certain?" Sonia could not keep the sharpness from her voice.

"Oh, quite," the gentleman from Kentucky said at his most urbane. "All things being equal, we will board tomorrow afternoon and she'll sail with the following dawn."

"How kind of you to keep us informed." She thought he relished being the bearer of the news, no doubt because he knew her reluctance to hear it. Not that he was crass enough to make an overt show of it; she would allow him that much. Still, there was something in the expression that played about his firm, well-formed mouth that set her teeth on edge.

"Since I have heard nothing to the contrary from your father, I will be on the *Lime Rock* at the appointed time. If I may be of any help with your baggage, I trust you will let me know."

"I'm sure that won't be necessary."

"As you please. Embarkation will mark the beginning of my duties then. I'll present myself when we get under way."

His voice was calm, without emphasis, yet she had the distinct idea that he was gratified her father had not dismissed him. She would not give him the satisfaction of realizing she knew it, so said nothing.

"We look forward to seeing you there," her aunt answered for her in tones a great deal more cordial than necessary. "No doubt the voyage will be as boringly uneventful as anyone could wish. But if not, we will rest easier knowing you are close at hand."

"I'll make every effort to be worthy of your trust, *madame*."

The bow Kerr Wallace made lacked true grace but was still gallant and self-deprecating. The look in his eyes was none of these things. It appeared sardonic yet alight with anticipation, from where Sonia stood. And disturbing, most disturbing.

For an instant, she was reminded of her pose as a virago a few days before, also the ruin of her carefully applied face paint by the rain. How embarrassing it had been to catch sight of herself in the mirror when she had returned from accosting Monsieur Wallace in the street. She looked nothing like that this evening. Surely the impression made in her ball gown would wipe the other from his mind.

Not that it mattered. She would not be on the *Lime Rock* when it sailed, would not require Monsieur Wallace's escort, had no cause to consider what he might think of her.

She would be elsewhere when the steamer for Vera Cruz left port and headed down the river to the gulf. Let the Kentuckian find gratification in that, if he could.

Four

Kerr lounged on a bench in the barrelhouse a few doors down from his salon with one long leg thrust out before him and a glass of beer at his elbow. Morose, disinclined to talk, he drummed on the scarred tabletop with the fingers of one hand. Christien straddled a chair across the table from him, while men of all stripes sat drinking, talking, filling the stale air with the smoke of cheroots and hand-rolled cigarettes. Kerr hardly noticed. He frowned, all too aware of the faint strains of a waltz from the hotel where the ball they had left an hour ago continued, and would until dawn. Something, some niggling doubt or presentiment, lingered at the back of his mind. He worried at it like a kid with a loose tooth.

Mademoiselle Bonneval had been too quiet, too self-possessed this evening. Her eyes were too veiled, her smiles too practiced. The aversion she had displayed at their first meeting had been set aside, or so it seemed. Yet she was certainly not resigned, he thought, not by a long shot.

The lady was up to something. He would swear to it.

He had almost asked her to dance. To take her in his arms, to hold her for a few short minutes as they whirled around the floor in the intimate contact of a waltz, had been a virulent impulse. What prevented him was the implacable set of her features. She would have turned him down flat, and he had no taste for public humiliation.

"You're all packed? Everything is arranged for this jaunt down to Mexico?"

Christien squinted at him through the smoke as he spoke, Kerr saw, his gaze assessing. A good friend but a bad enemy, was the half-breed. In the manner of those raised in the woods, he missed little of what went on around him, was damnably sensitive to the way the wind was blowing. It seemed he might have picked up his disturbance of mind. It would be as well to deflect him from it.

"All except the last bits," he allowed with a nod. "Have I thanked you for looking after the salon while I'm away?"

"At least a half-dozen times. Think no more of it. Just make sure you return."

"My fullest intention, I promise you."

"And I'll hold you to it. I've better things to occupy my time than disposing of your pitiful belongings to cover your rent."

"Shouldn't come to that, but if it does..." Kerr's shrug was fatalistic.

"It's a killing matter then."

"You might say so."

Kerr was not one to talk about himself or his business. The fewer who knew what he was about, the better. It was a family trait, that taciturn attitude; his father had been the same, and his father before him, all the way back to the Clan Wallace in the Highlands of Scotland. Stiff-necked pride and the need to keep a firm hand on the reins, his mother had always called it. She may have been right.

"The lady didn't look overjoyed at the news of the *Lime Rock*'s departure." The light from soot-dulled lanterns slid over the black waves of Christien's hair as he tipped his head.

"Not particularly."

"Can't say I envy you the voyage with her under your wing."

Kerr gave his friend a skeptical look. "If you think I believe that…"

"God's truth, I swear it. I prefer my women softer and more biddable."

"Careful, my friend. The old gods enjoy serving up a man's past words with trouble as a sauce."

"You're learning that, are you?"

"Meaning?"

"Aren't you the man who has dodged and ducked for years to avoid the matchmaking of his friends' wives? The staunch frontier gent with no use for a pampered Creole belle, no time for hanging on the sleeve of one? Now look at you."

"I signed on to deliver the lady to her wedding, and nothing else."

"But you'll be looking after her, keeping close watch,

making sure nothing happens to her. First thing you know, you'll be trailing after her like a sick pup."

Kerr gave him a straight look. "I wouldn't put money on it."

Christien went on as if he had not spoken. "Yes, or running up and down, swearing a blue streak and wondering where she's got off to while your back was turned. Mademoiselle Bonneval has the look of a lady with a mind of her own. She's not likely to stay put like a horse you can ground tie and expect to find when you come back."

"For that gem of wisdom I thank you, not being able to figure it out for myself."

"Oh, you're up to every trick, I don't doubt. The thing is, so is the lady, and she doesn't look happy with her lot. You and that papa of hers don't look out, she'll bolt on you."

The back of Kerr's neck tingled and alarm slid down his spine. Christien had just put into words the feeling that had him blue-deviled. It was what had bothered him about Sonia Bonneval's mood this evening, her composure, the unruffled way she had taken the news of the *Lime Rock*'s sailing date after her first start of surprise.

She didn't intend to be on that ship. She meant to run out on her wedding and on him.

The legs of his chair screeched on the flagstone floor as he surged to his feet. Thrusting a hand into his pocket, he tossed a few coins on the table and turned for the door.

"Hold on, where're you going?" Christien called after him.

"To check on my charge," he said over his shoulder.

"You saw her leave the ball before we did. She'll be at home, tucked up in her bed."

"I'll just make sure of it."

Behind him, Christien said something under his breath. Kerr didn't wait to hear it. But he thought it had to do with hearing old gods laugh.

Some hours later, Kerr was still turning that conversation in the barrelhouse over in his mind as he leaned against the plastered storefront across from the Bonneval town house. He'd got the wind up while talking to Christien, and that was a fact. He'd been so certain Mademoiselle Bonneval meant to leave him holding the bag. Sure as God made little green apples, she'd be packing her traps and sneaking out to hide with some friend or relative. Or so he'd thought.

Now he wasn't so sure. The night was almost gone, and he was still holding up the wall with one shoulder, loitering like a lovesick fool and watching her window. Hell, all he needed was a guitar and a song to yodel and he'd look as if he was courting the lady, Creole style. Not that there was any hope of that since he couldn't carry a tune in a sack. Maybe he should have found himself a Jew's harp or fiddle, something as an excuse for being still at his post next time the gendarmes made their rounds.

If he had a lick of sense, he'd slope off to his rooms over the salon, get himself some sleep. Another hour and he'd do just that. Dawn would be breaking by then. Chances of her making off in daylight seemed doubtful.

Could be she'd never intended such a thing. Where would she go, after all? Who would take her in when they knew they'd have to face Papa Bonneval?

What an old stick he was, her father. Marrying her off to a man she hardly knew was bad enough, but to send her away to a foreign country in the middle of a war? Anything could happen. Armies weren't known for being too polite when civilians got in their way, particularly enemy civilians. Being tied to Rouillard was downright chancy, too. Who knew how he might treat a woman? His wife would have nowhere to go, nobody to turn to for help if he cut up rough.

Not that it was likely to come to that. The marriage would be over before it began if he had his way. And he intended to have it.

Too bad he couldn't just tell her she needn't worry, that she'd be a widow before her wedding night. Problem was, he couldn't guarantee it; Rouillard might be the one to come out of this alive. For another, women were unaccountable. She might simply be miffed because her husband-to-be hadn't bothered to court her in proper style. If she learned of the threat to him, she could feel duty-bound to shout it out the instant she clapped eyes on him. Then where would they be?

At least she wasn't making the voyage alone. She'd have the support and comfort of her tante Lily. He had no idea if she meant to stay with her niece or return to New Orleans, but it still made him feel less guilty.

A shadow moved across the jalousie blinds that covered the French door of the second-floor bedchamber across the way. He knew it belonged to Sonia because he'd seen her earlier as she stepped to the French doors to pull the draperies across them. She'd had on a wrapper over her nightgown, and her hair had trailed down her back in a long braid that swung thick and heavy against her hips. Though he'd had only the briefest of glimpses, he thought the vision had scarred his eyeballs. Right now, just thinking about it, he felt such heat in his groin that he shifted uncomfortably against the plaster behind him.

What kind of nightgown would she wear? Something thin, lacy and easy to remove, like the handful of silk he'd taken off an accommodating actress from the Saint Charles Theater? Not much hope. It would be serviceable cotton lawn, he suspected, and buttoned up to the throat with the kind of pearl bits that made men cuss, plus scratchy with white embroidered stuff around the neck and wrists that was done by nuns. That would be it exactly.

So why in hell did the idea of it make his heart clang like a hammer striking an anvil?

As he watched, the lamplight faded away behind the blinds. She was going to bed at last. It had taken her long enough. The delay was the main reason he still stood there in the shadows. He wondered if maybe she'd been packing her trunk, possibly adding the evening gown and other unmentionables she'd worn this evening. Her shadow had crossed back and forth over the window a number of times with something in her arms.

Or could be she was pacing, trying to come up with

a way to escape his company. The thought did nothing to ease his mind.

Taking out his pocket watch, he glanced at it and put it away again. He'd allow her enough time to fall asleep then make his way back to his own bed. And what a double-damned shame that he'd be sleeping alone. The trip ahead of him looked to be a sore trial if he was going to catch fire like pitch pine at every sound or move made by Sonia Bonneval.

She had appeared pale this evening. It had made him uneasy. That was before he realized her face was free of paint.

Odd that she would use such artifice at home but not at an evening entertainment. He was forced to wonder if it was not usual for her, if it could maybe have been applied for his benefit. If she'd thought to entice him, she had gone about it the wrong way.

But, no, that was the last thing she would want. It followed then that her purpose might have been the opposite. She'd miscalculated there, too. Clean-faced innocent or painted sophisticate, she had the same unfortunate effect on him either way. Though having met Papa Bonneval, he could not imagine she had been given the opportunity to be anything other than a model of virtue.

She would, no doubt, sleep the sleep of the untried virgin, free of all burning, all temptations. Her future husband would relieve her of that innocence, some future gentleman she had not yet met. What a shame and a waste. But the man would not be Rouillard, not if Kerr could help it.

He'd not reached that exact resolve before in his ruminations. Why it should seem so imperative to prevent the wedding night now was something he'd just as soon not look at too closely.

He'd been wrong about the lady; she apparently had no thought of avoiding her fate. Why he'd been so sure she was up to something, he couldn't say with accuracy. It had been a notion, an instinct. Well, and maybe a fear. He couldn't allow her to get away from him, not after coming this far. He owed her an apology for his suspicion, he supposed. The gesture was impossible without exposing his distrust, and so it would be expressed in silent service. That was all he could allow himself, the reason he had been hired after all.

The thought had barely crossed his mind when he caught a flicker of movement at the French doors he'd been watching so assiduously. They eased open. A slender figure slipped through, one dressed in a dark coat and pantaloons and carrying a belled top hat in his hand.

The lady had been entertaining a midnight visitor.

Not so innocent after all.

The corners of Kerr's mouth tightened. He might have known. It certainly explained Mademoiselle Bonneval's strenuous objections to her arranged marriage, also her papa's arrangements for a guard to see to it she reached her groom. He had to be scandalously unsuitable, this lover of hers, to make such a thing necessary.

Kerr could almost pity the poor, dandified bastard, forced to make a last clandestine call by way of farewell. His ladylove would board the *Lime Rock* tomorrow afternoon—or make that this afternoon—and that would be the end of it.

It would be as well if he made certain the gentleman understood that point, Kerr thought. There must be no hysterical farewells, no last-minute rescue attempt or doomed heroics.

Kerr eased away from the wall and crossed the street in swift silence. As he reached the balcony of the Bonneval town house again, he heard a soft tread on the floor above him. He had lost sight of his quarry as he reached the cover of the balcony, but thought the gentleman headed toward the fluted metal support post at the near corner. Kerr positioned himself just under that point and set himself to wait.

The railing overhead creaked as weight was placed upon it. Booted feet appeared, first one, then the other. A pause ensued, then the feet were lowered, the ankles wrapped around the pole as the gentleman prepared to slide to the ground. Something about the trimness of those ankles, some warning, brushed the edges of Kerr's mind.

Too late. He was already moving, reaching out to grab the scoundrel in a bear hug and drag him to the ground.

His hands were filled with firm, resilient curves, his senses with the fragrance of soap and violets. His quarry yelped and let go of her hold. Kerr stumbled backward, sprawling on the ground. His breath left him in a hard grunt as Mademoiselle Bonneval, caught to him by a hard arm around her waist, landed squarely on top of him with her hips pressed to his groin.

Five

Sonia lay motionless for a stunned instant. Rage and terror burst over her then. She flailed, kicking at the man who held her, clawing at his arm as she tried to break his hawserlike grip on her midsection. Her breath came in wheezing gasps and the edges of her vision grew dim. It wasn't fair that she had escaped the house to be caught by some drunken seaman or sot reeling homeward. It wasn't fair…

"Be still, or I swear I'll…"

That voice, the damnably American-accented voice.

Kerr Wallace. It couldn't be, shouldn't be, but it was. She redoubled her efforts, managed to ram an elbow backward into his ribs.

"Bloody hell."

The world shifted around her in a whirl of black and red, tan and brown. She landed on her back, dragged a single whistling breath into her lungs before a hard-muscled form landed on top of her. Long legs tangled with hers, holding them straight. Her wrists were grasped in viselike fingers and pinned to the ground on either side of her face. A hard chest, banded with thick muscle, pressed into her breasts, holding her immobile.

She closed her eyes tightly, unwilling to look, not wanting to see. Through stiff lips, she said, "Get off me at once. Let me go."

"Go where?" he demanded as he pushed up to rear above her. "What are you about, dressed in boy's garb like some beardless kid on a spree, target for every scoundrel from here to Levee Street? You're lucky I was keeping an eye out for you."

"Lucky." Her lashes flew up and she glared up at the *Kaintuck.* "If it weren't for you, I'd be—"

"Not on board the *Lime Rock,* I'll be bound," he said as she came to an abrupt halt. "So where were you off to without satchel or carpetbag to your name? If it's an elopement, banish the idea from your mind."

"As if I'd have use for such a thing! The last thing I want is a husband or man of any kind."

Stillness gripped him, a strained lack of movement that seemed rife with things better left unspoken. She was suddenly aware of his heat and weight pressing against her, particularly the too-firm heaviness at the juncture of her thighs. His scent, compounded of starched linen, warm wool and clean male, surrounded her. She felt incredibly open to whatever he might do, vulnerable in a way so foreign to anything she'd ever known that it sent panic thudding through her. Her heart thundered against her ribs. Her chest heaved with her every breath, pressing her breasts against him so she wondered if he could feel their hardening tips. Fury, distress and wild yearning clashed so violently inside her head that the backs of her eyes stung with acid tears.

A soft curse feathered the air above her.

Kerr Wallace lifted off her with a wrench of hard muscles, getting one knee under him somewhere between her knees. An instant later, he surged to his feet. Retaining his grasp on her wrists, he hauled her up to face him.

Unprepared for the sudden upright position, she stumbled against him. His arms closed around her to keep her from falling. It was like being surrounded by a wall of stone. His chest was solid, ridged with muscle; his arms had no give in their support. For a single instant, she felt sheltered, protected, safe from all possible harm. The need to lean into him, to rest within that strong haven, was so urgent that she felt light-headed with it.

That lapse was more frightening than anything that had happened before. She shoved away with such revulsion that her back came up against the balcony pole behind her, rattling it in its supports. With a hand to her tight throat and her eyes narrowed to slits, she drew a knife-edged breath.

"What now?" she demanded. "Will you ring the bell and hand me over to my father?"

"Why? So you can climb down again the minute his back is turned?"

That had been her exact thought. It did nothing for her despairing resentment to have him guess it. "You could always recommend he tie me up until the *Lime Rock* sails. Only think what a lot of trouble that would save you. You could cart me off tomorrow like a pig to market."

"Now, there's an idea," he drawled.

She had thought matters could not be worse. She was wrong.

Bending toward her as if with some perverted bow, he grasped her wrist again and pulled her toward him. Her breath left her in an unladylike grunt as her solar plexus struck his hard shoulder. When he rose to his full height again, she dangled over it. He clamped a hard arm across her knees and swung around, heading off down the street in the direction of the river.

A strangled cry was torn from her as fury beyond anything she'd ever known engulfed her. She jounced and swayed with his every long step. His arm was like an iron barrel hoop around her knees and his long fingers bit into one thigh above it. The blood pooled to her head so her temples pounded and she had to swallow her gorge. Her hat had been lost in her fall, and now her hairpins began to loosen their grip. They pinged down on the banquette so the heavy coil of hair slipped its moorings. She beat on his back with her fists but he seemed not to feel the blows. The movement made her slide on her precarious perch so she had to grasp handfuls of his coat to keep from falling headfirst.

"What are you…doing?" she jerked out. "Put me… down. My father will…"

"He'll what? Give me a medal?" He hefted her forward from where she had slipped, so the cheek of her bottom was pressed against the hard line of his jaw. "Scream for your papa, why don't you? Unless you would rather not face him."

He was right. The last thing she wanted was for her father to see her like this, to learn what she intended before she could manage her escape. That knowledge was so devastating it left her throat too tight for sound.

It was infuriating yet terrifying, the ease with which Kerr Wallace strode along with her. He was like some unstoppable force of nature. A shiver moved over her, becoming a trembling that shook her from her head to her toes. "You…you have to listen, *monsieur.* I can pay…pay you. My grandmother—"

"That where you were headed, to your grandmother's?"

"She…she'll take me in if I can get to her. She lives—" She stopped, fearful she was saying too much.

"Not in New Orleans, I'll be bound, else you'd have thrown yourself on her mercy before now. Besides that, you'd not need britches to get to her? Where then? Upriver, maybe? Natchez, Saint Francisville? Or maybe downriver toward Mobile?"

She stiffened at his lucky guess; she couldn't help herself. If she'd hoped he wouldn't notice, she was soon disabused of the idea.

"Mobile, right. The packet for there arrived just before the *Lime Rock* and leaves tomorrow afternoon, now I think on it. Guess you were counting on that. Too bad."

Desolation shifted inside Sonia. Her grandmother, her mother's mother, had been her hope, her one chance for refuge. Her letter, delivered when the steam packet docked, had held the precious offer of shelter with her.

Mémère had never cared for the man her daughter, Sonia's mother, had married, had opposed the alliance when it was proposed, but been overridden by Sonia's grandfather. She blamed Simon Bonneval for her daughter's death. He had never cared for her properly, she said, had expected her to recover within mere days from the miscarriages that had plagued her so he could get her with child again. He had been disappointed at the birth of a daughter instead of the son he craved, and shown it too clearly. He had been an autocratic, judgmental husband, always finding fault, never able to see what had been done for pointing out what had not. He had taken the joy of life from her mother, so Mémère had told Sonia, and when she had lost yet another baby son, the sixth in the twelve years following Sonia's birth, she simply let go of living.

Sonia, who had taken her mother's place as her father's housekeeper in the past few years, thought the things her grandmother said might well be true. She had seldom, in all that time, managed to please him.

"Monsieur Wallace, I beg you," she whispered, her voice a mere rasp in her throat.

His stride broke for a bare second; she was sure of it. He didn't stop, however, gave no other sign he heard.

Her anger of moments before was nothing to the rage that consumed her now. She bitterly regretted her moment of weakness. This *Kaintuck* was a monster, a heartless, ignorant barbarian; she'd been a fool to imagine otherwise. For what he was doing, she would make him pay a hundredfold. This she swore on her mother's grave.

They reached the open area of the Place d'Armes, which fronted the cathedral and the Cabildo, or government house. Kerr Wallace turned there, making toward the levee. It was then she knew just where he was taking her.

A few minutes more and they were at the dock where the *Lime Rock* lay quiet and peaceful at its moorings. Her captor came to a halt. Bending forward, he set her on her feet but grasped her forearms for a second while she gained her balance. Giddiness assailed her as the blood pooled in her skull drained away, but she refused to show it, glaring up at him in half-blind defiance.

The levee was just coming to life at this predawn hour. Stretching away from them on either side, the long, curved embankment was lined with steamboats and sailing ships as far as the eye could see. Their signal lanterns gleamed like some earthbound Milky Way, bobbing with the wash of the river current, reflecting in its sliding surface. Stacks of merchandise, boxes and barrels and acres of baled cotton, sat ready to be loaded come good daylight.

Behind them lay the town in its orderly arrangement of streets marked by lamps at the corners, where cats and dogs slinked, pigs snuffled along and men walked with every sense alert for those who preyed on the unwary. From that direction, faint on the dawn wind, came the tinny and melancholy sound of a barrel organ.

They were so alone there in the dimness, she and the

Kentuckian. The knowledge brought an odd flutter in the pit of her stomach. His hold on her was not hurtful, but its firm pressure suggested that it could become so at the least sign of resistance. The power of it affected her like a drug, so she swayed a little where she stood.

It was maddening, that febrile awareness, when she wanted nothing more than to get away from him. Far, far away.

"We're going aboard the steamer, you and I," he said in tones like a sledge being dragged over gravel. "We can do it nice and easy or we can do it hard—you can walk up the gangway on your own two feet or I can carry you. Your choice, Mademoiselle Bonneval."

Refusal hovered on her lips. She longed to fling it in his face then jerk from his grasp and run like the wind.

The trouble was that she suspected he would catch her all too soon. Afterward he'd do precisely as he threatened. To be carried on board like a sack of flour, with her derrière turned up for all to see, was more than she could bear.

Pride demanded compromise, no matter how much it pained her. Besides, he could not stay with her every moment until the ship sailed, could he? She had a few hours yet before she need succumb to despair.

"The captain may not let us board," she said, the words stiff and graceless in her capitulation.

"I've only to show him the letter of intent written by your father that appoints me your escort for the voyage. If there's a problem, he can apply to him."

"But I'm dressed in male clothing. It will appear odd."

"You should have thought of that before you left off your petticoats."

She looked away. "Better to be mistaken for a boy than taken for a...a light skirt."

"I'd agree with you there," he said with a grim nod.

"Not that I care for myself, but your good name may suffer if I appear in pantaloons."

Reaching out, he picked up a strand of her hair that had tumbled down to lie across her shoulder, rubbing it between his fingers. "No one could take you for a boy while this flows around you. My reputation can only be bettered when you appear in full female regalia."

It was a compliment of sorts, if she cared to see it in that light. She did not. Snatching the strand of her hair from his hand, she flung it behind her back. "That will be difficult when I have no baggage."

"You're going to tell me you don't have your *chère* tante Lily all primed to come running with your traps whenever you send word? Don't be daft. I'll see to it she knows your change of direction."

"You are all accommodation." Her voice was tight in her throat, compressed by the tears she refused to shed.

"It's what I'm being paid for."

The words were abrupt and double-layered. He meant her father had commissioned him to see that she sailed on the *Lime Rock,* also that she remained safe, reasonably comfortable and, as with any live cargo, arrived in the same condition in which she embarked. Kerr Wallace would perform his duty. She could expect no more from him, and certainly no less.

He released his grip on one arm but retained her elbow as if he thought she might yet take off if he let her go entirely. It was possible he was right, Sonia thought; she could not be certain what she might do in her present mood. The resentment inside her was so powerful that she longed for a weapon, something, anything to use to annihilate him.

Turning with her, Kerr Wallace strode toward where the *Lime Rock* lay. She had to lengthen her stride to keep up with him. She tripped after a few yards, exclaiming as she nearly fell on her face. The Kentuckian brought her upright again, then slowed his pace. Even so, she had trouble with the boots she had found in the *garçon-nière* wing, left in the bottom of an armoire after a visit by one of her cousins. They were too big for her, as was the frock coat from the same source, though the panta-loons she'd borrowed from the cook's son were a size too small. She looked a fright, in fact. That she could care, after all, was almost as annoying as the rest.

At the ship's mooring, Kerr Wallace hailed the watch and requested permission to come aboard. An inter-minable wait ensued before the captain appeared and gave the order to allow it. The rope railing of the gangway was unhooked and they climbed the slippery planks with their nailed crosspieces. Sonia, leading the way, was horribly conscious of the unprotected view of her lower limbs. It was a great relief when they reached the deck and a ship's mate was detailed to show them below.

They stopped at the cabin presumably reserved for the use of her aunt and herself. The mate who had directed them nodded and went away. As Sonia put her hand on the door latch and pushed it open, Kerr moved to block her way.

She gave him a look of fulminating interrogation, but he only ducked his head and entered the small cubicle. Stopping in the center with his hands on his hips, he surveyed the dim corners, the Persian carpet that was its one spot of color, the bunks stacked one above the other with their tightly tucked sheets and blankets, the small commode table inset with a basin and pitcher and with doors underneath to conceal a chamber pot. It was not a difficult inspection since he could have touched the walls with his outstretched fingertips.

His gaze alighted on a small trunk sitting at the foot of the bunks. Without ceremony, he caught one handle and slung it out into the corridor. That done, he gestured for her to join him.

"What was that?" she asked in disdain as she crossed the threshold. "Someone else in occupation?"

"A mistake," he answered, his hands resting on his hip bones. "I'll attend to it."

No doubt he would, one way or another. "One you anticipated?"

"On some vessels it's first come, first served. I doubt you'd find the owner of the trunk an agreeable bunkmate."

She barely repressed a shudder. "No."

"Figured. In spite of the face paint the other night."

She had no one to blame for that remark except herself, as much as she despised acknowledging it. Turning from him, she held the door, standing stiffly beside it. "I hope you have no expectation of taking the trunk owner's place?"

"Never crossed my mind."

"You have seen me settled. I require nothing else except for you to leave me."

He pursed his lips but didn't argue. Nor did he try to hide the gleam of sardonic amusement in his eyes. Moving to the doorway, he ducked through it, inclined his head in a bow and took the heavy hatchway from her, pulling it shut behind him.

She let out the breath she hadn't realized she'd been holding, permitting it to sigh between her lips like a child's deflating pig bladder. She had almost feared…

What precisely had she been afraid of? That Kerr Wallace intended to stay with her as a guard? That he would make himself at home in one of the two bunks? That he would take liberties because of the peculiar situation in which she had landed herself?

He need not, of course, have made it so clear that he was disinclined. No, even if nothing he had done suggested his thoughts might take that direction.

Mon Dieu, but she could not remember when she had been so aware of a man's virile strength, his superior height and reach. If he had decided to stay, how could she have stopped him?

He had not, nor was he likely to in the future. To him, she was nothing more than a responsibility. It was only that he'd laid hands on her, carried her as if she weighed no more than a peck of dried beans, clamped her to him so her knit britches rasped against the stubble of his jaw.

She had felt the muscle in his cheek move as he clamped his jaws together from some reason she could only guess. She was not used to such treatment. Never in her life had she been in such an embarrassing position.

It wasn't that she had no knowledge of the rough-and-tumble ways of boys. She'd run wild for some years before putting up her hair and resigning herself to her lot as a female. Many were the mornings she'd sneaked out of the house with her cousins, the children of her father's younger brother. They had played marbles in the dirt, walked the tops of brick courtyard walls, jumped the ditches that ran muddy with sewage and slops after a rain and fought barefooted and bare-fisted with the gangs of rowdies from beyond the Vieux Carré. She'd learned to swim by paddling like a wild thing after being thrown into the river, but learn she had, that and much more.

Of course, her every antic had been watched over by old Fonz, her father's majordomo Alphonse, until he'd died three winters ago of the ague. She'd thought he was perhaps eighty years of age, but couldn't say for sure. He'd been sold into slavery as a boy by an uncle who had killed his father and older brother in order to assume the position of chief in their African village. He'd not repined, or so he said. Being a slave was no easy life but better than being dead, and it had brought her to him in his old age, his chick, his kitten, his girl-child in pigtails who had idolized him because he adored her in his grandfatherly way.

Alphonse would not have approved of this alliance with Jean Pierre. He would have stopped it, if only by shaming her father into abandoning the idea. White-haired, bent Fonz had been a quiet power in the house, creating a ring of protection around Sonia. Her child-hood would have been much harsher without him.

Such thoughts took no more than a second to slip through her mind. They were banished by a quiet grating of metal on metal, followed by a distinct click.

Sonia whirled, her eyes wide as she stared at the door. She reached it in a single stride, caught the handle and tried to turn it. She jerked once, twice.

Nothing, no movement whatever. It was locked.

She slammed the door panel with the flat of her hand, hitting it so hard it burned all the way to her shoulder, then spun and put her back to it.

For an instant, tears burned the back of her nose. She would not cry, she told herself with fierce resolve. No, she would not. Her impulse instead was to pound on the door at her back, to scream and shout curses after the *Kaintuck.*

That would be a waste of time as well as exhausting her strength and her passions to no purpose. She would need both if she was to find a way out of this dilemma. And if there was nothing to be done, then she would use them to make Kerr Wallace wish he had never been born.

Six

It was perhaps two hours later, when the morning light through the small porthole illuminated the dreary confines of Sonia's prison and danced in watery reflections on the ceiling, that reprieve arrived. It came in the clear tones of her aunt as she scolded someone for the handling of her trunk. Moments later, the sharp clicking of heels marked her progress down the passageway outside. The lock in the door turned and it swung open. Tante Lily swept inside in a froth of petticoats and lace and the wafting of fresh air.

"*Ma petite,* what is this? I cannot believe you are here. Are you all right? Please tell me everything is as it should be with you!"

Sonia scrambled from the bunk where she had been sitting and stepped into her aunt's rose-scented embrace. "Yes, yes, of course I'm all right, just so very glad to see you."

"Likewise, *chère,* believe me." Her aunt patted her shoulder, sniffing a little. "You cannot conceive of the uproar this morning when it was discovered you were gone. Your papa was about to send for the gendarmes when Monsieur Wallace arrived with news of your whereabouts. I've been throwing things into boxes and trunks like a madwoman ever since, for he insisted I must come with him at once."

"How very thoughtful," she said with irony as the huge *Kaintuck,* carrying a small trunk on his shoulder in a manner too reminiscent of her own transport a short time ago, loomed behind her aunt. His smile was brief, a mere movement of the lips, as he stopped in the doorway, fingering the key to it in his free hand.

"Well, I consider it so myself, for he need not have troubled. I mean, a message would have sufficed for most. Such courage he displayed, to come at the earliest moment to admit what he had done. I quite expected to see him clapped up in the calabozo. But, no, indeed. Your papa commended him instead, said he had done just as he should to prevent you running away. Naturally, I was sent with all speed to lend respectability to the escapade."

Tante Lily's spate of words was as much for Kerr Wallace's benefit as to let her know what had transpired, Sonia realized. Her aunt could not be aware of how much he had guessed of their plans. The dry appreciation that lurked in the gray shadows of the Kentuckian's eyes indicated he understood the act as well.

It was maddening, that perceptiveness, since it raised doubts of her ability to deceive him. Beneath the anger, however, ran a current of distress. Her father had shown not an iota of concern for her welfare, or Tante Lily would surely have related it for the rarity, if nothing else. No presumption that she might have had reason for her actions had apparently crossed his mind, no doubt of the sword master's word about the events that led to her incarceration, no inquiry after her safety and well-being. There was nothing from him, apparently, except condemnation and concern for propriety. She had expected little more, yet somehow his unfeeling attitude still took her by surprise.

She recovered in an instant, tilting up her chin as she drew a deep breath. Her eyes were half-blind with unshed tears as she held the level gray gaze of Kerr Wallace. If he felt any triumph, he hid it well. The look on his face turned somber, the set of his mouth grim.

Her aunt released her, fumbling for a handkerchief, which she pressed to her eyes. "But there, you will think nothing of your papa's temper. You know how he is, and I'm sure he will come and see you off. In the meantime, we must, we really must, do something about your toilette, *ma chère*. How could you go out in the public in such an ensemble as you have on? It's all very well in a child of twelve, though I never liked it. But you are two-and-twenty, practically an old maid. I'd thought you beyond such indiscretion long since."

Sonia knew her aunt as well as her father, knew the scolding was mere nervous chatter to cover her upset and concern. "Yes, certainly," she said without inflection. "That is, if Monsieur Wallace will allow us the privacy."

Her aunt whirled to stare at the sword master. "Are you still here? *Mon Dieu, monsieur,* can you not see you are no longer required? This is the cabin of a lady. You may not enter without her permission. Sonia's papa may overlook the familiarity you dared assume, but I do not. Put down that trunk and take yourself off. Away with you!"

The mountain of a man colored to his eyebrows, a phenomenon fascinating to watch. The cause might have been anger at being rebuked, but had every appearance of embarrassment. With a curt nod, he set the trunk in a corner and backed from the room.

"Wait!" Tante Lily moved after him in a flutter of skirts, putting out her hand with the palm up. "The key, if you please!"

It was handed over without a word. Sonia watched her aunt take it then close the door in Kerr Wallace's face. It was a pleasure to see him routed, but not quite as satisfying, somehow, as she might have expected.

"There now, tell me everything," her aunt said, attaching the key to the chatelaine at her waist as she turned back and took Sonia's hands in both of hers. Seating herself on the bottom bunk as the only resting place, she pulled her down beside her. "Did your *Kaintuck* behave like a complete brute? Did he hurt you at all? What conduct! I was never so shocked in my life as when I heard. Carrying you about, indeed. Quite abominable."

Sonia cleared her throat, looked down at their clasped hands. "No, he was…simply unstoppable."

"There I was, thinking you safe on the Mobile steamer and making ready to join you—in a quiet way, of course, so as not to alert the servants. When I learned what had happened, I nearly went into spasms. Are you sure he did not harm you, Monsieur Wallace? He didn't offer you insult of…of a personal nature?"

If she claimed such a thing, would her father remove him? Sonia wondered. It was a great temptation to put it to the test.

She couldn't do it. Kerr Wallace didn't deserve such an underhand trick. More than that, he would hardly keep silent if accused, and her father might well believe his version of events over anything she could fabricate.

"No, no, nothing like that."

Tante Lily closed her eyes an instant. "*Bien.* I am relieved beyond words to hear it. Something about his manner made me think…" She sighed, patted Sonia's hand. "But that's neither here nor there. He is not, perhaps, quite the barbarian that one might have expected."

As much as it pained Sonia, it had to be admitted. She shook her head.

"And now it seems you go to Vera Cruz, in spite of everything. Truly, *ma petite,* there are worse things for a woman than having a husband chosen for one. I shudder to think what might have happened if you had been caught on the street by some drunken lout. Yes, or if Monsieur Wallace had been any other kind of man. He might have taken the most dastardly advantage."

She knew very well what her aunt meant, could recall with biting clarity the moment when, lying pinioned by Kerr Wallace's weight without knowing his identity, she had feared it was to happen. To speak of that would only alarm her aunt again, however, without being useful in the least. "But he was not," she said, her voice not quite even.

"What a blessing your papa hired someone so trustworthy, so conscientious. Nonetheless, he may not always be so if you try him too far. Come, say you will be sensible."

"I suppose I must be." Sonia lowered her gaze in token of her resignation, but crossed her fingers where her aunt could not see them.

"Oh, *chère*, I do feel for you most sincerely, but we must all give up our childish yearning for our own way or even for fairness. Females cannot expect such things, for it's not the way of the world."

"What of our right to choose for ourselves where we will go, how we will live, who we may marry? You always said—"

"A lovely ideal, I must admit, and it's my dearest belief it should be so for all of us. One day it may, but the time is not yet."

"One day."

Her aunt reached to touch her face. "I fear we must be realistic, and make the best of what we are given. One becomes accustomed to anything in time, and the children of a marriage are always a great comfort. But never mind. You must allow me to help you dress for the day. A woman can always face whatever comes if she is properly turned out for it."

Her father, Sonia reflected, had always considered Tante Lily a flighty creature with little on her mind beyond men, clothes and entertainment, barely fit to chaperone a young girl. He was not always wrong. But neither was he entirely correct.

She was not a complainer, Tante Lily. She had endured an arranged first marriage without benefit of children to soothe her heart. Whatever grief and repining she may have felt, she had not attempted to influence her niece against a similar match. Regardless, Sonia thought her reluctance to acquiesce in her own fate came in large part from what she had gleaned about such marriages from her tante Lily. Though she seldom made direct comparisons, it had always been clear that her second marriage, a love match, had been far more agreeable.

On impulse, Sonia caught her aunt in a quick, fierce hug, suddenly intensely grateful for all she had done for her, and particularly her presence now. They smiled at each other in tremulous accord. Then they turned to the important question of what Tante Lily had brought to replace Sonia's disgraceful boy's attire.

In the midst of her dressing, a seaman arrived with the remainder of their trunks. He was followed by a stewardess bearing a tray with café au lait and bread served with butter and honey. Stolid, whey-faced and approaching middle age, the woman seemed to have little French, but gave them to understand in her broken mixture of German, English and Creole patois that the big American gentleman had sent their breakfast. She also made it clear that the courtesy would not be repeated.

When questioned, the stewardess seemed to have no idea of the present whereabouts of Monsieur Wallace.

She could not tell them if he had brought his baggage on board, nor whether he lurked somewhere nearby, on guard.

It was most unsatisfactory.

Sonia and her aunt spent some time arranging the cabin for best use of the confined space and access to their belongings. That it was likely a useless exercise was something Sonia kept to herself. Tante Lily was so relieved that she seemed resigned. It would be heartless to upset her again.

More, she was reluctant to embroil her aunt in further escape attempts that might lead to public scandal. Tante Lily was fun-loving and flirtatious, but conservative with it. Invoking the possible protection of her mother, Sonia's grandmother, was one thing, but true disgrace would horrify her.

It was near midday when she and her aunt finally left the cabin. Making their way to the top deck, they strolled the planking, watching as an endless stream of stevedores loaded bags and barrels, boxes and crates onto the vessel. Drays lined the levee and wound in a line back toward the Place d'Armes, each of them laden with more cargo to be stowed in the hold. Such a vast amount did it appear that it seemed the *Lime Rock* must sink under the weight.

The ship was a steam packet, one of the newer sailing vessels with twin paddle wheels to add power to its sails. Trim and rakish in design, with a single smoke-stack and three commodious decks as well as a pilot-house, she was elegantly painted with maroon and dark blue stripes on white above the waterline and black below. A model of speed compared to older sailing ships, she made a regular run between New Orleans and a number of South American and Mexican ports. Along the way, she picked up and delivered dispatches and news sheets, so spread the news to and from that hemisphere.

A few other passengers had arrived on board. Sonia and her aunt exchanged bows with a harassed young mother who had a toddler clinging to each hand and a maid carrying a baby in tow. A gentleman with a hen's nest of white whiskers concealing his lower face and a white clerical collar nodded to them from his place in the shade of the pilot deck. Farther along stood a distinguished-looking older man with a goatee, high collar and superior air in conversation with a rather *sportif* younger gentleman in a flat-crowned summer straw hat and a coat in black and green houndstooth check.

"Not a large complement so far," Tante Lily observed.

Sonia murmured a reply, but her attention was upon the gangway, guarded only by a single ship's officer in a dark uniform. His purpose, so it appeared, was to prevent unauthorized passengers from coming aboard. What would he do, she wondered, if she simply walked past him and off the ship?

"I suspect the fellow in the straw hat of being a Captain Sharp," her aunt said in low tones. "He has that look, don't you think? Rather daring yet blasé, and far too attractive for his own good."

"What?" Sonia had barely noticed the gentleman in question. She saw now that he was dark in coloring, with a bold cast to his features and trim mustache. Of average height, his general appearance was lean, almost hungry. A week ago, she might have considered his shoulders broad, but that was before she had met Monsieur Wallace.

"These ships usually carry a gambler or two," her aunt went on with a wise nod. "Captains wink at it as it relieves the tedium for certain passengers."

"I suppose."

Sonia kept to her aunt's idle pace only with an effort. She looked away out over the town, at the Place d'Armes backed by the crumbling Spanish towers of the cathedral, the barrel-tile roofs of the town houses lining rues Royale and Chartres and, through the treetops, the dome of the Hotel Saint Louis. She tried to appear as if idly enjoying the view, afraid Tante Lily might guess her intentions otherwise. Not that she thought her aunt would try to stop her, but she would protest, calling after her and generally drawing attention. That must be avoided if she was to have any chance of getting away.

Pigeons swirled above the Place d'Armes. Joyful descendants of escapees from *pigeonniers* where gentlemen raised squabs to grace their dinner tables, they soared in and out of the pall of yellow-gray coal smoke that lay over the town. Vendors of greens and berries, flowers and pralines called their wares on the cathedral steps and under the Cabildo's arcade, their voices making a singsong cacophony. Barrel organs played and children danced in hope of earning a few picayunes. Men hurried in and out of the government house on matters of business, or else stood in idle groups, chatting and gesticulating. Some kind of assembly was beginning on the flat, bare parade ground with its cannon emplacements. Men streamed from the barracks that lay on the downriver side, beginning to form ranks.

If Kerr Wallace was anywhere in the bustle, she could not locate his tall form.

"The gentleman may be only a planter from upriver," her aunt said with a light touch on Sonia's arm. "We must keep an open mind, though he looks a thorough rogue. I suspect we shall soon make his acquaintance, for he is staring at you, *chère.*"

She was still talking about the sporting gentleman, Sonia realized. For an instant, she'd thought she referred to the *Kaintuck*. "Is he?"

Her aunt tapped her arm again. "You must pay more attention to your surroundings, particularly when gentlemen are present. One never knows when such a one will make advances, as I've told you a thousand times."

"Yes, Tante Lily."

The answer was perfunctory as her attention was taken by a rather large man sitting in a deck chair just down from the gangway, his face hidden by a news sheet. She frowned even before he began to lower the large page of print.

"Ah, here is Monsieur Wallace." Her aunt's features relaxed into a smile. "We might have known he would not be far away."

It was indeed the Kentuckian. He folded the news sheet that had concealed his face and rose from his chair, a slow and endless movement that caused Sonia's heart to do a stutter step. His smile as he met her eyes had a sardonic edge, which made it clear Monsieur Wallace had been on guard, had suspected she might entertain some idea of flight.

There had been no chance whatever of it without being stopped. Recognizing that fact was infuriating, almost as much so as the painful heat of embarrassed remembrance that flooded her as she met the gentleman's watchful gray eyes.

She looked away at once, her gaze drawn to the levee where the foot of the gangway rested. Desolation settled, aching, around her heart. Freedom lay there in front of her, so close and yet so far away.

Kerr Wallace tipped his hat of glistening beaver as he drew closer. "Ladies," he said politely, "I trust your cabin is satisfactory."

"Perfectly." Tante Lily beamed at him as if she had not shooed him out of it not so long ago. "And you, *monsieur?* You are as comfortable?"

Sonia was grateful to her aunt for filling the breach, since she could not have formed a coherent, much less pleasant, answer.

"The *Lime Rock* is a cargo vessel, *madame.* Passengers are an afterthought. Only four cabins are available, and they are given over to you and your niece, a lady who travels with her children, a government official of some description and an elderly woman in bad health. The rest of us must make do as best we can in a pair of common cabins, one for the ladies and one for gentlemen."

"We are honored to be among the chosen then," her aunt said. "That was your doing, perhaps?"

"Monsieur Bonneval made the arrangements, though someone else was in possession when we came aboard earlier. It was only necessary to persuade the gentleman of your prior claim."

"With no great difficulty, I hope?" The sparkling look her aunt gave the Kentuckian made it obvious she expected otherwise.

Kerr's face remained grave. "None at all, at least not after the situation was explained to him."

"I was happy to oblige, I promise you, and am even happier about it now."

The sporting gentleman had left his companion to stroll toward their party. Skimming off his straw hat as he spoke, he swept the deck with its wide brim.

Tante Lily turned toward the newcomer, her gaze severe. "I beg your pardon?"

"Forgive the intrusion, I beg, but I couldn't help overhearing. It's presumptuous to introduce myself, but I hope it may be forgiven under the circumstances. Alexander Tremont, always at the service of two such lovely ladies."

Sonia's aunt offered her hand and a slow smile. "It's you we have dispossessed?"

"Only through an unfortunate misunderstanding."

"Then the informality may be permitted, I believe. We can hardly pretend not to know you for the length of the voyage."

Tante Lily might be fond of male company, but was usually cautious about admitting male strangers into her confidence, as witness her strictures on the subject just moments before. Sonia could hardly believe she was being so cordial now to a man she had labeled a gambler. She was up to something without doubt. It was likely nothing more than securing an amusing companion, someone to fetch and carry, shift deck chairs out of the wind or sun and make agreeable conversation over dinner. Sonia hoped that was the whole of it.

Monsieur Wallace did not appear happy with the turn of events. His face remained grim, his stance four-square and watchful as introductions were made all around. It was enough to reconcile Sonia to their new acquaintance, in spite of his presumed occupation.

Monsieur Tremont held her hand a little longer than was necessary as she was presented, but was quite well behaved otherwise. His remarks were addressed as much to Kerr as to her aunt or herself, and consisted mainly of when they would sail, the route they would take across the gulf, the experience of their captain and other such details. Tremont represented himself as owning a sugar plantation above New Orleans, though his main interest was investments in Mexico and Central America involving coffee and other such commodities. It might even be so, for all Sonia could tell, though in truth, she hardly listened.

Her thoughts inevitably reverted to how she was going to get off the ship. What a devil the Kentuckian was for vigilance. Still, he could not be everywhere. She might yet outmaneuver him.

Whatever she was going to do, she must hurry. Time

was leaking away. The packet for Mobile would leave its moorings in less than two hours. If she missed it, she might still hide away somewhere in the city until the next one left. But she had mere hours to get off the *Lime Rock,* for it would up anchor and sail away down the river at dawn tomorrow.

"Shall we walk, gentlemen?" Tante Lily said. "We are facing the sun here, and Sonia and I failed to bring up our parasols."

No one objected, least of all Sonia. She was eager to look over the ship for anything that might present itself as a screen or concealment for her flight.

The deck was narrow and cluttered with the preparations for departure and tools for ship's maintenance. Only a few steps beyond where they had been standing, a pair of seamen were scraping the railing and repainting it. Tante Lily took the arm of Monsieur Tremont as she stepped around a bucket of varnish. This left Kerr to steady Sonia while she held her skirts away from damage. She removed her elbow from his grasp as quickly as possible, disturbed by its effect upon her, like the tingling static shocks of winter where each of his fingers touched.

As they passed the two seamen, one of them tilted his head to look up. His gaze met Sonia's and he grinned, showing teeth stained red by the juice of the odd chewing tobacco that bulged in his cheek. Something in the widening of his mouth seemed unduly forward, and he licked his tongue over his lips as his gaze moved from her face down her body. Of a combination of nationalities from English and Spanish to Lascar, he appeared to be of that breed of seagoing men who kept the barrelhouses and brothels busy while their ships were in port.

Sonia looked away at once. Kerr moved closer and took her arm again in a possessive grasp as he stared down at the man.

"You there, Baptiste. Back to work."

The order came from a ship's officer who stood at a nearby hatchway, supervising the loading of flour barrels.

"Aye, sir. Right ye are, sir."

The seaman's answer, in the accents of dockside England, had an insolent ring to it, though he ducked his head and went back to his task as if his life depended on it. As they passed by, Kerr looked back, a frown lingering between his eyes.

The incident was so minor and quickly over that Sonia dismissed it at once. She was much too aware of the Kentuckian at her side. He did not release her a second time, but took her hand and placed it in the bend of his elbow.

She could feel the iron-hard muscles and tendons beneath his sleeve, sense the contained power in his tall form. In a frock coat of slate blue, worn with a cream and blue figured waistcoat and gray trousers fastened under his polished half boots by straps, he was a somber yet commanding figure of a man. The bright morning sun picked out the small fans of wrinkles at the corners of his eyes, glanced over the hard planes of his face and the indentation of a small scar on his chin, reflected silver in his eyes.

An odd frisson rippled over Sonia, leaving goose bumps in its wake. She frowned in disturbance. She was not some schoolroom *mademoiselle* to be thrilled by a set of fine shoulders and a prowling walk like some great mountain cat. What ailed her that she could see this *Kaintuck* as attractive in any fashion? It was ridiculous, especially when she preferred culture and refinement in a man. Yes, and some modicum of civilized discourse.

It was her duty to at least attempt conversation, of course; the precept had been impressed upon her from the moment she put up her hair. She might have depended on her aunt to supply the stream of chatter necessary to prevent awkwardness, but that lady had drawn ahead with Monsieur Tremont. Sonia was half inclined to remain silent since she had little to discuss with the man at her side. A moment's reflection dissuaded her. It would be prudent to convince him she was resigned to what lay ahead. He might then let down his guard.

"Have you been to sea before?" The question, couched in tones as even as she could make them, was instigated by the gentle movement of the deck under their feet as the ship rocked with the river current.

Kerr Wallace gave her a narrow look, though his answer came readily enough. "Only on coastal steamers, traveling between here and Mobile or Charleston."

"So you have no real idea whether you're a good sailor."

"No. And you?"

"My parents and I traveled to France when I was a child. I enjoyed the journey, loved the movement of the ship. But that was a long time ago."

"We must hope for the best then."

"Yes." That seemed to dispose of the subject. While she scourged her brain for another, she caught up the fan that dangled from a wrist cord and waved away the wood smoke that drifted around them, coming from an upriver steam packet making ready to leave the dock. It was bound for Natchez, she thought. Beyond it lay the Mobile packet that also had fired up its furnace, building steam in its boilers.

Resentment that she was not on that vessel washed over her in a wave. And with it came the vivid memory of the effortless way Kerr Wallace had lifted her, carried her the night before. It gave her a hollow feeling in her abdomen, and she could not prevent her gaze from flickering to his wide shoulder where she had rested. Her hip had pressed against the square line of his jaw, his large hand had clasped her upper thigh, coming perilously close to the softness between her legs in a way no man had dared before.

A heated, almost painful awareness of him as a man suffused her. It was disturbing beyond anything she had ever known.

If he felt anything similar, it was not apparent. Why should he indeed? She was his charge, a source of profit and funds for travel to Mexico, one he had no intention of losing. He had been the victor in their clash of wills and intentions so could afford to be at ease. At least for now.

"Something puzzles me, Mademoiselle Bonneval," he said in quiet tones. "You're not exactly hard on the eyes. You have family background and I suspect your papa can afford a good dowry. How is it you're come to—what was it, two-and-twenty—without being leg-shackled?"

"It's a dreary tale of little interest." The words were short as she summoned anger to combat her discomfort.

"We've nothing else to fill the time."

He was right, she was forced to admit. What harm could there be in relating these few details of her past, after all? They might soften his attitude, if such a thing were possible. Certainly, they would deflect her thoughts from the odd effect he had on her as he moved with lithe ease beside her, effortlessly buffering the wind off the water with his wide shoulders.

She looked away with deliberation, slowly plying the fan in her hand. "I was promised in the cradle to the son of our near neighbor in the country, Papa's best friend. Bernard was his name, Bernard Savariat. He and I grew up together, almost like brother and sister. He was, in fact, my father's godchild and intended heir."

"His heir?"

"Oh, Papa would not have disinherited me in a legal sense. He does care for my welfare, in spite of—" She stopped, began again. "Nonetheless, in his view a female isn't capable of attending to the business of a plantation. Bernard would naturally have taken control of whatever came to me."

Kerr gave her a keen look, perhaps for the carefully neutral tone of her voice. "I suppose Rouillard will do that now?"

"As you say." The words were stiff with distaste for the idea. Dismissing it after a moment, she went on.

"Anyway, Bernard was always at our house or I was at his. We did everything together, played house under the big tree in the courtyard, rode our ponies on the levee, fished in the river, swam, ate, napped—we were inseparable. He sometimes let me borrow his pantaloons and shirts so I could join the games played by him and his cousins—who were my cousins as well by grace of some common ancestor, in the usual way of such things among our people."

"A habit that came in handy, I see."

She inclined her head without looking at him, banishing once more the image of his hands upon her in her thin boy's pantaloons. With her gaze on the low houses of the town across the river, actually on its west bank as they neared the stern of the ship, she went on. "But then we grew up, or at least grew older. Bernard was an idealist. He had such exalted ideas about freedom and independence and the need to throw off tyranny. He thought everyone should be able to choose who should govern them, where they would live and how they would plan their lives."

Kerr Wallace tipped his head in a considered nod. "I knew someone like that once."

"A lot of young men feel these things, I suppose, and young women as well." She frowned a little, disturbed by the thought that the man at her side might have a dreary story in his past as well.

"So they do. But you were saying?"

"Yes. Bernard. One of his uncles had fought in Texas during their War of Independence against Mexico. He'd brought home Mexican silver dollars that he melted down to make a plantation bell, and often told stories about the land and the men who had opened the Texas frontier. Bernard was wild to see it before he settled down with a wife and family. He talked his father into letting him go off to join the Ranger company set up by President Lamar, the leader of Texas at the time."

"Yes, I recall." As she sent an inquiring gaze in his direction, he waved a hand in dismissal. "Nothing. Go on."

"There's little more to tell," she said with a shrug. "The company marched from San Antonio across the vast western reaches of the so-called Tejas country. Their object was to take Santa Fe."

"The luckless Mier Expedition."

"What?"

"So some name it, after the town where they fought the hardest, though it's labeled the Santa Fe Expedition as well."

"If you know that, then you surely know the rest."

"I prefer to hear your version."

She gave a small shrug. "Lamar was convinced those who lived in that part of the country, maybe even the commandant of the Santa Fe fortress, would join the Rangers in revolt against Mexico. It didn't happen."

"He died in Texas, your Bernard."

"He was one of those forced to surrender at Mier. The group was marched into the Mexican interior, but made a daring escape. They became lost, were recaptured. General Santa Ana decreed there must be reprisal, that one man in ten would be shot in ritual decimation. A pitcher was filled with a hundred fifty-nine white beans and seventeen black ones. Bernard drew a black bean when the time came to decide who would pay for their mistake, so was taken from the line of prisoners and—"

She stopped as tears rose to close off her throat. How very strange. She'd thought she had moved past the aching grief of that loss. Apparently she was wrong.

"My brother Andrew didn't have to face that ordeal," the man at her side said without looking at her. "He was one of those who died during the escape attempt."

She stopped, turned to him. "Your brother? I didn't know. I'm sorry."

"Could be they knew each other, your fiancé and Andrew."

"Perhaps. Jean Pierre, the man I am to marry, was also a member of that terrible expedition. It was he who told me about Bernard, making me a condolence call just after his return. He also gave me the message Bernard sent before he died. That—that was the only time I ever had what might be called a conversation with my future husband."

The Kentuckian gave her an odd look, opened his lips as if he meant to contradict her. Instead, he only said after a moment, "Not much to build a marriage on."

"No."

"The Mier Expedition was some time ago now. You've met no other man in the four years since? That is, you've formed no other attachment?"

He posed the question to allow some small distance from what was a painful subject, she thought, perhaps for both of them. She was grateful for it, though she preferred he not know it.

"Marriage being the whole reason for a woman's existence?" she asked with deliberate acerbity.

"It's usually seen as something to be desired."

"It appears a trap to me."

He turned to look at her. "That's how you see this match with Rouillard, as a trap?"

"One sprung by my own father." Her smile was brief and without humor.

"Why is he so set on the match? He think maybe you and Rouillard have something in common because he was supposed to be on hand when your fiancé was killed?"

"My father's thought processes are unfathomable. He has simply decreed it and expects obedience."

"Could be he's still after that heir."

"A grandson, yes. His lament since Bernard died has been that I didn't persuade him to marry me before he went off to Texas."

"Might have been better."

"What do you mean?"

"You could have avoided marrying Rouillard, not to mention this trip."

"There is that."

"Of course, you'd have been young for it, I'd say."

"Eighteen." She gave him a dark look. "Young marriages are quite common here. Any number of my friends have been wed since they were fifteen or sixteen."

"Too young to know what they were getting into."

"That's the point of parents arranging matters," she

said with precision. "They are presumed to have the necessary age and experience to make the right choice."

His frown remained. "That can hardly be the case now. What I mean to say is, you're old enough to know your own mind."

It could not be denied. What she could have told him, however, was that a French-Creole woman still unmarried at her age was considered a crone who might as well abandon hope, tossing her corset up on top of the armoire, as the saying went. She had refused so many proposals that her father had lost all patience. This alliance was his last chance, at least by his lights, to have her off his hands. To explain that aspect of the matter to the man at her side seemed an unnecessary humiliation, however.

"I was…reluctant to accept a substitute for Bernard," she said finally.

"It must have been hard for you, not knowing what had happened to him out there in Mexican territory, only learning of his death afterward."

"It was surely the same for you and your family."

He tipped his head in acknowledgment, his face set as he turned his gaze out over the yellow-brown water that raced past in flood beyond the railing, spreading its smells of mud and decaying vegetation.

After a moment, she spoke again on impulse. "The betrothal, mine and Bernard's, was merely understood between our families. It was never official, never celebrated with the usual gifts and parties. I could not go into black for him as my father would not permit the two years of seclusion that went with it."

"Two years of being out of the market for marriage, you mean."

She inclined her head by way of an answer since it seemed her voice might break. She had never mentioned that aspect of her grief to anyone else. It was peculiar that she had chosen to confide in this man. Or perhaps not. He was nothing to her. Their paths might never cross again after this day.

Ahead of them, Monsieur Tremont and her aunt paused to glance back. "I am told the captain has taken on a seaman with a talent for the violin," the sugar planter called, "one who may provide music for dining and dancing once we are at sea. Your aunt has agreed to do me the honor of a turn around the floor, Mademoiselle Bonneval. Perhaps you will do the same?"

"I am betrothed, you understand, *monsieur,*" she replied.

"But your fiancé is not here." His eyes were bright with audacity and he kept one brow lifted in inquiry.

"We shall see."

Beside her, Kerr Wallace gave the other man a hard stare. Sonia observed it with irritation that was increased in some manner by the odd rapport between them just moments before. His duties did not include the right to approve or disapprove of her dance partners, she thought.

At the same time, she felt a certain satisfaction in the knowledge that the Kentuckian was not happy in the association with Monsieur Tremont. She could see no reason for him to think everything would go his way. Besides, if Kerr Wallace was concentrating on separating her from what he believed to be unsuitable company, he would have less time to consider her other actions. And if he thought her in danger of being captivated by Monsieur Tremont's addresses, might he not feel she was becoming resigned to the voyage and her fate?

Sonia increased her pace, deliberately closing the distance that had opened between the four of them. Shaking off her introspection, she summoned her liveliest manner in the effort to appear charmed by the company of her aunt's newly met escort.

Seven

Tante Lily always swore she seldom closed her eyes at night, being a martyr to insomnia in its many forms. Sonia would not have contradicted her for the world, but had never found this to be true. Nor was it so on this, their last night at their mooring before an early-morning departure. Within minutes of blowing out the lamp, her aunt's gentle snores could be heard from the lower bunk.

Sonia had depended on that instant oblivion since it seemed her last opportunity to leave the ship. Kerr Wallace had been entirely too much on guard throughout the day. Every time she approached the gangway, he was there. If she attempted to join some group departing after seeing off a family member, he appeared at her side. She had come finally to realize that she was always under his eye so was forced to watch the Mobile packet sail without her. If she was going to escape him, these night hours promised to be her best, perhaps only, option.

Moving with the greatest stealth, she pulled out the pantaloons, shirt and boy's jacket she had secreted under her pillow and dressed in the dark. She climbed down from the upper bunk and pushed her feet into her borrowed boots, then felt for the small drawstring purse she had left under her discarded petticoats. With it thrust deep in her jacket pocket, she tiptoed to the door. She turned the key with care and peered out into the passageway.

The narrow corridor lay dark and empty in the pale light filtering down from the top deck. She sighed with relief, since she would not have been surprised to discover Kerr Wallace sleeping across the threshold like some servitor of times gone by. No doubt he had thought her aunt's presence would act as sufficient restraint upon her movements. That was his mistake.

Pulling the cabin door shut behind her, she stood a moment, allowing her eyes to adjust to dimness, listening for movement. All she heard was heavy snores from farther down the passage, the quiet creak of rigging and the lapping of the river along the ship's beam.

She should have been satisfied, even glad. Instead, a hard shiver of dread rippled down her spine. It was, just possibly, too quiet.

What was she doing? Was anything worth the acid doubt that poured along her veins? Was it really possible that she could make her way unnoticed along the dock with its piled crates, boxes and barrels, its tangles of rope and baling twine, its mounds of baled cotton creating tight alleyways where anything, anyone, might be hiding? Could she hide away until after the *Lime Rock* sailed, or until the Mobile packet returned? And what then? What then?

She would be free.

Free.

Free to go where she pleased, do what she wanted, live as she preferred without thought of anyone else's wishes or disapproval. She would be her own mistress, answerable to neither father nor husband but only to herself. That was surely an end worth striving for.

Swallowing hard, she lifted her chin and started toward the dim companionway. She kept close to the wall, stopped often to listen. At the bottom step she paused again.

Nothing, she could hear nothing, though it seemed she caught the faint whiff of tobacco smoke mingling with the dank odors of the ship's bilge and the muddy river. Could the smell linger from earlier in the evening, or might it be fresh? She couldn't tell which.

A watch would be posted. Where was he? That guard must be avoided at all costs, at least until she could make a run for the gangway.

Wherever the man was, he was making no sound. Perhaps he was patrolling at the stern or had fallen asleep. The last was surely too much to ask, but she could hope.

She could not discover the situation while cowering below. She closed her eyes, gathering her resolve. With careful steps and her back to the wall, then, she began to climb toward the deck.

The cool freshness of a night breeze reached her as she emerged topside. It was welcome after the stale air below. It brushed the tendrils of hair that had escaped from her long night braid so they tickled her cheek. She reached up to rake them back behind her ears as she looked toward the stern.

It was then she heard the whisper of cloth against cloth from behind her. She whirled to run. A hard, rough hand clamped down on her wrist, pulling her up short.

"What has us here now? Such a purty boy. I likes purty boys, I does."

It was the seaman she had noticed that morning, the one called Baptiste. In the gleam from a rigging lantern she caught the yellow-red gleam of his teeth, inhaled the foul odor of his body. She bit down hard on the scream that rose in her throat. Chest heaving, she wrenched back against the grip on her arm.

His hold tightened, radiating pain from her wrist to her elbow as the bones ground together. Sickness washed through her. She gave an instant to the throbbing ache.

Her captor used that momentary weakness to drag her against him. "Oh, ho, not a boy a'ter all," he said on a crude chuckle as he bucked against her softness. "Foine by me. Ol' Baptis' ain't partic'lar."

Disgust boiled up from inside her, sweeping aside caution and fear. "Release me this instant," she demanded in a hissing whisper.

"Now, why'd I be doin' 'at?"

"You can't molest a lady and hope to get away with it."

His laugh was obscene yet low, as if he was no more anxious for noise than she was. "I thinks maybe I can. Some ladies 'ould rather die nor say a hand was laid on their private parts by such as me. Knowed it to 'appen, I 'ave."

He might well be right. The shame of admitting such a thing could be worse, for one was soon over and the other unending. The knowledge only added to the sick fury inside her.

Abruptly, she lifted a foot and stomped down on his instep with a booted heel, then swung a fist at his grinning mouth.

It was a good effort, but his experience with rough-and-tumble fighting was clearly wider and more deadly than her own. He grunted and jerked his head back so her blow glanced over his cheekbone. In the same movement, he came around with a backhanded slap.

She caught the blow with a raised wrist, but stumbled back with its force. He came after her, slamming her against the bulkhead. Shoving against her, he pressed her to the grooved wood as he ground his lower body into the juncture of her thighs. Groping at her shirtfront with one hand, he tore its buttons free and pushed a hand in the opening to catch and squeeze a breast while his fetid breath assaulted the air between them.

"Now, my pretty, wha' think you of 'is?"

She stood rigid while a blood-red haze of pain and loathing clouded her vision. Furious impulses raced through her mind. Shifting her weight, bracing against the wall behind her, she made ready to ram her knee up into his crotch.

It was then that the slithering slide of metal on metal rasped the night air. "Release the lady, friend," a deep voice instructed in biting command. "You have two seconds before I carve your scrawny throat into a whistle for Davy Jones."

The seaman locked every muscle, going as stiff as the ship's mainmast. With virulent curses in a half-dozen languages and an abrupt, shuddering wrench, he pushed away from her. Slewing around, he faced the sword leveled at his neck.

Kerr Wallace shifted the point to the man's Adam's apple. His face was set in hard lines, his eyes a deadly gray-black behind the gleaming weapon in his fist.

The timbre of the voice, the lethal blade—who else should it be except Wallace? Nevertheless, the shock of his appearance was like a blow to the heart. With it came such despairing recognition of defeat that Sonia clenched her hands into fists and pressed them to the center of her chest as if that could stop the burning desolation inside her.

Kerr spared her a glance, his gaze resting on her torn shirtfront. His features hardened as he looked back to the man he held at the point of his sword. "Apologize to the lady."

The seaman spat on the deck, glowering his defiance.

As casually as if swatting a fly, the *maître d'armes* reached out with a flick of his wrist. A red line appeared under the jaw of the seaman. "Apologize," Kerr repeated in soft command.

"Gawd, man." Sonia's attacker wiped at his neck, stared at the blood on his fingers.

"How many scratches will it take to make you say you are a misbegotten bastard unfit to touch a lady?"

"She 'as leavin' the ship. You said look out fer 'er."

"And I was here to stop her. Had you forgotten I was also on watch, or did you expect me to share?"

"Could, still and all."

Another slash whipped across the man's jawline in a movement so fast the shining red of it seemed to appear by magic. "Apologize. To both of us."

The seaman stood white-faced and with murder in his eyes while breath whistled through his flared nose and blood dripped in black spots onto his bedraggled shirt. Then his gaze flickered to the sword point in front of him. It wavered, lowered to deck. "Sorry," he mumbled.

Kerr flicked his sword toward the railing. "Over it with you."

"What? Wait a mo'!"

"Now."

"I can't swim!"

"Learn. Fast."

"Fo' the love of God, man. She be only a skirt!"

Sonia closed her eyes tight as she saw the sword point flash once more. A hoarse cry sounded. An instant later, it was followed by the clatter of feet, a pause and a splash.

When she dared open her eyes again, Kerr was wiping the tip of his blade with a square of white linen. He paused as he met her gaze. His own hardened, then he seated the sword with a snap, twisting it into the sheath-like section of his malacca cane. His face grim, movements lethally silent, he stepped closer.

Nerves she hardly knew she possessed tightened in Sonia's chest, her stomach, low in her belly. Against her will, she sidled away from his advance. Angry chagrin boiled in her mind, becoming a single, near-incoherent cry. "Do you never sleep?"

"I'll sleep when we're at sea and you have nowhere to run," he said in grim reply. "Have you no sense whatever? Can you not imagine what might happen to you if you go prowling at night?"

"Imagination is no longer required." She made as if to push away from the bulkhead behind her.

He moved swiftly to block her way, slapping a large hand against the surface near her head. "But you're still willing to risk being taken for a lady of the night."

"What difference should it make to me whether the man who takes me is a seaman or a husband who is also a stranger?"

"Living to tell the tale, for one thing," he countered in hard tones as he leaned nearer. "Careful bedding rather than assault, for another."

"Careful." Her choke of laughter was layered with scorn.

"It should be nothing like what almost happened here."

"And I'm to take your word for it."

"All men are not the same."

"No, indeed! Some are worse."

"Yet some more tender."

"I can see you have never met Jean Pierre Rouillard."

"That pleasure has not been mine," he said, his voice grave, his eyes holding a steel-like shimmer in the uncertain light. "Nor have you known him as a husband."

"You don't understand," she said, her voice tight with the rage of despair. "You're a man. You're free. No one will ever force you to marry. You'll never have to come or go at the will of others, or because of events you can't control."

"None of us are as free as you seem to think. Events always move us, sometimes with our will, sometimes against it."

"Oh, yes, you're being forced to take ship to Mexico."

"As surely as you are."

"For the money."

"Wrong. I vowed—" He stopped. "But we were talking about you. Letting you go wandering the streets is like staking a lamb outside a wolf's den. Besides, how do you know you'll hate being married? You might find a husband's touch to your liking."

She might have known he would have no more consideration than to delve into the matter with her. She refused to play the coy maiden, however, in spite of the hot flush that rose to her hairline. "And I might be sickened by it."

"Have you never had a stolen kiss? If you liked one, chances are you'll enjoy the other."

The argument had logic, but she refused to concede it to him. "I should think that would depend on the man."

"Why would you say that?"

The sound of his voice, its deep vibrancy, seemed to seep into her, setting off echoes of longing that spread in waves to the very ends of her nerves. It was dangerous to stay here with him hovering so close above her. His nearness, some hard masculine power from inside him, seemed to sap her strength, leaving her oddly vulnerable, yet at the same time prey to a reckless need to defy fate, her father and everything she had ever known.

"Some people draw you to them," she said, her voice tight in her throat, "some have little effect and some repel for no reason."

His laugh was soft, short. "You have a point there."

"Of course, I could be wrong and you are right. It may be any man's kiss could be the prelude to…to love, of a kind."

"Of a kind?"

"Women are told they will come to care for their husbands no matter how they may feel in the beginning. That affection will grow as you come to know each other."

"But you don't believe it."

"And you do?"

"It seems reasonable."

Wariness edged his voice as he hovered over her. She refused to meet his gaze in the feeble light from the stern lantern. "If I could be sure…"

"You require proof."

"If…if you would care to provide it."

She caught her breath on the last word, stunned at her own daring. How strange it was, this moment in the gray night while the ship rocked with the river current and the shadows of its rigging wavered back and forth over the oaken deck. Mist hung in the air, rising from the water, curling upward to drift around them. In it, the man so close to her seemed not quite real, the figment of a dream. She would wake in a moment and discover she had not yet left the cabin and her sleeping aunt, that she had somehow missed the chance to escape the ship.

Kerr Wallace drew back a fraction, his features perfectly still. Then he dipped his head toward her. "I might at that," he whispered.

The words drifted over her lips in a warm current, waking them to tingling sensitivity. The first brush of his mouth was careful, a mere exploration of surfaces and intentions. The next was sweet, so sweet yet heady in its flavor that her breath left her in a soundless rush. Firm, smooth, a little rough at the corners from his day-old beard, his touch enticed her, made her dizzy and disoriented so she reached out to clutch a handful of his frock coat. He drew a quick breath, perhaps at her boldness. And she felt that cool inhalation before he settled his mouth more firmly over hers.

An experiment, she had thought, evidence against his conclusions about her and her marriage, refutation for society's ridiculous certainty regarding such arrangements. That was all she wanted.

She had not expected this intoxicating fascination with tastes and textures, the instinctive response to deep, inner need. A part of her mind stood aghast, disbelieving, while the remainder savored his kiss as she might hot, sweet morning chocolate, seeking the delicious stimulation, the awakening promise of sublime surrender, ultimate fulfillment.

He dropped his sword cane; she heard it clatter to the

deck and roll away. His hands closed on her arms to draw her against him then smoothed across her back. Blindly, she pressed into him, feeling the buttons of his waistcoat between her breasts, the loop of his watch chain beneath them. He surrounded and sheltered her with his innate power; he held her safe.

She wanted to consume and be consumed, to capitulate and forget. Most of all, to forget. The urgency of that need surged up inside her, burning behind her eyes. It pressed around her heart with such force that a soft moan of distress sounded in her throat.

Abruptly he dragged his mouth away. Breathing a fierce oath, he released her, took a fast step back.

She swayed an instant at that wrenching loss of support, the too-swift return to reality. He put out a hand to aid her, but she had already regained her balance and pretended she didn't see.

"That was…" he began, than stopped as though at a loss for words.

"Unwise? Dangerous?"

His eyes met hers in a searing glance before he inclined his head. "Both. Either. You had better go below before you are seen. Before you are missed."

It was a recommendation, not an order. He must be as disturbed as she was, Sonia thought. That was some comfort.

She drew a deep breath, let it out again. "Yes. You are perfectly right. It may be you are right in the matter of husbands as well. And wouldn't that be a farce?"

What he replied, she didn't know. She didn't wait to

hear it. Gathering her dignity around her like a cloak, she turned from him and walked away, back toward the blessedly safe confinement of her cabin.

Eight

Kerr watched the lady until she disappeared down the dark companionway. It was his duty as well as his pleasure. More than that, he could not have looked away if his life depended on it.

She had staggered him. Just when he thought he knew what he was about with her, she set him on his ear again.

This time he feared he had gone too far. Retribution had been in her eyes. Though whether for the kiss they had shared and her reaction to it or his role in keeping her a prisoner, he couldn't begin to guess.

He raked a hand through his hair and clasped the back of his neck as he turned his gaze heavenward. Lord, give him strength, because he knew he was going to need it.

The rattle of his sword cane rolling on the deck snagged his attention. Leaning, he picked it up in a stranglehold then stalked toward the stern of the ship where it jutted out into the river. His footsteps thudded on the thick planks. Above him, the ship's rigging clanked and jangled in the night wind, and a brown pelican, disturbed in its roost on a crossbar, squawked at him. Higher in the midnight black of the sky, the moon sailed, unconcerned with the problems of mere mortals.

What the hell was the matter with him? Had he lost all principles, every vestige of judgment? Had he slept so little in the nights since he'd taken on this post that his reason was skewed? Or was it just that something about Sonia Bonneval destroyed it?

What maggot of the brain had caused him to lay hands on her? She had put herself in danger, yes, but he had been in control of the situation. Never at any time had there been a chance of real harm coming to her. The run-in with the woman-starved seaman might even have been a good thing if it put the fear of God into her.

Or so he had thought at the time. Now he wasn't so sure.

Glancing around for the man he'd forced overboard, he saw him crawling from the river a few yards downstream where the current had taken him. Baptiste shook water from his hair and clothing like a dog as he got to his feet. Throwing a last, malevolent look over his shoulder, he trudged off toward the row of dives that lined Levee Street. Kerr, staring at where he'd disappeared among bales of cotton, wanted to nick the bastard a time or two more before kicking him overboard again.

How had that misbegotten devil's bastard dared touch Sonia? He should be whipped for the thought, much less the deed.

Yet Kerr himself had taken her in his arms moments

later. It must have been the last thing she needed after what had gone before. He should have been more considerate of her upset. Instead, he had taken advantage of it.

"If you would care to provide…"

The words she had spoken whispered through his memory along with the painful challenge in her eyes. Oh, he had cared, all right; every vestige of male pride inside him rose up to meet it. How was he to resist?

Somewhere in his mind, too, had been the memory of the paint on her face that first night. He had thought to test its hint that the lady had experience in the ways of men.

His mistake. She'd been as innocent as the most blushing of brides. Curious, yes, responsive in a way that told of sweet passion waiting to be brought to life, but innocent.

A groan rumbled deep in his throat. He should have stood firm against temptation, should have seen her to her cabin, turned her over to her aunt for comfort and said good-night. That he had not made him as bad as the twice-damned seaman squelching his way into town. The cause for both of them was the same and he knew it. Lust, it was pure, unbridled lust.

He would put a stop to it, Kerr swore in silent resolve. Another such mistake could bring his carefully laid plans to ruin.

He could not afford to feel attraction for the lady, had no use for the guilt that ate at him because of her. It wasn't his fault that she was on this ship or that her father had arranged a hateful marriage for her. Seeing her to Vera Cruz was a job, the means to an end. That was all.

Fine words. But who was holding her prisoner on the *Lime Rock,* guarding against her escape even now?

No, he was the one who had slammed the door on the trap that held her. It was he who intended to see to it that she was delivered safely to her groom. And what did that make him?

Kerr was still on deck when the dawn arrived in a glory of gold, lavender and rose that turned the river fog to opalescent mist. He was there when the order came to sail and crew swarmed from below to prepare the ship. He watched as the gangplank was swung in and the shout came to cast off, as the great hawsers were released from their dock cleats and pulled aboard, snaking through the water, while the steamer drifted away from the dock. He was there still, leaning against the deck housing with his arms crossed over his chest when Sonia Bonneval came up on deck and stood staring out over the sleeping city.

She was the consummate lady this morning in a gown of lavender blue over full petticoats and matching bonnet ribbons that twisted and fluttered in the morning breeze. Regardless, he was more aware than he wanted to be of the womanly form that lay beneath the layers of cambric and lace and behind the restriction of whale-bone corsets. Her warmth, her softness, the resilience of her female flesh under her boy's disguise were embedded so deep in his senses they might never leave him. His mouth was parched for another taste of her, his body as yearning as a drunk gone a week without the taste of liquor.

She was watching for someone, scanning the carriages that pulled up to the various river packets and sailing ships that were also making ready to sail this morning. Her gaze touched on the various gentlemen who stood about, lingering on those who were older.

Kerr didn't have to guess for whom she watched and waited. She thought her father, for all his displeasure over her attempt to avoid the marriage he'd arranged, would come to see her departure.

There was no sign of Bonneval. No one hurried from the still-dark streets; no one lifted a handkerchief to wave farewell. No one stood forlorn, as if reluctant to see her go.

The ship's deck shuddered as the steam engine began to rumble and the first turning of the side-wheel paddles sent river water cascading in wide falls. Coal smoke, already blowing in the wind, belched in black gusts from the big, single stack overhead, raining bits of soot onto the deck. The *Lime Rock*'s steam whistle blasted for their leave-taking. It was answered by others along the levee, and by ragged cries of farewell from well-wishers on the dock. The gangway was drawn in. A roustabout lifted a hand in an all clear.

They were moving faster, backing into the river's current. The *Lime Rock* was sailing, the grumble and thump of the steam engine growing louder as it surged into action. Still, Bonneval did not appear.

What kind of father would refuse to wave his daughter goodbye and look his last upon her face when it might

be years before he would see her again? What kind of
father would send her away at all to a man like Rouillard?

Kerr refused to think on it. He could only watch as
Sonia turned away from the railing. A female passenger spoke to her, perhaps in civil good-morning, and she
summoned a smile as she answered. It was a valiant
attempt, but even from where he stood, he could see the
sheen of unshed tears standing in her eyes.

Damn Bonneval to hell and back. It would not have
hurt him to rise early and make his way to the docks.

Damn Rouillard for demanding the hand of a lady he
barely knew and did not hold in regard. Damn him, too,
for expecting her to comply as if the careless proposal
was an honor.

Yes, and damn the man who had kissed Sonia last
night and made her stay, and wanted nothing so much
this morning as to kiss away her tears and tell her she
had no reason to cry.

That bastard was the worst of them all.

The steamer turned downriver and gathered headway.
Wharves, warehouses and anchored ships slid past. The
town fell away behind them. Plantations with their big
houses, outbuildings and river docks appeared like mi-
rages drifting past in the morning fog. Shanties built on
flatboats or raised on stilts edged the great waterway,
perched above their wavering reflections. These faded
away to endless stretches of trees. They were on their
way, gliding down the hundred or more miles of river
that would take them to the Gulf of Mexico.

The passengers wandered away from the railing,

some to promenade the deck, others to tidy their belongings brought on board or make ready for breakfast. Sonia disappeared belowdecks, perhaps in search of her aunt. Kerr, watching the last twitch of her skirts, pushed away from where he stood and let out a deep sigh of relief.

He could not think the lady was either foolish or desperate enough to leap from the moving ship. It would be nothing less than suicide even if she did know how to dog-paddle a bit, like the seaman he'd forced to swim ashore. The Mississippi River was wide, the shoreline impossibly distant. He could afford to rest and maybe catch up on his sleep knowing Sonia could not escape the ship.

He tried, he really did. Forgoing food, he took off his boots and lay down in his bunk, pulling the curtain closed around it for privacy in the common room. Eyes shut, he listened to the beat and thud of the engine, the swish of the water moving along the hull, the slap of cards and rumble of voices from a game in the gentleman's parlor next door. A short nap, he thought, that was all.

He couldn't do it.

What if he was wrong? What if Mademoiselle Bonneval so despised her proposed groom that she'd try any means to get away from him? She was no milk-and-water miss, apt to give up at the first setback. Oh, no. She'd spit in the eyes of them all—Bonneval, Rouillard, even him, especially him.

Besides, the steamer would not be keeping to the middle reaches of the Mississippi. Sandbars, islands and floating debris, even whole trees lifting leafless branches like drowning souls, would send them along channels closer to the banks. She might well throw herself off the stern.

Chances of her making it to shore were slim if she tried it in her heavy skirts. They'd drag her down to the muddy river bottom where she'd turn, pale and staring with her hair trailing around her, before settling among the scavenger catfish and turtles. And that was if she didn't jump from the side rail so she wound up battered by one of the paddle wheels.

Kerr sat up with a shudder, thrusting the images from him as he wiped his hands over his face. It couldn't happen. He wouldn't allow it.

Rolling from the bunk with a hard wrench of tired muscles, he pulled his boots back on and went topside again. It didn't help his feelings, not a whit, to find the lady stretched out in a deck chair with an open book on her lap, pages riffling in the breeze, and her eyes closed in the most peaceful of slumber.

Kerr took a chair a few feet down from hers and stretched out, crossing his booted ankles and folding his hands across his waistcoat. For some time, he lay watching Sonia, his gaze moving from the fine dark curls stirring against her cheek to the curves of her lips and soft mounds of her breasts that rose and fell so evenly. Her skirts covered her ankles, yet he caught a discreet display of neatly turned perfection in white stockings every time an errant wind lifted them as it gusted along the deck.

He stirred uncomfortably, cursing softly under his breath. Pulling up the split skirt of his frock coat, he folded it over him so it covered the front of his trousers a little better.

He had kissed her, held her, felt her breasts, belly and thighs pressed against him from chest to knees. The taste of her lingered in his head, a sweet intoxication beyond imagining. He wanted her with an ache that was three parts physical need, but one part something else entirely.

His enemy's betrothed. What was it in men that demanded they possess the women claimed by those they despised? Did it come from the instinct to hit where it hurt most, to go for the soft underbelly? Or could it be some ancient need to prevent their tribe from increasing?

Kerr had no idea. He only knew he was fast becoming obsessed with Jean Pierre Rouillard's bride-to-be.

She had been afraid of him the night before. It was momentary, he thought, yet he had seen her measure his size with a swift look and estimate her lack of chance against him, seen the terror in her face when she thought he would maim or kill the seaman who'd insulted her.

He hadn't enjoyed it. It made him feel degraded, that flash of dread, branded by it as an uncouth bully. And he deserved it, that he knew well, because he had deliberately used his size and strength of will to intimidate her. It wouldn't happen again, not if it was in his power to prevent it.

Nor would he touch her again. She didn't deserve to be made a pawn in the game between him and Rouillard. Except she was that already, had been from the moment he learned of her existence.

She would not suffer for it, at least not any more than was strictly necessary. This much he swore in silent vow. Like the swordsmen of the Brotherhood, he would fight to his last breath to keep her safe.

Exalted intentions, he thought with silent scorn. But he did not disavow them as he allowed his eyelids to close.

Nine

It might have been an hour later, but seemed mere minutes, when a clatter jerked Kerr awake. His neck was stiff and one arm hung down beside his chair with the knuckles of his hand trailing on the deck. More than that, the deck chair where Sonia had lain was vacant.

He came erect with an oath, swung his head to peer up and down. There she was, only a few paces away, strolling on the arm of Alexander Tremont. She seemed oblivious to everything except that gentleman as she chatted, smiling as if she had not a care in the world. Behind her on the planking, not two yards from Kerr's resting place, lay a fan of painted silk with ivory sticks.

It was the sound as she dropped it that had awakened him. Kerr climbed to his feet, stretched, then bent to scoop up the feminine trifle. Closing the distance between the couple and himself with a few long strides, he cleared his throat.

"Your pardon, *mademoiselle.*"

She paused, turned with the most innocent of faces. *"Monsieur?"*

"I believe you lost this."

"Oh, yes," she said as she took the fan from him. She spread the carved sticks, inspecting the silk for damage, before sending him a quick glance from under her lashes. "How kind of you to retrieve it. I am sorry if my letting it fall disturbed your rest."

She was nothing of the kind. The bit of silk and ivory had been dropped on purpose. It was, he thought, something in the nature of a thrown gauntlet, a declaration of war between them. He would not give her the satisfaction of knowing he understood it, however.

"Not at all," he answered with a brief nod of greeting for Tremont at the same time. "I was merely enjoying the air."

"As are we all, though this passage downriver to the gulf is a tedious business. Or don't you find it so?"

Kerr glanced at the glittering silver stretch of the river ahead of them. Great blue and white herons waded in the shallows, making the water ripple as shoals of minnows fled before them. Egrets festooned the moss-hung trees like great white flowers. A raccoon scurried out of sight as the ship neared, and an alligator or snake stirred a nearby eddy. Shrubbery feathered with rich green growth skirted the verge of the waterway, leaning out as if to see their reflections.

"I'm not sure I do." He turned back to smile into her periwinkle eyes. "There's much to be said for a slow and quiet journey."

"I might have known you would say so. A quiet life for you, at all costs." She glanced up at the gentleman next to her. "Monsieur Wallace is my escort, you perceive, hired by my father to make certain I arrive safely at Vera Cruz."

Tremont nodded. "Your aunt explained it to me. An enviable position."

"I'm not sure he would agree with you. I suspect it's been a trial for him to this point."

"It's had its rewards." Kerr kept his voice carefully neutral.

A flush bloomed on her cheekbones and her lips compressed in a flat line. He was gratified to see that she understood his reference, that she recalled the evening before even if her remembrance could not be as vivid as the one that seared his mind.

It was also satisfying, in some strange fashion, that she seemed to be playing fair with Tremont by frequent reminders that she was not free. He would not have put it past her to add the gentleman to her train in hope he might prove useful in effecting an escape.

That, he couldn't allow.

The gentleman's intentions toward Sonia were not likely to be serious or to extend beyond the length of the voyage, Kerr thought. A brief flirtation, a midnight tryst or two; he would look for nothing more. No doubt his handsome face and polished address had gained him many a similar conquest in the past, so he naturally expected another.

His next would not be Sonia Bonneval. Kerr felt no

particular ill will toward the man, but he would carve him up like a Christmas goose at the first hint that he meant to take advantage of her.

"I'll just amble along with you, if I may," he said casually, even as these swift conjugations ran through his head. "Nothing like a nice walk around the deck for warding off the fidgets."

Sonia made no objection. Primed as he was for another clash, Kerr was instantly uneasy. He leaned a little to see under her bonnet brim as he fell into step beside her, across from Tremont. The flash of burning lavender blue he caught did nothing to reassure him.

Moments later, while she discussed the passengers she had met thus far and the cargo they were carrying, one end of the shawl she wore looped through her elbows slipped to the deck. In reeling it in again while keeping her hold on the book she'd been reading, she somehow managed to entangle its fringes with Kerr's boot. He stumbled, trying to keep from ripping away the trailing silk threads, as she pulled them from under his foot. Only the most desperate of hornpipes prevented him from landing on his backside.

She smothered a laugh. He was sure of it. He apologized, anyway, while avoiding the grin of sympathetic understanding Tremont threw him. Let her treat him like a lackey and buffoon, he thought in wan acceptance. His shoulders were broad enough to take it, and they both knew where the authority lay. If the exercise roused her spirits, he didn't mind.

"Curious thing," the sugar planter said, manfully filling

the conversational breach as they began to walk again, "I came up on deck in the wee hours this morning for a smoke and look around. The ship's crew was loading, doing the work of stevedores. What they carried on board appeared to be crates and boxes of a special size."

Kerr inclined his head in agreement. "I noticed the same myself."

"I figured you might have, since I saw you at the stern. What did you think?"

"What was it?" Sonia asked. "What were they loading?"

She glanced from him to Tremont and back again as she put the question, Kerr saw. Since the other man had brought up the matter in front of her, there seemed no point in beating around the bush, even if it was not a subject usually discussed before the ladies.

"Arms," he answered, "or so it looked to me, rifles and ammunition."

"But that would mean—" Sonia stopped, frowning.

"Someone is either planning a large hunting party or sending a shipment of weapons to Mexico."

"Who would do such a thing?"

Her voice was thin and she stared straight ahead so it was impossible to see her face. Kerr wondered what she was thinking, wondered if, just possibly, she suspected the involvement of someone she knew. Rouillard, for instance.

"Some scoundrel who values gold over scruples, I'd say." He twitched a shoulder. "Not that there's any law against it. We aren't at war."

"A technicality," Tremont said. "There will be a law the instant war is declared."

"Agreed."

The planter tipped his head. "I suppose the captain could have a hand in it."

"Making a bit of extra cash on the voyage, you mean? It's possible." The vessel's master, Captain Frazier, had the look of an upright New England Quaker to Kerr, plain of dress, with a permanent frown between his eyes and side-whiskers like cotton bales on his jaws, untrimmed because it might appear vain to keep them neat. Not that it meant anything. The look of a man had fooled people before, and would again. "Might just as easily be in the charge of the American commissioner we have on board."

"As a peace offering from our government, you mean, or a bribe for the good behavior of whoever is president of the country by the time we get there."

Kerr nodded, understanding the last as a reference to the frequent changes in that high office. The most disturbing of these involved General Santa Ana, the man behind the decimation of the prisoners from the Mier Expedition, as well as the infamous massacre at the Alamo ten years before. He'd been in and out of the position at least twice, and looked to be back again any day.

"Might they not be for their protection?" Sonia suggested.

"You haven't seen the number of boxes, *mademoiselle*," he answered.

"Unfortunately not," she said in acid tones, "being otherwise occupied."

She meant that she had been confined to her cabin for all rights and purposes. "Just so," Kerr said in grave approval.

The exclamation she made was soft but virulent. At the same instant, the book she held slid from her grasp. Careening down the sloped bell of her skirts, it skidded across the deck where it lay with pages flapping in the breeze.

Tremont reached it first. As he leaned to pick it up, his frock coat fell open, revealing the shape of a pocket pistol against the lining. Gentlemen often kept such a weapon about them, but it was usually for a particular purpose, such as protection late at night or when carrying large sums of money. It was possible this voyage was excuse enough. Still, Kerr took note of it.

He wanted to snatch Sonia's book from the planter's hand. Perverse though it might be, given his suspicion it had been let fall on purpose, he resented Tremont's retrieval of it. The game was between him and the lady, after all.

Deliberately, he reached out and took possession of the volume. It was *The Legend of Montrose,* a historical romance by that purveyor of ancient Highland dramas Sir Walter Scott. The feudal settings and grand notions of honor had made his work wildly popular in New Orleans in recent years. This one was an elegant edition in bound leather stamped with gold and with its pages edged in gold leaf. "A fine tale," he said in judicious comment, "but not the equal of *Ivanhoe.*"

"You've read it?" Sonia lifted a brow as she held out her hand for the return of her property.

"We do read in Kentucky," Kerr answered, his voice dry.

"I didn't mean it that way," she said, her voice stiff.

Maybe she hadn't, maybe he was too ready to see insult where there was none. "You feel such high romance is not my style? My ancestors were from Scotland, you know. I'm reminded of the stories told by my grandpa, fine tales of cattle stealing and brawling in the heather for the glory of the clan. Well, and for the fun of it."

"Fascinating, I'm sure."

"So they were," he agreed, all affability as he handed over the book with a bow. "Being I'm the type, it could help if you picture me in the part of Scott's Robert McGregor. You might gain a clearer understanding of events."

"I understand well enough."

"Now, I'm pleased as punch to know that as it makes everything so much easier," he answered at his most obtuse, though he knew very well what the snap in her voice meant.

She gave him a fulminating glance then whisked around in a swirl of skirts and began to walk again. Tremont paused long enough to offer a quick shrug before hastening after her.

Kerr, his face set in grim lines, stared after them for long moments. He should give up, go below, have a shave and a wash.

He wasn't so inclined.

It occurred to him that he was far too intrigued by the

battle of wills between himself and the lady under his protection. Something in it made him feel alive, almost hopeful in a way he had not since—well, since before Andrew had died. Might just be that the long quest was nearing an end, that he was finally doing something that bid fair to let him keep his sworn promise to avenge his brother's death. Possibly it was because he was going to face Jean Pierre Rouillard at last.

Yes, and it could be he simply took pleasure in the lady's company. He took far too much pleasure in it, in fact.

He should back off, leave her be except for keeping watch to make sure no harm came to her. He should slope off now, find something, anything else, to pass the time. He could visit the engine room, look in on the bridge, have a word with the captain about when they would reach the gulf and the course they would set for Vera Cruz. He could slip down into the hold, poke around checking cargo markings, see if that shipment of arms and ammunition was directed to anyone familiar, say, a gentleman named Rouillard.

None of those things held the least appeal. They might later, but not just yet. Regrettable, but there it was.

Clasping his hands behind his back, whistling a Scots lament for Bonnie Prince Charlie, he sauntered after the irritating yet fascinating Mademoiselle Bonneval.

Ten

The arrogance of the man, to suppose she might picture him as the hero of some epic romance, a figure of nobility, chivalry and desperate courage. He hardly fit the mold, having hired out his sword to the highest bidder while taking on the subjugation of a helpless female. Not that she was as supine as all that, which the gentleman would discover to his cost, but the principle was the same. The McGregor indeed! His suggestion was enough to put her off finishing the book; now that he had instilled the idea of himself as a figure in it, she must continually force the image from her mind. How very provoking.

It was precisely what he intended, of course; she had seen it in the fathomless gray of his eyes. How odd, when she would have sworn subtlety was not his forte. Force, action, overt command, she might have expected, but not oblique challenge.

How very conscious she was of him behind her. His great shadow, slipping along ahead of him, fell over her so she walked in its gray, moving pool. The sheer magnitude of it would be intimidating if she allowed it to be. She was not a large female, but neither was she petite, and it nearly covered her.

To walk at anything approaching a natural pace was difficult with him so close on her heels. Why that should be was a mystery. It wasn't as if she cared what he thought.

Perhaps the problem was merely that he was always near at hand, or so it was beginning to appear, always aware of where she was and what she was doing. He was conscientious in his job; she had to give him that much. Her father was getting his money's worth. Too bad he wasn't there to appreciate it.

Or perhaps it was just as well. One of the few advantages she could find in her approaching Mexican exile was that she need no longer be under his thumb. Kerr Wallace was acting as his proxy for now, to be sure, but even that would end in time. And then…

Yes, and then?

She didn't know. It would depend on what she found when she reached Vera Cruz. She only knew it would not include a wedding, no matter what Kerr Wallace thought.

Sonia rounded the prow of the ship and paused to gaze down the river's winding channel. They had left all habitation behind other than an isolated trapper's shack or two with a pirogue bobbing in front of it. A thick growth of trees still crowded the waterway, but was beginning to be broken by small islands of shell where oaks grew, draped in their mourning rags of gray moss. Something inside her longed for the first glimpse of the gulf, as if freedom might lie beyond its blue waters instead of behind in New Orleans. What contradictory creatures people were that she should feel that way.

At the railing opposite where she stood was a slender gentleman. He appeared sunk in melancholy, drooping over the railing as he contemplated the water. As he caught sight of her, however, he straightened. Executing a creditable bow, he wished her and her companions a good-morning.

He was young, hardly passed into his majority, Sonia thought. Handsome in the traditional French-Creole fashion, with olive coloring that indicated a dash of Spanish in his bloodline, he yet had the fresh, open countenance of one who had not yet succumbed to cynicism. His soft brown hair curled back from a wide forehead, his eyes were dark, tender and intelligent, deep-set behind luxurious black lashes. His mouth was full and mobile, and appeared to smile as easily as it turned down in ennui. Attired in the most outré of current male fashion, in a buttercup-yellow frock coat edged with leather and *tan d'or* pantaloons, he wore the artfully careless cravat of the Bohemians, one dotted in yellow on tan and pinned in place by a Zeus-head cameo in the style made popular by the renowned Mulatto sword master Croquère. For all his casual elegance, something about him reminded Sonia of a puppy anxious to be noticed.

His appearance also seemed just short of effete, a result of the contrast with Kerr Wallace, she was sure. Compared to the undiluted masculinity of the Kentucky swordsman, every man in sight seemed too refined, somehow lacking in power and authority. It was not a comfortable insight when it should have been the opposite, with him appearing crude compared to the rest.

"Well, *monsieur,*" she said to this fellow passenger with determined brightness, "are we progressing as we should, do you think? Can the pilot be trusted to see us safely out into the gulf?"

"As to that, I could not say, *mademoiselle.*" He gave her a bashful smile. "We seem to be making good time."

"Always something to be wished, I agree. Do you travel alone?"

"With my mother, rather, Madame Marie Pradat. I am Gervaise Pradat, *à votre service.*"

Sonia, on an impulse of kindness and with the delicious knowledge that Kerr was unlikely to approve, presented the Kentuckian and Alexander Tremont then introduced herself.

"My mother will wish to make your acquaintance," the young man said. "I'm sure we have friends in common, and she will delight in discovering them. She was making ready for breakfast when I spoke to her, though not without difficulty."

"She isn't unwell, I hope?"

Gervaise shook his head. "Just not in the most robust of health, you understand."

"What a pity. So you are alone."

"As you see." He inclined his head, his gaze hopeful. To invite the young traveler to join their perambulations seemed the only course possible. When she began to stroll again, Sonia had three gentlemen in her entourage.

"I trust your aunt isn't under the weather, *mademoiselle*," Kerr said in a deep growl from behind her.

"Because she isn't here to act as chaperone?" She sent him a sparkling glance over her shoulder for his rather heavy-handed intimation that she needed such a thing. "No, no, it's her habit to lie abed until noon, and she was exhausted after rising so early yesterday. I saw no reason to disturb her. Though my dear aunt is as serene as any could wish under most circumstances, she can be most uncivil before she has her morning coffee."

"That's hard to believe."

"She would be delighted to hear you say so. You are free to wake her, if you like."

His reply was no more than a grunt, but he made no move to leave their little group. Exultation at the small victory ran in Sonia's veins like fine wine.

Contrary to her expectations, she could not feel entirely downcast this morning. A part of it was because she refused to give up hope, was too stubborn to accept her fate. The main reason, though, was the gentleman following on her heels. He made her so furious she had scant time for despondency. Matching wits with him was stimulating even when she could not win. It defied belief, much less understanding, but she was very close to enjoying their verbal exchanges.

Behind her, Kerr was engaging Gervaise Pradat in idle conversation. It seemed good sense to listen since it might reveal some piece of information that could be useful.

"You have business in Vera Cruz?" the Kentuckian was asking.

"Not at all," came the answer with all the proper horror of a Creole gentleman who would never think of turning his hand to trade. "My mother's brother is there. His wife, being from an old Spanish family, inherited a considerable amount of property in Mexico. They have investments on the coast, so keep a house in Vera Cruz."

"Your uncle looks after his wife's interests."

"Naturally."

Noting her attention to their exchange, Kerr sent Sonia an ironic smile. Undoubtedly, he was recalling their discussion on the subject of a husband's prerogatives. She rolled her eyes for the predictability of it.

"Naturally," Kerr repeated to Gervaise in grave acknowledgment. "You've made this journey before?"

"Several times. My aunt is the soul of hospitality, so makes us, *Maman* and myself, welcome every year. Vera Cruz, like New Orleans, is infernally hot and pest-ridden in summer. We travel with them to the mountains of the interior where it's much cooler."

"A pleasant escape. You go by carriage, I suppose."

"Alas, no. The roads are too bad. The usual mode is by litter for the ladies, while the gentlemen ride saddle horses."

Kerr's inquisition was not entirely idle, Sonia suspected. She could not be certain what was in his mind, but wondered if it might have some connection to the shipment of arms residing in the ship's hold. A gentleman such as the uncle of Gervaise Pradat would have the means and opportunity to engage in such commerce. She could see, as well, that the annual visit of a doting sister and nephew would make excellent cover for transporting the merchandise.

"And what of you, *monsieur?*" the younger man asked with the lively curiosity of those who preferred investigating people to exploring ideas. "You have affairs of business in Vera Cruz?"

"He is in charge of a prisoner," Sonia answered for the Kentuckian. "He escorts me to a wedding with a bridegroom I barely know."

Kerr gave her a hard look that she ignored with ease since she was becoming practiced at it. Gervaise clapped a hand to his heart while staring at her in comic dismay. "I am desolated, Mademoiselle Bonneval. Just when I become acquainted with a lady who might come to mean everything, I discover it can never be. For a picayune, I would make away with you before the wedding."

"For a picayune, I would allow it," she said at her gayest.

"May I inquire as to the man lucky enough to be your intended?"

"Certainly, if it's of interest." She gave him Jean Pierre's name and direction.

"Ah."

That single syllable held a wealth of meaning. Sonia could not let it pass unchallenged. "You know the gentleman?"

"I believe I've heard my uncle speak of him. He cuts

quite a figure in Vera Cruz, particularly in more cosmopolitan circles."

"Is that not a good thing?"

"It isn't a bad one by any means." The boy's face carried a plum-colored flush and he refused to meet her gaze. In an obvious attempt to turn matters in another direction, he said, "So Monsieur Wallace stands as protector in lieu of your father? The two of you are related, perhaps?"

Sonia's laugh was hollow. "Hardly. He is a *maître d'armes* of most fearsome reputation. You must be careful not to give offense."

"I shouldn't dream of it," Monsieur Pradat said with mock alarm, though a small frown remained between his eyes.

"It's the incessant talk of war, you see," she went on. "My father felt something more was required in the way of protection for the journey."

"Other than your aunt as your companion, I comprehend," he said. And perhaps he did, for his face was grave and his dark eyes liquid with sympathy.

Kerr understood as well, for he met her eyes, his own shaded a forbidding, storm-cloud gray. The smile she gave him in return was guileless. Still, it seemed a distraction was in order. Deliberately, she released her grip on her fan and let it fall for the second time.

She expected a small melee as her various escorts vied for the honor of retrieving it. Instead, Kerr leaned with pantherlike grace to catch it as it fell. In the midst of that swift move, he plunged a hand into the fullness of her skirts, skimming over her leg at the level of her garter.

She caught her breath at his audacity, the sound perfectly audible in the morning quiet. For an instant, they remained in frozen tableau, gray eyes locked to lavender blue, while the world slid past around them.

"So this is where you have hidden yourself, *ma chère* Sonia!" her aunt said as she descended upon them with brisk steps and a froth of windblown skirts. "Such a pleasant promenade, really—I quite see the attraction. Oh, you've made contact with Monsieur Pradat. How very providential as I've just been speaking to his mother. We were at convent school together, you know, though I've not seen her in an age. She quite longs to meet you, *chère*. Come, let us all walk together. I'm sure we will meet up with Madame Pradat again at the back of the ship where it's less windy."

There was nothing to be done except fall in with Tante Lily's wishes. Sonia had no real objection since matters had become a little strained. Still, she hesitated, waiting for the return of her fan, preparing a gracious acceptance of the courtesy that would put Kerr in his place as her servitor rather than her jailer.

The words went unspoken. The Kentuckian stared down at the silk trifle in his big hand while a smile curled one corner of his mouth. Lifting it to his lips then, he slipped it into an inside pocket of his frock coat as if secreting the most precious of love tokens.

She could have demanded the return of her property. She could have made a scene, refusing to budge from where she stood until the fan was in her possession again. Instead, she ignored it, taking the arm of her aunt and walking on beside her.

It was for the best, that retreat, she told herself. She wasn't confused by his unexpected gesture, wasn't misunderstanding it, and certainly wasn't acquiescing to it.

No, it was simply that she had no wish to call attention to something that had no meaning beyond the gentleman's annoyance at being treated like a hired servant.

It was only common sense.

That was all.

Eleven

Aboard the *Lime Rock*, meals were served for the convenience of the officers and crew rather than for the passengers, so timed to the changing of the watch. Breakfast was at sunrise or shortly thereafter, the midday meal at noon and that of the evening at dusk, with a scratched-up supper at midnight for those who required it. There was some grumbling at the change from more fashionable mealtimes, but the passengers soon grew accustomed.

Kerr had no preference himself. Though he was as fond of eating as the next man, he'd not yet developed the constant French-Creole preoccupation with the timing and composition of his next meal.

The dining salon was a long room with a coffered ceiling and an Axminster carpet woven in a green-and-brown pattern taken from Moorish tiles. A series of tables set in a row like one long board centered the space. Padded benches lined either side of them. Whale-oil lanterns swung on gimbals overhead, casting a sway-

ing yellow light, or else were attached to gimbaled girandoles along the walls. Between large windows were
gilt-framed mirrors, and more of them faced the center
support posts, endlessly reflecting for a sense of spa-
ciousness.

Dinner on this first official evening aboard consisted
of a bouillabaisse followed by pasta heavy with butter
and garlic. This was succeeded by baked fish with
steamed vegetables and tournedos of beef in a wine
sauce. Plain cake improved by a side dish of dried
cherries flamed in brandy served as dessert, along with
the usual cheese and nuts. The seaman doing double
duty as a violinist gave them several lugubrious tunes
designed to aid digestion. While they ate, they sometimes
noted the red spark of another steamer passing upstream,
or else saw the wavering lights of a settlement clustered
near where a winding bayou emptied into the river.

It was an uncomfortable meal. Several times, Kerr
caught Madame Pradat, Gervaise's mother, staring at
him with disapproval in the lines of her palely severe,
aristocratic features. He noted also when she put her
head close to that of the dispirited young mother traveling alone, one Madame Dossier, while speaking in a
sibilant whisper. Afterward, they both glared at him
before turning away with their chins in the air.

He felt like a pariah. It wasn't something he enjoyed,
though he had learned to live with a similar isolation
since putting out his shingle as a sword master. His kind
was not, in the main, acceptable company at the tables
of the crème de la crème. His skill with a blade usually

prevented the more obvious expressions of disdain. At least from the gentlemen.

What did these French-Creole ladies expect, that he would rise and turn tail, taking his meals with the crew for the remainder of the voyage? It wasn't in the cards. They could get used to his presence, as could the lovely Mademoiselle Bonneval. He was going nowhere.

Kerr looked down the long table to where Sonia sat, wondering if she had noted the success of her campaign to make him conspicuous. The glance of unsmiling satisfaction she sent him was answer enough. He gave a soundless grunt before turning his attention back to his food. She would have to do better if she hoped to get under his skin. Likely, she would be more discomfited than he was by talk of having him as her guard.

Following dessert, the tables were cleared and set against the walls with their benches under them. The smells of food still mingled with the fishy reek of whale oil from the overhead lanterns when the dancing commenced.

Kerr watched for a while as Sonia was steered around the floor by the captain, a ship's officer or two, the American commissioner, Tremont and young Pradat. He considered joining the line waiting for the privilege, but was in no more mood for a public refusal than he'd been in New Orleans.

He opted instead for a cheroot on the deck while watching the sparks that shot from the ship's smokestack as they trailed across the night sky behind them.

He didn't often indulge in tobacco, but there were times when its soothing effect was required.

They were coming close to the gulf, he thought. The terrain had grown more flat and watery, and the smell of brine came in windblown gusts. Gulls had appeared at dusk, following their progress in hope of scraps from the galley or a roost in the rigging. Captain Frazier, or rather the pilot he'd taken aboard, was using the more southwesterly of the various passages to the gulf. Word from the bridge was that they would emerge into open water by midnight, if not before.

Kerr intended to wait up for it. He had little to do otherwise, and it was always a milestone. This time around it meant even more than on his coastal excursions. He could finally let down his guard since the open gulf heralded an end to any possibility of Sonia trying to swim for the riverbank. He'd have that worry off his mind once and for all.

Contemplating the glowing end of his cheroot and the way its fragrant smoke was whipped away by the wind, he let his mind wander to the munitions in the cargo hold beneath his feet. They bothered him out of all proportion. He didn't consider himself more than an average patriot. He'd signed up to march in the Legion, true, but more with the idea of fitting in with the swordsmen and young bloods of the town, maybe getting a lead on the bastard responsible for his brother's death, than for any other reason. He cared little enough whether the border between Texas and Mexico was fixed at the Rio Nueces or the Rio Grande.

Nevertheless, the idea of some yahoo selling weapons to Mexico that could be used against his friends in the Louisiana Legion didn't sit well with him. Looking a bit deeper into the matter was, just maybe, a fine way to pass the time.

Sauntering, pausing now and then, trying to look like a gentleman with time on his hands and an idle mind, he moved along the railing to the vicinity of the cargo hatch. When he was sure the watch was busy elsewhere and no passengers or off-duty crew were nearby, he opened the heavy cover and slipped inside, closing it noiselessly behind him.

The hold was dark and close, the air heavy with the musty scents of old coffee, molding spice and spoiled fruit, of raw timber, cottonseed and wheat chaff. Bales and barrels, kegs and boxes were stacked to the ceiling, held secure against rolling seas by ropes and railings that formed narrow aisles barely wide enough for a man to pass through without his shoulders touching the merchandise. In this close space, the wash of seawater along the hull was an endless, sibilant rush, with the gurgle of the bilge and squeaking of rats joining in obbligato.

Kerr eased crablike down one aisle with his back to what felt like grass sacks packed with dried corn. At a corner, he paused, moved forward a step.

Instantly, he whipped back again.

Someone was in the hold with him. A seaman, maybe, sent to inspect the cargo against shifting before they reached rougher water? Impossible to say, but he wasn't inclined to explain his snooping.

Whoever it was appeared to be going at a crate or box with a crowbar. The quiet shriek of nails being dragged slowly from wood was easy enough to recognize.

The man kept at his job, apparently unaware he had company. Kerr stepped backward, reversing his path, taking a different aisle as he sought out the sound. He moved with greater care as it grew louder, also as he caught the faint gleam of a shuttered lantern. Reaching a corner behind the worker, he stopped. He eased forward with care, leaning just enough to see.

It was no seaman who pried at the long, narrow crate that topped the stack of similar boxes. The swing of a skirted frock coat and sheen of polished boots marked him as a gentleman. His back was to Kerr, but his face gleamed with sweat and the curses he muttered under his breath were as inventive as they were rough.

The wooden box top gave with a splintering shriek. The man went still, his head cocked, listening. Long seconds passed. Finally, he lowered his crowbar, dragged off the lid. With a soft whistle of appreciation, he dug his hands into loose packing straw and lifted out a rifle. Turning his upper body, he held the weapon to the faint lantern light.

Tremont.

Kerr had not expected it. A frown pleated his forehead as he considered the concern he'd heard in the man's voice when he first mentioned the shipment. Something didn't quite fit. Was the planter as surprised as he sounded, or only appreciative of the weapon he inspected? Had he mentioned the arms earlier as a concerned citizen, or only because he knew Kerr had seen them loaded and he meant to disclaim any connection?

This wasn't the time to get to the bottom of it, Kerr thought, nor was it his place. Captain Frazier could handle the situation when they reached port. That was assuming, of course, that the captain wasn't in on the deal.

Easing backward, Kerr retraced his footsteps to the cargo hatch. He was soon dawdling along the promenade deck once more.

It might have been a half hour later when the ship began to dance upon the waves to a stronger rhythm. They were drawing nearer the gulf, though still somewhat protected by the last trailing fingers of marshland. Kerr moved nearer the prow.

As if attracted by the sea change, someone stepped out onto the deck just down from where he stood. The light from inside silhouetted a female shape. The pale skirts that flapped around her in the wind of their passage could have belonged to anyone, but he knew only one lady who might brave this midnight hour on deck. More than that, some primeval knowledge tightened his stomach muscles into knots, allowing him to recognize her with an instinct he had not known he possessed.

She had not seen him there in the shadows, he was almost sure of it. Should he make his presence known or leave her to her solitude? It was difficult to say with Mademoiselle Bonneval.

She appeared pensive as she stood running the fingers of one hand back and forth in the blown spray that dampened the railing. He wondered what was in her mind, whether dread of what lay ahead or yearning for what lay behind. Surely she was not so downhearted that jumping could seem the way out, not here, not now?

No, the fighting spirit burned too hot inside her. She also had sense enough to realize there was no place to go even if she made dry land. Yet rousing her from her low mood might be a good thing, even if fury at him must take its place.

Pushing away from where he propped up the bulkhead with his shoulders, he walked toward her with a lounging stride. "You run through the whole gamut of dancing partners already? Or is it just that none are up to your standards?"

She whirled to face him. Her expression was merely startled rather than shocked or frightened, which led him to think she expected him to be about somewhere. That struck him as a good thing.

"You can have no idea of my standards." The words were quiet, her features guarded.

"I know they can't be low since you despise me."

"I don't—" she began.

"They have to be high or you would be wed by now."

"I told you the reasons for that."

"So you did. Your Bernard was fine and noble, I'm sure. I wonder if Gervaise Pradat is like him, if that's why you struck up a friendship with him so fast. Or was it to spite me?"

"Your conceit is beyond anything if you think my conduct has any bearing on you," she said in acid rejection. "Why should I care what you may think? Or what you may say or do, for that matter?"

"Now, there is a question, isn't it? But you might want to take it into account unless you're prepared to leave a litter of dead bodies in your wake."

"I haven't the least idea what you mean."

Her gaze was so frigid there in the starlit dimness that it should have chilled him to the bone. That was better than her dejection, in Kerr's considered opinion.

"Gervaise Pradat is precisely the kind of young idiot who would think it fine and noble to spring to your aid if convinced you were being wronged by someone, namely me. To draw him into our quarrel was short-sighted. That is, unless you don't care if I run my sword through him."

"You wouldn't."

"Only if forced to it by whatever you may do or say."

"I would never instigate such a thing."

"I'm happy to hear it. You will, in that case, do every-thing possible to keep him from offering me a challenge. Well, or an insult I'll have to respond to with one of my own."

"That's all well and good, but you should refrain from conduct which might lead in that direction."

It was his turn to scowl. "Meaning?"

"The little byplay of yours when you picked up my fan—which I must ask you to return."

"Which byplay is this?" He was intrigued by what had every appearance of high color burning on the pale contours of her face. The question of the fan he ignored completely though that bit of feminine frippery weighted his frock-coat pocket.

"You know what I mean."

"I'm not sure I do."

"You…you touched me. You know you did. Through my skirts."

"Why, Mademoiselle Bonneval, what are you accusing me of?" He was enjoying this far too much, he knew. Withdrawing immediately would be his best bet. Yet the flash of her eyes and quick rise and fall of the white curves of her breasts under her silk bodice were too enticing. More than that, she made teasing her so rewarding. He could no more resist than he could stop breathing.

"Nothing. It was done only to annoy me, as I am well aware. But you can't be surprised if another admirer chances to take issue with it."

"*Another* admirer, is it?"

She gave him a glare of exasperation, though her features seemed to have taken on a deeper color. "An admirer, period. I do realize you are not in that camp."

"Just so," he agreed, inclining his head. "As to my…encroachments, I will promise to be more discreet. Will that suffice?"

"By no means."

"You don't want me to be discreet?"

"You are not to encroach! You are not to touch me at all. Do you understand?"

Oh, he understood all right, but some devil inside him refused to make the concession.

It was not required. With the inevitability of tides and

timing, they finally left the Mississippi behind at that moment, broaching the first swells of the gulf. These were sizable where they clashed with the great river's final surge into the sea.

Sonia's attention was on him instead of the water. As the ship lifted with the first wave, she tottered a step in her heeled slippers, trying to keep her balance.

There was only one thing to be done. With a tight grin curving his mouth, Kerr clamped one hand to the railing beside him and snagged her narrow waist with the other. Contracting muscles gone suddenly as hard as steel, he snatched her against him.

She was a glorious armful in her silk and lace and whalebone, delicious with the scent of violets, fresh sea air and warm female. She went to his head like the finest cognac, tripping impulses he hardly knew he possessed. He wanted to plunder her mouth, to taste the very essence of her. He would give his soul for the right to take her below to some private cabin and peel away all the feminine furbelows that protected her. He longed to hold her as she turned to him, naked, willing and languid in her passion. He yearned to trace with hands, lips and tongue every sweet curve and delectable hollow of her body, delicately questing while she panted, writhing with need in his arms. Need of him.

Her eyes were darkly mysterious, her face was open and vulnerable, her lips parted with unconscious entice-ment. Her heart throbbed against the wall of his chest, between the resilient mounds of her breasts.

She was temptation personified.

She was forbidden to him.

The effort required to release her strained sinew, made rigid muscles creak with protest. He did it because he must, because he had taken on a commission and would not abandon it, because she was likely to scream and demand he be clapped in irons if he didn't. He did it because it was right.

"Thank you," she whispered, when she stood on her own feet once more, holding to the railing for support.

Kerr gave her a truncated bow of acknowledgment though uncertain whether her gratitude was for saving her from a fall or for abandoning his more ferocious impulses. That she suspected them, he had no doubt. She was neither stupid nor insensitive. He could only hope she was not so desperate for escape that she thought to forge them into a weapon against him.

It cost nothing to hope.

He watched her turn away without another word between them, moving toward the companionway that led to her cabin. Only when she disappeared from sight did he swing back to the railing, grasping its chill, damp wood with hard hands while he stared into the darkness. Ahead of him lay the black and heaving surface of the sea and the limitless horizon.

Oh, yes, and Mexico, where Rouillard waited for his bride.

Twelve

On the morning following the *Lime Rock*'s entrance into the gulf, Tante Lily refused to rise from her bunk. It was more than her usual inclination to lie abed until well after breakfast. Moaning about the terrible wallowing of the ship and her imminent death from *mal de mer,* she squeezed her eyes shut and turned her face to the wall.

Sonia did everything in her power to make her aunt more comfortable, bathing her face with a cool cloth, holding the china slop jar while she was thoroughly ill, bringing watered wine and dry biscuits to help settle her stomach. Nothing made any difference. When she offered to rub her aunt's temples with perfume, Tante Lily begged her to go away and stop tormenting her so she could die in peace. Sonia complied, since it seemed she might rest better if left alone.

The fresh wind sweeping along the deck was a vivid reminder of how close and noxious the air had become below. Sonia stood breathing it with gratitude while watching the steady rise and fall of the horizon with the ship's movement. The motion caused her no discomfort. Truth to tell, she enjoyed it. The deep blue waves that stretched to the horizon also pleased her. There was a profound sense of peace in their eternal movement and the light that danced over them.

It was impossible to sink into true reverie, however. She was too aware that Kerr could appear at any moment. She wasn't anxious to face him after the night before. It had to happen sometime, but the longer she could put it off, the happier she would be.

How the man unsettled her. She would like to think it was deliberate. The turmoil that shook her to her feminine core when he was near would be more excusable then. She was sure that brand of practiced seduction had never crossed his mind, however. As with last night, he simply responded to the moment.

So had she, and far too easily.

The feel of his arm around her, the unfaltering strength of his hold and incredible security of being caught against him had seeped into her dreams during the night. The promise of sweet, hot bliss had been there as well, beckoning with painful intensity. She feared she might have surrendered in sleeping fantasy but could not be sure, refused to be sure. Still, the urgency of the need had returned since she was awake, as it did now while she stood near where it had happened, as she breathed salt-flavored air into her lungs and felt the soft sea breeze in her face.

It would not do. She shook her head, forcing such visions from her.

She must keep her mind on what lay ahead, when she reached Vera Cruz. Three possibilities existed, as far as she could see. The first was simply to do nothing and hope that Jean Pierre had changed his mind. Second, she could attempt to elude her escort in the confusion of docking, hiding away until she could arrange passage to Mobile. Finally, she could allow herself to be escorted to her new home while trusting some avenue of escape would present itself once Kerr had gone.

Of the two men, Jean Pierre and Kerr, she fancied her future husband should be easier to deceive. He would not dream she objected to the match, so was unlikely to be on his guard.

That was, of course, unless her father had sent some advance warning along with the message to expect her arrival. The possibility of an alliance had been explained to her months ago, before Christmas, along with instructions to complete the trousseau that every young girl began to collect the moment she was born. She could not think that had been the first her father knew of it. There would have been negotiations concerning her dowry, terms and agreements sent back and forth about her personal allowance, the budget for housekeeping, the allocation of her property and the sum that would come to her one day by inheritance. Yes, her recalcitrance could easily have been mentioned at some point.

What if Jean Pierre met her at the docks and hustled her off to the church and a priest? That would be the end of it, the end of everything.

"Good day, *mademoiselle*."

She turned with a start to greet Alexander Tremont as he strolled toward her. Hatless in deference to the brisk wind, he touched his brow in token of what would have been removal of his headgear in her presence. He was dressed in shades of brown and cream, the only discordant note being orange flowers embroidered among the trailing vines on his waistcoat.

"I understand from the dining-salon steward that your aunt may be a bit under the weather."

His smile was as warm as the look in his dark eyes as they moved over her. It was a shade too calculating, Sonia thought, his perusal of her form beneath the sea-blue poplin of her day gown a little too comprehensive. "A touch of seasickness," she replied. "I'm sure she will soon recover."

"In the meantime, you are also without your large, sword-wielding protector. Perhaps you will allow me to keep you company. I could read to you, sort your embroidery silks or some such task. Oh, and pick up whatever you drop."

"I don't expect to be clumsy today."

Amused comprehension curved to his lips. "A great disappointment, but I'll survive it. As long, that is, as Monsieur Wallace remains at cards in the gentleman's parlor."

"Is that where he is? I did wonder."

"No doubt you did, having grown used to walking in his sizable shadow. May I ask…? But, no, it's none of my affair."

"What isn't?"

He seemed to take that as permission to continue. "If the gentleman isn't related, perhaps he's a friend of your father's that he's entrusted with your welfare?"

"By no means."

"I will admit it seemed unlikely. On the other hand, he's hardly the sort to hire out his services."

"What sort would he be instead?" She searched his face even as she tried valiantly to remain unmoved by the thought of how she and Kerr had met, and all that had happened since that moment.

"Independent, able beyond most, a commanding personality—"

"Ruthless, stubborn to the point of pigheadedness," she supplied.

Tremont accepted her additions with a brief inclination of his head. "His size must give him a fearsome presence on the fencing strip. His concentration would be hard to match as well. I'd have thought his salon would be overrun with clients."

"Assuming he has any skill with a sword."

"That's a given. I mean to say, he'd not have earned a place on the Passage de la Bourse otherwise."

She hesitated then plunged ahead with the question in her mind. "You seem to have some knowledge of swordplay, *monsieur*. Have you perhaps spent time in the Passage?"

"I can claim some small facility, though it was gained in other venues."

"So you have never faced Monsieur Wallace with sword in hand."

"Thankfully, no." His expression turned wry and he averted his gaze to the sea around them. "It was more than enough to face him over the card table this morning."

It was a change of subject, but she was inclined to allow it. "He defeated you there, did he?"

"Let us add the devil's own luck to the list of his assets. But my question is why he is here with you. With all due respect for your charm and beauty, it's difficult to understand what attracted him to the post."

"He's being well paid for his trouble."

"Yet will almost certainly lose as much or more in the time spent away from his salon."

It was a point she had not considered. Resentment had kept her from any attempt to understand Kerr Wallace's presence. She essayed it now with some reluctance.

Why had Kerr applied for the position as her escort? It was nothing personal she was certain. He had hardly been aware of her existence before arriving at the town house, and she had known nothing of him beyond mention of his name as a notorious sword master. If her father was acquainted with him at all, she had no knowledge of it, and nothing in their manner at that first meeting suggested it.

She frowned as memory stirred. Hadn't Hippolyte, on the night of the ball at the Hotel Saint Louis, suggested Kerr might be in search of some man in a personal vendetta? The sword master himself had made some reference as well, something about a sworn oath.

"It may be he has reasons of his own," she said finally.

"So we must suppose."

"And the question exercises your mind because you have so little else to occupy it?"

"As you say," he answered, then hesitated a moment before he went on. "I also had it in mind to…to issue a word of caution."

"Did you." Her tone was not encouraging, but he was not deterred.

"Men such as Wallace are not always bound by the rules that constrain the rest of us. They are too used to putting their lives on the line for a whim or misspoken word, carving their own paths by main force, so matters turn out to suit their ends. They have little regard for the tender or the innocent. In short, Mademoiselle Bonneval, your protector on this voyage could become your greatest danger."

"It's kind of you to trouble yourself." The comment was perfunctory as Sonia's thoughts moved in rapid surmise about the purpose behind Tremont's warning. She acquitted him of mere flirtation; his manner was too serious, his face too grave.

"You are a lady to whom it's impossible for a true gentleman to be unkind."

She inclined her head in acceptance of that bit of gallantry, but walked on without reply. Nor did her frown lighten.

It was peculiar, but serious regard on the part of the gentleman at her side left her unmoved. Her heart kept to its sedate beat and her breathing remained even. Though she was aware of him, it was merely as a person with whom she felt reasonable accord. Unlike the devil of a sword master, he stirred nothing inside her, no doubt or alarm, indignation or fury—certainly not the near-unbearable exhilaration of battle.

It was disconcerting. She had not thought the physical presence of two men unrelated to her could affect her in such different ways. Was it possible that women stirred men in a similar fashion? Was there some basic difference that called to one and not to another?

Oh, she had known the thrill of secret infatuations during her teenage years, had whispered of such things with her friends in retiring rooms at house parties. All had agreed they soon passed, could have nothing to do with the enduring love between husband and wife which must be based on shared expectations, mutual respect and consideration. These were things that came with time, or so they had been told, and would be felt for whoever was chosen for them as a partner for life.

What if they were wrong?

What if Alexander Tremont felt something for her regardless of her response? His purpose in speaking to her of Kerr, then, could be to discredit him so he might take his place.

Yes, but to what purpose? He knew any acquaintance between them must be short-lived. What could he expect of her once they reached their journey's end? That was, if he expected anything at all.

Her pace slowed as her mind ranged in wider circles. Suppose Tremont knew Jean Pierre and had set himself to look after the betrothed of his friend. It was not impossible since they both had business interests in Mexico—

or so Tremont had said, though Tante Lily still insisted he had the look of a wastrel. Yet if it were so, would he not have claimed the acquaintance and spoken of their good fortune in traveling to Vera Cruz together?

It occurred to her, abruptly, that the munitions the gentlemen had noticed being loaded before they sailed might have been on Tremont's mind. Did he suspect some connection to Kerr? It was a startling concept, but not impossible on the face of it. The qualities that made the swordsman a formidable opponent on the fencing strip would stand him in good stead should he turn to criminal activity.

What a farce it would be if her father had sent her off on her wedding voyage under the protection of a traitor. She was almost willing to believe it was true for the fine jest it would make.

Anything was possible as a cause for Tremont's concern, including genuine distrust of Kerr, genuine concern for her well-being while in his company. If that was his position, might it not be to her advantage? An ally in eluding Kerr's escort when they touched land would be most welcome.

"I am grateful for the warning," she said after a long moment, "but fail to see what use I'm to make of it. Monsieur Wallace was chosen by my father, so stands in his stead. Added to that, we are fixed on board here until the ship reaches port. Naturally, I shall be safeguarded from that point on by my future husband."

"Forgive me, but you don't seem overjoyed at either prospect."

"How discerning of you." She could not prevent a dry note from creeping into her voice.

"Am I to assume you would escape both if you could?"

"Readily, though I have little hope of it."

"Your future groom is quite unknown to you, then. Or is it rather that he's known but not highly regarded?"

"My father esteems him."

"A telling indictment if ever I heard one." He gazed out to sea an instant before turning back to her. "I should think it would be almost intolerable to know you must marry a virtual stranger."

"You can have no idea."

"Being a man, you mean. It happens. Though not, generally, without some...some fault in the matter."

If her aunt had been there as chaperone, he would never have spoken of such a possibility, never ventured a hint at such misconduct. Sonia was torn between appearing worldly enough to understand his allusion to unwed passion between men and women and a disinclination to encourage more of the same. Uncertain how best to answer, she allowed silence to speak for her.

"Arranged marriages are not unknown where I'm from back East," Tremont went on, apparently oblivious to her reticence. "Still, they seem to happen more often in New Orleans."

"Perhaps."

"Wealth and position tend to marry wealth and position the world over. It's the way dynasties are formed." He lifted a neat shoulder. "Men on the western frontier post notices in news sheets for wives, too, and women answer them. Now, there is courage, to risk everything on a mere printed notice."

"Desperation, rather. Such women must be destitute or have abandoned all hope of finding a husband in the normal manner."

"Many are alone in the world, granted, or else moral condemnation forces them to leave everything behind."

He meant to suggest these desperate brides were often in a family way. Did he think, perhaps, that was her condition? "I can assure you the last is seldom the cause in New Orleans. Nevertheless, I agree it's a great gamble."

"Yes, which leads me to suggest…"

"What, *monsieur?*" She stopped walking as she waited for what he might say, waited to see if he meant to offer her succor.

At that moment, Kerr stepped from the companionway ahead of them, paused for a moment, looking up and down the deck, then came toward them. Glancing at him, then back to Sonia, Alex Tremont shook his head. "Nothing for the moment, *mademoiselle.* But if I may be of service in the future, I hope you will call upon me."

With that she had to be satisfied, for he inclined his head in farewell, nodded briefly to Kerr and left them. After so abrupt an abandonment along with all else, Sonia wasn't at all sure she could rely on him. Nor could she hold too firm a belief in his concern.

"Setting up a tête-à-tête with Tremont?" Kerr inquired, his gaze sardonic as he watched the other man's retreat.

"Enjoying a civil discussion for a change." She could

feel the annoying heat of a flush rising in her face, a direct result no doubt of her thoughts moments before. Or it might have been her sudden recall of being pressed against the hard body of this man while his heartbeat pounded drumlike against her breast. She had not enjoyed that instant of acute vulnerability, certainly not, yet it threatened now to turn her bones to water.

What to do with her hands suddenly became a discomfiting problem since she had no fan, no parasol, no book or handkerchief to occupy them. The best she could do was inspect her gloved fingertips for signs of soot from where she had clutched the railing earlier.

"I'd like to have heard that," he said, the words shaded with caustic amusement.

She met his eyes for a tried instant. "It might have proven educational."

"Or not, for those of us who are less than civilized. I wouldn't put too much dependence on anything he may have told you."

"Why should I not?" That he had come so close to echoing her own thought made her voice sharper than she intended.

"If I tell you he is less than trustworthy, will that make you determined to add him to your conquests?"

"I hope I am not so unreasonable."

"So do I, since that's exactly what I mean to say."

"You have a good reason, I suppose."

"An excellent one."

She waited, but he did not go on. "Which you don't intend to impart to me?"

"I prefer to keep my own counsel for the time being."

"A fine excuse." She surveyed the hard planes of his face, wondering at their grim cast. "It might surprise you to know he feels much the same about you."

"Said I wasn't to be trusted, did he?"

"He did."

"Since he spoke first, and we are at outs, you believe him."

"I didn't say that."

"Unnecessary. I can see it's so."

"What an infuriating man you are."

She turned her head, staring out over the shifting waves that buffeted the steamer, throwing themselves against its prow and surging through the paddle wheels. He could have tried to convince her at the very least, she thought. The contradiction of wanting to be persuaded she was wrong in spite of preferring to think the worst did nothing to relieve her temper.

His gaze rested on her face, for she could almost feel the heat of it. She longed to know what he was thinking, if he cared at all for how she might view him or had revisited at all the moment when he had held her close.

It was unlikely she would ever know.

Stifling a sigh, she began to walk again. Kerr Wallace, ever the faithful escort, fell into step beside her. They circled the deck until they were enticed inside by the wafting aromas of the noonday meal.

Since the indisposition of her aunt left Sonia without a female companion, she gravitated toward the table that had been claimed by Madame Pradat and her son.

As she approached, Gervaise half rose from his bench seat with an expression of shy welcome on his face. The urge to respond to the admiration in his eyes, flouting Kerr's warning, was strong. She had no wish to be the cause of a confrontation, however. Still less did she care to play upon whatever feelings Gervaise might have conceived for her. Kerr might think her heartless, but it was not so. Well, except toward those who had given her cause.

She changed directions, taking a place farther along the extensive board, across from young Madame Dossier who had her babe on her lap and a youngster on either side of her. Kerr waited until she was settled, then stepped over the bench and seated himself next to her.

From the corners of her eyes, Sonia saw Gervaise's olive skin turn dusky red and his teeth press into his bottom lip. Her chest ached in sympathy with his obvious embarrassment, but it could not be prevented. Better that than having his death on her conscience. She only hoped no further discouragement was required, for she wasn't sure she had it in her to accomplish it. Swallowing hard, she reached for the water glass at her place, taking a sip to help dissolve the knot in her throat.

"He will recover," Kerr said in low tones. "You've only blighted his morning, not his life."

"It was not my intention to injure him at all." She plunked her glass back on the table so hard that water slopped over the rim to wet her fingers.

"It can't be helped. That is, unless you would expect to marry every gentleman who yearns after you."

"Don't be ridiculous!"

"No, only making a point. You'd have had to let him down before we make landfall. It might as well be now."

What he did not say, but she knew well, was that it had been wrong of her to encourage Gervaise Pradat in the first place. She would not have except for Kerr's presence on the ship. Giving him the satisfaction of admitting it, however, was more than she could face at the moment.

"I take it you have never been disappointed in love," she said, the words quiet as she dried her fingers on her shawl fringe.

He was silent so long that she finally looked up to meet his eyes. Their steel-gray depths held a brooding expression before his thick lashes came down to conceal it. "Why would you say that?" he asked in curt tones.

"It would undoubtedly have given you more consideration for the feelings of others." Her answer was a moment in coming and the words had a random sound, as if she'd almost forgotten their import.

"Take heart," he said in stringent irony, "you may yet live to see it."

"I should doubt it, since we are unlikely to be in each other's company so long."

"You're right. How could I forget?"

How indeed? That they would part in Vera Cruz was engraved on her mind. She could not wait for that moment to arrive.

Thirteen

The fine weather did not last. By midafternoon of that second day out, the *Lime Rock* began to wallow through an endless series of swells. Its smokestack waved back and forth against a leaden sky and the sails billowed and strained overhead. A gray bank of clouds gradually took away the light, draping everything in gloom. The sea, tinted by sky reflections, became a dull blue-gray as it shifted in troughs around them.

Nor did matters improve. Walking became difficult, a matter of lunging from one handhold to another. Lamps burned day and night in passageways and in the common rooms. And so it continued without let up.

Tante Lily burrowed deeper into her bunk, taking a few sips of water now and then but moaning at any mention of food. Sonia urged her to dress and come above decks with her embroidery or a book as it seemed fresh sea air would be better for her than the rank miasma below. Her aunt could not be convinced. Any attempt to set foot on the floor brought on another bout of retching, she said. It was a calamity that there was no priest on board to hear her confession. And, no, the Reverend Smythe would not do. She had no faith in the man, no dependence on his prayers to get her into heaven.

Nor was Tante Lily the only person to succumb to the movement. Madame Dossier and her children were absent at mealtimes, as was the American commissioner and a half-dozen others. Even one or two of the crew took to their bunks or hung over the stern with a green tint to their faces.

On the morning of the third day, the captain gave it as his opinion they were being overtaken by one of the northerners that plagued the latitude from winter through late spring. Accordingly, preparations for it began. Lines were strung along the passageways and across the dining salon, and seamen went from cabin to common rooms to make certain the lower portholes were securely battened down. Buckets half filled with sand were set out at all doorways. Condiments and other unnecessary articles were removed from the dining tables. Cuspidors vanished from beside the chairs favored by gentlemen, forcing any man using snuff or chewing tobacco to go topside and spit carefully downwind.

Sonia was only marginally affected by the motion. She didn't feel actively unwell, but her appetite deserted her. That was no great cause for concern since she had not felt really hungry since her first sight of Kerr Wallace.

That gentleman was faithful in the pursuit of his duty, appearing at regular intervals to see how she fared. Sometimes he lingered for a question or two, though more often he retreated again to the gentleman's parlor. A card game of some duration seemed in progress there, one only postponed for meals instead of being brought to a close.

Monsieur Tremont sometimes sat in on this game, but more often found his way to her side. Sonia might have been flattered at the attention except for being well aware that she was the only female of even semi-unattached status on the vessel. Add to that the fact that most of the exchanges between the two of them revolved around Kerr in one way or another, and she could be forgiven, she hoped, for suspecting it was the Kentuckian's activities that held the planter's interest.

There were gentlemen, she well knew, who doted on the *maîtres d'armes* of the Passage. Their prowess, muscular strength and ability to face death with sang-froid roused intense admiration. To be admitted to their company for an hour was a prize that might be talked of for weeks. Young boys trailed after them on the streets, the beaus and bloods about town aped their manners and articles of dress, and older gentlemen considered it a high honor to be allowed to stand them a drink or a meal. Rather like the heroes of one of Scott's novels, they were endowed in imagination, if not in truth, with ideal strength, power, courage and honor.

It was difficult to accept that Alexander Tremont could succumb to that kind of awe, especially given his misgivings about Kerr. Nonetheless, she could fathom no other reason for his fascination.

She did little to discourage Monsieur Tremont's

attentions, but was friendly in a noncommittal fashion. It seemed appropriate to have a sympathetic admirer in reserve for when she might require aid. The run from New Orleans to Vera Cruz took no more than a week in the normal course of events. Soon, too soon, she would have to decide what she would do when she arrived.

The uncertainty was maddening. It shortened her temper while making her listless and inclined to headache.

She wasn't alone. The general malaise and outright illness caused by the surging rise and fall and side-slipping of the steamer set everyone's nerves on edge. The captain snapped at the officers, the officers shouted at the seamen, and the few passengers left upright ran the gamut from chill politesse to irascibility and down-right surliness.

On the evening of the fourth day, the tables in the dining salon were set for fewer guests than ever. Soup was removed from the menu because of the difficulty in serving it, and the sound of breaking dishes from the direction of the kitchen came with hideous regularity. The appearance of a cold fish course cleared out several more passengers, as they took one whiff of the odorous dish and left the long room.

Among those affected was Kerr. He was grim of face and pale around the mouth as he departed, Sonia noticed. She was sympathetic, of course, but also bemused. That so invincible a man could be laid low while she remained able to function was a small irony of the kind that appealed to her female soul.

Halfway through the dessert, as the wildly swinging

whale lamps threatened to strike the ceiling at the peak of the ship's roll, a pair of crewmen swept through the salon, extinguishing lamp flames and unhooking the globes to prevent fire. The wicks in a single pair of girandoles at each end were left burning, but the flames danced and wavered, casting more shadows than light. In the semidarkness, the flash of lightning was almost constant. Thunder rolled overhead and wind whipped across the decks along with the surge of building waves. The tops of wind-torn waves dashed against the diningsalon windows. Rain began in a downpour so violent it was almost impossible to be heard above it.

Sonia felt sure the salon would empty when the meal came to an end, and it very nearly did. No one troubled to clear the space for dancing and the violinist departed with the passengers who straggled out. A few hardy souls refused to give in to the elements, however. Those who remained behind were Tremont, the Reverend Smythe with his prickly beard who had turned out to be on a mission to the Yucatán, an elderly lady knitting on a lapful of puce wool and a trio of card players who commandeered the far end table and laid out a hand of euchre.

Sonia and Tremont talked in a desultory fashion for perhaps a half hour, lifting their voices above the storm while sitting on facing benches with the table between them. The reverend left then and, shortly thereafter, the elderly woman gathered up her knitting wool to go. As she passed by where Sonia and Tremont sat, she gave them a small sniff of disapproval.

The lady's feelings were easily deciphered. To be left

the only female among a company of men was highly irregular. It was also uncomfortable for Sonia. Retreating to the noisome cabin she shared with Tante Lily held no appeal, however, and she had no reason to think insult would be offered her under the present circumstances. More than that, she was accustomed to late hours, was often up until dawn during the hectic social round of the *saison des visites*. She would not be able to sleep for some time yet, even without the wind and rain.

On the other hand, her position was awkward enough without inciting gossip that might attach itself to her skirts wherever she finally settled. She frowned in indecision.

"Don't go," Alex said, reaching out to catch her hand.

"It would be best if I did."

"I'll look after you in Wallace's absence. Surely I can't be any less suitable for the post."

She wore no gloves as they were always removed before dining and she had not donned them again. She had acquired casual habits as the days passed, as well, as if the ship had become home territory. His thumb stroked the fine skin on top of her hand in something very near a caress.

"I can see how suitable you intend to be." Firmly but without rancor, she removed her fingers from his grasp.

"I beg your pardon," he said, instantly contrite. "It seemed so natural I hardly noticed what I was doing. I will apologize a thousand times, I swear, if you will only stay."

"Shall I count, or will you?"

"Fiend. Charming, yes, but a fiend in lovely human form. I believe you would enjoy watching me grovel."

"Immensely, I assure you."

It was mere banter, of course, the kind of meaningless exchange that eased formal meetings between men and women. She meant not a word, nor did he. Nevertheless, the accord between them was real enough, as were their smiles.

Tremont's faded first. Leaving his seat, he moved around as if he meant to join her on her side of the table. It was not the most graceful of maneuvers due to the rolling of the ship. The deck pitched upward. He caught the table corner and swung around it, coming down hard beside her.

The bench on which she sat rocked backward. She cried out, snatching at the table's edge.

It wasn't enough.

The bench tipped over in a slow arc, then slammed to the floor as the sea lifted the ship again. Sonia's head hit the carpeted decking with a solid thump. Alex landed beside her, cursing. She lay for a stunned instant in a welter of petticoats and skirts and with her slippers pointing at the ceiling.

The ludicrous picture the two of them must have presented struck her, along with the vivid memory of a less disastrous incident not so long ago caused by wind and water. Her escort had caught her then, but this time he was not here. She began to shake with silent laughter.

"Sonia—Mademoiselle Bonneval—are you hurt? Here, allow me…"

Alex rolled toward her, trying to find a place to put his hands for purchase, trying to get his feet under him. His way was impeded by the layers of silk and lace-edged cambric that spread over them both. He reached across her to brace himself against the heaving of the deck under them, but could only grip her shoulder.

She attempted to help by grasping his sleeve, but the position was so awkward, and she was so weak with tremors of mirth, that she only fell back again. It was then that a shout came from the door behind them.

"*Monsieur!* Release her! Release her at once."

Gervaise.

Alex muttered an oath as he twisted his head to look over his shoulder. A groan rose in Sonia's throat, though she clamped a hand over her mouth to hold it back. Of course it was Gervaise, exactly the kind of quixotic young idiot certain to make a bad situation worse. At least it wasn't his mother or, worse, Kerr.

"Release her, I say, or you will answer to me!"

She sobered instantly as the possibility of blows or even a duel surfaced between the two men. Hot embarrassment caught up with her as well. She bent her knees, struggling to right herself in spite of her corset stays that prevented her from bending her upper torso. "No, no, really, Gervaise," she protested.

"Why, you impudent pup, I'll flay you alive for daring to think…" Alex began.

Another voice, deeper, richly caustic, joined the fray. "And I will be forced to take on both of you for neglecting the lady."

Sonia closed her eyes in dismay. It was Kerr, of course. The man could always be depended upon to show up where he wasn't wanted.

An instant later, the sense of his words reached her and her eyes flew open again. He wouldn't challenge both Gervaise and Alexander Tremont over this ridiculous incident. Surely he would not.

Would he?

"The scoundrel has been manhandling Mademoiselle Bonneval," Gervaise said in outraged condemnation.

"Nothing of the sort." Alex's expression was pained. "It was an accident from the rolling of the ship."

Gervaise drew himself up. "He has compromised her and must be brought to account for it."

"I doubt it," Kerr drawled. "The lady is unharmed so far as I can see, the bench in one piece, and Tremont more in need of sympathy than a lesson in manners."

"I insist."

"That's my place, I think. Unless you'd care to face my sword, being you're so set on a fight."

The Kentuckian's manner might be offhand, but his words held a slicing edge of danger only a fool could disregard. The difficulty, Sonia feared, was that Gervaise might be just the sort of heedless young idiot who would consider his pride more important than his life. Fighting her skirts, she tried again to draw her feet down off the bench's seat so she could achieve a sitting position. The stiff crinoline of her petticoats threatened to fall into her face, even if her corset would allow it. Caught like a turtle on its back, she could not right herself without displaying more of her limbs and undergarments than any had seen thus far.

"Gentlemen, if you please!" she said in acid annoyance.

Tremont was closest, with Gervaise a near second. Neither of them moved, nor did they take their regard from the sword master who stood somewhere behind her. She wondered what communication passed between them.

She was not left long in doubt. A solid tread sounded as Kerr rounded the bench. Leaning over her, he batted her skirt hems aside with more purpose than finesse, then closed long fingers about her waist. She put her hands on his forearms in purest reflex movement, so felt the muscles underneath his coat sleeves as they tightened into steel hawsers.

A moment later, she was free of the bench and standing on her feet with his firm grasp binding her rib cage like the cruelest of corsets. She stared into the dark, storm-sea gray of his eyes, swaying with him to the wild rhythm of the tempest-tossed ship and some deep, internal upheaval that was like the world shifting on its axis. They anchored her, his eyes, while she hovered between chagrin and unbidden relief that he was there to take charge. Yes, and also the sudden, blind terror that he would always be there and she could never, ever escape him.

Fourteen

Everyone began talking at once—Tremont, young Pradat, the card players who had witnessed the whole thing, even a seaman who had been passing by. Kerr barely heard them. He was only aware of the pale face of the women he held, and the wine-dark pools of her eyes. More dangerous than the deepest riptide, they drew him like a spell. He could drown in them with never a regret, he thought. He could spend a lifetime following where she led, keeping her eternally safe. How much of a fool could he be?

"Let me…let me go," she whispered. "I can't… breathe."

He realized then that she was gasping, her lungs laboring for air under his hands, even as he maintained balance for both of them in the swaying dining salon with its dark, rain-washed windows. He released her at once, his big hands flying wide like a sprung lock.

She caught his forearms, teetering a little since she could barely move with him in front of her and the bench behind. He took a step back but thought it best to stand firm there while she used him for support until she was steady on her pins.

"You are unhurt, *mademoiselle?*" Tremont asked.

He should have been the one to ask that, Kerr knew. That he hadn't was not from lack of concern but because the answer seemed obvious.

"Perfectly," she said, releasing her grip on him and shaking out her skirts. "My head aches a bit from hitting the floor, but I believe my hair prevented any serious damage."

She looked at neither of them nor her young would-be defender, but kept her head bent as she saw to her flounces. Kerr's gaze rested on the intricate knot of hair at the back of her head. It appeared thick enough to cushion any blow. It was also listing to one side, in danger of slipping its mooring. The need to see that happen, to watch the silken length unfurl down her back in a dark and shining river while he removed the pins tangled in it, to feel its warm weight sliding over his fingers, was an unexpected ache inside him. He clenched his hands at his sides with its force.

"I'm relieved, since the upset was my fault." Tremont's expression was a model of self-blame. "You will want to retire, I expect, *mademoiselle.* I'll see you to your cabin."

"You've done enough for one evening," Kerr said, his voice as hard as the stare he gave the planter.

"Oh, but surely…"

The urge to punch the man in the face was so strong

that Kerr took a step toward him. Besides, he'd used up his store of reasonableness on Pradat. "You heard me," he said in quiet menace. "I'll take Mademoiselle Bonneval to her cabin."

Tremont searched Kerr's face. Something he saw there apparently convinced him protest was not a good idea. Shifting his gaze to Sonia, he said, "I shall make my apologies in the morning, if I may. I hope most sincerely that you will feel well enough to receive them. For now I'll bid you good-night."

Sonia murmured some reply, said a general good-evening and accepted the bows of the gentlemen at the card table who stood to see her go. Placing a hand on the arm Kerr offered, she allowed him to lead her from the dining salon.

The passageway leading to the cabins was a dark tunnel lighted only by a single whale-oil lamp swinging in its gimbal. Their shadows dipped and swayed to the ship's movement, stretching ahead of them, multiplying around them. The sound of the wind and rain was a constant roar.

Kerr kept one hand on the single brass railing attached to the bulkhead, and Sonia clung to him. Though she walked with her usual smooth glide, he could feel a slight tremor in her fingers that gripped his arm.

"You sure you're none the worse for your fall?"

"I said so before, didn't I?"

"Doesn't make it so."

"I'm not going to faint, nor am I going to be ill."

Kerr wished he could say the same. He'd not had

recourse to a slop jar as yet, but the food smells lingering in the dining salon had made running for one a near thing. What had caused him to crawl out of his covers and hie off to the dining salon, he couldn't say. It might have been the sound of the bench falling over, but could just as easily have been the quiet after the meal ended and an instinctive feeling that his charge had lingered long enough. Now that the excitement was over, he wanted nothing more than to crawl behind the curtains that enclosed his bunk and close his eyes.

No, that wasn't strictly true. What he'd really like was to take the lady at his side with him and hold her while the sea tossed them back and forth, rocking them both to sleep. He could be sure she was safe then, instead of plotting some other start that would make all his carefully laid plans as useless as Mexican sand. The best way to make certain of it would be to strip away the layers of clothing that encased her so she was naked against him. She would be warm and soft, tender and wild under his hands, under his body, surrounding him.

"If you're going to be unpleasant, you may as well get it over with," she said, her expression strained and mutinous in the dimness.

"Now, why would I do that?"

Kerr clung to the railing as a particularly vicious wave lifted the ship on one side. He could hear the whine of the paddle wheel on the canted port quarter as it spun uselessly out of the water, and the groan of its mate to starboard as it plunged so deep turning became almost impossible.

"I can't imagine, seeing you have no right. It seems a habit with you."

"My job is to see you to Vera Cruz. One way or another."

"And heaven forbid that you should fail." The last word was a short gasp as the ship wallowed again and she caught his arm with both hands.

"I don't intend it."

"Monsieur Tremont made an interesting observation. You are not, he said, the kind of man to take on such a commission for money alone. Why is it, again, that you wish to reach Mexico?"

"I'd think you'd have better things to discuss with Tremont." He flexed his bicep to prevent her from being dragged away from him, aware of ten spots of fire that were her fingertips pressing into it.

"That's an evasion, I think."

"Like your question, you mean? I've pledged not to be unpleasant, but am curious as to how you came to be entangled with Tremont and a fallen bench."

"Purest mischance. Oh!"

Her exclamation came as the ship was tossed in the opposite direction, throwing her against him. He freed his arm in a swift move and swept it around her waist to clamp her to him. A glancing suspicion touched him that she had taken advantage of the moment to distract him. Was it possible? Had she arranged this reenactment of their embrace of the other night?

He didn't know, nor did he care as he pressed his shoulders to the wall and spread his feet, holding her wedged between his thighs while the sea tried to drag the ship to the bottom. He'd learned something since their last such encounter. Yes, and since seeing her lying in a welter of petticoat ruffles, stockings of whitest silk and rosebud embroidered garters. He would take any opportunity to hold her that came and damn the consequences. He might well make another himself, if it came to that.

She stared up at him, her eyes like drowned violets, lips parted, lush and moist, as if begging to be kissed. That was only in his mind, he was almost sure, but it mattered not a whit.

He took her mouth like a man dying of thirst. The surfaces of her lips were smooth, so smooth and cool yet lusciously inviting. He swept inside, seeking remembered sweetness and delicate intoxication so subtle it destroyed mind and will in an instant, obliterated every good intention. Her sigh whispered over his beard-stubbled cheek, lodged in his heart. It wasn't surrender but felt like its cousin, a flammable curiosity that defied logic.

She despised him, longed to be shed of him with a fierceness that made her a warrior woman, and yet she caught the lapel of his coat and twisted it in her grasp as she met his desire, yielding to it in all the small ways women used to say they might yield completely. He drew her closer, needing the press of her breasts against him, dying to feel her pulsing heartbeat, the heat and scent and glorious promise of her. And all the while, his mind retreated, growing cooler, more distant, as he asked himself a single burning question.

Why?

He didn't want her to come to him for a purpose. Well, yes, he wasn't really that choosy. He would swallow every objection and bury himself in her to the hilt if she took his hand and led him to her cabin. But he wanted her to want him, not simply to use his undeniable attraction to her as a part of whatever scheme her fertile mind had hatched this time. And the chances were about as good as those of a drunken seaman stepping overboard into this gale.

The *Lime Rock* righted itself, shuddering like a dog shaking off water, then continued with the steady beat of its engine. Kerr braced himself and caught her wrist, pulling it away from his lapel, holding it captive in the prison of his fingers. Lifting his head, then, he gazed down at her, at the rosy moistness of her mouth, the dazed look in her eyes, the flush that mantled her skin.

His slow-drawn breath burned in his lungs with furnace heat. Then he set her from him.

"Listen to me," he said, his voice husky yet lethal in its seriousness, "because I won't be saying it again. I'll not allow you to use any man on this ship to make good your escape. If you want to cause the death of any one of them, then tempt them and set them against me and I will oblige you. We are going to Vera Cruz, you and I. The only male who will be on any kind of close terms with you is the one you're looking at right now. Forget it, and I refuse to be responsible for what happens."

"Close terms," she repeated as if the words were in a foreign tongue.

"Talking, walking, dancing, always beside you morning, noon and, especially, nighttime."

"And nothing else?"

Calculation was rising in her eyes, for he caught its cool gleam. He saw and chose to ignore it. "Nothing else. I will deliver Rouillard his bride, one unharmed, unsullied and unrepentant. Whether the rest of the trip turns out uncomfortable is up to you."

Her chin rose to a pugnacious angle. "You're very sure of yourself for a man who has just indulged in something requiring more closeness than mere idle flirtation."

"If I choose to *flirt* with you, Mademoiselle Bonneval," he said in soft promise, "the last thing it will be is idle."

She moved not a muscle, yet her features congealed into such hauteur that he felt a distinct shiver run down his spine. "If you choose, *monsieur?*"

"Don't let the prospect trouble you. I'm not that reckless or that much of a fool. More than that, I took your father's commission, shook his hand on it, and I keep my word."

"How very noble. You do realize such nobility can have its price?"

What was going on behind the sea-blue shadows of her eyes with their shading of purple darkness? He'd give his right arm to know, even if something told him he'd not like it worth a damn. "I've noted it every time I've faced a man on the dueling field, *mademoiselle.* And the price for some gestures can be higher than others."

"You have no idea how high it can be. Not yet."

She turned and left him with those words ringing in his ears, making her way down the passage in an oddly graceful zigzag progress that followed the tilting of the carpeted floor beneath her feet. He watched her go with narrowed eyes, and felt, suddenly, a hollow ache in his chest where his heart should be.

Fifteen

Dawn brought fog and more rolling seas, but at least the howling wind and rain seemed to have passed them by. The rigging still splattered water down onto the wet planking and dripping rails, the occasional thunderous clap of the sails that aided the steam engine sent mist flying behind them, but the seas were calmer.

Kerr stood swaying to the ship's movement, his hands braced on the railing. He drew the storm-washed air deep into his lungs, feeling it oust the queasiness caused by rougher water. He'd never make a deepwater sailor, but that was fine since he was a farmer at heart like his father and grandfather before him.

He was certainly more of a planter than Tremont, in fact. A question here and there while they played cards had made that clear.

The boxes of armaments below, and what would become of them, slid across his mind, and he grimaced. He'd waited to see if Tremont would mention his inspection. So far, it hadn't happened.

The arms would have to be reported. Question was, to what authority? There was no American envoy in Vera Cruz since Slidell had been turned back from the port. Who did that leave?

Kerr could think of no one at the moment. He'd keep a watch on the cargo when they landed, make certain someone didn't spirit it away before the situation could be cleared up. Whether it would be by Tremont or someone entirely different remained to be seen.

A shrieking cry from overhead drew his attention. It came from a seagull that circled the mast then drifted down to roost on a crosspiece. It was followed by three more, like bits of swooping silver against the sky. They signaled land, and he turned to squint into the fog-shrouded distance at a blur that could be low-lying clouds but was most likely the Mexican coastline. They had made good time due to the storm wind on their beam. With luck, they would be in Vera Cruz in a couple of days, maybe less.

He couldn't wait.

A yawn caught him unaware, almost cracking his jaws. He might as well not have gone to his bunk last night after leaving Sonia. He'd lain staring into the heaving darkness, listening to the rush of the sea along the hull, the hiss of steam through the pipes below, and particularly the monotonous thump of the crankshaft. That steady beat was maddening in its rhythm, its hard and endless thrust homeward followed by withdrawal. It matched his more primitive impulses far too exactly for comfort, torturing him with images and impulses

concerning the woman in his care that were something
less than protective.

Dear God, but she could get under his skin. She was
annoying but fascinating, part spoiled darling and part
lioness, genteel lady and Lorelei. The pale and tender
valley between her breasts lingered in his mind like a
heavenly vision; her scent haunted him. The shape of
her shoulders, the turn of her waist that fit his hand so
perfectly, the delicate shadow cast on her cheekbones
by her lashes—these images and a dozen more of
similar nature played in his mind's eye like a magic-
lantern show. And any one of them was capable of
throwing him into such rampant lust that he hovered on
the brink of social embarrassment.

He'd once had more control. What had become of it?

The wind buffeted the skirt of his frock coat, slapping it against the railing where he stood. Something
heavy in the pocket bumped the support post then
banged against his thigh. As he reached deep for it, the
first thing he came across was his ivory-handled pocketknife. He tucked that into his trouser pocket then
dived down again to draw out Sonia's fan he'd captured. As he spread the sticks, the ghost of her violet
scent assailed him. The thin fabric of it, unfolding, fluttered in his hands like the wings of a butterfly, the
silken span quivering in the wind as if it tried to break
free of his hold.

Freedom.

That was all Sonia wanted, or so she said. And who
could blame her? It was what he craved himself, the

freedom to get on with his life that he'd finally earn by running to ground the man who'd caused his brother's death. He had been on the trail so long it seemed the end might never come. It had felt at times like an aim as impractical as the one that drove Sonia.

Somewhere behind him, a door creaked open, followed by footsteps on the decking. There was no mistaking that light tread. Kerr snapped the fan closed while concealing the movement with his body, and buried it in its hiding place. By the time Sonia came to a halt a few feet down the railing, his hands rested on the long stretch of polished teak.

"You're up early," she said, her voice light, even if not quite friendly.

"Makes two of us." Kerr discounted the presence of the watch since he doubted she took them into account.

"I trust you'll be able to face breakfast now the seas are calmer."

"Could be."

She sent him a quick glance, as if to judge his mood. "I confess I was almost glad to know you have some small weakness in that area."

"Were you now?"

"It makes you more…approachable. You are rather daunting, you know."

He would like to tell her that she could approach at any time but it seemed unlikely to improve matters. "I wouldn't make too much of it. It changes nothing."

"So I apprehend after last night. Your arrival was timely, even if you were unwell." She paused. "I don't believe I thanked you for resolving what had become a…distressing situation."

"It's what I hired on for."

"So you said before." Her tone verged on sharpness before she stopped, drew breath with a sound of tried patience and went on again. "I do appreciate being removed from it, no matter the reason. I'm also thankful for your patience toward Monsieur Pradat. That was well done."

He turned his head to look at her while grimly aware of his pleasure at the respect in her voice, and the approval. "You think so."

"Without it, you might be defending yourself here with sword in hand at this moment."

"I'd have thought you'd enjoy that prospect."

A small shudder ran over her, one that appeared entirely natural. "Your mistake, *monsieur.* I abhor even the idea of sword fighting."

What was she up to now? It was something; he didn't doubt that for a minute. Trouble was, the idea of meeting it felt a lot like facing a worthy opponent on the fencing strip. The challenge sent the blood boiling through his veins and turned every muscle in his body iron-hard with determination.

"Sword fighting in general," he asked, shifting to face her with one elbow on the railing, "or only as it applies to me?"

"Either. Both."

"The sentiment does you credit. I'm sure Pradat would appreciate it."

She gave him a frowning glance. "You don't believe me."

"I believe you're reluctant to cause injury to your young gallant."

"You needn't sneer at him. He was only attempting to ensure proper conduct toward a lady."

"I realized that at the time, which is why I intervened. What I don't understand is why it was necessary."

Disdain flashed in her eyes. "You can't actually think he had cause?"

"What I think doesn't matter. The affair is between you and your conscience."

"It was the storm, I promise you. Monsieur Tremont joined me on the bench just as the ship rolled and—" She stopped, looking away from him while hot color flushed her cheekbones and her gloved fingers gripped the railing. "I would not have you think I am so careless of my good name, or that you must report misconduct to Jean Pierre."

"Now wait a minute," he began, straightening to his full height as anger stirred inside him.

"You are going to say you would not do that?" She sent him the briefest of looks before returning her attention to the sea. "Well enough. Let us cry quits then. I don't care to quarrel with you any longer."

He had not expected such an easy victory. He waited for gratification, but it didn't come. With some surprise, he realized his main feeling was disappointment that their sparring might be at an end. That was less than wholehearted, however, since beneath it ran a vein of pure suspicion.

She gave him no time to dwell on it. Turning toward him so her skirts brushed the polished vamps of his boots, she studied him. "You are not a very talkative man, are you?"

"I talk when I have something to say."

"But you aren't fond of conversation for its own sake, the exchange of ideas or small talk simply to pass the time."

"Don't have much use for it."

"So I apprehend," she said, her voice bone-dry. "But you have no objection, surely, to a question or two?"

He shrugged. "As long as you don't expect fancy answers or high-flown compliments."

"Neither is required, but only honesty." She went on before he could comment on the implied slur upon his integrity. "Will you be returning to New Orleans? That is, have you no plans to remain in Mexico?"

"Depends."

"Upon what? The war, perhaps? Or is it a question of money and opportunity?"

"On what I find when I get there."

"What do you expect?"

"A meeting with a man I've been in search of for some time."

She frowned at him. "By meeting, do you refer to an ordinary call upon him or something more...fatal?"

"Depends," he answered again at his most laconic.

"I take it you would rather not say." She paused, waiting. When he made no answer, her lips tightened and she tried another venture. "Are you alone in the world that you can come and go with so little regard for who might be waiting elsewhere?"

"If you're asking whether I'm married…"

"Certainly not!"

"I'm not," he went on as if she had not spoken. "I've been on my own since I was old enough to leave home, but have the usual set of family members—father, six brothers, a whole passel of aunts, uncles and cousins."

"They will all be back home in Kentucky?"

"Here and there over the state and in Tennessee."

"You didn't mention your mother."

"She and my father, my pa, live apart."

"Do they? He must be your pattern card for behavior as she could not remain with him." She closed her eyes with a quick grimace. "I'm sorry. That was unkind."

She was attempting to be conciliatory. Kerr's guard went up another notch even as he studied the soft color that mantled her fine-grained skin; the way a cat's paw of a breeze flattened her bodice against the soft curves of her breasts. Looking away abruptly, he replied, "You may be right. She blamed him for my brother Andrew's death on the march to Santa Fe. He and our pa were always at loggerheads. Andrew tore out of the house after the last shouting match came to blows. He wound up in Texas."

"You followed after him, so it seems."

"You might say that. I set out for Texas when he didn't come back."

"How did you arrive in New Orleans?"

He hesitated, tempted to tell her the whole sorry tale,

including the letter from Andrew that had set him on Rouillard's trail. It could be so easily used against him, however, and reticence was a hard habit to break. A half truth seemed the better choice. "It's a place I'd wanted to see since I was knee-high to a jackrabbit. Pa used to talk about it around the fire on winter nights. He was with Jackson when he came down to fight the British back in fifteen, his one big adventure. He never forgot the place or the people."

"He knew Andrew Jackson?"

Kerr tipped his head in assent. "Ol' Hickory himself. They were neighbors in Tennessee at the time, though my pa left the family place and moved west after he married, bought acreage of his own in Kentucky."

"He bought a place."

"You needn't sound so surprised," he said, though it pleased him to see the perplexity in her face as she took in the fact that the life of a sword master might be a choice for him instead of a necessity.

"I suppose he farmed."

"Some, though he mostly raised horses, purebred racing stock. He and Jackson exchanged breeding animals on occasion."

"So you belong to the landed gentry."

"I wouldn't put it that way." He gave a brief shrug. "Wasn't exactly born in a log cabin, either."

She stared at him as if he had sprouted horns, though what she might have said in answer was lost as the watch bells rang out. Since they also signaled breakfast, he offered his arm to lead her below. That she took it was more a symptom of her preoccupation, he thought, than a sign that she accepted his escort. It felt like a victory anyway.

The dining salon had been set to rights after the debacle of the night before. Quite a few passengers seemed to have recovered from their seasickness; at least they straggled into the long room to face whatever fare was on offer. Among them was Sonia's tante Lily, looking washed-out but determined to perform her duty toward her niece. Madame Pradat bristled with disapproval as she followed Kerr's progress with Sonia toward a seat next to her aunt. Her son, at the lady's side, avoided looking in Kerr's direction though the tops of his ears turned the color of brandied plums. On the opposite end of the table, Tremont and the Reverend Smythe discussed tides and ocean currents, but that did not prevent the planter from inclining his head in ironic acknowledgment of his entrance with Sonia. Other passengers greeted their arrival with a beehive murmur of comment that all too obviously concerned the events of the night before. Sonia gave no sign that she noticed, though her voice was stilted as she made some light comment about the aroma of morning coffee.

Kerr seated his charge next to her aunt then rounded the end of the table to take the bench facing her. It was a compromise of sorts, one that avoided the appearance of familiarity that might come from seating himself beside her yet allowed him to discourage anyone else from assuming that place.

The dining-room stewardess, her moon face still

sallow and mouth grim, arrived with platters laden with hard rolls, ham, conserves in crystal pots and butter shaped to resemble seashells. To this was added the usual café au lait. Within moments, all conversation died away as appetites depressed by the storm revived with the ship's relative stability.

Kerr would not have been surprised at some repercussions from the near duel, a tedious scene of contrition and apology enacted by Gervaise Pradat, maybe, or a social cut by his proud *maman*. Yes, or even a supercilious comment on his dog-in-the-manger attitude from Tremont.

It didn't happen. He was just congratulating himself on the prospect of a peaceful breakfast when Sonia reached across the table to take one of his breakfast rolls. Breaking it in half, she buttered a portion and put it back on his plate. Leaning back where she sat across from him, she ate the other half with delicate nibbles while smiling into his eyes.

Kerr almost choked on the bite of ham he'd just put in his mouth.

"Are you all right, *mon cher?*" she inquired with spurious concern as she reached for his water tumbler. "Here, you should drink something."

His fingers brushed hers as he took the glass from her. He felt as if he'd been stung by an electric eel. Setting the glass down again without tasting the contents, he sent her a warning glance.

If she recognized it, the effect was nil. Gently, so gently he could not swear he actually felt it, she reached with the toe of her slipper and caressed the booted calf of his leg. He swallowed hard while heat ran up his spine, blazing across the back of his neck with such intensity that he thought his collar and cravat might catch fire. *"Mademoiselle,"* he began.

"Yes, *monsieur?"*

What could he say? He looked at his plate. "Nothing."

"Such a pity," she murmured.

Her voice was as dulcet as her smile. The need to be alone with her to demonstrate the folly of what she seemed to be doing was an ache inside Kerr. On second thought, that might be unwise given the hot anticipation the idea caused in his lower body.

She took her slipper-covered toe away. Smiling with eyes like sunlit bluebells, she reached to pick up a sliver of ham with her fingertips and bent forward to hold it to his lips. Mesmerized, he leaned to take it. At the last second, he curled his tongue around her thumbnail, licking so the essence of her mingled with the flavor of ham on his taste buds.

Her gasp was perfectly audible. She snatched her hand away, then made a valiant try at a laugh as she glanced around, noticing the attention the two of them had garnered. In a low murmur, she said, "What big teeth you have."

Kerr opened his mouth to answer her, but once more thought better of it. Some answers, particularly the more obvious ones, were best left unspoken.

"For pity's sake, *chère,"* her aunt said in sotto-voce protest.

Sonia turned a limpid gaze in her direction. "I assure you it is quite acceptable, even expected, *ma tante*. The gentleman has forbidden me the company of other men, demanding that I concentrate my flirtatious impulses in his direction."

"Has he?" the older woman asked faintly, putting one frail hand to her temple. The look she flung in Kerr's direction was both apologetic and accusing.

"I assure you, he has. What else am I to do? A lady must have some distraction, and he is quite immune, you know. He gave me his word on it."

Kerr suppressed a heartfelt groan. What maggot of the brain had made him put such an idea into her head? He was going to regret it, for she would see to it.

Hell, he regretted it already. His head felt as if it might explode from the pressure building in his veins as she nudged his calf again.

Down the table, Gervaise and his mother were involved in low-voiced disagreement. Kerr thought Madame Pradat was remonstrating with her son over his urge to rally to Sonia's defense yet again. He tensed, waiting to see if it would be necessary to give the young idiot a lesson in swordplay after all.

It was then that a ship's officer entered the dining salon and walked briskly to where the captain sat at the head of the table. He handed over a message then stood back while it was read.

Captain Frazier glanced up at his officer with a frown. Crumpling the message in his hand, he thrust back his chair and rose to his feet. With the briefest of requests to be excused while they continued with their breakfast, he went quickly from the salon.

"What do you suppose that was about?" Tante Lily asked with a worried frown.

Tremont, on her far side, patted her hand that lay beside her plate. "Nothing that need concern us, I'm sure."

Kerr was not so positive. It seemed he could just catch the distant thump and splatter of another steamer somewhere to the rear of the *Lime Rock*. That they would meet a vessel in what was a regular shipping lane was not unusual, but it should not require the presence of the captain on the bridge.

His mind went once more to the arms shipment in the hold. Could they be about to make a transfer at sea? If so, the master of the vessel would have to be a party to the gunrunning.

Kerr looked down the table to where Tremont sat. The erstwhile planter returned his gaze an instant through narrowed eyes before dropping his napkin beside his plate and rising to his feet. He stepped over the bench and left the room on the captain's heels.

It was too much. Kerr surged upright and followed in his turn. He was not moved solely by curiosity, however, or even suspicion. He was also glad to leave what had become a torturous situation.

There was indeed another ship. It hovered nearby, paddle wheels barely turning, looking ghostly in fog. The flag that flapped from its masthead showed the colors of Mexico but it was no merchantman. It was, rather, a man-of-war with its gun ports hanging open and the snouts of its guns pointed at the *Lime Rock*'s waterline.

Pennants were being hauled up by both vessels, appearing and disappearing in the drifting smoke from the stacks as the *Lime Rock* slowed its engine, losing headway. The captain stood on the forward deck with a spyglass to his eye, watching a signalman on the far ship. Taking the glass down, he closed it with a snap.

Kerr stopped a few feet away, next to Tremont. He had his own ideas about what was taking place, but thought it best not to leap to conclusions.

"What's going on?"

Tremont nodded toward the man-of-war. "The Mexican commander there demands we heave to and allow ourselves to be boarded."

"Why in God's name should we do that?" Kerr could not, somehow, be surprised that Tremont knew how to decipher the signals.

"Two reasons," the other man answered in driest irony, "the first being we are unarmed and they have guns at the ready."

"And the second?"

"The United States Congress has finally bestirred itself. We have declared war on Mexico."

Sixteen

The thunderous boom of a heavy gun brought Sonia to her feet. She was not alone. Tante Lily jumped up with a shrill cry. Madame Pradat screamed and fell back into Gervaise's arms. Madame Dossier clasped her children to her and bowed her head over them.

The Reverend Smythe put his hands together as if in prayer. The reaction of other gentlemen was less pious.

"Calm yourself, *Maman,*" Gervaise told his mother while craning his neck to see out a side window where another vessel could just be glimpsed. "We haven't been hit. Judging from the powder smoke, I believe it may have been a warning shot from a bow gun."

It seemed a likely explanation to Sonia, though she could not imagine the reason for it. The need to find out for herself welled up inside her. With a glance from the strange ship to the door, she stepped around the bench.

"Wait, *chère,* where are you going?" Her aunt reached to catch the back edge of her shawl. "We should stay here."

"I only want to see what's happening."

"You'll be in the way if danger threatens. Besides, Monsieur Wallace will surely come tell us what transpires."

No doubt he would, in his own good time. "I will only be a moment. I promise not to linger if there's trouble."

She tugged her shawl free and went swiftly toward where the gentlemen were already crowding out onto the deck. Even as she made her way among them, she could hear the ship's engines pick up their beat, feel the surge as the paddle wheels spun with more force, gathering speed.

It didn't seem at all normal. Fearful doubt ran through her mind, particularly as she recalled the grim set of Kerr's face as he left them moments ago. She suddenly longed to be near him, anchored at his side where it was safe.

That impulse brought her to a stunned halt. Where had it come from? Could it, just possibly, be the result of her deliberately distracting him, testing him and discovering his mettle last evening? Was that when she had begun to trust him so much?

No time was allowed for an answer. A ship's officer brushed past her, heading toward the stern. His shoulder struck her, so she stumbled against the bulkhead, though he hardly seemed to notice. It did nothing to reassure her about whatever was going forward.

Regaining her balance, she stared around her but could see little for the bulk of the side paddle wheel. Moving past it in the direction of the stern, she stepped to the railing and peered around the crowd of men there.

Blown sea spray, swirling smoke and the nose-burning stench of gunpowder stung her eyes. She squinted against it, gathering the flying ends of her shawl as she stared toward the open water behind them. Steaming to their rear, just off the port side, was the pursuing ship. Painted in hues of black, red and yellow, it had a solid, dangerous look to it. Its identity came to her in snatches as the men around her shouted back and forth, leaning over the railing, staring, pointing.

A Mexican vessel, a man-of-war, and it had fired at them.

They were at war.

This was it. War had come at last, after years of threats and skirmishes, posturing and diplomatic maneuvering. How hard it was to believe. The threat had hovered so long she had never expected to see it, in spite of railing about it to her father.

Even more difficult to accept was that she was caught in the middle of it. What could a Mexican naval commander want with the *Lime Rock,* a mere packet ship carrying mail, cargo and a few passengers between New Orleans and Vera Cruz? Unless, perhaps, it was to seize the American commissioner who traveled on her?

The paddle wheels churned, moving faster and faster, leaving twin wakes of roiling, foam-streaked water behind them. The Mexican man-of-war was giving chase. Both ships wallowed in the lingering storm swells with their masts describing violent arcs against the gray sky.

It almost seemed to Sonia that she could sense the

increasing heat of the boilers beneath her feet as they poured steam power into the pounding machinery. Certainly, she felt the constant shudder through the railing as the thudding crankshaft thrust the paddle wheels in ever more frantic revolutions.

Gervaise, standing just down from her with the Reverend Smythe, called out something and pointed landward. Putting up a hand to protect her eyes from the increasing wind of their flight, Sonia gazed in the direction he indicated. All she saw was the coastline she and Kerr had watched earlier. It was closer now, for she could make out the blackish green silhouettes of palm trees and what appeared to be a white line of surf.

The explosion of another shot echoed over the water. It flashed in fire-brightness and smoke from the muzzle of a small cannon mounted on the Mexican ship's bow, as Gervaise had suggested before.

A geyser spouted up just off their stern. The water from it splattered down, scudding away on the rising wind that whipped the fog from the tops of the waves and tore the mist along the shoreline into drifting gray rags.

Men ducked away from the aft railing. As they scattered, Sonia saw Kerr with his feet spread as he braced there. He stared at the pursuing ship, his face so grim it seemed he meant to leap the barrier and stop the oncoming vessel with his bare hands. If the shot had come just a little closer…

No, she wouldn't think of that.

Sonia shivered convulsively. She was damp and cold, her moisture-laden skirts whipping around her like wet washing on a line. She was the only female above decks, the only one braving the elements and the peril. It might be best if she returned to the dining salon with the other ladies. Tante Lily would be beside herself with anxiety about her and concern for their plight. She could at least relieve her mind.

She could, she should, but it was impossible to drag herself away.

Watching the events was far better than huddling below. Besides, what if they were hit? She could not bear the prospect of being trapped if the ship should sink.

The *Lime Rock* appeared to be drawing ahead of the man-of-war; the stretch of ink-blue water between the two ships was widening. The packet was the lighter vessel with perhaps more efficient steam power. Captain Frazier must be throwing everything he had into the furnace, for they were fairly flying over the waves. It seemed they might well outrun their pursuer.

Sonia clung to the railing, staring at the oncoming Mexican ship until her eyes burned. Her heart pounded in her throat and her hands ached from the hard grip of her fingertips. Terror poured along her veins like acid, yet with it ran fierce exhilaration. She could not recall when she had last felt so vividly alive.

What would happen if they could not shake off this attack? Would the *Lime Rock* have to surrender? Would they be taken to another port as a prize of war? She had longed for something to happen that would prevent her marriage to Jean Pierre. For better or worse, this might well be it.

Another blast from the Mexican bow gun thundered across the water. The shell arched toward them in a smoking parabola. It seemed to slow as it neared, though its scream grew louder.

It crashed into the stern. The lower deck of the *Lime Rock* exploded in a fountain of splinters that spread, rising, pulling the planking apart at the seams.

Cries rang out. Men flew in all directions. The ship's stern rose up, sending buckets and rope coils, spars and bits of broken rail plummeting toward Sonia.

A wooden pin of some description struck her and she fell to her knees. She snatched at the railing post, but it was torn from her hand as the ship crashed down again, deep into the sea. Tumbling, sliding, she came up against another post farther along the deck. She grabbed for it, holding on as soot rained down from overhead along with splinters and a deluge of seawater.

She could hear the gurgle and rush of incoming water and the ominous crackle of what could only be flames. A great burst of steam poured from the back of the packet. On either side, the paddle wheels slowed to a grinding, cascading stop.

The captain shouted in hoarse command. Ship's officers ran here and there, shoving people aside. Passengers poured from the dining salon, crawled from the cabins below. Women prayed and shrieked and children cried. Crewmen swarmed to the upper deck where they dragged down a launch that dangled crazily from its davits.

Sonia glimpsed her aunt. She could hear her calling her name. She answered, but her voice was drowned by the rumble and crash of falling objects and the dying blast from the ship's steam whistle.

She got to her knees, dragging her skirt from under them as she staggered upright. Though she scanned the men crowded amidships, scrambling away from the downward slant of the stern, there was no sign of Kerr. She turned to look behind her.

The ship jerked, listed to starboard with a mighty groan. Sonia latched on to the railing again as the pitch of the deck threatened to toss her overboard. Two men rolled past her, slipping under the railing in a shower of splinters and dirt. They struck the water and went under.

The Mexican man-of-war surged ahead as the crippled *Lime Rock* settled to a halt. Sonia could see it as the packet broached, slowly turning its bow into the wave troughs. The armed vessel seemed to be coming about, swinging around to perhaps finish them off.

There was no need. They were sinking.

Saltwater surged around her ankles, wetting her hems so they dragged at her waist. If she loosened her grip on the railing, she might dash up the canting deck to the steps that gave access to the upper deck. With the slant of the ship, she could see the crew preparing to set afloat at least three of the four available lifeboats.

If the law of the sea was women and children first, however, it was not being followed. A good dozen male passengers were trying to wrest the launch from those about to swing it over the side.

Both crew and passengers lost control of one lifeboat. It shifted, screeched along the railing and then shot over it into the sea. Immediately, men began to clamber after it, diving into the water.

The ship rumbled, creaking mightily as it settled deeper into the waves. Something, a falling sail or rope with dangling pulley, swung past Sonia then slapped into her head from behind. She lost her hold and pitched forward, falling over the railing. The cold turbulence of the sea reached up to catch her and drag her down.

It closed over her head, burning her eyes. Her shawl wrapped around her. It was wet, clinging, confining her arms. Panic burst in her mind as she felt herself sinking.

She fought the cloth, dragging it from her face, her neck, her wrists, thrusting it from her, into the murky depths. It followed her retreat, tangling around her like a net. Lungs bursting, she dived away, finally leaving it behind. Almost immediately, she began to rise, bobbing to the surface in a balloon created by her skirts.

The ship was dying. She could hear its death rattle, the choking, burbling rush of water through the cabins and salons, the muffled thunder of machinery and cargo letting go of their moorings, slamming into the bulkheads. And above it all, like the cries of seabirds, came the calls and screams of those still on board.

Horror poured over her in an icy wave. She cried out with it, and in rage against fate, in woman's ancient curse for barbaric war and senseless destruction. The sound, thin and pitiable, was lost in the melee.

Air trapped in her skirts was keeping Sonia afloat. It would not last. She could feel the wetness seeping closer, sense the drag of waterlogged cloth as buoyancy faded away. She had to get free of the layers or they would drag her down. She reached deep, digging for the hem of her skirts, tugging at the sodden cloth to reach under it for her petticoat tapes. She wrenched at them with all her strength.

One or two came free, but others turned into wet and stubborn knots. Sobbing, she tried harder as water began to lap at her breasts, slapping wavelets against her chin. She could see the shoreline, almost believe she could hear the surf. Or was it the rush of blood through her veins?

The water around her seethed with air bubbles rising from the ship. Boards and splinters floated, bumping into her, along with a chicken coop, a wooden pail, a belaying pin, a half-drowned pillow, a child's rocking horse. She saw a man swimming, another floating. Somewhere, she could hear the squeak of oars.

None of it seemed quite real. It could not be. Could it?

The water was circling her neck. She could feel it lifting her hair that had come free of its pins, floating it around her like seaweed. She kicked free of one petticoat, then another. Her slippers were gone. Her bare foot touched something soft and warm as she kicked, and she shuddered away from it.

Abruptly, she was snared by a hard, warm rope. It wrapped around her waist, pressing the stays of her corset into her ribs, forcing the air from her lungs. Flailing in the water, she grasped at that constriction with both hands.

"Be still. Let me help you."

Kerr.

She inhaled in sharp amazement, swallowed saltwater, coughed. That deep voice soothed, excited, galvanized her. She could feel his warmth, his heat and contained power along one whole side of her body. She turned her head so quickly that her hair tangled around them both.

"My skirts," she gasped, "they—"

"I know. Don't breathe."

She glanced down, saw something flash silver in the water. An instant later, she felt the press of a knife blade at her waist. She froze as it jerked once, twice. Then he was ripping at her clothing, dragging her tight-sleeved bodice and clinging skirts from her. He thrust them away, letting them sink so she floated light and free beside him.

"I—I can swim," she said, trying to push away from him as he supported them both.

He released her, though his warm fingers trailed over her back, along her arm. "I remember. Come on, then."

They struck out, breasting the waves shoulder to shoulder. Dodging floating debris, skirting other swimmers, they made for a clear stretch of water and the promise of land beyond it.

It was only when they were some yards away from the ship that Sonia realized neither had given a thought to the lifeboats. There would be no room, she was almost sure. More than that, the Mexican man-of-war was making ready to pick up the survivors. It was unlikely they would allow those in the launches to escape. The rescued might well become prisoners of war, particularly the men.

To avoid that uncertain fate seemed the best course. If they drowned in the attempt, it was still worth the chance.

Before they had gone a dozen yards, Sonia realized she was slowing Kerr down, that he could easily have outdistanced her. It was not surprising given his superior strength, but it distressed her all the same.

The shore was also farther away than it had seemed from the ship's deck, farther than she had ever tried to swim as a skinny teen wearing her cousin's pantaloons. The waves that lifted her were higher, deeper and stronger as well. More, it had been years since she last paddled in the river. Her arms were losing their strength, the back of her nose burned and her breath was labored from the strain of trying to keep up with Kerr.

She rolled over, changing to a backstroke. "Leave me," she said in hoarse recommendation as a wave slapped into her face. "I…need…rest a minute. I'll come…behind you."

"Not likely."

"But you…"

"I made a promise."

"Don't be…ridiculous. It was never meant…for this."

"You're wasting your breath." With barely a pause, he reached across her and grabbed her wrist. Flipping her to her stomach again, he tucked her fingers into the waistband of his trousers. "Hold tight. Help any way you can."

She grasped the cloth, feeling against the backs of her fingers the warm flesh of his muscle-wrapped side. He surged once more for the shore.

It should have been humiliating, being towed like a

child. Instead, it felt right, somehow, and gratifyingly secure. Matching her pace to his then, she pulled with one arm, kicking mightily, as they cleaved through the water.

Time ceased to have meaning. Fear, doubt, concern for her aunt and the other passengers was an ache in Sonia's heart, but the need to help was banished from her mind by its impossibility. All of existence narrowed to the watery world around her and the man at her side. Their goal of the far-off line of trees, the rhythm of their progress and the need to breathe and stay afloat were the only realities. It seemed they might go on and on forever, caught between ship and shore, making little headway but striving, earnestly striving, to live.

All clamor from the *Lime Rock* and the Mexican ship died slowly away behind them. Wisps of fog drifted over the water, gathering, thickening again, above their heads. The splashes as they dug into the waves, the rasping of their hard breaths were muffled sounds held close around them. Sonia gave thanks that it was so, hoped that their existence would be forgotten in the excitement, that they would be presumed drowned.

The waves turned to foaming surf around them. Gritty, powdered coral shifted between Sonia's legs and the water seemed to grow thick with finely ground gold. She and Kerr struck the shelving brown sand beach at the same time. He staggered to his feet, pulling her upright beside him. Holding on to each other, they waded from the surf with faltering steps, falling face-down as they reached the tide line.

Solid ground.

It felt miraculous, even if the wave-packed sand was littered with broken shells, fish bones and bits of rotted wood. Its greatest virtue was that it didn't move. Sonia could have lain there, slept there, for aeons.

Kerr groaned, then pushed up on his hands and rolled to his back. Propping on his elbows, he stared back out to sea.

"What is it? They aren't…"

"No," he said in answer to the question she could not bear to complete. "The Mexicans seem to be searching for survivors, though it's hard to tell."

She sat up to glance around, seeing at once what he meant. The fog had grown denser along the shoreline where the land blocked the wind. The Mexican ship and what was left above water of the *Lime Rock* were like ghost vessels with their masts appearing and disappearing in the mist.

"You don't think they will look for us?"

Kerr turned his head to stare at her a long moment. His gaze brushed the deep décolletage and shirred cap sleeves of her corset cover under her corset that protected it from perspiration and kept it from pinching her skin, the bedraggled and semitransparent batiste of her ruffle-edged pantaloons. Something hot and disturbing unfurled inside her. She lifted her chin a fraction while blazingly aware of her seminude state.

His face tightened and he turned away. After a second, he hauled himself to his feet with a wrench of vein-traced muscles. "Best not wait to find out."

The abrupt move startled a sandpiper so it scuttled

away, leaving an embroidery trail of tracks on the wet sand. It did not excite the flock of pelicans that perched on a rocky outcropping some dozen yards away. They sat watching them like wise and suspicious old men, waiting to see what they were going to do. Moving slowly to prevent startling them into flight that might alert those around the foundering *Lime Rock,* Sonia pushed to a crouch and eased behind the outcropping for concealment. She straightened then, turning toward the junglelike wall of greenery beyond the beach. Kerr joined her, his fists on his hip bones as he narrowed his eyes to search the towering growth.

It was a dark green tangle of frond-crowned palms hung with lianas, of exotic-looking shrubbery, luxuriant, sensual flowers and clumps of plants wrapped around the crotches of trees like diapers on babies bottoms. Anything could be hiding in there from the look of it, particularly if it was poisonous, venomous or dangerous to the touch.

"What are we going to do? Where can we go?" she asked in a whisper.

A deep breath swelled Kerr's chest before he squared his shoulders. "We'll do what we have to," he answered. "As for where we'll go, the only direction I see is inland. There should be a river or stream of some kind, judging from maps I've seen. Find it, and we can follow its course. With luck, it should lead to a village of some description."

"And if there isn't one?"

He didn't answer, nor did he attempt to persuade her to his idea. He simply strode off, making toward the dense jungle growth. Sonia stared after him with her lips parted. Then she narrowed her eyes. "Monsieur Wallace!"

He stopped. "What now?"

"Did you never hear of ladies first?"

"This isn't a lifeboat."

He had seen that mass breach of conduct and disapproved of it, judging from the grim note in his voice. It made Sonia feel marginally better. "It isn't a promenade, either, but manners still apply."

He took a deep, tried breath, for she saw it lift his chest. "You know where you're going, do you?"

"Does it matter? The point is—"

"The point, *mademoiselle,* is that whoever goes first will meet head-on with whatever is waiting for us in there." He waved toward the green wall of growth. "The one walking behind will have a good chance to run for it. You want to break trail, be my guest."

She swallowed hard as she considered it. "No," she answered after a long moment. "That won't be necessary."

"What I thought," he muttered. Or Sonia thought he did. She couldn't be sure since he walked away again.

His shoulders were so impossibly wide, tapering to a narrow waist and hard-muscled thighs like a statue of some ancient gladiator. He moved with that same athletic ease in his own body and with the innate grace that came from limitless strength. His oak-brown hair, slicked back by seawater, glistened with copper highlights in the morning light. He seemed so sure of himself, so positive about what they should do, also when and how they should go about it.

It was supremely irritating.

It was also a vast relief.

Moving with care, stiff in every joint and strained in muscles she had never expected to use, Sonia took a step after him. Once begun, she followed without complaint.

Seventeen

Walking away from Sonia was the only way Kerr could keep his hands off her half-naked body. What kind of brutish idiot was he that he could see her prostrate on the sand, exhausted from the ordeal just behind them, and want nothing so much as to take her in fierce possession where she lay?

Men had such impulses after facing death, he knew; he'd felt them himself following dawn meetings at the dueling oaks. This was more than that primitive need to prove he still lived. It had in it a touch of the elemental, a pledge that he would allow nothing to harm Sonia Bonneval, not now, not for all eternity.

He of all men had no right to such a vow. It must, no doubt would, cancel out one he had held before him like a grail for more than four years. And what use was a man who would discard one obligation for the sake of another, like a child taking a lick from every bonbon in the box?

She was so tender, so impossibly smooth and pale where no sun had ever kissed her skin, and certainly no man. He longed to touch her, to run his hands over every inch of her in the lightest of explorations, smoothing his way into hollows, dipping into crevices while she sighed and moaned and gave him access to all she had. His fingers burned with the need so he shook them as he walked. His neck ached with the urge to turn and impress the sight of her in wet, clinging dishabille upon the backs of his eyes for all time.

No. He could not look, dared not look.

He had made her half-naked, had cut her clothing from her body as she swayed with the waves, yielding in his arms. It was his ultimate fantasy come to life. When old and toothless, rheumy-eyed, half-blind and lost to all physical pleasure, he would remember that moment and he would smile. It had been, in some strange manner, like slicing away her defenses, leaving her at his mercy. To strip away what was left, the few tattered scraps of unmentionables and damnable corset that he should have taken care of before, would be no more than a moment's work. And then…

No.

Yes, and the swim through the heavy sea with her breasts pressing into him with every stroke she made and her thighs, the softness between them, twining around and against him. He could feel the sensation down his side still, like the burn of stinging nettles. If he checked, he thought he might find scars from it.

That, too, would remain.

God, he was just a man. What was he supposed to do? He wanted her with a desperate ache that nothing less than her surrender could assuage, had longed for just that since he had wiped black tears from her face while rain fell around them.

It was the one thing he could never have.

He had promised to deliver an unsullied bride.

He would do it if it killed him.

It well might.

He tramped ahead, blind to everything except the hot thoughts that ran through his head. Sonia followed, keeping up better than he expected. It was all the walking about the Vieux Carré done by ladies like her, he thought, from town house to market, cathedral to modiste, shoemaker to milliner. That and the endless daily visits between friends during the season, the promenades on the levee and nights of dancing until dawn.

It was perhaps a long, hard hour after they left the coast that a movement caught his eye, a shift of mottled color sliding away on his right side.

The hair on the back of Kerr's neck stirred, rising in the awareness of danger as he halted. He turned to stone in place, barely breathing.

It was a rattlesnake as big around as his arm and twice as long. The reptile eased away, sliding over the forest floor with the faintest of dry rustles, disappearing between one patch of shadow and the next.

Cursing under his breath, Kerr wished passionately for his sword cane now sinking beneath the waves with the *Lime Rock*. He hated being without it. Seldom had a blade of some kind—épée, foil, rapier, saber or sword cane—been out of his reach these past few years. A

pocketknife was no substitute, though it weighted his
trouser pocket where he'd thrust it after divesting Sonia
of her heavy outerwear.

He glanced back at Sonia. She stood quite still.
Whether she had seen the snake or only taken her cue
from him, he wasn't quite sure. The first, he suspected,
since her eyes were wide with alarm and she breathed
quickly through parted lips.

He had better put what couldn't be helped from him
and collect his wits, he told himself in silent resolution.
If he didn't, they could both die here in this Mexican
jungle and never be heard from again. The pelicans and
parrots would shriek over their bones, the ants would
carry away all the rest, and that would be the end.

Summoning a smile, he held out his hand. "Might be
best if you keep close. I wouldn't want to lose you now."

She came forward, stepping daintily in her stocking feet
that were already filthy and showed red scratches through
the rents in the silk. Her hand slid into his, clasped, held.

Kerr's heart lifted inside him, but he said nothing.
Turning, he walked on with every sense honed to such
slicing alertness it was near pain. He welcomed that ache
as an antidote to the craving he could not bear half so well.

"Have you any idea where we are?" Sonia asked
after a moment. "I mean, where along the coast."

"Somewhere below Tampico, judging from a quick
look I had yesterday at the captain's charts."

"So we will try to head north?"

He stared ahead, his gaze quartering the undergrowth. "Vera Cruz is south."

"Yes, but Tampico is a port. If it's closer…"

"By the time we make it that far and wait for a ship, then wait again for the right tide and weather conditions so it can clear the bar that blocks the harbor, we can be where we were going in the first place."

Sonia stopped, snatched her hand from his grasp. "You can't mean we are still going to Vera Cruz!"

He let silence stand as his answer. What had she expected? Could she really think the sinking of the *Lime Rock* canceled out all obligations so they could sail for New Orleans from Tampico?

Maybe she was right, after all. They were half-naked, coated with sand, their skin itching from dried saltwater. Marooned on a strange coast where every bloodsucking critter known to man whined around them, they were days away from where they should be. They were also without food, water, map or even a compass to get them there. The smart thing would be to seek civilization and throw themselves on the mercy of anyone who looked able to help them out.

Kerr couldn't do it. He'd come this far and wouldn't turn back now. He had his knife, the silver from Bonneval that he'd been too wary to leave where he'd bunked, a decent knowledge of wood lore and a handy sense of direction. Mexico had a longer history than the United States, particularly in this southern region. The Spanish had been here more than four hundred years, so it must be chock-full of towns and villages where they could barter for food and some kind of transportation to Vera Cruz. All they had to do was find one.

"You are the most heartless man I've ever encountered," she said, her hot gaze searching his face. "Have you no thought at all for how I feel, no understanding of the escape we just made? Can you not think beyond this stupid loyalty to my father? He will not appreciate it, I promise you."

"It's nothing to do with him."

"Then it's this man you're so determined to find. Why is that? What do you want from him that you'll walk into a war to get it?"

She had the wrong idea by the tail, but he didn't intend to correct it. "War may have been declared," he said in evasion, "but I doubt it will mean much to us."

"I daresay you would not have predicted the attack on the *Lime Rock,* either."

"The battle lines have all been on the northern border. To send an army by ship to this neck of the woods will take weeks, even months, even if the generals decide on Vera Cruz as the logical port of entry to take Mexico City. I'll be in and out long before then."

"But I won't."

He shook his head. "That's up to your future husband."

"In other words, you refuse to be responsible for what happens to me."

She had him there, though he had no intention of admitting it. "We talked about this once already. No need to go over it again."

"Then I see no need to follow along meekly where you lead."

He dropped his voice to a threatening rumble. "I could always carry you."

"You wouldn't find it so amusing this time, or so easy."

"You're quite sure of that, are you?" He waited, poised on the balls of his feet, to see if she meant to run. He almost wished she would for the excuse of catching her, hefting her over his shoulder as he had on that night outside her papa's town house. Anything that would allow him to touch her seemed a fine excuse at the moment. He wanted that, needed it with pure dumb longing so strong his muscles clamped into rock hardness to prevent him from reaching for her.

Thank God there was only disgust for him in her face. If there had been invitation in any form he could not have been responsible. How in hell he was supposed to keep his hands off her until she was decently covered again, he had no idea.

A mosquito was feasting on the curve of her breast just above the low neckline of her corset cover. Without thought or plan, he reached out in swift reprisal, crushing the insect into a mere gray streak tinted with blood.

She flinched, her eyes widening, until he showed her his fingertips. Before she could speak, he stripped the buttons of his waistcoat from their holes and slipped it from him. Removing the studs from his shirt and cramming them into his pocket, he shrugged from it and held it out to her. His frock coat would have been better, he thought, but he had discarded it in the sea, along with Sonia's fan in the pocket. He'd miss the coat as it was his Sunday best. The fan, he mourned. One could be replaced, but the other was gone forever.

She took the shirt in reflex action, but immediately pushed it back at him. "I can't take this."

"Do you have to make a to-do over everything?" he asked in strained patience as he slid his bare arms back into the waistcoat with its dangling watch chain. "Put it on before you're eaten alive."

"If you think—" she began.

"Believe me when I tell it will be best if you're covered." A muscle in his jaw flexed as he clamped down on the urge to tell her exactly why it was best that she displayed fewer of her manifold charms. He refused to look at her as he spoke, refused to allow his gaze to return to the silken, heat-flushed curve of her breast that he had touched so briefly.

She searched his face for long moments. Something she saw there made her eyes widen a fraction. She looked at the shirt then. Giving it a hard shake, she thrust her arms into the sleeves and jerked the front edges together over her chest.

It was too big. The cuffs fell over her hands and the tail hung halfway to her knees. Kerr was just as glad to see it. The more of her that was covered, the easier he breathed.

An odd pleasure bloomed in the center of his chest. She might not acknowledge his right to protect her, but at least she accepted his shirt for cover. It felt like a victory. It felt, in some small degree, like an acceptance of him.

"Look," he said, deliberately removing his gaze from

her damp womanly curves, scanning the woods around them. "We need to put distance between us and the Mexican navy. We have to find water, food, shelter and some way out of this mess we've been handed. Now, we can feud and fight while we do it, but to my way of thinking we'll have a better chance if we declare that truce you mentioned on the deck there earlier. We can always take up where we left off when we get back to civilization."

Slow color rose in her face. For an instant, he thought it was from anger. He realized then that where they'd left off had been with her tormenting him with loving attention and a game of footsie under the table. Well, he wouldn't mind that, come to think of it.

Her lashes swept down, veiling her eyes. "You're quite right."

"What?" The capitulation was so unexpected that he was taken aback, wondering what he'd missed. Or maybe it was the distraction of remembering the feel of her toes in her thin slipper running up the back of his calf.

"It will be best if we put aside our differences, as you said. It would be foolish to do otherwise since I have the most to gain. I'm quite ready to admit," she finished with quiet bitterness, "that my chances of getting out of this are much better with you than on my own."

It sounded well enough. He wanted to believe it.

Instead, it worried him. She looked much as she had when she'd decided to torture him with her seductive wiles.

He allowed nothing of his suspicion to show in his

face. Holding out his hand, he waited to see just how sincere she was in her agreement.

She took it, sliding her slim fingers into his again as if it was the most natural thing in the world. Maybe it was, for her hand seemed to fit his as if made for it. The thought slipped through his mind about the same perfect meshing of other parts of their bodies, damp, heated, tight, with or without friction.

That wasn't the kind of ceasefire she'd had in mind, and he'd better remember it. Turning with determination so strong it made the tendons in his knees crack, he started off through the thick woods again.

Eighteen

"I will deliver Rouillard his bride, one unharmed, unsullied and unrepentant...."

Those words, spoken by Kerr, echoed in Sonia's mind time and time again as she walked and trotted and walked again, trying to keep up with his long strides that covered ground hour upon hour, putting distance between them and the coast. He had referred to the possible attentions of Tremont at the time, or so she had assumed. Now she could not help wondering if it might not have been his own impulses that disturbed him.

He forged ahead, aiding her, supporting her, half dragging her with him. So single-minded was he that he seemed not to notice the branches that slapped at them, the green-and-red parrots that flew up, squawking, ahead of them, or the small creatures that scuttled away into the undergrowth. Perspiration gilded his skin and made his hair curl on the back of his neck. It glistened on the hair of his chest as well, plainly visible as his waistcoat hung open, unbuttoned as a concession to the heat. For all the good that garment did him, he might as well have given it to her with his shirt. Between its swinging edges, she glimpsed the musculature of his upper body, the power of it and the round coins of his nipples. In fact, she was privy to more male nakedness than she had ever thought to encounter in her life as he twisted, turned and ducked his way through vines and around thornbushes. It affected her with a species of perilous awareness that made her toes curl into the soft leaf mold of the forest floor.

What would it take to persuade him to abandon his good intentions toward her? The question had nothing whatever to do with her recognition of him as an attractive male, of course, but could be vital to her future. Kerr was determined to deliver her to Jean Pierre. If she was less than pure when she arrived finally on her betrothed's doorstep, would he repudiate her?

The possibility, though enticing, was not without its dangers. Her father would inevitably learn of the disgrace. Chances were high that he would not allow her under his roof again. That would be no great tragedy, but the reason for it would soon become common knowledge, and she would not care to be at the center of such scandal. Her grandmother would no doubt take her in, but Mobile and New Orleans enjoyed close ties and the story would follow her. Her grandmother would be aghast to know her granddaughter could be so shameless.

Could she be?

Sonia wasn't entirely sure. It seemed possible as a last resort.

The question was, could Kerr be brought to cooperate? Beyond the question of honor—and she did not discount its value to him—it seemed something more was at stake, something that might make him immune to any overt appeal. She would need to come at it from a different angle.

"That shipment of arms you found," she said to his broad back, "it must be at the bottom of the sea by now."

"No doubt about it."

"Do you think it had anything to do with the Mexican ship's interest in the *Lime Rock?*"

He sent her a brief glance over his shoulder before returning his attention to the rough game trail he was following through the trees. "Who knows."

"You might hazard a guess."

"Not much point. It's nothing to me."

"You seemed interested when the subject first came up."

"That doesn't make me a gunrunner."

"I never said it did."

"It's what you were getting at, wasn't it?"

She frowned at him in annoyance before looking away again. "I suppose it may have been. Are you sure you know nothing about it?"

"Only that Tremont was interested."

She considered that. "He did bring it up, didn't he?"

"I wouldn't run away with the idea that he was the one meant to profit. Could be he was only curious."

"And you weren't?"

"I checked out the boxes in the hold."

"Yes?" When he failed to answer, she said in astringent inquiry, "So what did you find?"

"Nothing much. Just Tremont doing the same thing, maybe for the same reason."

"Or he could have been making certain his merchandise was secure."

"Maybe."

"You don't seem anxious to accuse him."

He shook his head. "I prefer to give a man the benefit of the doubt."

Admirable as that might be, it told her precious little of what she wanted to know. She opened her mouth to question him further. What came out instead was a short cry as something sharp jabbed into her heel. Her knee buckled and she stumbled to a halt.

"What is it? Here, sit down." He pressed her to a seat on a pile of stone blocks that jutted up from the forest floor, one of several they had passed.

"My foot," she said, lifting it to rest on her knee. "I came down on something."

Without so much as a by-your-leave, he went to one knee in front of her, pushed up her pantaloon leg and unfastened her garter. Sliding it up his arm to his bicep like some exotic bracelet from ancient times, he stripped away the torn rag of her stocking. His swift competence at that task made her frown, wondering where he had acquired it.

"Thorn," he said, turning her foot in his hand and leaning to peer at the heel.

"You see it?"

He wiped blood away with his thumb. "Broke off, and a good inch deep, maybe more. It's a wonder we haven't got on one before now. Here, I'll get it out."

Straightening, he dug into the pocket of his trousers. An instant later, he had his pocketknife in his hand.

She set her foot flat on the ground, wishing she had skirts to cover it. "It will be fine, I assure you."

"More likely it will fester so you're not able to walk. Let me see it again."

"It isn't necessary." She eyed the razor-sharp blade he had unfolded from the knife's haft. "Really, it isn't."

"Lie down and put your foot on my knee."

"I don't believe so."

"It will only hurt a moment, I promise you."

"You aren't sticking that thing into me."

"I could hold you down while I do whatever I want, and there's nothing—" He stopped, a flush staining the hollow of his throat. Pushing to his feet, he turned away from her. "Never mind. Suit yourself. Just don't blame me if blood poisoning sets in."

She was startled by his volte-face. That was, until she considered the possible connotations of the exchange between them. She blushed in her turn, a hot flood of color that threatened to set her skin aflame. Despite the embarrassment, she was encouraged.

"Wait," she called after him.

He stretched his neck as if it was stiff and set his hands on his hips. As he shifted a half turn in her direction, his gaze was opaque, the generous curves of his lips firmly pressed together.

"Please." She dandled her foot. "I'd like you to—to do what you wanted, after all." Without waiting for his assent, she lay down on the broad rock and turned to her stomach.

Quiet settled around them for long seconds. Then she heard the rustle of his footsteps in the decaying leaves as he came back and eased onto the rock near her ankles. He picked up her foot in his strong fingers.

Sonia pushed her arms out in front of her and folded them, putting her head down on them. The movement pulled his shirt she wore upward, but she refused to allow it to matter. Willing herself to relax, she waited for the bite of the blade.

It was a long time coming. Kerr simply sat with her foot in his hand, one thumb smoothing the same place on her ankle over and over.

"Can you see it?" she asked, her voice muffled by his shirtsleeve that concealed her face. He seemed to surround her as she inhaled the scent of the shirt that was compounded of warm linen, starch and virile male.

"I can see," he said, a strange note in his voice.

"Well?"

A soft sound, like a cross between a snort and a grunt, left him. Taking her heel in a firm grasp, he pressed the area where the thorn lay between his fingers.

She inhaled, lying perfectly still as she fought the need to snatch her foot free, fought the poisonous ache where the thorn was embedded. She felt so incredibly vulnerable to what he might do. It was disturbing in some fundamental way she could not quite grasp.

He gripped harder, pinching the flesh around the wound. She closed her eyes tight. Then came an instant of hard pressure and a flicker of slicing pain.

"There," he said. "It's out. It's over."

The need to see was strong inside her. Just as imperative was the instinct to end her supine submission to his aid. She lifted her head, started to turn.

"Just a minute." His voice was strained as he spoke. An instant later, he squeezed her heel again so something hot and warm ran down her ankle.

"What are you doing?"

"Making it bleed since we have no other way to wash out any bits that might fester—hold still."

The last command was given as she turned her head quickly to look over her shoulder. He was still clasping her foot, but as she watched, he put it down, reached with his knife to slash at the ruffling that edged one leg of her pantaloons. With a quick twist of his wrist, he wrapped the fabric around his hand and ripped free the long strip. He made a pad and pressed it to her heel, holding it in place while he wrapped the extra ruffling back and forth around her ankle.

"You need shoes," he said abruptly, his fingertips lingering on a long scratch that crossed her instep.

"So do you."

Her answer was sharp. The soothing caress on that most sensitive part of her foot brought a clenching sensation to her lower belly. As she met his intent regard, she thought his eyes darkened, gathering heat in their black centers. Deliberately, or so it seemed, he let his gaze rest on her ankle, travel to her calf then along her pantaloon-clad leg to where the curve of her hip began.

It was only then that Sonia remembered the thin batiste fabric of her pantaloons, also the possibility that their split crotch might have gaped open a trifle.

She twisted around with a gasp, pulling her foot from his hand as she sat up. "I'm sure I will be quite all right now, thank you. Don't you think we should go on in…in case we are being followed?"

"Stay here and rest a bit longer," he told her with a shake of his head as he rose to stand over her. "I'll backtrack a mile or two and find out."

A species of panic touched her. "What if they are there?"

"Could be I can slow them down."

"But you will come back?"

"Oh, yes, I'll be back. You can count on it."

His gray gaze smoldered with banked heat as he stared down at her. Then he backed away with his hands fisted. Turning, he disappeared back along the way they had come.

The woods around her had a breathless hush for long moments after he had gone. The insects began again finally, followed by frogs and then birds. None of them had the familiar sounds Sonia knew from the swamplands around New Orleans. They were louder, more raucous and insistent. Some cries had the shrill edge of screams. As the minutes slipped past, they seemed to be encroaching, gathering near, possibly making ready to pounce.

What would she do if Kerr left her here alone? She

might survive after a fashion, she thought, could blunder on until she came to a waterway and followed it as he had suggested. But success was much less certain.

She trusted him to find the way out for them, she really did. It was a strange thought. Strange, yet somehow unsurprising. He was a most capable man.

If he wanted to, if he could be persuaded to want it, he could extricate her from her arranged marriage. All she had to do was present the advantage to him in it. Or else discover what he might require in return and give it to him.

She thought she knew one thing he desired. However much he might try to hide it, he wanted her.

It troubled her to contemplate exchanging her favors for his help. What a wicked compromising of her principles, her upbringing and her future; she cringed to think of it. Yet what else could she do? It was men, her father and Jean Pierre, to be precise, who had entrapped her in this coil. Why should a man not release her from it?

Time crept past. The burning sun climbed overhead, reaching past midday and waning into afternoon. Her heel throbbed with a deep ache. She closed her eyes in exhaustion but was too keyed up, too wary and uncomfortable, to drop off to sleep.

She was beginning to think she had been deserted after all, when some shift in the air, some faint sound, made her bolt upright. Kerr stood in the tree shadows some twenty feet away. He was so still, so watchful that he might have been a ghost. She met his gaze with a suspended feeling inside her while her heart tripped into a faster beat. It seemed something hovered between them, something as untamed and dangerous as the tropical forest around them.

Without her volition, Sonia's lips curved into a slow smile of relief and gladness, a reaction without subterfuge. And the slashing dimple that appeared in his lean cheek in return was almost worth that moment of unguarded dependence.

He came toward her, carrying a sheaf of wide, flat leaves in his hand. Kneeling as before, he dropped the leaves beside him, then selected a layer and began to wrap it around her foot.

"What is it, what are you doing?"

"Making shoes of a sort." He kept his eyes on the green, solelike padding he was fitting over her bandage. Reaching for her stocking he had removed, he wrapped it quickly around her ankle and foot like the lacing of a Greek sandal.

She turned her foot this way and that in inspection. It seemed amazingly secure. "I must thank you for the thought," she said without quite looking at him. "It was…a kindness."

"Don't mention it." He paused while he adjusted the wrapping, and his voice was gruff when he spoke again. "It's best if I deliver you in fair condition."

"Yes, of course." What else? "But…where are yours?"

"My feet aren't as tender," he answered as he began to work on similar makeshift protection for her other foot. "I went barefoot from spring to fall as a boy. Even now, I sometimes give lessons on the fencing strip in stocking feet. Takes away the unfair advantage of my height."

A quick glance at the tough skin on the bottom on his foot that was turned up as he knelt confirmed what he'd said. She absorbed the rest, with its intimation of fair play, while watching him work.

After a moment, the quiet began to feel uncomfortable. She snatched a glance at his face. It was inscrutable as he concentrated on his task. His hands were warm and sure on her ankle, around her instep. The sensations they set off radiated up her calf, settling heavily at the juncture of her thighs.

She licked her lips that were suddenly dry, saying the first thing that came into her mind. "Did you see anyone on our trail?"

"Not a soul. Didn't hear anything, either. If we were followed at all, it seems we lost them."

"They may have been too busy with the others to notice us."

He tipped his head in agreement.

"I can't help worrying about Tante Lily."

He gave her a brief look from under his brows. "She was picked up with the others, I would imagine."

"If she made it off the ship." Her voice was subdued as she surveyed the flat knot he had just tied at her instep.

"She did, you know. I saw Captain Frazier handing her into his lifeboat."

Hope rose inside her, along with her spirits. "Truly?"

"Thought you knew, or I'd have mentioned it before. Madame Pradat and Madame Dossier and her children were in another. Gervaise fell overboard, but his mother was doing her best to pull him in, last I saw of them."

"Merci, le bon Dieu." She made a quick sign of the cross. "And Reverend Smythe?"

"God saw fit to put him in the first lifeboat lowered," Kerr answered, his tone dry.

"I suppose they will be all right."

He looked up, perhaps at the doubt in her voice. "What, you don't believe in your papa's ideas of Mexican gallantry?"

"Do you?"

"To a point. The ladies pose no threat so will probably be put off at the nearest port, maybe even at Vera Cruz since it's a military-supply point. Could be they'll make land ahead of us. Besides, your aunt is the kind of woman who always lands on her feet."

Was he saying those things to relieve her mind or because he believed them? Either way, they were good to hear. "And the others, the men?"

"They may have to answer a few questions, but the results should be the same."

"I pray you're right."

"Depend on it."

What else could she do? In any case, she preferred his view. To say so was going a little far, however. She made no reply but only rose and followed after him as he struck out again.

The improvised sandals were a great improvement over bare feet, but she still had to stop now and then to wrap them tighter, retying the stockings that held them. Kerr made no further offers of assistance, but seemed to be keeping his distance. That was an encouraging sign, she thought with some optimism. He wouldn't be so wary if he wasn't attracted to her.

He had kissed her, of course, which might be proof of a kind. She did not set great store by it. Her aunt had told her even the most refined of gentlemen would take advantage in that way, given the right circumstances. It was simply their nature. Such attentions were a compliment of sorts, even if they must be turned aside.

Sonia had no intention of spurning any advance the sword master might care to make. If the opportunity arose, she might create one of her own. And if the prospect made her breasts tingle and her lower abdomen feel heavy with anticipation, that was her secret.

How very strange, she thought with a minute shake of her head. Only a week ago, she would have laughed any such idea to scorn. Now it seemed not only reasonable but necessary.

It would not do for her acquiescence to come out of the blue, she realized. His suspicions would be aroused rather than his emotions, and who could blame him? They had made some small progress toward greater accord, but she thought further give-and-take between them might be helpful. She limped on for several yards while searching her brain for topics that might lead to a more accommodating mood.

What came to her instead was another surge of niggling doubt. Her plan could well make matters worse. It troubled her sense of fair play as well. But the alternative was to give up and accept her fate, becoming the bride of a man she despised. A little guilt was a small price to pay for freedom.

"I've been thinking," she said as she avoided a low-hanging branch to which clung great wads of wiry gray-green plants. "About this man you were going to see in Vera Cruz, I don't believe you mentioned his name."

"No."

"What do you mean, no?" She frowned at his broad back, allowing her gaze to shift for an instant to her garters that he still wore on either arm.

"I didn't mention it. Doesn't matter just now."

"I can't say I agree as he seems to be the reason I'm here."

He grunted by way of answer, and she thought his pace increased as if he meant to outdistance her curiosity. A disquieting thought struck her, but she dismissed it almost at once. Jean Pierre had been in New Orleans for only the briefest of visits in the past four years. It was unlikely he and Kerr had met.

"You can't tell me," she said finally, "that you would have accepted the job as my escort except for your quest to find this gentleman."

"Right now my quest, as you call it, is for water."

"Which I pray you find, since I'm so parched my tongue is sticking to the roof of my mouth. Still—"

"Not so as a man could tell." The glance he gave her over his shoulder had an ironic edge.

"You prefer a silent companion, trailing along behind you like a Choctaw and his woman at the French Market? Forgive me, but that isn't my way."

"I've noticed."

"Excellent," she said with a bright smile. "Then you won't be surprised if I put my question again."

"Surprised, no." He paused as they emerged from a tangle of greenery onto what had the look of another jungle path. Whether it was made by animals or human was impossible to tell. That it was in use seemed plain since otherwise the rampant vegetation around them would have closed it off in short order.

"You should have an answer ready for me then," she informed him. "We have disposed of the issue of the guns. At least so I suppose since you seem set on going on, and you wouldn't be if selling the lost arms had been your object."

"Thank you for that much."

"I do try to be fair, as difficult as it may be with some people. As I was saying—"

She stopped abruptly as he made a slicing signal for quiet. For a split second, she was incensed at the imperious gesture. His stance was too rigid, however, his attention too focused on the jungle around them. She stood listening to the hum of insects, distant calls of birds and the rustling of some creature moving away from them, deeper into the trees. She was about to demand the cause of his order when she saw it.

A mere spotted shadow, it hovered at the edge of the trail, blending so beautifully with the sun-dappled foliage around it that it was almost invisible. It was a great cat, resplendent and powerful as some beast of legend, the jade-green stare unblinking.

"Jaguar," Kerr said, the word a mere breath of sound.

Untamed, preternaturally alert yet unafraid, with physical perfection in every line of his body, the great cat reminded Sonia irresistibly of the man at her side. Sudden death was inherent in the animal's stance and stare; only its will held it in check. Her breath caught in her throat and her heartbeat thundered in her ears. Her every muscle turned to stone.

Leisurely, as if in disdain for such poor prey, the jaguar glided into movement. It crossed the path in the glow of the afternoon sunlight before vanishing into the thick growth on the other side.

Sonia released the air from her lungs in a sigh. Beside her, Kerr eased his stance. It was only then that she noticed the knife in his hand, the open pocket-knife he had used to such good purpose since the sinking of the *Lime Rock*. He had meant to meet the great beast with that puny weapon. It was all he had, yes, but what manner of man was he that he could even think of trying?

She could hardly imagine, didn't want to consider it. If she thought too much she might lose all hope, might give up and let him take her where he would.

Moistening her lips with the tip of her tongue, she asked, "You don't think he…might come back?"

"Who knows?" Kerr shrugged. "If he was a swamp panther, I'd say not. That is, unless he was too old to chase down his usual fare."

"You're such a comfort."

"My purpose in life."

He threw the words over his shoulder as he set out down the jungle track once more. Sonia, following after him, was pensive as she stared at a spot between his shoulder blades. His true purpose, as she well remembered, was to see her safely to her destination. He was prepared to do just that no matter what he had to face. She would not forget it again.

No, she would not. Neither would she forget that he had avoided, yet again, the answer to her question.

It began as a whisper, a distant murmur not unlike the wind among treetops or the tumbling surf they had left behind. Slowly, it grew louder, more definite.

Kerr increased his pace. Sonia kept up with him, walking faster, running a few paces, though her feet ached with every step and she felt light-headed with heat and thirst. Neither dared speak their hope for fear of making the disappointment greater if they were wrong.

The game trail turned, winding downhill around rocky outcroppings, almost fading away among them. It snaked past enormous trees with exotic flowers growing in the crotches of their limbs then wound down an embankment. Without warning, it broke from cover, stopped at a fern-covered lip.

Water.

A few steps more and it lay before them. Cool and inviting, it was a pool tinted viridian and raw sienna as it reflected its basin of moss-covered rock. A thin waterfall spilled over a rocky, wall-like cliff above it and clouds of dragonflies danced over its surface. At its far end, it flowed away around an obstacle course of rocks as part of a stream that might be wide enough to be called a river, if one were charitable.

They were so inclined since it promised a direction to follow, maybe even rescue.

"Wait here," Kerr said, placing a hand on her arm, the first time he'd been within touching distance in the hours since he had tied her sandals onto her feet.

Sonia's tongue was swollen, her eyes burned, and her skin itched from the saltwater that still coated it. Her clothing, scant as it might be, was so stiff from its salt-water soaking that it had chafed her raw in places she didn't want to think about. Every inch of her body cried out for the cool, clear water that lay in front of her.

She didn't move. With compressed lips, she watched as Kerr made his way down to the pool. Leaping from one rock ledge to another, sliding in a wash of gravel before recovering his balance, he moved with lithe caution to the water's edge. Kneeling, he scooped up a handful of the clear liquid, sniffed it, tasted it.

He looked back up to where she stood and gave a slow nod. She smiled in return, holding his gaze.

The slashing indentation in his cheek took on intriguing depth as his mouth curved in a grin of thankfulness, triumph and a frank need to share them with her. And the light in his eyes was like the sun rising bright and glorious over a gray sea.

Nineteen

Sonia needed no other invitation. Slipping, sliding in her makeshift sandals of leaves, she made her way down the bank and plunged into the water. She gasped as its chill struck, but did not stop. Wading out until she was hip deep, she scooped up the fresh sweetness in her cupped hands, splashing her face and neck so it ran over her shoulders and into the valley between her breasts, drinking her fill. It was only when her initial thirst was slaked that she realized she was alone in the water.

Swinging around in sudden panic, she scanned the rocky bank. Kerr was there where she stepped past him, sitting on his haunches.

"Aren't you coming in?" she called.

"I'd rather watch…keep watch until you're done."

The penetrating look in his eyes made her self-conscious. She backed away a step, skimming her hands back and forth over the water's surface. "I won't be long."

"Take your time."

It seemed better to put distance between them, which

was strange considering her intentions of not so long ago. She didn't care to look into it too closely, however, not while her hair was stiff with salt and her skin cried out for the cooling wetness that surrounded her. She moved deeper, dipping her head into the water and drawing her fingers through her hair to wash away the salt stiffness. She submerged, swam, floated with her eyes closed. She used her hands to rinse her corset cover, corset and pantaloons, also Kerr's shirt while the soft linen clung to her body. She drank, scrubbed her face, wrung the excess water from her hair while standing neck deep in the coolness. And all the while she worked her way back toward where Kerr rested, mindful that he must be as anxious to plunge into the pool as she had been herself.

Streaming water from every stitch, every strand of her hair, she rose up before him like a naiad, her smile beatific. "Now you," she said, her voice husky, "while I watch."

He blinked, as if her offer required mental processing. An instant later, his gaze flashed down her body.

A white line appeared around his mouth. Rising to his feet in a single fluid movement, he backed away from her.

She had half expected him to offer his hand for her support as she covered the last few steps to where mud and rock met, but he did not. As her knees cleared the water, he stripped off his waistcoat and let it fall. With a muscular leap off the slope, he launched into a flat, fast dive that took him three-quarters of the way across the pool.

Sonia glanced down then gave a hissing gasp. She had thought the shirt she wore covered her. She was mistaken. It gaped, exposing the wet transparency of her unmentionables. Beneath the fabric, the rose-pink areolae and beaded nipples of her breasts were clearly visible, as was the shadowy dark wedge where her thighs came together.

With stunning clarity, she recognized that if her body was so plain to be seen now, it must have been even more so when she and Kerr first crawled out of the gulf. She had just been too stunned by the disaster, too exhausted, to notice.

No wonder Kerr had sacrificed his shirt. She must have appeared the most complete wanton. But if so, why had he not taken advantage of it?

Wrapping the linen covering closer around her, Sonia moved up the bank and dropped down on a rock ledge protruding from the grass. She listened, she looked, but saw nothing that hinted at danger. Leaning to prop her elbow on her knee and her chin on her palm, she returned to the puzzle of Kerr Wallace.

The only thing which made sense was that the control of his emotions that allowed his success as a swordsman also allowed him to remain unmoved by her near nakedness. Well, perhaps not unmoved, she amended, thinking of his haste in getting away from her just now, but at least the training reinforced his will to resist. That could be a problem, one that must be surmounted.

She would have to bend her mind to it.

The waistcoat Kerr had discarded lay just below her. With a quick glance toward where he swam at the far side of the pool, she stretched to grasp an armhole and pull it toward her. The fabric, a light blend of cashmere and silk, was warm to the touch, though it was impossible to say if from the sun or his body heat. She closed her hands on it for an instant, all the same.

The movement dislodged his pocket watch so it slid onto the ground. She caught it by its chain, gathering it into her hand. Of silver chased with gold, it was engraved with scrolls around a pair of crossed swords in a design peculiarly significant. She stared at it with a cool feeling around her heart before pressing the release for the lid.

The watch had stopped not long after they plunged from the *Lime Rock* into the sea. She had expected no less; still it was a disappointment. Time had little meaning while they were lost here, but it was a symbol of events that must be, surely were, proceeding without them.

What would Jean Pierre do when he discovered the ship bringing her had sunk, or when her aunt reached Vera Cruz only to report that she and her escort were among the missing? His first act would surely be to send a message to her father by the next packet to New Orleans. That was, of course, if such vessels were being allowed to leave port.

What would her father think? How would he feel? Yes, and how would he react when he discovered she was alive? What would he do when he learned, finally, that she had miraculously escaped the disaster at sea? Would he appear at Vera Cruz to take her away from a country at war with their own, or only send a demand that the wedding go on as planned?

A silent laugh left her. She had no doubt of the answer.

Tucking the pocket watch away again, returning the waistcoat to where she had found it, she lifted her injured foot to her lap and began to repair the leaf sandal that had loosened. It was a moment before she glanced at the pool again.

Kerr was swimming strongly back and forth, his shoulders slashing through the water in a white-edged wave, long arms reaching with powerful strokes. Concentration furrowed his brow, and his eyes were closed. Some instinct caused him to turn just before he reached the smooth stone cliff, however, reversing with a flip of his body powered by a hard kick.

She wanted to look away, to pretend unconcern or boredom. It was impossible. The westward-leaning sunlight striking through the trees fell around him like a shower of daggers, so he flashed in and out among them as if avoiding their danger. The muscles across his back rippled, gleaming with a silver sheen. Sleek, powerful, almost primitive in his masculine beauty, he seemed to suit the time and place in a way she did not. His eyes, as he lifted spiked lashes and caught her gaze upon him, were as opaque as those of some carved river god.

He changed directions, surging toward the shallows where she sat. Sonia averted her eyes in quick reflex, though she could still see him through the shields of her lashes. She knew perfectly well the moment when he touched bottom, gained his feet and began to wade toward her.

His trousers, she was gratified to see, offered scarcely

more concealment than her pantaloons. The weight of the water draining down his body dragged them low on his hip bones, exposing a considerable expanse of hard, flat belly with an arrow of dark hair pointing downward. Below that, scrupulously molded by wet fabric, was an outline she recognized as corresponding to the male member of stallions seen at pasture.

Like some satyr of legend, half man, half beast, he lifted his arms that were circled by her wet garters and used both hands to rake his hair back from his face. The resulting furrows of wet hair relaxed into waves and wild ends that looked like a crown of tarnished copper leaves.

The closer he came, the harder it was to breathe and more furious grew the race of the blood in her veins. Something about him, some untamed impulse in his face or purpose in his stride, made her breasts tingle and lower body ache with reckless yearning. She didn't move, had no thought of retreat. Never in her life had she felt so alive or so in need of human closeness. The urge was so desperate that even the hint of menace in his approach could not disturb her.

His movements slowed, came to a halt. She met his eyes, sustaining the steel-hardness in their silver-gray depths. Her lips parted, and she inhaled with a soft, tried sound that might have been either trepidation or anticipation.

His gaze dropped to her mouth, and lower to where the shirt she wore had fallen open, revealing the enticing curves of her breasts above her corset cover and the drops of water that dripped from her hair to jewel their swells. It moved lower still, to her lap where she cradled her foot.

"You're bleeding," he said abruptly.

So she was, an ooze of red from under the leaves protecting her injury. Her voice had a trace of huskiness as she answered, "It's just from being in the water."

The rigidity of his muscles eased, his stance became looser. "More than likely, though I should take another look. It must be sore to walk on, too. Maybe we had better stop for the night."

"Here?" She glanced around at the stone walls that enclosed the pool except for the slope down which they had gained access. The question was almost at random in the confused disappointment that gripped her. She had thought, had expected...

But, no, it must have been only in her mind.

He gave a quick shake of his head, looking past her shoulder. "This is the jaguar's stomping ground and we don't want to get between him and his watering hole. I thought I caught sight of a cave higher in the rocks above here."

"That sounds useful," she said with some strain. "That's supposing it isn't his den."

His face remained impassive. "As you say. Best I take a look."

"I could go a little farther if necessary."

"A mile or two more shouldn't make a difference. At least we have water here, and we may need the daylight that's left."

He didn't explain further, and Sonia didn't ask. She

had made her effort toward cooperation and was too grateful that it had been turned down, too desperate for the prospect of rest, to care.

It was just as well they had not entered the opening he spoke of in darkness. It was not a cave, after all, but the overgrown doorway of what had once been a dwelling or pagan temple of enormous size. The stone blocks of which it had been built were tumbled and broken, leaving a usable space larger than the average room. Tree roots and vines covered the rubble, insinuating their tendrils into the cracks caused by storm and earth tremors so they grew down the walls inside. Lichen and fungi coated them in spreading crusts, almost obliterating the oddly convoluted characters and symbols that were incised into the rock. Lizards enameled in green, red and blue darted over the surfaces and spiders made nests like silken tunnels in the seams. And over it all hung a breathless, thunderous silence, as if something or someone long vanished would return momentarily.

Kerr checked the dark and echoing interior. Turning back to where she waited just inside the door opening, he pronounced it safe enough. Though it had been used by animals in the past, he said, the signs weren't recent.

"I've heard tell of lost Indian cities," he went on with a slow shake of his head as he studied the terrain around the opening. "Never expected to run up on one."

"You think there are other buildings?"

"Bound to be." He nodded toward where the ground rose behind where they stood. "That rock pile doesn't look natural. Must be lots of other ruins farther on, half buried and covered over with all the greenery."

She shook her head in amazement as she stepped deeper into the shadowy refuge. There was fascination for her in the idea of all those who had lived here, who had laughed and cried, played, sung, loved, hated, fought and died. It may have been long ago but their spirits seemed to hover in the stifling heat and silence. To take shelter where they had trod seemed a sacrilege, yet also a privilege.

How long she stood there, peering around the cool, dark space, absorbing its dusty mysteries, she didn't know. When she looked toward where she had left Kerr, he was kneeling in a small area he'd cleared under shelter of the doorway. Before him was a pile of dry leaves, shredded bark and what appeared to be fibers from the hems of his trousers. His ruined pocket watch lay next to him while he held the thick, concave crystal from it in his hand, directing a ray from the sun through it and onto the tinder he had prepared. A small smile touched her mouth as she understood, abruptly, why they had needed sunlight enough to stop while it was still available.

By the time she reached his side, a thin curl of smoke was rising from the pile in front of him. She dropped to her knees and leaned to blow gently on that hot spot. Seconds later, a tiny blaze appeared. They fed it with care, placing another leaf or two on it, a handful of rotted bark, a few twigs. When it was crackling, reaching upward for more fuel, she looked across the yellow-red flames and smoke, beaming.

Kerr smiled back at her, his eyes silver bright.

Perilous delight suffused Sonia. The two of them had survived enemy fire, drowning and jungle danger to find a safe shelter. To be alive was such a miracle. Inside her, some odd, internal barrier seemed to give way. Careless of the smoke and her damp hair strands that dangled near the small fire, she leaned impulsively to press her lips to his.

He came to his feet in a single, swift movement, taking her with him, swinging her away from the flames. Releasing her just as fast, he spun away from her. "Keep it burning," he said over his shoulder. "I'll be back soon."

"But where—"

She was talking to empty space. He was gone, and she was left to contemplate the difficulty of persuading a man to make love to her who was forever leaving her.

It was dusk, and thunder was rumbling in a darkening sky to the southwest, when he returned. As before, there was no sound; he simply stepped out of the fading evening into the firelight where she sat.

Hanging from one hand was what appeared to be a small, dressed chicken. He had cleaned and washed it, perhaps to keep the smell of the fresh kill a safe distance from their haven, but the green feather stuck to his shoulder was a fair indication of what was to provide their supper. His other hand held a handful of plantains. Clasped with them was a tree branch sharpened to a point and a sheaf of leaves that might serve as plates.

It occurred to her, in the instant before she smiled her pleasure at his safe return, that no other gentleman of her acquaintance could have provided food and shelter with such lack of fanfare in this situation, much less have found water or offered protection for her bare feet. That he should have some skill as a woodsman was not especially surprising, considering his birthplace, but watching it put to use was still impressive. She owed Kerr Wallace her life, her comfort, her promise of safety. The degree of respect she must concede for these things was uncomfortable but also inescapable. Though it was best if it remained silent, she could not stint on it.

Barely had their meal begun to roast on the spit Kerr arranged for it when lightning burned across the heavens and rain swept down on them. It came in windblown, tropical fury, lashing the earth while the trees creaked and swayed and muddy rivulets snaked away on all sides.

Sonia and Kerr retreated deeper into the interior of the ancient ruin. She sank down, putting her back to a dirt-encrusted wall while Kerr sat against what appeared to be a couch of stone located just inside the door, so closer to the glowing coals of the fire. An odd peace settled between them as they watched the slanting rain while absorbing the rich smell of roasting fowl that pervaded their lofty chamber. Food, water, shelter and someone to share them, these were the basics of life, she thought. What more did anyone need when all was said and done?

"If people lived here once," she said after a time, "I suppose they could again."

"You thinking of taking up residence?" Kerr broke a twig from a limb, one of a pile they had gathered, tossing pieces of it into the flames.

"Would it be so bad?"

"No balls, soirees, theater or opera, no baker or butcher, no modiste or milliner? How would you survive?"

She closed her eyes, made weary by the mocking note in his voice. "I enjoy all those things, yes. But they aren't necessary to me."

"So you think now. You'd miss them like hell if you had to do without for a few months."

"You may think you know me. I promise you, you don't."

"Works both ways."

"Meaning I don't know you? That's difficult with someone who never speaks two words when one will do." She stared out at the storm-tossed forest beyond their shelter, her contentment draining away to be replaced by infinite weariness.

"You sure you want to know what I have to say?"

The grim timbre of his voice drew her attention. His eyes were shuttered, his face like a mask gilded by fire-light. "How can you think otherwise?"

"That you asked doesn't mean you'll like what you hear."

"I think I must hear it anyway," she said in quiet certainty.

He flipped the rest of his twig toward the coals and leaned his head back against the stone behind him. His expression was reflective and a shade bitter when he finally began. "I told you about my younger brother— told you, too, about my old man's one trip down to New Orleans. Andrew, named for General Jackson, was as much taken with the idea of the city as I was, maybe more. He used to talk of heading down the Mississippi the way some men talk about looking for El Dorado. It's my guess that's the reason he took up with a yahoo who hailed from New Orleans when he joined Lamar's Ranger company in Texas. He wrote of the man and all the things he'd told him about the town, the way people lived there, how they thought, what they called themselves."

"The crème de la crème." She whispered the phrase he had flung at her on the first night they met, though she feared an instant later that the interruption might have caused him to withdraw again.

"You're right, I heard it first from him. Andrew and his new friend got to be like brothers, or so he said. They shared mounts, rations, canteens—everything except bedrolls."

"He told you his name?"

"Oh, aye, he did that."

She waited a second, but when he failed to give it, she did not press him. "Your father thought you should have gone with your brother, I believe you said."

"If I'd done that, he'd have had no need for a so-called friend. Or I might have died instead of Andrew."

"What happened?" she whispered, her voice blending with the falling rain that had begun to die away, tapering to a drizzle.

"They were sent on the march to Santa Fe that became the Mier Expedition. It was a tough go from the first—hot, dry and plagued by attacks from the Comanche and Apache allied with Mexico. Truth to tell, it was a stupid blunder, that trek, a bid for glory by President Lamar that was bound to fail."

"And fail it did."

Kerr gave a short nod. "At Mier, where they were finally cornered. What was left of the force was rounded up and marched off to Mexico, destined for Perote Prison no great distance west of Vera Cruz. A bunch of them escaped the guards and went hieing off into the desert. That's where it really got ugly."

"How do you mean?" She'd heard the story in part, but never the details.

"They were low on supplies, sun-blistered, footsore and lost. A handful decided they were never going to make it the way they were going, but couldn't talk the others into giving themselves up. So they took everything they could lay hands on and hightailed it. First town they came to, they bartered what they knew about the escaped prisoners to save their wretched hides."

"But…but not your brother."

"Not Andrew, no, but their ringleader was the man he'd called his friend. The man, not incidentally, who took everything with him that the two of them owned— mounts, rations, water. Especially the water."

"Your brother was left with nothing."

"Only the need for exoneration because some of the others thought he must have known about the trick but got left behind. Being Andrew, he had to do something to redeem himself. He convinced them he might be able to stop the deserters, bring them back. They gave him a horse and let him go. His horse was found later. He wasn't."

"You think…you suspect he caught up with the others and they killed him?"

"God knows. He may have been thrown or snake bit, might have drunk from an alkali spring, been killed by Indians or a dozen other things. But it would never have happened if not for the betrayal of Jean Pierre Rouillard."

Sonia drew a sharp breath, though as much for the abrupt denouncement of her betrothed as from real surprise. It stood to reason that he would be mixed up in the affair in some fashion. Once or twice, it had crossed her mind that he might because he had been a Ranger like her Bernard and Andrew Wallace, but the idea had seemed too terrible to contemplate.

"I don't understand it," she said after a moment. "Jean Pierre said…I mean, he must have been recaptured at Mier with the others because he told me about Bernard, told me how he died."

"He lied."

"But he knew Bernard drew the black bean."

"He was told it by his Mexican friends, or else was with the Mexicans when the decimation of the Rangers was carried out. I give you my word he wasn't among the survivors. I can do that because Andrew wrote before he went off on the trail of the deserters, giving what happened and where, naming names. He gave the letter to his captain, a man who drew a lucky white bean. He managed to get the note to Kentucky."

"I see." Tears rose up inside her for the deaths of those two brave young men, Bernard and Andrew. Strong, smiling, full of life, they had ridden off to fight a war as they might have to some house party and never came back. Gone, they were gone as if they had never been, living only in the memories of those who had loved them.

Yet the man she was to marry, the man who had betrayed them both, caused the death of both, still lived.

"You are going to Vera Cruz to kill Jean Pierre."

"To force him to face me, sword in hand, and explain what he did and why."

"And then kill him."

Kerr looked at his hands that he had clenched into fists. "Probably."

"That's the reason you have been so determined I must go through with this marriage."

"It is."

Pain tightened her throat, so it was a moment before she could go on. "The reason you laid hands on me, locked me in my cabin on the *Lime Rock,* kept me from finding a way to go ashore."

"That's it," he agreed, his voice even.

"Forgive me, but I don't see why it was necessary to accept my father's offer of employment. Why could you not have simply boarded ship for Vera Cruz to find him?"

"I've been on his trail for years now. Figuring he'd hang around Santa Fe after he deserted, I left Kentucky for Missouri, joined a caravan of traders heading overland and down the old mountain-pass route. I was right, but your fiancé found out I was asking around for him. He took off across the border for Chihuahua. I followed, as you might expect. By the time I got there, he had disappeared again. I knew he was from New Orleans, figured he might go to ground there, so that's where I showed up. I couldn't get a line on him and was short of ready cash. It seemed reasonable to spend time at the trade of sword master, one that would let me earn my keep and give me contact with the men in the Vieux Carré who might know something of Rouillard. Now and again I'd hear he'd been in and out of town, or had been seen in Mobile, Havana, Galveston or somewhere in between. I checked out every lead but was always too late to catch up with him."

"So you didn't know about Vera Cruz."

"I don't think he was down here the first couple of years. He moved around, had no settled base. Later, I heard rumors about connections in the area. Then the word was that he had chosen a bride from New Orleans, one sailing to join him for the wedding. It seemed her father wasn't anxious to make the trip and had a mind to hire an escort. If I could get myself hired so I showed up with the bride, there was a chance I could finally meet face-to-face with the man who'd caused Andrew's death."

The simple way he put his long quest said more about the man than any amount of bombast and threats. It also said much about the depth of his feeling for those he loved.

Sonia took a deep breath and let it out with a shake of her head. "You may be admitted to Jean Pierre's house as my escort, but I will be surprised if he agrees to meet you on any field of honor."

"Could be I'll have to find a reason he can't ignore."

"Suppose," she began, stopped, moistened her lips

with her tongue and tried again. "Suppose you brought him a bride-to-be who was not as represented in the marriage contract?"

He stared at her, his brows gathering above his nose in a scowl. "What are you suggesting?"

"Think," she recommended. "A bride can be returned to her family if she has more…experience in the bed-chamber than might be expected. I haven't that, which seems an unlucky state of affairs at this stage. But it might, perhaps, be…arranged."

His gaze flickered and he turned to stare into the gathering darkness. Quiet fell in which the crackling of the fire and drip of rain from trees seemed to jar the eardrums. He swallowed with a quick slide of his Adam's apple in his taut throat. "I promised otherwise."

She tilted her head, her gaze on his rigorously averted face, or what she could see of it in the firelight. "A promise made to whom? Not my father, for he would not have insulted you by requiring it. Not to Jean Pierre since he has no idea you're coming. If it was to me, then I release you. Who else is left except you? And if it was made to your own self, then what was the purpose?"

"I couldn't take so underhand a revenge."

"Very noble, though where is the harm if I have no objection? Or did you intend to sacrifice me by waiting until after the wedding to confront him?"

"Sacrifice?"

"You can't think," she asked with precision, "that I look forward to the wedding night."

He still would not look at her, though his lips made a flat line in his face.

"Of course, I could claim to be compromised due to this little jaunt of ours anyway," she went on in relentless reason. "That's in the event that you are the one to be killed in any meeting between you and my fiancé. But it seems better to be able to speak with the proper authority and…and knowledge." She swallowed, went on with valiant hardihood. "Yes, and present the proper evidence in…in case it must be proven."

"You want me to make love to you."

Her smile was wan and not quite even. "You did promise to protect me. I'm not asking that you refrain from taking me to Jean Pierre, merely that you give me this safeguard against becoming his wife. That is, if it isn't too much trouble."

Twenty

The look he gave her had the scourging strength of lye water. His lips parted, but he made no reply, only took a quick, close-held breath while silence gathered again between them, around them.

The rain had stopped now. It had been no more than a tropical shower, after all, much like those that fell in New Orleans during June and July. With its passing, a fresh breeze sprang up, bringing the scents of flowers and wet vegetation and a feeling of renewal. As the cool wind swirled in at the door opening, it brought tendrils of smoke and the smell of roasting meat. It also brushed the surfaces of Kerr's shoulders and arms with goose bumps, for she could see them rise on his skin.

Hot juices sizzled as they dripped into the fire. Kerr wrenched away from where he sat, moving to squat beside it and turn the spit holding the bird. He frowned at his task as if it required all his powers of concentration. Done, finally, he used a stick to nudge the plantains deeper into the coals. His gaze was on what he was doing when he spoke finally with a meditative sound in his voice.

"What about afterward?"

"I don't know what you mean." She did, perhaps, but it seemed best to be certain.

"What will happen when this is over? Where will you go? Will your papa receive you again in this proper, or maybe improper, state achieved at my hands?"

An undercurrent in his voice, his choice of words, brought the rise of compunction. In quick defense, she said, "I didn't mean—"

"I know. Let it pass. But for the rest?"

"I see no reason my father should know."

"Too optimistic, I think. The story will come out."

"Then my grandmother's house in Mobile must be my destination, as before."

He fed a few more limbs into the fire, his face glazed in shades of orange and blue by the flaring coals. The licking red flames were reflected in his eyes as he turned his gaze to her. "Let's be clear. You don't aim to…leave me with any obligation."

She thought other words had been his first choice for describing what she might intend. What would they have been? She could not think in her need to reassure him that she would not be a burden in his life. "Naturally not."

"Naturally."

He came to his feet with such violent swiftness that she shrank back a fraction, pressing her head to the stone behind her. It was unnecessary. He didn't so much as glance in her direction, but scooped up his pocketknife from beside the cook fire and walked into the night.

She should be accustomed to these abrupt retreats. This one was more disturbing than any before, for it had the feel of rejection.

She closed her eyes, biting the inside of her lip to contain the tears that pressed behind her eyes. It had required all her courage to speak the words that would leave her without protection against anything he might do. That he wanted nothing from her, would take nothing, was a blow. The pain of it was not only from the defeat of her dream of avoiding her wedding. She had thought, had hoped somewhere in the back of her mind that Kerr desired her. That he would allow her to taste a form of surrender that had nothing to do with two bodies joining out of duty and vows spoken in church, but came from mutual attraction, mutual joy.

He didn't want her, or at least not enough to lay down the burden of his revenge for an hour while they were alone here in this paradisiacal wilderness. It had been a gamble and she had lost. The humiliation of it was blighting, but worse still was the pain. That was something she had not expected. She was grateful that he had left her, for it allowed her to become accustomed in decent and welcome privacy.

It was some time later, after she had tested the bird for doneness and removed it from the fire, that Kerr returned. She heard the soft scuffle of his footsteps and looked up from where she was dividing the plantains and placing them on leaf plates alongside sections of roast bird. He strode toward her, his gaze ferocious. His bare arms, crisscrossed by scratches, were filled with palm fronds.

At least he had not deserted her. Amazingly, it was enough to lighten her spirits. Her appetite had been absent until that moment, but now it returned.

She gestured toward the food. He gave a brief nod and walked past her to dump his load against the interior wall. Moving back to hunker beside her, he ate with economy and speed, licking his fingers before rubbing them on his trouser legs.

Sonia consumed her share of what had been laid out, and licked her fingers in her turn. When she was done, she threw the green leaves of their plates into the fire and watched them blacken and curl before bursting into flames.

"Come," he said. "I'll walk you back down to the pool before we turn in."

It seemed a good idea. She went with him, content to trail a step or two behind in case the jaguar had a similar idea. Along the way, they had recourse to a thicket of brush, as they had at times during the long day. Or at least she did while Kerr kept watch. She could only imagine he had attended to his own needs earlier.

The pool was alluring in the light of the rising moon, but they did not linger. After washing their hands and faces and drinking their fill, they turned away and climbed back toward their shelter.

Sonia's footsteps flagged. She was tired, almost desperately so. Her fatigue grew worse as they came closer and closer to their chambered ruin. A part of it was the effort of the day, but disappointment and loss of hope dragged at her as well. Conversation seemed too much effort. What else was there to be said between her and the man who walked ahead of her, after all? She could not insist that he make love to her and had too much pride to beg.

Where would she be this time a week from now? Would she be waiting for Jean Pierre to come to her as her bridegroom or mourning, at least officially, his death? Would she be waving goodbye to Vera Cruz or grieving the demise of a gray-eyed sword master?

Shuddering away from the last thought, she kept her gaze on the ground until she could see the red coals of what had been their fire, and the dark maw of the ancient room where they would sleep.

Kerr went ahead of her into the opening. She followed more slowly, hesitating just past the entrance as she saw him crouching over the palm fronds he'd brought earlier. He seemed to be shuffling them into some semblance of a bed, but there was only a single pile. One stocking-covered foot was thrust out behind him. Its bottom was ragged and bloodstained, mute testimony to cuts and scratches he'd taken without flinching or complaint. Gazing at it, she felt an odd pain just under her breastbone.

A movement behind him caught her attention, along with a soft scratching noise that had nothing to do with the mat of greenery he was arranging. The low firelight behind her stretched into the darkness, highlighting a shape that crawled along on spindly arms and with a raised, crooked tail. Her eyes widened as she recognized the form, and the threat.

If she called out, Kerr might move directly into its path. Yet she had to do something.

Crouching with the slow flex of aching muscles, she closed her hand on a chunk of broken stone that lay to one side. She eased forward with consummate patience, careful not to make any sudden moves. Kerr glanced at her with a lifted brow, but she paid scant attention. Finding her position, she lunged, smashing the stone down with all the speed and strength at her command.

It slammed to the floor, crushing the scorpion with its tail raised to strike. The blow wakened echoes that rumbled into dark space and dust so old and dry that it caught, choking, in the lungs.

Kerr came erect, spinning in his inimitable swordsman's stoop. His gaze centered on the dying scorpion at his feet, lifted to Sonia's face.

The dust settled. Dense quiet drew in around them, and still he didn't speak. His features were immobile, watchful, yet held a thousand uncomfortable questions. The crushed scorpion writhed a last time in its death throes and then was still.

Sonia shrugged with a valiant try at nonchalance, though her lips trembled. "I couldn't lose my escort."

"No," he said, his voice even as he straightened slowly to his full height, "that would never do."

"But you won't be surprised, I hope, if I'm not overjoyed at the thought of sleeping with that thing's kin?"

"I see your point."

Bending, he caught up the palm fronds and removed them in a sweeping gesture to the slab of stone he had rested against earlier. He spread them like a particularly primitive altar cloth, then stepped away and stood waiting.

She appraised his handiwork. Slowly, she lifted her lashes. "Mine," she asked in tones like tinkling glass chimes, "or yours?"

For answer, he took out his pocketknife and flicked it open, then made a swift gesture with the blade before his face like the salute of one duelist to another. "Turn," he said quietly.

She held her place. "What?"

"Unless you don't trust me, after all."

It was a challenge and a reminder. To both, there could be only one answer. She revolved slowly to put her back to him. Then she held her breath while she waited to see what came next.

The legs of his trousers whispered together as he stepped closer. With gentle fingers, he lifted the weight of her hair that spilled down her back and moved it aside, looping it over her shoulder so it tumbled down over her breast. He skimmed his shirt from her shoulders and down her arms, then tossed it to the foot of their bed. Inserting the fingers of one hand between her skin and the top of her corset where it fastened up the back, he pulled that undergarment taut. With a single, quick move then, he dragged his knife blade down through her corset laces.

They parted with a sound like distant pistol shots. Her

corset sprang open at the back, the release so sudden that she gasped with a hoarse, strangled sound.

The whaleboned span of fabric fell to her waist. She caught it with an arm across her middle, but he pulled it from her grasp with a quick tug and tossed it after his shirt.

"I've wanted to do that since we left the *Lime Rock*," he said with satisfaction.

She faced him again, searching his face in the light of the dying fire. Her voice a mere wisp of sound, she asked, "And what else?"

He eyed the knife in his hand, looked with narrow-eyed speculation at the corset cover.

"No," she said in haste, clapping a hand to the space between her breasts. "I need some cover left to me."

"Too bad," he murmured, and closed the knife, slipping it into his pocket.

Was she reading him correctly or was his only intention to add to her comfort? She had no way of knowing. All she could do was ask. "You have decided…?"

"That you are right. An excuse for a meeting is something to be valued."

"And afterward?" She deliberately repeated his words spoken earlier.

"Afterward I'll ask no more than you are willing to give."

It was the answer she had wanted. Why did it seem so empty? She would not refuse it, however, could not afford that gesture. Greatly daring, she crossed her arms and reached for the hem of the corset cover. With a swift movement, she drew it off over her head.

He was still for the space of a deep, slow breath while his eyes darkened to secretive pools. His lashes swept down and he reached with care to spread the long fingers of his left hand over her rib cage, smoothing upward until he cupped her breast. His touch was sure but gentle, with something in it of reverence. Bending his head, he blew warmly on the nipple, touched it with his tongue, drew back enough to watch with hooded eyes as it beaded, nudging against the web between his thumb and forefinger. As if drawn, unable to help himself, he dipped his head again and took the knotted berry of it into his mouth. He laved it with his tongue, testing it carefully with his teeth, before drawing it deeper into his mouth as if savoring the most succulent of fruit.

The sensations that rippled through her were ravishing, incredible, too urgent to resist. She swayed toward him, her knees losing their strength. He caught her with one arm under her thighs, the other behind her back. Straightening, he swept her high against him, held her for a long moment while his gaze turned possessive, devouring. Stepping to the bed he had made, he put her down with care. He vaulted up beside her then, stretching his long length out on the frond-covered stone altar and drawing her close so they were molded together from chest to ankle.

Sonia's doubts vanished while glad anticipation rose in their place. Drawing air deep into her lungs, she let it out in a sigh as she pressed closer, needing to feel his power, the strong columns of his legs against hers, the faint abrasion of his chest hair on the sensitive curves of her breasts, the heat and firmness at the juncture of his thighs. Shivering with the unexpected gratification of impulses she barely recognized, she smoothed a hand over the hard curve of his shoulder, clasped the rigid bulge of his upper arm, the corded strength of his forearm. In that moment, she understood why a Roman woman might have slipped away to lie with a gladiator before he entered the arena. There was something deeply seductive in male perfection of form allied to deadly strength.

There was more to Kerr than brute power, however; this she knew well as he slipped the bow on her pantaloons and pushed them from her. Intelligence and sensitivity informed his movements; he knew not only what he was doing but why and how. Nothing distracted him, nothing made him forget. And that was the most seductive thing of all.

Lifting her hand, she eased his waistcoat from one shoulder. While he shrugged from the rest, she rubbed her hand over his chest in circles as she gathered sensations inside her like a miser storing gold. Sliding her fingers into the hair at the base of his neck then, she turned her head and offered her mouth for his kiss.

He accepted, moving deep in fast, sensual possession. He swept her lips with his tongue, testing their moist corners and fragile inner surfaces. Searching, tasting, he drew her tongue into his mouth, seeking the slick underside, sipping from it as from a blossom heavy with nectar. And she felt heavy, felt languorous and content yet drowning in sweet intoxication. It spun through her bloodstream, left her lower body lax, moist and open, poured molten and dizzying around her heart. Her will quiescent, she hovered, following his lead and most virulent inclinations without thought or care for the consequences. They could only be what she wanted, what she needed now and in the future that hovered so close. And if some pleasure could be wrung from necessity, who was to know or care?

He kissed the tip of her nose, between her eyes, the point of her chin, then slid his tongue, warm and slick, down the valley between her breasts to where his big hand was spread wide over the flat surface of her abdomen. He dipped into her navel, licked the quivering surface of her belly, and then returned to her breasts while he made forays into her lower regions with his long and supple fingers.

Enthralled, embarrassed, beguiled and bedeviled by turns, she allowed whatever access he required, moved against him, with him, in mounting fervor. His mouth on her breast sent fiery longing cascading downward to pool in liquid heat against his palm. He caressed the small mound at the apex of her thighs, separated delicate folds, penetrated in small incursions that grew ever more bold, went deeper.

She trailed her fingers over the taut muscles of his back, skimmed them with her nails in her extremis though sane enough, barely, to refrain from clawing at him. She turned her head back and forth, stifling her moans, her breath sobbing in her throat. She wanted more, hovered on the brink of claiming it, but would not demand it for fear of missing what else he might do.

It came, his hot, whispering breath over the exquisitely sensitive surfaces of her inner thighs, the touch of his tongue, its soothing sweep over places rubbed raw by the travails of the day, and into moist curls. The perfervid suction, sure, warm and endless at the center of her very being. Yes, and then the plunge, deep, deeper so she could not hold back her cry or inner convulsions.

He lifted above her then, skimmed from his trousers and fitted their slick bodies together. She stared up into his face, watching wide-eyed as he pressed into her, as he shuddered with the prickling rise of goose bumps under her hands. He lowered his head and took her mouth in a swift, marauding kiss, stifling the cry she made as he found the internal barrier and sank through it with firm power.

He was still for a few seconds, easing her with inventive kisses and fiercely gentle hands while her body accepted him, stretched to accommodate him. Slowly then, with infinite control and the contraction of strained muscles, he began to move.

His shadow cast by the fire swooped over her, rising and falling in gigantic multiple images painted in shades of black and gray upon the stone walls. She opened to him like a virgin sacrifice, holding him, urging him with feverish need. With powerful, surging movements of hips and thighs, he answered her tentative guidance, pressing deep, abrading, until she lifted against him, finding his pace and matching it.

And it was not a simple mating of a man and a woman but something more elemental, the primitive tumult of life at its most basic, most true. It caught them, held them in its grip, and rewarded them at last with the paramount gift such mating has to offer.

The heart-pounding glory burst over them in hot waves. Sonia clenched upon him, every muscle cramped and burning as her very being contracted around him. He bent over her in protective embrace, giving her all he had. She took it, trembling, and with salt tears streaming into her hair for the unselfishness of the gift.

It was less than she desired at her heart's core, but more than enough for her need.

Twenty-One

Kerr lay on his side with his head resting on his bent arm and his free hand holding Sonia against him. She was tucked into his long length, the soft roundness of her hips pressed against his groin and one breast perfectly enclosed within the trap of his fingers. Her chest rose and fell in the rhythm of deepest sleep and her feet were cool where they touched his shins. The top of her head was just under his chin and a single hair tickled his nose with a maddening itch.

He exerted rigorous control over his need to shift position, ease the cramp in his side. For one thing, she might wake and she needed her rest. Mainly, he wasn't ready to let her go.

Dawn was turning the light outside from blue-black to gray. He could hear the distant, squawking chorus of a flock of parrots. Soon the sun would climb above the trees to herald another sultry, too-bright day. They should be moving, taking advantage of the morning cool, but he didn't stir. From where he lay, he could see the quiver of Sonia's lashes and the way their shadows deepened the dark circles under her eyes, see her lips that were parched-looking from their long day without water and the slight twitch of her hand now and then where it lay open on the palm fronds. She was dreaming, he thought. Could be it was one worth keeping.

He preferred his waking dream.

She had come to him. She had her reasons, yes, but they hardly mattered against the miracle of it.

He'd nearly spoiled it, stalking off in a fit of wounded pride because she would grant him no place in her life when this episode was over. What else had he expected? She was who she was, and so was he. Their worlds seldom met, much less merged. He was a fool for wanting more, especially when he had so little to offer in return.

She wasn't cut out to be a farmer's wife. He'd bought a fine place in Kentucky with his earnings as a sword master, a full section of rich bottomland where two rivers met and a white house sat under sheltering oaks on a hill. Living there would seem barren to a woman used to the luxury and entertainment New Orleans had to offer. She was sure to be bored to distraction in a month, no matter what she'd said earlier.

No, Sonia Bonneval was not for him. She was quite a woman, nonetheless, quick-tempered, headstrong, heedless of consequences, but also fair-minded, considerate of others and quick on her feet. She was soft where he was hard, tender where he was tough, but had inner strength that matched his in every degree, and maybe surpassed it.

God, he would never forget the sight of her with a stone in her raised fist, like some avenging fury as she killed the scorpion. He'd thought for a second that he was her target. The prospect had so stunned him that he'd been half inclined to let her strike.

She'd saved him instead. Scorpions in this latitude were twice as large as their American cousins. He would have been painfully sick from the poison, if not dead. Most women he knew would have screamed and hopped around in a panic. Sonia had crushed the thing and watched it die.

Would she do the same to him if he got in her way?

Who could say? But he'd rather not take the chance.

A woman in a thousand, that much he had to admit. He was amazed at the way she had trudged after him, keeping up with him even if it was at the slower pace he'd chosen to travel because of her injured foot. She hadn't complained or begged to rest, had not whined over the lack of water, heat, injury or even the sting of scratches and scrapes. She ate what she was given and helped when she could. What else could a man ask?

Well, yes, she'd given even that, and with a generosity that made his heart swell to remember. Not to mention other parts of his damnably susceptible carcass. He'd taken advantage of it in a shameful manner, covering her with his body twice more before they slept, driven by a desperate insatiability unlike anything he'd ever known. It was as if he must cram a lifetime of possession into a single night.

He would give all he owned to stay where they were

for another day, maybe two. It wasn't possible. Food was not the problem; he could provide ample for them using the woodsman's lore he'd gained as a kid hunting with his old man. Their haven here kept off the rain and sun and protected them from animal attack. As for water, it was best he didn't think too much about the pool and its uses. Though he thought the picture of her floating in it, as near naked as God ever made a female in spite of her underclothing, would be something he'd carry to his grave.

No, the problem with lingering lay behind them. Sonia was worried about her aunt's safety and where she might land. He was concerned with what Tante Lily would do once she set foot on dry ground. Vera Cruz, as he'd told Sonia, was a likely docking place for the man-of-war. Once there, she would go to Rouillard. She knew no one else, after all, and would expect her niece, if she survived, to eventually make her way to her future husband. What could be more natural than that Tante Lily, inestimable lady that she was, would embark on the story of the wedding voyage and the misadventure that had caused the loss of the bride-to-be, including the name of the man who had traveled with her?

Rouillard would recognize the threat he represented, Kerr was sure; the man hadn't stayed one step ahead of him all this time without knowing he was on his trail. The question was what he would do then. Would he wait to see if Sonia turned up or send out a search party in hope of discovering whether she was alive? Would he lead the effort himself or wait at Vera Cruz, barricaded in his stronghold, until he discovered if her protector had died?

Kerr's grip tightened fractionally in response to his thoughts, as if to keep what he held for this brief space of time. Sonia stirred, pressing back against him as she stretched a little. Her eyes flew open. She stared straight ahead while remembrance surfaced in her face.

"Morning," he said into her hair with its trace of violet scent overlaid by warm female. Releasing her breast with some reluctance, he smoothed his hand down until his fingers were splayed across her abdomen. Rubbing gently, and in ever lower circles, he asked, "Are you all right?"

"Yes, I'm…fine."

He felt the catch in her voice as much as heard it. The increasing tempo of her heartbeat throbbed under his arm as well, and he could feel the rapid rise and fall of her breathing. His brain was suddenly boiling in his skull, his blood coursing through his veins like steam from an engine. Every point where his body touched hers felt marked for life. He fought the urge to simply roll her over and shove into her in rampant fornication. And he was winning, until she moaned under the press of his questing fingers and pushed against his palm.

He couldn't help it, and didn't try. It was no ordinary desire that drove him, no simple need. He was like a man obsessed as he sought the soft, hot core of her, filling her, seating himself so fully inside her that it seemed they must merge into one. He plunged again and again while sweat ran into his eyes and he ground his teeth to prevent the consummation that would crown his rampant ecstasy but also end it. So he strived until the edges of his visions blurred and were tinted red, until her cries mingled with his groans and she grasped his thighs with both hands as she rose to meet him and there was nothing, nothing more that either could hold in reserve, nothing he could hold back at all except promises he could not keep and she had no wish to hear. And so he let go, finally, in certain knowledge that the last thing he could ever hold was the woman in his arms.

An hour later, they were on the trail again. They kept within hearing distance, if not in sight, of the stream that fed what had been their bathing pool, while following the animal path that paralleled it. Neither had much to say. There was no need. They had established a routine the day before and followed it by rote, walking in lockstep with Sonia one pace behind him, bending as one to duck under limbs, avoiding briars, climbing over rocks, stopping to catch their breath and then going on again as at some mutually recognized signal.

They were climbing, though so gradually that it was almost imperceptible. The forest remained the same, however, and the heat. Nothing changed much at all until the sun passed its zenith and began to slant toward afternoon again.

A sharp crack was Kerr's first warning. He came to a stop with his hand on Sonia's arm. She looked at him, a question in her eyes. He only nodded at the winding trail ahead of them with his head cocked, listening.

"Ax," she whispered after a moment of following his example.

It was what he thought himself. "Best to make sure," he replied before looking down at her. "You wait—"

"I'll wait here. But don't be long."

He had to smile; he couldn't help it. Not long ago, she would have spat in his eye at any hint of an order from him. Now she looked for the reason behind it. She still might not like it, but accepted the necessity regardless.

He wanted desperately to kiss her as a reward and also for the taste of her lips. He didn't dare. Once started, he might not stop until he had her backed against a tree with her legs around his waist while he took advantage of the split in the crotch of her pantaloons.

His mind went back to the day before as he moved quietly away down the trail from where he'd left her sitting on a rock. God in heaven, what it had done to him, that damnably convenient slit of an opening. The sight of it as she stretched out before him, unaware of the sweetly naked white curves so innocently turned up for his inspection, had nearly made him swallow his tongue. He deserved sainthood for taking only a quick glance. And it was a thousand wonders he hadn't cut off one of his own fingers while he removed the thorn from her foot.

He'd been in a bad way already, after hours of tramping along knowing she was the next thing to naked and he had made her that way. Sacrificing his shirt to cover her earlier had been the purest self-preservation.

Sacrifice.

Her word choice last evening, and a good one, too.

She'd been right in accusing him of planning to throw her to Rouillard in order to get what he wanted. He'd known it all along, but refused to face it. Hearing it from her had brought it home in a way he hadn't liked. So he had made a burnt offering of his vow to deliver an un-touched bride by taking her on an ancient, palm-strewn altar, turning a necessity into an honored privilege.

She was right again, in thinking it made a fine reason for forcing Rouillard to a dawn meeting. Cowardly traitor that the man was, it could be the only thing that might achieve it.

Why then, Kerr asked himself for the hundredth time, did it feel as if he had committed a colossal blunder, one he might regret all his days? Not that he had made love to Sonia Bonneval, no, that wasn't it. Rather that he had done it for the wrong reason.

He almost walked up on the woodcutters. So much for his woodsman's skill. If not for the thudding hack of an ax, his absorption in the events of the night would have left him at their mercy. As it was, he slid behind a tree, studying them, their weapons and their purpose, from its cover.

They were mestizos, judging from their flat fea-tures, black hair and eyes and dark skin, and wore the simple homespun clothing and wide straw hats of their kind. They were cutting up a fallen tree, chopping off branches, splintering away what they could of the larger limbs with the single ax they shared between them. The resulting firewood they were bundling onto the backs of a string of donkeys. They talked between themselves in guttural syllables that bore no resemblance to any language Kerr had ever heard, laughing and making an occasional gesture that was ribald but not obscene. If there was any harm in them, much less menace, Kerr saw no sign of it.

He had a choice. He could approach them and offer payment for the use of a donkey to carry Sonia to wherever they meant to return, or he could hang back, following after them as they turned homeward. Left to himself, he would have opted for the second. He wasn't alone.

"*¡Hola!*" he called as he stepped from his cover.

They rounded on him, ax at the ready in the hands of the younger of the two. Father and son, he thought. They were remarkably similar in appearance, short by his standard, but wiry and strong.

They were also more than he felt like tangling with in his present condition. Not that he'd back down if it came to that, but he preferred negotiation. Digging into his pocket, he took out a silver coin, a Mexican cartwheel of the kind often seen in New Orleans these days, and began to barter with more signs than words.

A short time later, he and Sonia were both seated on donkeys, plodding along on their way to a place call La Casa de las Flores.

Nightfall fell like a blue velvet stage curtain just as they came within sight of what seemed to be their destination. The donkey train, scenting their home corral, picked up the pace to a trot. Kerr, more sore from straddling the scrawny beast between his legs than he'd have been from the walk, was just as glad to see the adobe

walls and passel of dogs and children that ran to meet
them in a hubbub of growls and shouts. That Sonia felt
the same he never doubted, not only from the heartfelt
moan she gave as he helped her down, but from the way
she rested her forehead on his chest as she stood in the
circle of his arms.

"We're here," he said around the ache in the back of
his throat, "almost back where you belong."

"And where is that?" she asked in a tired whisper.

Or at least he thought she did. He could have been
wrong.

Light bloomed from the direction of the house,
becoming a bevy of lamps that dipped and swayed as
they drew closer. It was, Kerr saw, a welcoming com-
mittee of sorts.

Four or five Indians carrying lanterns led the way,
followed by a trio of buxom females in identical blue
dresses and aprons. In their midst moved a majestic
figure clad in a black silk gown that featured a bodice
low enough to display breasts like a pair of white doves
and a skirt formed of cascading ruffles. A lace scarf,
covering glossy black hair that was held in place by an
enormous comb, framed a face of surpassing beauty
though no longer youthful.

"Good evening," the lady said, speaking in the lisping
accents of Castile. "I, Doña Francesca Isabella Cordilla
y Urbana, welcome you to my home. Manuel, who ran
ahead to warn of your coming, tells me you are victims
of misfortune. Please to come inside and allow my
people to serve your needs. You will rest and regain your

strength for a few days, yes? Or stay as long as you desire, for *mi casa es su casa*."

"You are very kind," Sonia began.

"*Parbleu,* you are French. How stupid of my man not to perceive it." Doña Francesca switched at once into that language, her manner pleasant but alive with curiosity. "How long it is since I last heard it spoken. You are doubly welcome for the opportunity. Come, now, *madame,* you and your magnificently huge and so handsome husband. Come inside at once."

Aristocrat called to aristocrat, Kerr thought in sour recognition. It might have been his own fault for standing like a stump, but he resented being bypassed as if he wasn't there. Of course, it could be that Manuel, who had jogged off in advance of their arrival, had given their hostess to understand he had used sign language instead of Spanish, so she had assumed he had no French either. He had both, thank you, after traveling from pillar to post on Rouillard's trail.

Sonia understood the situation perfectly, of that he had no doubt. Yet she hadn't corrected the mistake that named him her husband. Now, why was that?

The home they entered was a combination house and fortress, a two-story dwelling built in a horseshoe shape around a courtyard that was enclosed on its fourth side by a tall, gated wall. The general aspect was in keeping with the houses of New Orleans in that its gate was of strong yet ornate wrought iron and galleries on both lower and upper floors looked out onto the courtyard.

This open space was shaded by palms and leafy trees,

and made cooler by the trickling sound of a fountain. Bougainvillea climbed the walls, dropping petals of garnet and ruby from massive bloom stalks to the stone floor below. Huge water ollas sat under the eaves, and a polished silver bell and doors carved with religious figures marked the entrance to a private chapel in one corner. Kitchen, laundry and servants' rooms where children played faced it across the way. A wide staircase of some exotic wood, located beneath the gallery directly facing the gate, mounted to the main living quarters.

Doña Francesca led the way upstairs, holding her wide skirts well above fine ankles, while Kerr stalked along behind her and Sonia. At the top, the lady directed them to a suite of rooms at the end of the gallery. Indicating that Manuel would arrange water for bathing and clothing for their needs, she bade them refresh themselves and rest until they were summoned to supper. Inclining her head in a regal nod, she left them.

Kerr scowled as he stood in the center of the bedchamber they had been given. It was all very well, this grand hospitality, but he would have preferred the offer of horses and directions to Vera Cruz.

Nagging unease gripped him. Staying in one place too long didn't seem a good idea. As soon as Sonia had rested and they found a little more decent covering, they would be on their way.

"What is it?" Sonia asked, turning from her inspection of the salon that led off the room where they stood. "Don't you like it here?"

"It's fine," he said shortly. He glanced at the tester

bed with its white coverlet and mosquito netting then away again.

"But you would prefer another ruin."

He set his fists on his hip bones, a belligerent gesture that suited him at the moment, suited also his spread-legged stance. "You could put it that way."

"Why?"

"I don't care for being looked over like a prize bull, for one thing."

Amusement and something more crept into her face and she put a hand to her mouth, probably to hide a grin. "You feel Doña Francesca may want to put a ring through your nose and shut you up in her pasture? Metaphorically speaking, of course."

"Heaven forbid." He barely suppressed a shudder.

"She was quite taken with your size."

"Huge, she called me." He grimaced.

"Yes. And handsome."

"Do you think I'm huge?" The words popped out before he could bite them back.

She flushed a little. "I've had cause to be glad of it these past two days." Her color deepened. "That is to say, a smaller man might not have made the swim to shore…"

"I know what you mean." Obviously, she thought of him as overlarge in a number of ways. He hardly knew whether to be gratified or irritated.

"I fear it's unlikely there will be anything available in the way of clean clothing that may fit you. I'll repair your shirt so it may be washed. And if you'll take off your trousers—"

"I doubt that's a good idea," he interrupted.

"But why— Oh."

Her sudden comprehension was preceded by a glance at the front of said trousers.

"Oh, indeed. Not that anyone will be surprised if we spend our time in bed. Why didn't you tell Doña Francesca we aren't man and wife?"

"It seemed awkward, and I doubt we will ever see her again."

"Awkward."

"Explaining everything, you understand. She might feel that our state of undress and the night spent alone together would mean I have been hopelessly compromised. You did see the chapel attached to the house?"

"She can't force us to marry."

"No, but refusing would be—"

"Awkward. I see."

"Especially if she has her own confessor here. Because of the chapel, I mean."

He hadn't considered that possibility, didn't particularly like thinking of it now. "The plain fact is," he said slowly, "that you *have* been compromised."

"Surely being shipwrecked will serve as an excuse."

"There are those who would deny it."

She lifted a brow. "But you don't feel that way?"

"And if I did?" Why he was pushing it, Kerr hardly knew. It wasn't as if he wanted to be held responsible. Was it?

"I did release you from any obligation," she said, turning away from him.

So she had.

He wished she hadn't. He really did.

Kerr fastened his gaze on the dark fall of her hair, the shifting thinness of her pantaloons that showed the color of her flesh through their fine batiste, at the back of his own shirt that covered the rest of her. His eyes burned and his stomach muscles cramped as he sought to imprint the image on his mind. This might be the last time he looked on such a sight.

Good Lord, he was as randy as a ram let loose in a pen of ewes. He wanted to lay her down on the Turkish carpet beneath their feet, to see her spread out under him with the vivid colors at her back, to discover just how long he could drive into her before the wool burn on his knees became unbearable. He wasn't sure he'd feel it at all.

A knock heralded the arrival of their bathwater. Kerr walked to a window and stood looking out while the parade of servants carrying brass pails marched back and forth, filling the tub that sat behind a screen in the dressing room off the bedchamber. He didn't move again until they were gone, until Sonia had availed herself of the warm water, until she called him to take his turn at washing their jungle idyll from his skin.

She lay in the middle of the great bed with its dark wood tester and filmy mosquito netting, when he stepped out of the dressing room. She was turned away from him with her hair spread out behind her to dry. A linen sheet edged with heavy lace covered her. She appeared naked beneath it, though a nightgown and wrapper draped the arm of a nearby slipper chair. He moved toward the bed as if drawn by invisible chains. On the far side, he stopped.

She was asleep. Her lips were parted, her eyelids sealed, her shoulder that rose from under the sheet had a childlike smoothness yet carried an apricot tint of sunburn in spite of the shirt that had protected her. Signs of exhaustion were still there in her face: the under-eye circles, the paleness.

His chest filled and he felt an acid sting behind his eyes. He had pushed her so hard, too hard. He had taken so much from her, giving nothing in return that he was not obliged to by his agreement with her father.

Sacrifice.

He rubbed a hand across his face and down over the back of his head as the word echoed in his mind again.

What she required now was her aunt and the re-spectability that lady could provide. She didn't need to be escorted home after long days of being alone with him. That way lay ruin. She would be an outcast from polite society or else married off to a man she despised, namely him. Her father would demand it, and rightly so.

There had to be a way to make things right for her. All he had to do was find it.

In the meantime, he was more tired than he'd thought, and it seemed from the sounds coming from the court-yard that it might be some time yet before dinner was ready. Discarding the towel he wore around his waist, he brushed aside the netting, climbed onto the bed and lay down. He turned to Sonia, stretching an arm above her pillowed head, curling his body around her without quite touching her. He watched her breathe for endless moments while inhaling the scent of soap and fragrant woman. A long while later, he finally closed his eyes.

Dinner was about as uncomfortable a meal as Kerr had ever endured in his life. For one thing, the dark suit he had been furnished was so tight in the shoulders that he couldn't take a deep breath for fear of splitting the seams, and the trousers so snug he needed an apron to preserve his modesty. The bones of his wrists protruded from the cuffs and he'd abandoned all hope of actually buttoning the waistcoat that went with the outfit, letting it hang open instead. More than that, the only shoes found to fit him were rough sandals of the kind worn by the house servants. All in all, he didn't cut a dashing figure.

Sonia, on the other hand, was elegance personified in sea-blue silk trimmed in lavender and with a black mantilla on her severely coiffed hair. The ensemble could never have looked so well on their hostess, in Kerr's considered opinion.

Doña Francesca was well enough, however, in brocade of such sumptuous heaviness that it looked as if it should be able to stand on its own. If it appeared too rich for a meal in the wilds of Mexico, rather than at some European state dinner, it was an observation he kept to himself. In the same way, he gave no sign that he considered more than peculiar the cheroot the lady smoked with delicate puffs of her full lips. He'd known mountain women who sometimes smoked or used snuff, but they were older and past caring what anyone thought of them.

Kerr sat at Doña Francesca's right hand while Sonia was farther down the table, sandwiched between the priest who had inevitably appeared, Father Tomas, and a man and his wife introduced as Doña Francesca's son and daughter-in-law. The son was upright, dapper and mustachioed, his wife thin and sallow. Neither appeared delighted to entertain guests.

Also at the table was an elderly gentleman with yellow features and a constant, vinegary frown. He turned out to be the father of the daughter-in-law. Next to him was a dumpy and chattering yet shrewd-eyed woman who seemed to be a poor cousin being provided with a home in typical Latin fashion.

Three children also graced the board. Though they were of an age to belong to the son of the house, it seemed they were Doña Francesca's children by a marriage that had occurred after the death of her second husband, her son Javier's father—her first husband having died mere weeks after the wedding. She had since been widowed and remarried for a fourth or maybe fifth time. It seemed the lady was most unlucky in the men she chose to marry. Or maybe lucky, if the size of her estate was any indication.

All that was, of course, if Kerr had understood the rambling story told of how she had come to be living in isolation at the jungle's edge. He was by no means sure, considering it had been given in volleys from everyone at the table, and in a bastard combination of Parisian French, Creole patois, Castilian Spanish and Mexican country dialect.

"In a few weeks or a month, when you are well rested," Doña Francesca was saying, "you will like, perhaps, to go to Xalapa. This is the only village of size near to us, a lovely place with a nice mountain aspect. If it pleases you, you might take the air there for a few days. Then you may hire a litter to transport you to Vera Cruz. Though, truly, I can't imagine why you would wish to go there with the season of heat and storms upon us."

"The diligence," her son said in flat contradiction as he sipped his wine.

"Oh, no," his wife began, but was quelled by a look.

"The diligence is a mere public coach and quite impossible." Doña Francesca removed the ash from her cheroot by rolling the end in her bread plate. "Not only do these conveyances smell, but you will be shaken to pieces, thrown about until you are bruised from head to toe, and forced to ride with persons you will not wish to know. Tell them, Father Tomas."

"Just so, my child," the priest intoned without raising his eyes from the tournedos of beef smothered in hot peppers and tomatoes that he was forking into his mouth. The calmest of men, with an unlined face and small, cherubic lips, he appeared to have enjoyed the beneficence of his God all his life, and to expect it after death.

The son turned a stolid eye on his mother. "If they take the litter, they are sure to be flung down the mountainside. I know of six people who died that way."

"And I know of ten who were robbed on the diligence," his mother returned in languid certainty. "One unfortunate woman was carried off and never heard from again."

"She probably took up with the bandit captain."

"What an unkind thing to say." Doña Francesca turned to Kerr. "Do you not agree, *monsieur?*"

"As to that…"

"I knew you would. You are all amiability." The lady put her hand on his arm, caressing it, squeezing the muscles, through the sleeve of his coat. "And so strong, too. I'm sure you would be able to discourage any bandit who tried to make off with your lady. Nonetheless, you would be more comfortable in a litter."

"He'd require extra mules to carry him," her son said, his expression jaundiced as he let his deep-set eyes slide over Kerr. "And still they may drop him down a ravine."

"I would prefer mounts if they can be bought in Xalapa," Kerr said a little loudly. The attentions of his hostess made the tops of his ears burn and left him without an appetite. The son had not, so far, appeared to resent the glances of his mother in Kerr's direction, but he would not be surprised if it came to that eventually. The sooner he and Sonia were gone, the better.

"That's all very well, but you don't know the way through the mountains. You would need a guide. These men who hire out as such are very well in their way, aware of all the trails and watering stops, but are sometimes discovered to be cousins of the bandits." Doña Francesca spread her hands in a gesture that seemed to say it was only to be expected, after all.

"Regardless of how we go, we can't tarry. We will not impose on your hospitality past tonight."

"Oh, but you cannot think of leaving so soon." The

lady clasped his arm again as if she meant to hold on to him by main force.

"I fear we have little choice," Sonia said, her voice firm as she entered the fray. "Though we are honored by your gracious acceptance of us into your home, it's a matter of some urgency that we move on."

"But what can be so important? Pray tell me, so I may join you in bringing it to pass."

"Are you, by chance, acquainted with an American gentleman by name of Rouillard?"

Uneasiness passed over the lady's features and she exchanged a swift glance with her son. "I may have heard the name."

Kerr watched her, every sense alert as he took up the subject. "In what regard, if I may ask?"

"He has many connections in the government, for a foreigner."

"He's a scoundrel," her son said, wiping his mustache with his napkin as if disposing of Rouillard in the same movement.

"Javier, please!"

"He advises, he schemes and worms his way in everywhere. He should be crushed like the low creature he resembles."

His mother threw a look of embarrassment at Sonia. "It's said this Rouillard is close to that great rogue General Santa Ana, you perceive. Though the general is from Xalapa, Javier has always preferred the politics of his rival, President Bustamente. We really know little of the gentleman from New Orleans except by reputation."

"Which is quite enough," her son said with finality. He threw Kerr an oblique glance. "You are not related?"

"By no means," he answered.

"An excellent thing." The Mexican shrugged. "One would not like to insult the relative of a guest."

"There can be no possibility. We have never met, as it happens."

"There," Doña Francesca said, her gaze as caressing as her fingers, "I knew you were a man of good sense."

The cousin, following the conversation with her black eyes bright in her plump face, spoke then in intrigued tones. "I do believe Señor Wallace is no more fond of Señor Rouillard than Javier is of Santa Ana."

"Can this be true?" Doña Francesca watched him, her eyes bright.

"We aren't friends," Kerr allowed.

"You will remove him, perhaps, from Mexico and from this life?"

"Doña Francesca, please," the priest protested, though it seemed a matter of form.

It would be foolish to answer with the truth, Kerr thought. "I doubt it will come to that."

"But you could." The eyes of his hostess fairly glowed and she clutched his arm with both hands, kneading it.

"Of a certainty, he could," the cousin said in forthright tones. "He is a swordsman. Only look at his hands."

The table fell abruptly silent. Every eye turned in Kerr's direction. Without intending it, he curled his hands into fists with the calluses on his palms and the edges of his fingers folded inside.

"Have you killed your man, *señor?*"

The question came from Doña Francesca's younger son, a sallow waif in hot-looking black velvet. It referred to a fatality that took place in a duel, and could apply to any gentleman forced to defend his honor. Kerr could have answered without going into detail, but refused to deny his calling. "I have," he said quietly, "and may be forced to do it again, being a sword master by trade. But it isn't a matter for boasting."

"Naturally not," Doña Francesca said with a frown for her son. "Nor is it a suitable subject for the dinner table." She turned back to Kerr. "Now that it's been broached, however, you must tell us what it is like."

"You would be bored, I'm sure," he answered, searching his mind for a diversion. "A better topic might be the war declared between our two countries."

Consternation swept along the board as the diners looked at each other in frowning dismay. Not surprisingly, it was Doña Francesca who recovered first.

"War? We are finally at war? Tell us at once, for we are so out of touch here that we have heard nothing of it."

In her excitement, his hostess carried his hand to her full breasts, pressing his knuckles between them. Sonia's lips tightened as she met Kerr's eyes, and she gave him a look chill enough to cover him with frost from top to toenails. It was she who came to his rescue by answering the query.

"We know little more than the bare fact that open war

has finally come after so many months of hostilities. Still, it's the major reason we must leave as early as possible for Vera Cruz."

That was not the end of it. More questions, more pleading that they stay came Kerr's way. Nevertheless, he was glad to see that Sonia agreed with him on something, even if it was only the need to go.

It was well after midnight before the interminable meal was over. Kerr was invited to smoke a cheroot and sip a brandy on the gallery with Javier. In this pleasurable pastime they were joined by Father Tomas. He expected the interrogation into his plans to continue, but it did not. Instead, they discussed the consequences and probable direction of the war.

Javier, for all his refined lack of animation, seemed to have a good grasp of the fundamentals of the conflict. It was his opinion that Vera Cruz would be the point of invasion for a march on Mexico City. His countrymen would fight with much honor and tenacity, so he said, but he could not envision victory if the United States was determined to take what belonged to Mexico, namely, Texas, and the country that stretched from there to the Pacific Ocean.

Kerr, sitting on the gallery railing with his back to a post, watched the red glow of the cheroots in the hands of the other men and the smoke from his own as it drifted into the night. It was so peaceful here, so quiet and pleasant a life. He wondered if the much-married status of Doña Francesca was responsible for the isolation of her house and her family, or if it was simply a matter of choice. He'd probably never know. Still, it seemed obscene that such a paradise should be disturbed by the ambitions and petty posturing of men and their wars.

Was that how Sonia saw his involvement with swords as a master at arms, a matter of posturing and ridiculous gestures for the sake of pride? He supposed she did—and so it was, in its way. He could give it up, he realized in some surprise, for the sake of a home like this, one where a lady graced the head of his table, ordered their meals, their children and their lives according to her lights and his occasional request.

The lady he saw in his imagination was Sonia. How big a fool could he be?

Tossing away the stub of his cheroot, he excused himself with all the polish he could manage and went to find her.

She had left the company of the ladies, retreating to their rooms. When he joined her there, she had already undressed for bed and was sitting on a window seat in nightgown and wrapper, staring out into the darkness.

He leaned in the doorway, watching her, looking at the scratches on the bottoms of her bare feet that were turned toward him, also her knife slash that had begun to heal. Until she whipped her head around as if sensing his presence.

"I didn't expect you for some time yet," she said in waspish tones. "Could Doña Francesca find no more excuses to paw at you?"

"Seemed best not to give her the chance." He began

to shrug out of his tight jacket. A seam parted, but he didn't care.

"Too bad. I suspect you could have been husband number five if you wanted to try for the job. Or would it be six?"

"Didn't take much notice as I wasn't in the market." Tossing the coat in the general direction of the slipper chair, he began to unfasten his shirt studs, dropping them on a nearby table.

She moistened her lips as she watched his busy fingers. "I can't imagine why not. She must be a wealthy woman, and I had it from one of the maids that she's barely forty."

He paused in the act of pulling the shirt from his trousers, caught by the scorn in her voice. The cause that presented itself stunned him. She sounded almost jealous, maybe from thinking that he might have considered making love to the widow. As if he could think of such a thing while she was in the same house, the same country, maybe the same world.

"Lady must have married early," he answered, his voice mild and to the point as he dropped his shirt on the floor.

"At fourteen, to a man thirty years her senior who promptly died. She liked being wed so well, however, that she made a habit of it."

"But she would not, I imagine, care to add a Kentucky mongrel to her list." The words were carefully chosen to see how Sonia would answer. It was suddenly important to know if Doña Francesca's preference might have encouraged her to see him as an acceptable entrant in the marriage stakes.

"You aren't—" she began then closed her lips tightly on the words.

"Oh, but I am," he answered, his mouth curving with satisfaction as he kicked out of his leather sandals. Unfastening his trousers as he walked toward her on bare and silent feet, he went on, "I am the dirtiest of dogs because I fully intend to take advantage of the borrowed title as your husband."

"You do."

"Oh, yes." He went to one knee in front of her, bent his head to lick the cut made with his knife on the bottom of her foot, washing it with the hot, wet heat of his tongue before rubbing it gently with his thumb. He kissed her knee, put his hands on her thighs as he insinuated two thumbs between them and rubbed slowly up and down, widening the space between them. His eyes were dark, rich with purpose, as he raised them to meet hers. "If you're going to object, it had better be now. In a minute or two it's going to be too late."

"It was too late when you came through the door," she whispered, and drew him into her arms.

Twenty-Two

It was another full day before they could shake off the fetters of Doña Francesca's hospitality. Even so, they were forced to accept the escort to Xalapa of her son, Don Javier, who felt it incumbent upon him to transport them in his carriage. Doña Sonia, the lady wife of Don Wallace, would be more comfortable, he said, and she could only agree. Since Kerr did the same, they entered the mountain town in conspicuous style, with several outriders and a servant in livery riding on the back.

Don Javier was most pleased that they intended to take his advice concerning journeying by diligence to Vera Cruz. Unknown to him, his recommendation had no bearing. Time of travel was the deciding factor. Closer questioning had revealed that the *literas,* or litters, swaying contraptions not unlike sedan chairs though they were slung between two mules, would require some eight or nine days of tedious travel, while the diligence could make the trip in only four, five at most.

Don Javier's approval of them was so great that it

seemed he might insist on conducting them to Vera Cruz in his carriage for the continued joy of their company. Only the sad reflection that this fine vehicle would likely be shaken to pieces on the rough roads dissuaded him. To compensate, he insisted on procuring their seats in the diligence departing the following morning, also arranging their room at the small inn where he left them. He might have stayed with them through the night, waving them off with the dawn, except for the need to gather the items on the list handed him by his mother on his departure. At last he bowed himself back into his carriage, and they were alone.

"Your conquest this time around, I think," Kerr commented as they stood waving goodbye.

"Don't be ridiculous," Sonia said on a laugh. "Don Javier is married."

"Doesn't keep him from sighing after what he can't have."

She turned her head, searching Kerr's face. He was watching the dust kicked up by the carriage, his gaze clear and uncomplicated. If he meant anything more by his comment, it was not apparent.

The air in Xalapa was cooler than at the Casa de las Flores. The flowers were brighter and more highly scented as well, no doubt from the increase in altitude. Streets in the town were narrow and winding, branching off without plan into mysterious alleys and culs-de-sac. Clouds seemed to hang low, enveloping everything in a fine and floating mist that their landlady called the *chipi chipi,* though she promised a view of the ancient volcano of Citlaltépetl, lord of mountains and tallest in the country, should it lift.

They were not so blessed. The mist drifted over the town, dripping from the eaves of the inn throughout the night. She and Kerr listened to it as they lay together on a rough mattress of corn husks slung on ropes. To Sonia, it had the sound of falling tears. And it was still with them at dawn when, shivering in the chill mountain air, they climbed into the heavy diligence and began the last leg of their journey to Vera Cruz.

The trip was every bit as horrendous as Doña Francesca had warned. The wide iron wheels of the coach ground through deep sand, jolting over hidden rocks with tooth-rattling thuds. The great wooden body, minus any pretense of springs, swayed in a sickening manner, leaning out over chasms and tipping forward as they descended inclines. Its leather seats smelled of sweat, chicken feathers, the moldy hay that covered the floor and the manure scent of the mules that wafted back to them. The hooves of the mules also threw up great clouds of dust that settled in a gray-brown and gritty pall over every surface. No other passengers shared their misery due to the good offices of Don Javier who had apparently hired the entire conveyance, but that was the only consolation.

Sonia was jostled from one side to the other, jounced high so her head hit the coach ceiling, and thrown to the floor when she failed to catch the knotted rope that served as a handhold. After the third or fourth time that she slid off the seat, dangling only by the rope, Kerr caught her up and disentangled her hand before plunking her down beside him. He encircled her with a hard arm, clamping her to his side while bracing his feet on the forward bench.

She tried to sit up straight so he need not support her weight. He only growled and drew her close again, throwing over her the serape he had acquired at the inn.

She was just as happy to subside against him. His chest on which she lay was broad and padded with muscle, his arm unyielding in its hold. From that more secure vantage point, she was able to take greater interest in what slid past the diligence windows.

It was an exotic panorama, from the cloud-shrouded peak of Citlaltépetl, pink-tinged in the morning light, to the mountain track that led to Perote Prison from which those who had been captured during the Mier Expedition had recently been released. In it moved donkeys with panniers slung on either side in which rode bright-eyed, dark-skinned children, also mule trains driven by horsemen with wild faces and saddles decorated with silver, tumbling waterfalls and a bird with a tail so long it seemed impossible it could fly. But these were the highlights in a landscape that was otherwise the same, made up of trees, rocks and the winding road that stretched ahead of them. After a time, Sonia grew sleepy. Closing her eyes, she kicked off her borrowed slippers, lifted her feet to the seat and snuggled into Kerr's side.

So the long days of travel passed, in a blur of fatigue and swaying, jouncing progress. They alighted now and then to stretch their legs while the mules were changed. At night they slept at small inns where the only comforts were cold water to remove their dirt, scrawny chickens cooked with oil, garlic and *frijoles,* and a wooden plank for a mattress.

Gradually, they descended into warmer levels where lovely green valleys appeared, palms thrust their umbrellas of fronds toward the sky and trees hung with vines dripped spent blossoms onto the roadway. Though the land flattened by degrees, the road did not improve but grew dustier still. The heat steadily increased as well, becoming a stifling pall. At last, at the morning stop on the fifth day, the coachman announced that they would sleep that night in Vera Cruz.

Vera Cruz.

Sonia could feel her nerves winch tighter at the very sound of the name. Dread formed a hard knot in her stomach as the diligence jerked into motion once more. Kerr reached for her, and she leaned against him, letting her head fall back on his shoulder, feeling the strength of his protection, listening to the steady beat of his heart.

She should not be so compliant. She should be planning some way to escape him now that they had returned to civilization. It would have been less than intelligent to chance it on the long trek down from the mountains to the seacoast, but surely it might be managed nearer to Vera Cruz? Vessels left from there to other parts of the world every day. The war had not changed that unless there was a blockade, and it seemed unlikely such a thing could have been set in place already. If she could arrange passage to Havana, it should be easy enough to transfer there to a packet bound for Mobile.

She had no money.

That was a drawback, yes, but not an insurmountable one. With luck her aunt might have arrived at the port. She would know how to apply for funds, even if she had not managed to save her small hoard when the *Lime Rock* sank. It would require time and some subterfuge to gain her father's assistance but, once it was forthcoming, she and Tante Lily could go where they wished.

That was, of course, if she could avoid Jean Pierre while she remained at Vera Cruz. Yes, and Kerr as well.

How very tiring it all sounded, and childish as well. Hiding, lying, sneaking about like a thief, worrying that someone would snatch her back into some variety of imprisonment. Where was the freedom in that?

No, she was done with such things. She would face whatever came. She would do it standing at Kerr's side while he achieved what he had come so far to do. She owed him that much for the care he had given her. Whatever happened, he had shown her what love could be like between a man and a woman, and loving.

Love.

She loved him. It was strange but true.

When had it happened? She could not be certain. It might have been when she first caught sight of him in the lantern glow at the town house. Yes, or when he gave her the choice of walking up the gangway of the *Lime Rock* instead of being carried. It could have been the night he forced the seaman overboard for daring to lay hands on her, or the afternoon when he had swum in the pool with dragonflies floating above him. So many choices, so many memories that she could not separate them. She would save them, however, pressed in the memory book of her mind to be taken out when she was very old, and sighed over as she sat before a winter fire.

Stirring a little, she tilted her head so she could see his face. He was staring out the open window, his gaze unfocused. His hand, where he held her to him, smoothed over the turn of her waist in an endless caress. She wondered if he realized it.

Alerted by her gaze, he turned his head to look down at her. "What is it?"

"I was thinking, wondering what you intend to do when we reach where we're going."

"Discover if your aunt is in residence, and her direction."

"And if she is with Jean Pierre?"

"Then we'll go there."

She searched his eyes, trying to guess at the thoughts that moved in their shadowed gray depths. They were as closed to her as before she knew she loved him.

The thought of a confrontation between him and Jean Pierre was disturbing, more so than anything she could imagine. "Do you think…" she began, then stopped.

"Probably not, but what?"

"Do you know if Jean Pierre realizes you blame him for your brother's death?"

"He'd not have run from me all these years otherwise, wouldn't have left New Orleans so soon after I arrived. Or stayed away, for that matter."

"He doesn't know you're coming, or didn't. Suppose Tante Lily *is* with him. Suppose she has let fall that you are my escort?"

"It can't be helped. He'll either run again or stand and face me."

"What then?" she asked, the words so soft they barely stirred the air.

"Depends on what passes between us, and what he does about it."

She could not think the outcome would be anything less than a duel. Nor was it possible to imagine that Jean Pierre would prevail against Kerr's superior strength and skill with a sword. The best she could hope for was that the meeting would end at first blood and with, perhaps, an apology from her future husband.

Would that suffice? Would Kerr accept it and go on his way?

She opened her lips to ask him not to leave her with Jean Pierre, no matter what happened, but to take her with him wherever he went. The words would not come. She could not risk a refusal. Hearing it would be too great a disappointment to bear.

"Don't look like that," Kerr commanded, his voice gruff, made uneven by a jolt of the wheels into a hole in the road. Hard on the words, he lowered his head and took her mouth.

She opened to him as naturally as a flower to the kiss of the sun. Yet her manner was not so calm or innocent.

Frantic need gripped her. She wanted him as she had wanted nothing else in all her days. Her heart ached with it; her breath was strangled by unshed tears. Every inch of her skin tingled in anticipation of his touch. It came, the light clasp of his hand on her hip as he drew her against the lower part of his body, and she shuddered with the pleasure that swept through her.

His serape had been discarded that morning, becoming a pillow for her to rest against. The edges of his waistcoat parted as she slid her hand between them, flattening her palm on his linen-shielded chest. She smoothed over its hard planes while a soft moan of frustration sounded in her throat. She wanted to press against him, needed to feel the heat of his naked skin against her breasts, the abrasion of the curling hair that grew there. A moment later, she twisted her fingers in the placket of his shirt, jerking the studs from their holes.

He groaned, every muscle tensing, hardening under her hands. She dragged open the edges of his shirt, even as she nipped at his lower lip, trailed a string of kisses down his chin to his neck. The hollow at the base of his throat enticed her and she dipped inside, tasting the salty flavor of him, feeling his pulse throb against the tip of her tongue.

She could not be sidetracked for long. Shifting, she angled her head and laved the hard bead of his nipple with her tongue, worried it delicately with her teeth while reaching lower to press her hand to the hard, hot length that stretched the front of his trousers.

His harsh gasp, barely heard above the clatter of

hooves and rattle of harness, was her reward. Also the feel of his hand sliding down her thigh, gathering her skirts, finding warm flesh underneath them.

She inhaled with a soft sound as he found her, parted moist and heated folds. Without volition, she pressed against him, seeking the incursion of his long fingers. And it came, so quickly, so surely that she melted, straining to take him deeper.

With a soft curse, he dragged her higher, brought her up to straddle him. Releasing the waist of his trousers, spreading them open, he urged her to cover him. She sank upon him, moaning, bending her neck to press her forehead to his. The sense of control the position gave her was astonishing, the increase in sensation astounding. She wanted to stay there, locked upon him forever.

"Kerr," she whispered, *"mon coeur."*

"Command me," he said, though his temples were damp with perspiration and the trembling of fierce restraint ran over him in fine waves. "Have it as you will."

Never in her life had she felt so powerful or so free. Stronger still was the fierce gratitude she felt for his instruction in this miracle of joining. No other man could have shown her so well. Never again would she know this miracle of entwined bodies and melding souls. This was likely the last time they would be together like this, the last time he would hold her, last time she would taste him, feel him so fully seated inside her, hotly throbbing against her capturing tenderness with every beat of his heart.

The diligence rocked, bounced, fell into a pothole and jounced out again. As she lifted and fell upon him in vital imitation, she felt the burning ache of tears. Felt also the raging desire inside her to drive upon him, absorb him, make him a part of her. The need overcame all thought and control. She moved upon him with aching muscles. Her lungs burned, her heart flailed against her ribs. She drew back, staring fearfully into his eyes.

He said her name as if it were a prayer. Then his long fingers sank into her hips and he rose beneath her with deep, hard thrusts, once, twice, a third time.

Her very being coalesced around him. She cried out her wild joy and grief as hot, liquid pleasure crested inside her. He caught her to him, burying his face between her breasts as he shuddered, pouring his being into her, and what felt like his love.

A mile farther along the road, or perhaps two, she stirred. She was still sitting astride him. Anyone glancing in upon them as they whirled past might see her there, spy her open bodice. She eased from him, began to do up her buttons while he fastened his trousers then leaned to help push her skirts into place.

Abruptly, a thudding explosion shook the air. Hard upon it came a shouted order.

Sonia's gaze flew to Kerr's. His grim nod confirmed her fear even as another shot whined above the coach. The diligence jerked as the coachman grabbed the brake handle.

Dust billowed, catching up and surrounding them in a dirty cloud as the heavy vehicle slowed. A horseman appeared, galloping toward the head of the mule team. Another followed, and another. They shouted, cursing in Spanish. The diligence came to a rocking halt.

The door beside Kerr was snatched open. He paused in the act of replacing the studs in his shirt as a familiar face, swarthy and decorated by a thin, newly grown mustache, thrust inside. Just below it appeared the silver bore of a wicked-looking pistol. It did not waver as it centered on Kerr's chest.

"Step down, if you please," Alexander Tremont ordered with a chilling blend of menace and manners. "Take care how you go about it. I'd hate like hell to shoot you, my friend, but will if you give me cause."

Sonia sat for an instant in stunned incomprehension. It was routed as red-hot rage swept through her. "What is the meaning of this, *monsieur?*" she demanded, even as she searched for her slippers and pushed her toes into them. "By what right do you dare stop a public diligence?"

"You will also step down, Mademoiselle Bonneval." Tremont dipped the pistol in her general direction.

"I'll do no such thing. We are on our way to Vera Cruz, and you cannot—"

She was stopped in midtirade as Kerr reached to lay a finger across her lips. He met her gaze, his own dark with warning before he pulled away. Taking her arm then, he drew her with him as he alighted from the heavy coach. When her feet touched the ground, he stepped in front of her, using his body to shield her from the men who milled around them on horseback.

What was Kerr thinking? His face was set in hard lines. Every muscle was rigid as he stood waiting. With his tremendous size and agility, he appeared deadly savage, the very epitome of a master at arms.

He had no weapon save a pocketknife.

"Step away from her, Wallace," Tremont ordered as he retreated out of arm's reach. His pistol was steady of Kerr's chest.

"I don't believe so."

"No harm will come to her at my hands, I swear to you. I am only delegated to escort her to her future husband."

Kerr gave a short laugh. "To think I actually hoped you hadn't drowned."

"Oh, we were all rescued and treated most courteously, including Tante Lily who anxiously awaits her niece at Rouillard's town house. Unfortunately, you won't be a welcome guest."

Sonia felt an easing inside her. Her aunt was really alive. She wasn't at the bottom of the sea or in a Mexican prison. The longing to see her, hear her bright chatter, was so strong that she swayed a little with it.

Kerr must have felt the whisper of her relieved breath past his shoulder. He reached to clasp an arm around her waist, even as he gave Tremont a speculative look. "Rouillard knows I'm here."

"As you say. And he prefers to avoid a meeting."

"It may be postponed but won't be avoided."

"He thinks differently." Tremont's voice hardened. "I said step away."

Kerr held his place.

Something flickered across Tremont's face that might have been regret. Then he looked past Kerr's shoulder and gave a nod.

A horseman wheeled in close behind them, lifted his

rifle like a club and struck. The blow thudded into the back of Kerr's head. Sonia cried out, clutching at his arm as he staggered. A second blow landed between his shoulder blades. She went down with him, pulled by his great weight. Scrambling to her knees, she reached toward the dark wetness already matting his hair.

She was snatched from behind by a hard arm around her waist. She kicked and fought, shrieking like a madwoman, striking backward with her elbows. A grunt told her the man who held her was Tremont and she had hurt him.

It made no difference. A moment later, one of his men trotted up with his mount. She was hefted across the saddle. Seconds later, Tremont swung up behind her. Wrenching her upright so she sat across his lap, he shouted an order. Then he swung the horse in a neighing, pawing turn and kicked him into a hard run.

Sonia strained against Tremont's hold, bobbing, jerking with the horse's hard gait as she craned her head to look back. For an instant, she could see nothing except four or five of the brigands milling around the diligence and its open door.

A space cleared between them then. She saw Kerr sprawled on the ground with blood seeping into the dirt beside him.

Twenty-Three

A groan, low and heartfelt, roused Kerr. It was a moment before he understood it had come from his own throat.

Hell, but his head ached as if a thousand blacksmiths banged away at their anvils inside it. His back hurt, his eyes hurt. Damned if even his teeth didn't hurt.

Flashes of images danced in his mind in backward progression. A slow ride in a cart with squeaking wooden wheels under a blanket that smelled of dogs. Dirt in his mouth and eyes. A man with a silver pistol. A diligence with the door thrown wide. Sonia, livid with anger yet with fear welling up into her eyes.

Sonia…

He came up off the cot where he lay so fast that his head swam. A chain running from the wall to a shackle on one ankle caught him. He tumbled to the floor, catching himself on his hands and knees. Sinking back to a sitting position, he braced his spine on the edge of the cot and pressed the heels of his palms to his eyes.

God, where was she? What was happening to her?

Tremont had said he would take her to Rouillard. Was it the truth, or did he want her for himself?

Tremont and Rouillard.

It was difficult to credit, the pair of them working together. He'd thought better of Tremont after a few days at sea with him. The guns aboard the *Lime Rock*—he and Rouillard must have partnered in that trade. One shipment had been lost, but there might have been more, could still be more.

Tremont wouldn't hurt Sonia, surely he wouldn't. The same couldn't be said for Rouillard. A man who discovered his bride-to-be had been consorting with his worst enemy would be in no mood to welcome her with open arms.

Thank God for that.

Or maybe not.

Kerr couldn't decide which might be worse in his head-pounding confusion, that Rouillard would fold her to his bosom with glad kisses and a hasty wedding or that he might beat her.

A shudder ran over him as sick rage washed through him. He'd slice Rouillard to ribbons and leave him fluttering in the wind if he hurt her. Nothing would prevent him, not stone walls or bars, not the shackle that held him or the sanctity of vows spoken by a priest. If Rouillard put a mark on her, he was a dead man.

His fault, Kerr thought with another groan. If she was in danger for being with a man before her wedding, the blame could be laid squarely at his door. He should never have taken her, never tasted her, never held her.

Yet how could he not? She was so lovely in her passion. Her skin was smooth as satin under his hands, sweet and warm under his lips. Her smile as she rode him in the diligence had been tender yet wicked with delight. He had wanted to stay buried in her for aeons, feeling the hot silk of her depths, counting the fervid pulsations of her heart. And her breasts—their tender skin under his eyelids, the sweetness of her nipples hardening under his tongue made his mouth water at the memory. To take her in the diligence had been the height of stupidity, yet he would not trade even a second of it for his dearest hope of heaven.

He had made love to her in the beginning because she had asked it, and because he had thought to provide for Rouillard a reason to challenge him, one he could not ignore. It had seemed a form of protection since her fiancé might well call off the wedding she dreaded after it was discovered.

He saw now the reasons were mere excuses, and weak ones at that. He had wanted Sonia in the most desperate way, and was sure it was the only chance, only time, he could ever have her.

Now it was over. Done. He only prayed he hadn't harmed her more than Rouillard ever could.

Kerr opened his eyes, squinting at the opposite wall and the door that centered it. If she was with Rouillard now, the job he'd been paid to do was at an end. He was freed of any obligation to her father. He could take her away if she wanted to go. She deserved that choice.

First, he had to find her. That was after he managed to get himself out of this coil.

Taking a deep breath, his first in what seemed a long time, he gazed around him. He was in a small room with four walls, three of plaster and the fourth of stone with a slit of a window let into it well above the height of a man. The only furnishings were the cot and a bucket. The floor was of stone, and the door that gave access of heavy wood. There was no lock, which suggested it might have a bar and padlock on the outside. Stains on the floor and a lingering scent of vinegar and corn made him think the place had been a storeroom at one time, or maybe a wine cellar. That it was part of a house or barn was plain enough, for somewhere in the distance he could hear the cooing of doves, children at play and snatches of voices in rumbling conversation.

The knowledge was no good to him. He wasn't sure he could stand up just yet, and there was no give in the chain that held him.

He let his eyelids close again as he listened. His head swam and he nodded. He must have dozed off or maybe passed out sitting upright, for his chin was on his chest and the door in front of him was opening when he came to himself again.

The man who stepped into the cell-like room was running to seed. His sandy hair was thinning, his face shiny and centered by a purple-veined nose and with a second chin hanging under the first. His tailor had done his best to conceal the man's expanding waistline, but nothing could disguise the sag of his trousers in the back. The blue of his eyes had a faded quality that dimmed the cunning in their depths, and they darted here and there as if he suspected an ambush in every corner.

He wore neither hat nor gloves, a circumstance that led Kerr to think the storeroom could well be located in whatever dwelling he'd acquired for himself. That meant, in turn, that he had undoubtedly arrived in Vera Cruz.

This was the man who had ordered Sonia sent to him as he would a parcel of linen or jar of pomade. This was the man who intended to bed her every night for the rest of his life, the one who would get his children on her, grow old with her and lie beside her for all eternity.

"Rouillard, I suppose."

Kerr made no attempt to disguise his utter contempt. Dragging himself up by bracing on the edge of the bed, he pushed slowly to his feet. The move made his head reel and his stomach heave, but it didn't matter. His visitor seemed inclined to loom over him and it went against the grain to allow it.

"At your service," Sonia's fiancé said with a snort.

Rouillard had left the door open behind him. A second man stepped through it just then. It was Tremont, dressed more formally than when last seen. Kerr's hands clenched into fists and he took a short step toward him. His chain scraped and plaster dust sifted from the wall where it was fastened, but he was still brought up short by the shackle.

"Where is she?" he demanded, his gaze hot on Tremont's face. "What have you done with her?"

That gentleman said nothing, but only moved to prop his shoulders against the wall beside the door.

Rouillard advanced farther into the room. "You refer to Mademoiselle Bonneval, I imagine. She is quite well and resting in my care. And I might add that she is pathetically grateful to be with me at last."

"You lie," Kerr said in quiet certainty. "Sonia—Mademoiselle Bonneval—was never pathetic about anything in her life. I'll be bound she wasn't grateful to be carried off against her will, either."

Rouillard gave him a narrow look and opened his mouth to speak, but Tremont forestalled him. "She is well enough. Certainly she came to no harm from me. I believe she's resting at the moment."

She was well. Kerr wasn't sure why he accepted that assurance from Tremont when he doubted Rouillard. Something tight and hard inside him dissolved at the news, an indication of how fearful he had been.

"I can't see why she had to be dragged out of the diligence and brought here," he said. "We were on our way, had been since the shipwreck."

"Don't be a fool." Disdain was heavy in Rouillard's voice. "The necessity was to separate her from you."

"You know why I'm here." It was a threat as much as a question.

"I've known from the moment I heard your name on the lips of Sonia's aunt. Not that I wouldn't have recognized you on sight. You have the same size and coloring as your brother, the same stiff-necked pride and damn look of being ready to take on an army by yourself. How Bonneval came to be taken in by you, I can't imagine. You'll find me more wily."

"No doubt. Look how you fooled Andrew."

Purple color appeared in Rouillard's face. "I did what I had to do. He could have come with me when I left the Rangers. The idiot refused as a matter of honor. As if that was worth shit when we were all about to die."

"But you lived."

"I lived, and I've done well in spite of you. Oh, I've always known you were on my tail. Now look where it's got you."

"Just look," Kerr agreed with irony. He had come up with his quarry, after all. That was something after all these years. "What will you do now?"

"I thought we should talk, see if there isn't some compromise. I have a great deal of money and will have more when my wife's fortune is in my hands. You could buy a sizable piece of property in South America and live like a king."

"I don't figure I'd make much of a monarch," Kerr said softly.

Rouillard pushed out full lips. Putting his hands behind his back, pushing them under the tails of his coat, he took a turn around the small room. "Everybody likes money. You'll change your mind after a few days in here."

"I doubt it."

Disappointment and trouble were plain in the man's petulant frown. "I should have let Tremont kill you."

"Why didn't you, just as a matter of curiosity?"

"I thought he would, didn't know he expected me to actually give the order." Rouillard shot Tremont a hard stare as he took another turn, his manner as offhand as if the topic had no more importance than a misplaced invitation to a soiree.

The man was a coward, Kerr saw. His methods were the sly, underhand ones of a weakling, someone too squeamish to get his hands dirty. He'd always known it in the back of his mind, but never quite the extent of it.

More than that, Rouillard had no conscience. He gave not a thought to the hopes, the dreams, the very lives of those he used or who got in his way.

He was hardly worth killing.

And this was the man Sonia was to marry.

Disgust raged through Kerr at the thought. Rouillard would never appreciate Sonia's courage and independence. He'd try to break her; his ego would demand it. He'd confine her, use her, treat her no better than a dog to be kicked or petted at his whim. All her lovely passion would be wasted, for such a man would see it as something to be deplored or even feared, a threat to his feeble manhood.

The thought sickened him to the bottom of his soul. It could not be allowed to happen.

"Release Mademoiselle Bonneval from the marriage contract between you," he said abruptly. "In return, I'll give my pledge to return to New Orleans and leave you in peace."

Rouillard stopped, turned to face him. A bark of a laugh rasped in his throat. "I suppose I'm to take your word for that."

"I am no less a man of honor than was my brother."

The small room was quiet while the other man

stared at him. Tremont, against the far wall, gazed at his fingernails as if in boredom, though it may have been a pose.

"You want my bride," Rouillard said finally.

God, yes, he wanted her, Kerr thought fervently, but it would be crass to say it, and stupid as well. "Allow her to set up her household, if that's what she wants. Or send her back to her father on the next ship with or without escort. It's all one to me."

"Let her go, when she came here expecting to be married?"

"She would rather be free."

"And you would rather see it, would trade your hope of revenge for it." Rouillard gave a wheezing snort. "I'm amazed, I must say."

"It seems a fair exchange."

"So you say, but there is her dowry to be considered."

"Marry her first and keep it when you let her go."

"Now, that's an idea—or would be if you were in any position to be a threat. Fortunately for me, you aren't."

That could not be denied, at least for now. "She doesn't want this marriage, she's said so time and again. Why would you hold her to it?"

"Her family is one of the most distinguished in New Orleans and it may suit me to return there one day. She is her father's only heir, an important consideration. As for what she wants, I like to think I can change her mind."

"You won't. If she fought so against making the voyage here, think what grief she'll give you."

"Fought?" Rouillard cocked his head.

"Why else do you think I was hired?"

"I did wonder. We had no such agreement, Bonne-val and I."

"She wouldn't be here except for me." The words were gall and wormwood in Kerr's mouth, bitter beyond imagining.

"I can guess your reasons for taking the job, for what good they did you. But tell me, why is the lady's welfare so important?" Rouillard glanced over his shoulder at Tremont before turning back again. "Just how well do you know my betrothed, Wallace? What happened between you in the days between the sinking of the *Lime Rock* and yesterday afternoon?"

"Nothing that need concern you." It was the truth as far as it went. Sonia's innocence or lack of it had not, apparently, been of paramount importance in Rouillard's offer for her hand. Why should it matter now?

Yet Kerr knew full well that it did matter. That the bride-to-be would be untouched was implicit in the arrangement; it had been that way for centuries. If Rouillard learned she had been thoroughly touched indeed, and by him, might even now be carrying his child, the bastard would be fit to be tied. Women had died for that breach of trust.

"I will deliver Rouillard his bride, one unharmed, unsullied…"

He had failed to keep his solemn vow. He should be horsewhipped for it.

Rouillard turned to Tremont once more. "What do you say, my friend? You saw them together aboard ship and again when you stopped the diligence. Should I be concerned?"

Kerr met the dark eyes of the erstwhile sugar planter, seeing in them the swift weighing of evidence, the sifting of advantage. He frowned a warning, or tried. Tremont had been attracted to Sonia, had walked and talked with her, laughed with her, knew her rare combination of beauty and spirit. Surely he would say nothing that might put her in danger?

The man against the wall lifted a shoulder, the picture of callousness. "Who knows. But you're unlikely to get the truth from Wallace. My suggestion would be to ask the lady."

No!

The protest shouted in Kerr's mind, though he clenched his teeth to keep it inside. Sonia would never deny it. Such discretion would not serve her, or so she thought. She would throw the truth in her betrothed's face in hope of release, if not for the satisfaction of it.

And whatever the result, Kerr thought as he closed his eyes, he would have to live with it. At least long enough to wipe from the face of the earth the man who dared hurt her.

Twenty-Four

Sonia stood at the window of the bedchamber to which she had been brought in the night, staring down onto the street below. It was alive with people: mestizo women with braided hair and colorful skirts swishing around their ankles, boys and girls racing here and there, vendors of coffee and vegetables and herbs crying their wares, gentlemen on horseback and men and ladies perched behind them with their heads covered by scarves instead of bonnets. In the gutters were vultures, great black and gray scavengers she had heard called *zopilotes* in Xalapa, birds tolerated because they served to keep the streets clean.

Across the rooftops she could see the blue gleam of the sea, also the port guarded by the gray mass of Fort San Juan de Ulúa.

Nothing held her attention. She might as well be blind. All she could see was Kerr lying in the road with his blood turning the sandy dirt to rust-red mud.

Was he dead? Could he be, and she not know it? He

seemed too strong for such a puny fate, too indomitable of will and spirit.

She could hardly believe what had taken place. Tremont, of all people, riding to stop the diligence and make off with her. He had not hurt her in any way, but his vigilance had not relaxed for even an instant during the long ride to the city. She had found no chance to get away from him.

They had traveled hard through what remained of the day and half the night. His arms had been around her, she had been forced to lean into his body. She had been as close to him as a woman could be without the kind of intimacy she and Kerr had shared. Regardless, she had felt nothing. His day's growth of beard had prickled against her scalp, his chest had been too narrow, his arms too tight.

Nothing about it had been remotely like being held by Kerr.

Oddly enough, she had not felt threatened by their former shipmate. He answered no questions, gave her no inkling of his intentions, but neither did she have the feeling he might harm her.

Where he was taking her had been a mystery right up to the moment when they rode into the courtyard of this walled house in Vera Cruz. He'd answered no questions, barely looked at her. It was as if retrieving her was an unpleasant duty, one he wished to be done with as soon as possible. The most she had gotten from him was the admission that this house belonged to Jean Pierre.

Like the Casa de las Flores, it was a large edifice in

typical Spanish colonial style. The scale was grandiose, however, with furnishings in the overdone opulence that was sometimes mistaken for taste. The thought that she might be forced to pass the remainder of her life within its walls was almost intolerable.

She couldn't leave, not yet. First, she must speak to Jean Pierre. He had not been in the house when she arrived. She had thought to wait up for him, but sank into sleep moments after falling into the bed in this chamber. She had to tell him…

Tell him what? What could she say that would not make matters worse if Kerr was alive? And if he was dead, what did it matter anyway?

A tap sounded on the chamber door behind her. She swung her head toward the sound, pulling the wrapper closer around her that she had found on the foot of the bed. Before she could give permission for entry, the door was flung open.

"Ma chère!" her aunt cried as she rustled toward her with open arms. "At last you are here! I have prayed so for this moment that my knees are sore and my rosary in pieces. If I had been told last night, if only I'd known—but no one came to inform me, no one said a word."

The warm arms, the scented bosom and dear, familiar face brought a hard knot of tears to Sonia's throat. She sniffed valiantly as she clasped her aunt, accepted and gave the ritual kiss on either cheek. "I missed you, too," she said with a watery chuckle.

"I had almost given you up, I swear it. You have no

idea how I despaired when the lifeboat filled and you were not there, or when the Mexican captain sailed from that accursed spot and you and Monsieur Wallace were not among the rescued. I had seen you swimming, both of you, but lost sight of you in the waves. My one hope was in him."

"Tante Lily, you know I can swim."

"Yes, yes, but truly, *chère*…"

"You are right. I owe Kerr my life."

"Where is he that I may thank him? He did bring you?"

The tale must be told from the beginning since her aunt would never rest until she had every detail. Hearing about the snake and huge scorpion and the night spent in what might have been an ancient temple, she looked appalled. On learning of the discovery by Doña Francesca's woodsmen, the arrival in Xalapa and the holdup of the diligence, she sank onto the bed with her hand over her mouth and her eyes wide.

"Oh, *chère,* such an adventure. Yes, and such horror, the stuff of nightmares. I've felt such terror myself, night after night, reliving the sinking of our steamer, worrying about you, where you were, what was happening to you. To think you were in such distress makes me feel quite ill. Are you—are you all right?"

"As you see." Sonia's smile was no more than a quick movement of her lips.

"No, no, my dear child. I mean, that is to say, you have spent considerable time in company with a man while alone and under great strain. It would not be surprising if, that is, if you were…if you were not intact?"

At one time, Sonia would have told her aunt everything. Now she felt oddly protective of the moments spent in Kerr's arms. She gave her a straight look. "I can't believe you would ask such a thing."

"Well, depend upon it, your betrothed will wish to know," her aunt returned in warning tones. "He has been like a madman. I don't know what was worse in his mind, the thought that you might have drowned before becoming his wife or that you may have been saved from it by a man he holds in dislike. Though to be sure, I didn't realize he and Monsieur Wallace were acquainted until I arrived here."

"They had not met before," Sonia returned, and told her with as little circumlocution as possible about the connection between them.

Her aunt's face turned grim. Rising, she moved to the bellpull, which hung beside the bed, and gave it a sharp tug.

"What are you doing?"

"You must bathe and dress at once. It will not do for your betrothed to see you looking so unkempt."

Sonia turned back toward the window. "I have nothing to wear."

"Indeed you do, for I have been to the shops since I arrived here. I know your measurements as surely as my own, and there are always decent garments to be had for these emergencies."

"I also don't much care how Jean Pierre sees me."

"But you must, really, you must! It's armament, as I've told you before. A woman barricaded behind whalebone and layers of petticoats is a different proposition from one who is naked under a mere wrapper."

"You feel I require armor?"

"I'm sure of it. I didn't wish to tell you, but…"

Sonia's heart kicked against her ribs in response to the dread she saw in her aunt's face. "Tell me what?"

"Monsieur Rouillard is frightened of your Monsieur Wallace, I think. If an injury has been done to him, then he is the cause. I heard him say to Monsieur Tremont that someone must be stopped, though I had no idea who was meant at the time. Now, if you are without your protector, if he is—"

"Don't say it!"

"No, no, but don't you see that the first question Monsieur Rouillard will ask when he sees you must be about what took place while you were with Monsieur Wallace? If you are to pass through the ordeal unscathed, you must be ready for it."

Her aunt was correct; Sonia saw that easily enough. What was not clear was just how she would answer the all-important question.

It was less than an hour later, as Sonia sat before her dressing table in a gown of brown-and-gold-striped silk while a young maid put up her hair in a braided coronet, that the door burst open. It smacked against the wall and bounced nearly shut again, so that Jean Pierre slapped it out of his way as he strode into the bedchamber.

"Get out."

The vicious order was for the maid, who scurried from the room with a frightened glance over her shoulder. It may have been intended for Tante Lily as well, but that intrepid lady blithely ignored it as she hung Sonia's wrapper away in the corner armoire that already contained another day gown, an evening costume and shawl and, on the top shelf, a hat and bonnet.

If her fiancé expected her to cower before such a violent entry, Sonia thought, he would discover his mistake. She did not rise, but turned on her stool, sitting it like a throne. "As charming as ever, I see, Monsieur Rouillard," she said in opening attack. "I cannot be surprised since you had me snatched from the Xalapa diligence and delivered to you like a crated pullet."

He blinked and stopped where he stood. "I do beg your pardon. I was eager to see you. You should have been with me long since."

"Yes, and would have, no doubt, except for running afoul of a Mexican warship. A small matter, but vexing. Where were you last night that you weren't on hand to greet me?"

The guilty flush that rose to his face told its own story. "I had an engagement."

"No doubt," she said in repressive tones. "I hope she was pretty and not too greedy."

"Mademoiselle Bonneval!"

"Are you shocked? Ah, well, I can see how you might be. We are barely acquainted, after all, so you have no idea of my character. Perhaps you will explain why you thought you must have me and no other as your wife?"

A pinched look appeared around his nose. "The arrangement suited me when it was made, and that's all you need to know. Whether it pleases me now is another matter."

He had regained his composure and sense of male privilege with it. That was not a good sign. She got to her feet, reaching for a fan that lay on the dressing table. Unfurling it, she gave her attention to the crudely painted cotton stretched over the wooden sticks. "I'm sure you will tell me when you decide," she said negligently.

"That will depend on your answers to my questions. I demand to know what passed between you and Kerr Wallace while the two of you were without a proper chaperone."

"You demand?" she said softly, raising the fan to her face in mock coquettishness, gazing at him over top of it.

"It's my right to know."

"If you had come to call upon me in New Orleans and courted me in the usual form, if we had spoken solemn vows at the cathedral before sharing this tragic sea voyage, you would not have to ask."

"Naturally you would have been overjoyed to have my proposal," he said, a snide look appearing on his round face. "You would not even allow me a space on your dance card five years ago."

She had not recalled that incident until this moment. He had been like a bluebottle fly buzzing around her, ignoring all polite efforts to avoid him. She had been forced to resort to the polite lie that Bernard had commandeered all her free dances. Obviously it still rankled with him. She might have realized except the incident had been so insignificant, at least to her.

"That's the reason you applied to my father, to pay me back for denying you a dance?"

"Added to the fact that he could hardly refuse the favor." Self-satisfaction lit his smile, and he clasped his hands under his tailcoat, rocking back on his heels.

Could hardly refuse…

That phrase presented her with a stunning possibility. Was it possible her father had not wished to be rid of her, had not been happy with the betrothal he had arranged? "What do you mean?"

"Why, only that he is a partner, silent, of course, in my import concern. He entered into the arrangement willingly enough since it carried no stigma for him of dealing in dirty commerce. That we should become in-laws was only a single step more. He would not, I felt sure, attempt to discredit his daughter's husband since to ruin me would be to ruin you."

"Why should he wish to discredit you?"

"Nothing that should concern you, only a minor disagreement over sundry items being shipped. In the end, I was able to make him see that he would be more suspect than I in any investigation, given his wealth and social standing. Who would suppose he was not the brains behind the scheme?"

Sonia stared at him while the chill of stunned comprehension shivered down her back. "The rifles," she whispered.

"You know about them?" Amazement twisted his face and he flung a hunted look at Tante Lily. "But why not? Yes. Tremont said Wallace found them, after all."

He stepped closer, caught her wrist in his plump, moist fist. "What else did he tell you, and what were you doing while this American bastard talked about my business?" He gave her wrist a hard wrench. "Were you spreading your legs for him? Is that it?"

Agony burned its way to Sonia's elbow. She bent at the waist in an attempt to ease it while frantic thought moved in her mind. At the edges of her vision, she saw Tante Lily turn from the armoire and start toward them. "You must be mad!"

"What do you expect when my betrothed spends days alone with a strange man and won't answer a simple question about it? I'm told you looked the most debauched creature alive when found, bedraggled, ripe and half undressed. As for Wallace—"

"Who told you such a thing?" she asked, gasping as he twisted her wrist farther.

"The man who knocked your lover in the head with a rifle butt, the captain of my house guard. You can be sure I rewarded him well for it."

That it was not Tremont surprised her; she had thought him in charge of the expedition. She had no time for more than a glancing thought. Tante Lily was creeping up behind Jean Pierre. Morning light glinted along the shaft of the hat pin in her fist. Abruptly, she thrust out her arm.

Jean Pierre howled and jerked upright. Releasing Sonia, he grabbed for his backside.

"You bitch!" he snarled, swinging on Tante Lily.

Sonia's aunt jumped back, the hat pin held before her

like a sword. "You are not yet married to my charge, *monsieur!* My duty is to protect her. Leave this room immediately."

"Meddling old biddy. Where were you when she was acting the whore with my worst enemy? What of your duty then?"

"They were lost and alone, the two of them had been shipwrecked and almost drowned. What could be more natural than that they should cling to each other? And whose fault is it, pray, that this happened? You and your rifles! It would not surprise me to know we were chased by the Mexican warship because of them!"

"Tante Lily, no," Sonia said in protest.

"He asked, so let him hear," her aunt said with barely a glance in Sonia's direction. "You, *monsieur,* are the greatest hypocrite alive. You fornicate as you please, but dare condemn a single misstep by my niece in the face of death? You should be ecstatic that she is here with you now. And you should thank Monsieur Wallace that it's so, for otherwise my dearest Sonia would be fleeing from this marriage, fleeing from you. It's only through the alertness and strength of Kerr Wallace that she was brought to board the *Lime Rock* for the wedding journey, and I would not be surprised to learn that she is here only because he made certain they traveled to Vera Cruz instead of homeward."

Sonia bit back a groan. She might have guessed her aunt had not been fooled by her evasion. She was wise about people, for all her tendency to chatter. She should also have realized Tante Lily, once provoked, would not be able to keep quiet about her feelings toward the marriage.

"Oh, yes, Wallace meant for her to arrive. He wanted to catch me napping, the better to kill me."

Tante Lily's eyes flashed. "Another example of your perfidy, *monsieur*. I know of your conduct on the march after the Mier Expedition, you see. You are a pathetic excuse for a man, and I believe it will be best if I do not permit my niece to be married to you."

"You can't do that. The contracts have been signed."

"Tante Lily," Sonia tried again, reaching out to place her hand on her aunt's arm.

"Not by my niece, they haven't. And you will see what I can do when I send for the priest. I have yet to meet a good father of the church willing to marry a woman against her will, especially when the matter has been explained to him."

Jean Pierre's face turned purple and his eyes narrowed to slits. "She will marry me," he said, "or Wallace will die."

The sudden quiet in the room was stifling. Heat was growing outside as the day advanced, beating against the windows. From the street below came the *clip-clop* of hooves as a horseman passed, the song of a flower vendor and the cries of children. Sonia's pent breath, as it left her lungs, was also perfectly audible.

"Kerr is alive?" she asked. "He's here?"

"Your concern is touching," Jean Pierre said, "though it might have been better if you had pretended indifference."

"What have you done with him?"

"Oh, he's quite comfortable at the moment. It occurred to me, given what he said, that he might be of more use to me aboveground than below it."

She clenched her teeth to hold back the tumble of questions about Kerr's injury, whether he was conscious or in pain. "You've spoken to him?"

"Indeed, and it was quite illuminating. Do you know, he swore to give up all notion of revenge and leave me unmolested if I would release you from our betrothal?"

Tightness invaded her throat. Kerr had offered to abandon the quest he had pursued so long, relinquish his vow to avenge the death of his brother, to gain her freedom? It was hard to believe. Even more difficult to accept was what might lie behind it. "He really said that?"

"Stupid of him, when he was no longer a threat." Jean Pierre laughed. "One thing he didn't say was that he intended to be your escort for the journey home. Do you think he has perhaps had enough of your charms? Or was it merely that he has no hope of escaping his chain."

Chain. Kerr was shackled somewhere. The fan she held quivered with the trembling of her fingers. She closed it, dropped it on the dressing table and curled her hands into fists. "I would not be so sure of holding him. He is a most formidable man."

"Your faith is touching, though I assure you he is quite powerless."

She said nothing, but was grateful when Tante Lily came to her, placing an arm around her shoulders.

"The question of what to do with him now I have him is worrisome, of course," her betrothed went on without visible sign of concern. "My thought, after what has just passed here between us, is for how you might remedy the matter."

She raised her chin, wary of the satisfaction she saw burning in his pale eyes. "Yes?"

"Oh, yes. What I need from you is careful, very careful, thought about just what you may be willing to do to save your lover's miserable life."

Twenty-Five

Tante Lily's hat pin, or more accurately the one she had bought to go with the new hat in Sonia's armoire, seemed to have punctured Jean Pierre's anger. He did not linger after throwing his malicious suggestion at her.

Sonia dropped down on the bed when he had gone. Absently she rubbed her arm where he had bruised the flesh. She was supremely weary of a sudden, aching in every joint and muscle from the hard effort of the past few days, the long ride during the night, and despair over winding up here in Jean Pierre's power. She ached, too, at the thought of Kerr shut up somewhere nearby, injured and alone.

Her aunt came to sit beside her, touching her hand. "Don't look so *désolée, chère*. There must be something that can be done."

"Kerr may need help. Jean Pierre won't see after him, will never send for a doctor. He would be just as happy if he were to die."

"I fear you're right."

In her aunt's face was the sadness of resignation, the inevitable bowing of women to things that couldn't be changed. Sonia refused to accept it.

"I have to do something," she exclaimed, beating a fist on her knee.

"But what? Forgive me, but you are virtually a prisoner yourself. Do you think Jean Pierre will allow you to see Monsieur Wallace, much less tend him? No, and no again. If you should ask, it may make matters worse."

Her aunt was right. The last thing she wanted was to push Jean Pierre into disposing of the man he recognized as his enemy. It pleased him to have the upper hand over him at the moment, but how long would that last?

"You have been here for several days," she said finally. "Have you seen the house? Do you have any idea where a prisoner might be kept?"

"I've only walked in the courtyard and gone from room to room along the galleries." Tante Lily paused, frowning in concentration before shaking her head. "No, I don't know. It's a house like any other in a tropical climate, with the kitchen, laundry and servants' rooms on the lower floor and family quarters on the upper for air. The main rooms are obviously ineligible as they have too many doors and windows to serve. My only thought is one of the storerooms near the kitchen. They are sometimes used in New Orleans to confine those who go mad or become violent, you know."

Sonia nodded, hope rising inside her in spite of the difficulties that still lay ahead. "If he's there, then the door will be bolted."

"Without doubt, I should think. It may be guarded as well."

"Does Jean Pierre have guests other than you and Monsieur Tremont?"

"You are thinking of our fellow passengers from the *Lime Rock?* No, we are all that are left in Vera Cruz now. Madame Pradat and her son, Reverend Smythe and the others went on their way as soon as arrangements could be made."

"What of servants? Are there a great many?" It seemed a good idea to know when they were all accounted for if the need arose.

"A cook and her helpers, of course, also a valet for Jean Pierre, a pair of maids for general cleaning and a man and his helper whose job it is to keep the courtyard tidy—call it eight or nine, plus another half dozen of what Monsieur Rouillard is pleased to call his household guard. Many in Vera Cruz have such in these troubled times, it seems, particularly those who like to appear grand. Your fiancé has become more of a Spanish grandee, I believe, than those with a right to the title."

Fourteen or so servants were a large number to avoid. At least it was unless she knew exactly where she was going and what she would do when she got there.

Shoving off the bed, Sonia paced the room, kicking her skirts from under her feet in irritation for their stiff fullness after only a few short days of being largely unfettered by them. Yes, and she was heartily sick of being unable to move for the restrictions imposed upon her by men. Her father, Kerr and now Jean Pierre—it was too much. No matter how benevolent the intention, the resulting loss of the freedom to direct her own life was galling beyond words.

Trapped. She was trapped.

Her prison was made up of walls and obligations, yes, but also of debts. Kerr had not left her behind after the sinking of the *Lime Rock* or during the long trek through the jungle when he could, she knew, have moved faster alone. Even if she could escape, how could she desert him now?

She would not submit. She would not stay here a moment longer than necessary, would never become Jean Pierre's wife. But first she had to make certain Kerr didn't suffer for her decision.

Somehow, she had to set him free.

The day wore on. Sonia spent it, in part, testing the limits of her confinement. No one objected when she left her bedchamber, nor did they seem to care if she explored the salon, the dining room or even the other bedchambers. She strolled the galleries at will, even descended to the courtyard to sit in the shade, dipping her fingers in the fountain, inhaling the fragrance of flowers.

The kitchen was not off-limits to her; in fact, she was encouraged by the cook to suggest dishes she might care to taste at dinner in midafternoon. The kitchen's long table seemed overcrowded with men with little apparent occupation. Rough men with long mustaches and knives in their belts, she recognized them as those who had stopped the diligence. None offered any sign they had seen her before, but she was appraised so thoroughly that she felt naked.

Jean Pierre was no longer in the house, so she discovered, but had left soon after the contretemps between them. Tremont had gone with him. Sonia was relieved beyond words. Anything that put off further discussion between her and her betrothed was to the good. She only wished he might stay away forever.

She begged a bread crust from the cook and sat for some time in the courtyard, shredding it to feed the birds that gathered around her. From her vantage point, she could see that the huge entrance gate was secured by an ornate padlock. Few came or went through it, though an elderly man who crouched beside it, snoozing in the shade cast by his enormous hat, seemed to be the gatekeeper.

Three other doors appeared to be padlocked, all in the wall that stretched beyond the kitchen. They corresponded almost exactly to the storerooms in the houses of the Vieux Carré, which, after two great fires and years of Spanish governance in the previous century, owed more to Spanish design than to the original French. No one approached these heavy doors, however, and she heard no sound from them.

The silence was disturbing, even a little frightening. She had no idea if Kerr was actually in the house and scant prospect of anywhere else to look. What if he was lying alone and too injured to move? What if he had died or been killed after speaking with Jean Pierre?

She tore off more bread crumbs, dropping them

around her feet. The vividly colored birds became only a blur as they swooped here and there to retrieve them. The flashes of the wings wavered in front of her eyes, their colors almost painful in the mirror-bright sunlight.

It was after sunset, as the gray-blue twilight descended into night, when Jean Pierre returned. The event was signaled by a great clatter of hooves and harness as his town carriage swept into the courtyard and wheeled to a stop.

Sonia watched from her bedchamber window as he alighted, looking as if he had enjoyed a day of surpassing pleasure. Tremont followed him. He had discarded his rough garb, appearing soigné once more in a double-breasted coat of the kind made popular by Britain's Prince Albert, as he stepped down behind his host. She turned from the sight with her lips set in a flat line.

The request for her presence at the ten-o'clock supper came a short while later. Sonia sent her refusal by the same maid who had brought the invitation.

Let her aunt go and make her excuses, soothe Jean Pierre's ego and keep bright conversation circling the table. Sonia wasn't hungry and had no stomach for sitting in the same room as her fiancé and his traitorous friend. Moreover, she had better use for the darkness that had fallen.

She waited until she could hear the clink of silverware on china and the murmur of voices from the dining room farther down the gallery. Leaving her room then, she eased along the gallery in the opposite direction. Keeping to the shadows near the wall, she drifted as noiselessly as a ghost while keeping watch for movement in the courtyard below. Her mission was to find a weapon. She would prefer a pistol, but anything would do.

A set of French doors stood wide to let in night coolness. She listened outside for long moments. Hearing nothing, she slid inside.

She stood in a bedchamber of feminine appearance, with rose-colored silk on the walls and ruffled white bedcovers. Though large and airy, it had an unused air. No bits of feminine frippery were lying about; there was no brush and comb on the dressing table or water in the dainty pitcher and bowl on the washstand. Connected to it was another bedchamber, with only a great sweep of white curtain dividing the two for increased airflow, and she moved inside without hesitation. Given the self-conscious magnificence of this one, she suspected it belonged to Jean Pierre. She became certain as she stepped into the dressing room beyond it, for the frock coat draped over the back of a chair was the one he had worn earlier. Signs of a quick bath and change of clothing lay here and there as well, including shaving things still out on the washstand. She glanced quickly around, hoping to locate something more lethal than the razor noticed at first glance, but nothing was readily apparent.

Something, a familiar shape, drew her gaze back to the shaving things. Half hidden behind the soap cup was Kerr's pocketknife. Anger moved over her at the thought of it being taken from him. Her fingers shook a little as she picked it up.

The smooth feel of the ivory handle, the memories

of how he had used it, the knowledge that he had touched it, soothed her in some fashion. It seemed to retain some of his heat, as if it had been kept near him too long for it to quickly dissipate. She opened the blade, slid a finger carefully along the well-honed edge.

Footsteps sounded from the connecting room. It would be the valet, most likely, coming to turn down the bed for the night. His next task would be to put the dressing room to rights. There was no time to search deeper. With the knife held tightly in her fist, she tiptoed to the French window and stepped out onto the gallery once more.

The staircase to the courtyard lay at the end of the gallery. She moved toward it, halting at the top as a maidservant, with long black hair worn in a single braid down her back and large liquid eyes, came up from below. She carried a tray holding a silver water pitcher that sloshed as she stood aside. Sonia smiled and spoke a low-voiced greeting as she passed her. Descending the staircase, she trailed her free hand along the banister with a *triste* air, as if resigned to whatever befell her.

A torch burned at the foot of the stairs. The only other light came from the open door of the kitchen and the glow of candles from the rooms on the second floor. Shadows lay deep under the lower galleries that surrounded the courtyard. The warm air was scented with flowers overlaid by the smells of roasted meat and seared vegetables. Somewhere a dove called. The center fountain made soft water music. A cat strolled from the kitchen and crouched to lap water from the paving where it spilled over the basin's edge, but nothing else moved in the dimness.

Avoiding the kitchen, Sonia crossed to the lower gallery that extended beyond it. The line of doors she had noticed earlier loomed before her. They were solid, heavy behind their wrought-iron hasps and stout locks. Nothing moved inside that she could tell. These storerooms remained dark and hushed as she strolled past with her shadow slipping along before her.

Turning at the end of the building, she paused. Something about the last door seemed odd, she thought. Retracing her footsteps, she stopped before it. Unlike the others, it had a long iron bar as part of its hasp. She leaned closer, listening, but could hear nothing. She lifted her hand, about to tap with the backs of her knuckles.

"Inspecting your domain, *chère?* Perhaps I may be of service as a guide."

Sonia swung in a swirl of petticoats. It was Jean Pierre who had spoken, his voice laden with irony. He stood on the landing of a service stair hidden away in this back corner. Descending as the words left his mouth, he came toward her. His footsteps were ponderous, deliberate, as if he expected to incite fear.

"You startled me. I didn't see you there." Using her wide skirts for cover, she hastily slipped the open pocketknife into the ornamental pocket that hung from her waist. She lifted her hand to her bodice then, trying to slow the hard, uneven beat of her heart.

"Otherwise, you would have returned upstairs at once."

That much was certainly true. It seemed best to provide a distraction. "Is supper over already? I had thought I might join you for dessert."

"We are between courses. I decided to see if you couldn't be coerced into leaving your room. Naturally, I was concerned when you weren't there."

"I'm sure you were," she murmured.

"To have you join us will be a delight. What sweet do you crave this evening?"

"Anything will do."

"You have only to express a wish and I shall order it done. I can be indulgent when I choose, though you will learn in due time that I am master in my house."

His boast had a purpose, she was sure, something more than an attempt to demonstrate his power over her. What it might be eluded her. "I expect you think so."

"You may mock me now, but you will learn to speak softly when we are married," he said, his hand curling into a fist as he stepped closer. "And we *will* marry. You need not think your *Kaintuck* lover will interfere. I hold his life in the palm of my hand."

From somewhere nearby came the quiet clink of metal against metal. Was it the rattle of a chain? Had it come from the room just behind her? "So you suggested before," she answered, "but you have not produced him and that makes it doubtful."

"You wish to see him? Perhaps you would like to touch him to make sure it isn't his ghost?" He reached out to run his fingers along her arm.

"Don't," she said, backing swiftly away from him.

"Why not? Soon I will have the right to do much more. How I will enjoy that, having you naked and begging under me." He followed after her, put his hand out to snag her waist and cover her breast with his hot, damp hand.

"Monsieur!" Beneath her exclamation, she distinctly heard a chain dragging over stone in the room behind her, not quite masking a soft curse.

"Don't sound so shocked," Jean Pierre said, his voice growing thick. "We both know you will be no virgin bride. I fail to see why I shouldn't anticipate the wedding by a few days. What will it matter when all is said and done?"

The chain clanked, a hard, abrupt sound followed by the clatter and slide of what might have been broken plaster. It was Kerr in that dark storeroom, jerking against his bonds. The thought of him in chains sent a surge of black anger through her. For a brief, mad instant, she considered bargaining for his release, her acquiescence for the key to the storeroom and promise that he could leave unharmed.

Jean Pierre would never agree. He was satisfied with matters as they were, thought he would have everything his way in the end. But the end was not yet.

She brought her arm up, knocking his hand away from her body. "It will matter to you when my aunt comes at you with her hat pin again."

Jean Pierre stiffened, stepped back a pace. "Interfering old witch," he growled, his face suffusing with dark color in the uncertain light. "I should have locked her up for attacking me. I may yet if she dares come between us again."

"Touch one hair on her head, and I'll never be your

wife." Sonia lifted her chin as she spoke, her gaze hard on his face.

"That may be, but you'll still warm my—"

"Good evening. Fine night, isn't it?"

The greeting came from the shadows farther back along the gallery. Tremont strolled into view a moment later, one hand in his coat pocket and the other holding a cheroot to his mouth while the tip glowed red. The smoke left his lips, drifting away in a fine gray cloud as he came up to them.

"Tremont." Jean Pierre's acknowledgment of the greeting was surly.

"Monsieur." Sonia's cool greeting covered her fervid appreciation for his timely appearance.

"We missed you at the supper table, *mademoiselle.* I trust you have recovered from our ride?"

"Quite."

"I regret that it had to be undertaken, but it was necessary to reach here in haste."

He was watching her with narrow interest, or so Sonia thought, though he might just as well be squinting against the smoke that made a gray veil around his head. The look she gave him in return was hardly cordial.

"Not forgiven, I see." His smile turned wry. "Ah, well, it's hardly to be expected." When she made no answer, he ground out his cheroot on a nearby post, inspected the end then tucked it into his waistcoat pocket. "I believe I heard you mention dessert. Allow me to escort you to the dining room. A dish of flambéed bananas over ice cream was carried up from the kitchen just now. It should not be wasted."

She murmured her thanks, the words only a shade less frigid than the promised treat. She put her fingers on his arm and moved closer to his side. Accepting his offer was far better than staying behind with Jean Pierre.

Her fiancé took a hasty step after them. "Just a minute here."

Tremont paused, looked over his shoulder. "Yes?"

Jean Pierre stared at him. It was no wonder, perhaps, for the American's voice carried an unexpected note of steely impatience. Sonia looked from one to the other, her attention caught by the tension that vibrated between them. At the same time, she realized she had heard nothing from the dark storeroom since Tremont's arrival.

"I will join you upstairs shortly," Jean Pierre said, his voice stiff, almost petulant. "We will talk again later, Sonia, *ma chère.*"

She made no answer. There would be no opportunity later, not if she could help it.

They moved along the lower gallery without speaking, she and Tremont. When they passed the open door of the kitchen, crossing the rectangle of light that lay on the stone walkway, he put his hand on her fingers where they lay on his arm. "An impulsive man, your betrothed," he said in tones too low to be heard behind him. "First he sends for you based solely on past infatuation, and now he can't wait to claim you."

"Infatuation?"

"So he has said."

"And you believe it."

He smiled down at her. "Don't you?"

"I think it was for spite, and balm for his pride that I wounded by refusing to dance with him."

"Men survive such slights. They don't, as a rule, take retribution for them."

"Not most men, no." She went on before he could comment. "Who are you, really? I mean, you sound as if you barely know Jean Pierre, certainly never mentioned the acquaintance on the ship, yet here you are with him."

A grimace crossed his features. "I knew interfering back there was a mistake."

It was a reminder, if she needed one, of how much she owed him. "I'm grateful you did, and sorry if you object to the questions, only—"

"Only you are curious? Say your fiancé and I are recent acquaintances then."

"Because of money, I suppose, and the traffic in rifles."

He stopped, staring at her with a frown between his eyes. "What do you mean?"

"You needn't pretend. Kerr saw you in the ship's hold when you checked on them."

"He saw but didn't tell Captain Frazier."

"Perhaps he thought it none of his business."

Tremont began to walk again. "It's a good thing he kept the information close to his chest or I might have been in the brig when the *Lime Rock* went down. I suppose I owe him for that."

"If you feel any obligation, then I beg you will help him," she said, halting and turning toward him. "He's being held in that storeroom back there, I'm almost sure of it. It would be—"

"Impossible."

"But why? It's such a small thing."

"It isn't small at all. Don't ask it. Please."

The hard finality in his voice cut deep, the more so because she had allowed herself to hope. Sonia snatched her hand from under his, releasing his arm. The main staircase lay ahead of her. Picking up her skirts, she ran toward it.

On the second step, she stumbled, half blinded by a film of tears. Blinking hard, she went on. Even as she climbed toward the dining room, however, she listened again for some sound, some evidence that she was right, that Kerr was in the dark storeroom below. Some proof that he was alive.

There was nothing.

Nothing at all.

Twenty-Six

Kerr drew his first easy breath as he heard Sonia's footsteps recede along with those of that bastard, Tremont. God, the raging fear of being forced to listen to Rouillard accost her while powerless to stop it. He'd been sure he meant to rape her there outside the door. He'd tried to tear the chain out of the wall, wanted to rip the door off its hinges with his bare hands. He was still shaking with fury, certain in the knowledge that Rouillard had wanted him to hear, had meant him to taste the fear.

It was to be his punishment for taking Sonia back there in the jungle. Only, *she* was the one meant to pay.

This was the bastard she was to marry, an immoral cretin who held nothing sacred, cared for nothing except what he wanted. A small man who needed to lord it over everybody around him so he could feel big. An idiot who could not be grateful for the lovely bride given to him, but had to punish her for not wanting him. Worst of all, he seemed set on enjoying his revenge.

From what he'd heard, Kerr thought the wedding must still be going to take place. That meant his offer had been rejected. Rouillard had said so before, but this was final confirmation.

Good enough. He was now under no obligation to spare Sonia's promised husband. Nor would he, not when it meant a lifetime for Sonia with such a man.

Backing to his cot, Kerr sat down on it. He ran his hand over his head, probing gingerly at his skull. Hard-headed, he'd been called more than once, and a damn good thing he was, too. His scalp was sore, the hair stiff with dried blood where the rifle butt had hit him, and he still had a headache, but the sick feeling in the pit of his stomach was gone. He thought he would be all right.

The question was, would Sonia? She was at Rouillard's mercy here in his house. He did not have the look of a man used to controlling his appetites. Soon he would simply kick down her door and take her.

Kerr's hope was that he'd decide to settle with him first. He was waiting for that moment. It would be his chance, maybe the only one he'd get.

All was quiet now out in the courtyard. Kerr turned to the wall that held his chain. Winding the links around his wrist, he swung it, wearing on the bolt, trying to loosen it from the rock wall as he'd been doing most of the day. It was disheartening work, especially in the dark; he had only a small pile of rock dust to show for his labor. Keeping at it relieved some of the rage inside him. Besides, what else did he have to do?

It was a quarter hour later, possibly less, when he

realized he was able to see what he was doing. Lamp-light was approaching, showing through the cracks around the door. Seconds later, he heard the rattle of keys and the creak of the bolt.

The door swung open. Kerr was on his feet with the length of chain draped in his hands. The captain of the guard stepped inside, preceded by his shadow cast by the lantern left on the stone floor outside. He was followed by a detail of six men.

For a fleeting moment, Kerr met the gaze of the man who had clubbed him. Wariness flickered across the captain's face. He rapped out an order, and two of the detail raised the rifles they carried, sighting on Kerr's chest.

"Step aside. We are ordered to release you and deliver you upstairs."

That sounded a vast improvement over his current occupation, Kerr thought. Could be it was the opportunity he'd been waiting for. He gave a nod and moved to one end of the bed to allow access to the chain's wall bolt.

He wasn't to be set free of his chain. It was left connected to his left ankle. The extra length dragged along behind him, rattling on the stones of the courtyard as the detail advanced on the staircase to the main floor. It trailed, banging on every step, as he climbed upward, made a high-pitched clatter on the tile floor as they entered the dining room.

He saw Sonia at once, seated on Rouillard's right where he held pride of place at the head of the table. She turned ghostly pale and half rose from her chair as the detail crossed the threshold with him a prisoner among them. Rouillard seized her arm, dragging her back down beside him.

She shimmered in the candlelight, a vision in silk and lace and with flowers nestled against the coiled coronet of her hair. The consummate lady, refined, delicately scented compared to his vinegar-and-corn-husk smell, his bearded face and ragged hair. She was so far above him that he grew dizzy from the height. Nevertheless, the longing to take her somewhere, hold her close against him, skin to skin, heart to heart, slammed into him like a sledgehammer blow. The sight of Rouillard's hand on her arm, holding tight around pale skin that already carried bruising, was a knife thrust to his vitals.

Kerr knotted his fists, took a step forward. Crossed rifles came up to block his way. It was the reminder he needed to lock down his rage, to wait, to plan.

Across the space that separated them, he met Sonia's eyes. For that moment, she was the only thing that existed in his world. No one else mattered, not Tremont who sat on the other side of her, not her tante Lily next to him. No, there were only her eyes, wide, dark, filled with a thousand memories.

Those same moments bombarded him like so many thrown stones in that instant: her tears in the rain, the moment when she slid down a drainpipe and into his arms; a kiss with fury and desire behind it; the swim to shore after the shipwreck; the deathly stillness of the jungle as she let him cut the thorn from her foot; her surrender upon an ancient altar, her riding him with the fierce pleasure of a Valkyrie. Memories to last a lifetime, or reason enough to die without regret.

"Well, look what we have here." Rouillard released Sonia and pushed back his chair, slouching down in it. "The entertainment of the evening."

Kerr fastened his gaze on the man's face. He wanted to wipe the snide smile from it, smash his loose, wet mouth that might have touched Sonia's lips, grind him into the dust.

"What do you mean?" he heard Sonia ask, the words even enough though he could hear the dismay that lay beneath them.

"Why, just what I said, *chère*. You ought to find it amusing since it was this man who forced you to board the ship that brought you. I should be grateful to him for that much, and would be if he had not forced so much more upon you."

"No," she whispered, a strangled sound.

"Monsieur!" Tante Lily said in protest, while Tremont, next to her, looked grim.

"No?" Rouillard shook his head. "You'll have to be more explicit, I think. Are you saying no force was required, that unlike with my invitation to dance, you did not refuse this barbarian?"

"Leave her alone," Kerr said in a warning so gruff it hurt his throat.

Rouillard turned his bulbous gaze on Kerr. "But how can I? These things must be made clear before marriage. A man should know what kind of woman he's taking to wife."

Kerr couldn't stand this deliberate humiliation for Sonia. "You know or you wouldn't have demanded she be sent to you. Let it be."

"But her condition is not the same as when she left her father's care, now, is it? I want to know the extent of it, and whether she went willingly to your bed or was hauled there."

Sonia drew a sharp breath, a perfectly audible sound in the quiet.

"Mon Dieu," Tante Lily whispered.

If he said she had come to him willingly, Kerr saw, she would be branded a wanton. If he said he had taken her against her will, he could be hanged out of hand for it. The law might wink at such summary justice by a wronged fiancé in the United States. How likely was it to notice such a thing here in a Latin country like Mexico?

Once more, he met Sonia's eyes, saw the terror that had surfaced there, half drowned by tears. He chose his course in the blink of an eye.

"Mademoiselle Bonneval is without fault."

"Stop this, *monsieur,* stop it at once," she cried, turning on Rouillard. "You have no cause to hold Monsieur Wallace. Release him now, tonight, and I give you my word I will speak my marriage vows at your side tomorrow."

Her terror had been for him, Kerr realized. So was this greatest of all sacrifices. It was the most precious gift he had ever received. It heated his heart, closed his throat so he could find no words for the protest inside him.

It also set his brain in fierce motion. It gave him the bare glimmer of a way out.

Triumph spread over Rouillard's face. "How magnanimous of you, my own Sonia. I am delighted. Tremont, my friend, you heard the bargain."

Tremont waved a hand, though his distaste for the scene did not leave his features.

"There, that's done." He gave Sonia a snide smile. "Shall we plan the nuptials, you and I, and the breakfast afterward? Or should I leave it to you and your aunt?"

"Not so fast," Kerr said, his voice carrying the lash of a whip. He went on at once in the manner prescribed by the code duello. "You have impugned my honor, sir, and that of the lady. I demand satisfaction."

Stillness pervaded the room. The guard next to Kerr sent an uneasy glance across him to his counterpart.

"You demand?" A guffaw broke from Rouillard. "In case you haven't noticed, Wallace, you're in no position to demand anything."

"Meet me or stand recognized as a coward before every man in this room, and also before the lady you are to marry."

Craftiness appeared in the other man's face. "You're a master swordsman. It would be legal murder."

"Leave on the chain." He gave it a contemptuous shake, making it rattle as it trailed behind him on the floor. "That should even the odds."

"No," Sonia whispered, a mere zephyr of sound as her gaze lingered on the blood-stiffened area of his hair. "Not now, not after—"

"Wait, *chère*," her aunt said, her fine eyes narrowing as she looked from Kerr to her niece and back again.

"It's a start," Rouillard drawled.

"What more could you want?" It should be enough, Kerr thought, given the headache that had returned to pound across the top of his head. Apparently, he had not allowed for the depth of the man's self-interest.

"It's my privilege as the challenged party to propose the terms of this duel. I claim the right to choose a champion to fight in my place." Rouillard waved in the direction of the dark-haired man on Sonia's right. "My friend here has some skill with a blade, I believe. I choose Monsieur Tremont."

Kerr's gaze flashed to that of the other man. Tremont appeared thoughtful, almost as if his mind was elsewhere.

"Well, *monsieur*," Rouillard asked, "do you accept the substitute?"

It wasn't what Kerr had intended. His idea, as far as it went, had been to convince Sonia's fiancé of the stupidity of moral blackmail in persuading a woman to become his wife or, at the very least, injure him so badly it would be some time before he could perform the duties of a husband. That was, if he didn't kill him.

The last was his preference.

None of these aims applied to Tremont, yet the man had stopped the diligence and carried off Sonia. It would be no hardship to give him reason to regret both moves. Any meeting was better than none.

He still didn't like it.

"Hiding behind Tremont, Rouillard?" he queried.

The man grunted. "Call it what you will. I freely admit to a lack of skill with the sword, and you're far taller than I so have an advantage in reach. It would be suicide to face you."

The admission was a good move; Kerr had to give him that. It even sounded reasonable to him. The arrangement seemed as much as he was going to be allowed under the circumstances, especially when he had expected to be refused any chance at all. At least he would have a sword in his hand, which was the main point.

"I accept your terms," he said with a hard nod. "That is, if the meeting can take place at once."

Rouillard smiled, his eyes gleaming. "I see no objection."

It was what the man had intended, Kerr thought. Why was that, unless he wanted Sonia to see what he expected to be her lover's defeat? Kerr glanced around, weighing the lighted room with its limited space as a venue against the open courtyard with limited visibility. The room would suffice. First things first, however.

Turning toward his countryman, he sketched a truncated bow. "Sir?"

"As you will." Tremont sighed, then straightened and pushed back his chair. The answering bow he gave then was a model of grace and resignation.

It was also a gesture of respect of the kind one swordsman accords another. Kerr's eyes narrowed as he saw it. He wasn't quite sure, suddenly, just what he had gotten himself into, but one thing he knew for certain. The only thing he could do was fight his way out of it.

Twenty-Seven

Sick disbelief hovered in Sonia's mind. This could not be happening. Quarrels might end in duels, but there were strict rules to be followed, safeguards to be set in place. The arrangement going forward was like some barbaric forerunner of such practices, a mere bloodletting in which the hand of God must decide the victor.

Jean Pierre sent the captain of his guard for a matched set of rapiers. Tremont, with apologies to her and her aunt, removed his long frock coat and waistcoat and began to turn back his shirtsleeves. Maidservants scurried to clear the table and push it to the wall then remove the chairs. Jean Pierre led Sonia and her aunt to one side of the dining salon, next to the table, and Kerr's guard ranged themselves alongside the other.

Kerr stood alone.

Sonia's heart ached to see him there in the empty center of the room, surrounded by enemies. His hair was matted to the back of his head by dried blood; his shirt was spotted with rust-red stains, his trousers torn and crude sandals loose and split. Despite it all, he was more valiant than any man in the room, more armored in dignity and courage. He faced them down and waited for his fate with his fists knotted at his sides. And his silver-gray eyes, as he met hers, were clear and steady. They promised he had not forgotten his vow to keep her safe, and would not abandon it even now.

Or so she wanted to think. It might be nothing more than a fancy brought forth by her need.

"Sonia, *ma chère,*" Tante Lily said with compassion in her voice as she leaned close, "I believe we should withdraw. This is not a spectacle for ladies."

Rouillard turned his gaze upon her. "By no means. I won't allow it."

"But our presence cannot be necessary."

"I disagree." His smile held cold spite. "It's essential."

Sonia had suspected as much. Jean Pierre wished her to witness what he expected to be Kerr's defeat. It was the main point of the exercise.

It wasn't the whole point, however. That much was soon made clear.

"Shouldn't you send for a blacksmith to remove the shackle from my opponent?" Tremont made the inquiry in grave tones, his gaze on Jean Pierre as he folded his sleeves to the elbow.

"I don't believe so." Sonia's betrothed did not bother to hide his amusement. "He offered to meet me wearing it. He can do the same with you."

The captain of the guard returned then with a sword box under his arm. Placing it on the table near Rouillard, he unfastened the latch and laid back the lid. Tremont picked up one of the pair of rapiers and sighted along its blade as he spoke again. "You can't be saying you think me unable to prevail unless my opponent has a handicap?"

Some intimation in Tremont's tone, pleasant as it had been, drove a degree of the satisfaction from Jean Pierre's face. "Certainly not. But why throw away an advantage when it's given to you?"

"Fairness," Tremont said, setting the first rapier aside and taking up the other. "Honor."

"Oh, those. Very useful at times but a liability when life or death is at stake."

Sonia, hearing the deadly intent in her fiancé's voice, felt her blood congeal in her veins. Frantically, she tried to think of some way to stop the madness.

Tremont flicked a glance toward where Kerr stood with his feet spread and his chain curling behind him. "Life or death, is it? What of the concept of first blood?"

"What use is that to me?" Jean Pierre gave an abrupt laugh as he looked at Kerr and away again. "The *Kaintuck* devil will never leave me in peace. I prefer to be rid of him, once and for all."

A soft snort left Tremont. He turned slowly, rapier in his hand as he sighted down it, turned until it was pointing at Jean Pierre's belly. "This duel is irregular enough, taking place as it is without mediation, minus seconds or a doctor. More isn't required."

Jean Pierre eyed the rapier, licked his lips. "What are you suggesting?"

"I am not a murderer," Tremont answered with quiet precision. "Remove his shackle or fight your own duel."

Tante Lily gripped Sonia's arm, her nails biting into the skin. She barely felt it as she waited for Jean Pierre's answer.

He darted a look toward Kerr and back again. "You can't mean it."

"I assure you, I do."

The quick anger of a weak man appeared in his eyes then. "Have it your way. It's your funeral."

Tremont replaced the rapier in the case, smiling grimly down at it as he seated it in its satin bed. "Or not," he said.

Time ceased to have meaning. Events moved forward at an alarming pace even as they seemed to take an age to be accomplished.

A maidservant was sent for the key to the shackle on Kerr's ankle. She returned with the valet who made short work of removing it and hauling it away with its attached chain. At Tremont's request, lines were drawn on the floor in accordance with accepted practice for meetings of honor, markers to show the limits of advance and retreat. The two principals took their places. Each chose a rapier. Their blades swept up and down in salute.

"Mademoiselle Bonneval," Tremont called from where he stood. "Have you a handkerchief?"

She fumbled one from the pocket at her waist, her fingers sliding over the pocketknife that weighted it before she drew out the bit of lace. "I do, yes."

"Excellent. You will call for the guard position, pause

until we are ready, and then drop the handkerchief as the signal to begin."

She didn't want the responsibility, couldn't bear to think the two men would fight on her command. Still, who else was there for the office? Not the guard captain who had joined his men where they had propped their weapons against the wall as they exchanged spirited wagers over the outcome. Her aunt was too high colored, as if on the verge of apoplexy. Jean Pierre could hardly be trusted to make it a fair start.

No, she had to do it.

They were waiting, Kerr and Tremont. Shoulders squared, heads high, they watched each other, assessing—what? Will, perhaps, along with stamina and intention. Nothing in the stance of either man hinted at the desperate nature of the contest, nothing gave notice that in a few minutes one of them could die.

Sonia cleared her throat with a low rasp, swallowing against the tightness that threatened her breathing. Closing her eyes, she drew a quick breath, called out in clear instruction.

"En garde!"

Two blades flashed upward in unison, coming together at their tips with a bell-like clang. They held steady, welded in place by the muscles of both men that corded their forearms under layers of skin and coverings of fine dark hair. Their eyes clashed as well, narrowing in concentration that seemed to exclude all else. Breathing in steady repose, they waited.

Sonia's fingers on her handkerchief trembled, tightening into a death grip as she lifted it high. They would not unclench. She could not make them, could not bear to begin this vicious contest.

Her hesitation lasted a moment, became two. A murmur ran back and forth across the room.

Kerr allowed his attention to stray in her direction. He met her eyes once more, his own dauntless in its encouragement. He gave an almost imperceptible nod.

The handkerchief dropped from her fingers, fluttering free. It rippled in a draft of air from the open French doors, swayed, sank to the floor.

Tremont sprang into an attack. Kerr parried with a hard scrape of blades that struck sparks in an orange rain. With a powerful bunching of shoulder muscles, he threw the other man back.

"Well done," Tremont said. "I had wondered at your level of expertise. Now I know."

"It's a beginning," Kerr said.

Tremont laughed, a short sound of real amusement. "As you say."

They settled into a round of moderate advances and retreats as they felt each other out for strengths and weaknesses. The tapping of their blades was rhythmic, like a clanging of bells as it bounced off the walls and out the doors to echo in the stone-walled courtyard below. Neither man was breathing hard as yet, but the sheen of perspiration washed their faces and dampened their shirts in a triangle across the back.

Sonia didn't want to watch but neither could she look away. She was mesmerized by the display of raw male power, fascinated by the speed with which they moved and the bright, flickering dance of the swords.

They seemed tireless, almost inhuman in their endurance. They lunged, feinted, shuffled back and forth with their footsteps whispering on the floor. Attack, parry, riposte, the moves they made were as formal as a minuet. Advancing and retreating again and again, they seemed to see nothing except the blades in front of their faces and their opponent's eyes behind them. They drove each other, invited and defended as if they had no audience, and needed none.

Following a particularly hard-and-fast exchange, Kerr laughed, a breathless sound. "You have some skill yourself, Tremont. Are you sure you aren't a *maître d'armes?*"

"My father had that title but not I. He trained me for other things."

"Congratulate him for me. He's a good teacher."

"I would do that, but he's dead."

"Not by the sword."

"Rather by an idiot with a pistol and a quart of strong drink in him. There was not an ounce of honor in it."

Jean Pierre, at Sonia's side, exclaimed under his breath with impatience. "End it," he called out. "For the love of *le bon Dieu,* end it."

Sonia felt very nearly the same. The snick and grating slide of blades tore at her nerves. The whistling of them made her cringe. The leaping twists to avoid a thrust, the sway of the torso to let bright death slide past made her heart jump and shudder as if her own body was at risk.

More than that, she thought Kerr was tiring. His frown came and went, deepening with every passing moment. Sweat trickled along the taut muscle of his jaw. A wet, red trail slid down his neck, staining his shirt in a widening patch. And it was impossible to say whether it was from the dissolving of the matted blood in his hair or the reopening of his scalp wound. Almost without noticing, she slid her hand into her waist pocket and closed her fingers around his pocketknife as around a talisman, for the comfort and the trust in the miraculous.

Tremont's gaze rested on Kerr's stained shirt for an instant. He redoubled his efforts, becoming more aggressive in his attacks. Kerr parried, but his movements were not as clean, his ripostes lacked their crisp edge.

Abruptly, Kerr slipped on the tile floor, or so it appeared. Sonia screamed. Tante Lily moaned and clamped her hands to her mouth while Jean Pierre exclaimed in triumph as if he thought the match at an end.

Tremont thought it as well, for he leaped forward.

He met a snapping strike like the whip of a scorpion's tail. A rent appeared in his shirt at the waist, and rapidly turned red. Kerr recoiled with no sign of faltering. He lowered his blade, waiting.

"Touché," said Tremont, pressing a hand to his side, exhaling on a short laugh as he looked down at his reddened fingers. "You fooled me."

Kerr inclined his head, his features perfectly composed. "But is it enough?"

"Never!" Jean Pierre shouted. "Begin again."

"Shall we?" Tremont asked.

"Your call." Kerr's face was impassive, the tip of his rapier resting on the floor.

Tremont looked down at the blade in his hand, turned it back and forth so it caught the light. "My curiosity is satisfied, I believe. And I can think of better uses for a sword."

"Curiosity?" Kerr stood loose limbed and at ease, though no one seeing him would make the mistake of thinking him unwary.

Their voices dropped so low then that Sonia had to strain to hear them. The guard looked at each other and shrugged their puzzlement while leaning on the rifles they had lowered as the duel progressed. Jean Pierre scowled, inclining his upper body closer as if he could not make out what they were saying at all.

"My besetting sin, curiosity," Sonia heard Tremont say. "It's time to put it aside and return to the business that brought me here."

"Contraband? Specifically arms and ammunition?"

"You might say so. Actually, it was the traitor who has been running them between Mexico and our sovereign nation, the sometimes great and often benighted United States of America." He lifted a shoulder, his smile a model of irony. "My employer, if you will."

There was more, but Sonia missed it. Hope burst inside her, crowding out all else.

Immediately thereafter, the two duelists turned as one and strode, shoulder to shoulder, toward Jean Pierre. Their swords were ready, their eyes merciless, and there was no one to stop them.

A hunted expression appeared on Jean Pierre's face.

He cursed, flinging a panicked stare at his guard. His mouth opened to let a scream burst from his throat. "Fire your weapons! Fire! Shoot them for the love of God!"

Sonia moved like a silk scarf unfurling, swinging where she stood and drawing out the pocketknife she held in the same moment. She stepped against Jean Pierre and pressed the lethally sharp blade to the pulse that hammered in his thick neck.

"They fire, and you are a very dead man," she said in clear sincerity. "Countermand the order. Now, *mon cher.*"

Twenty-Eight

On a sultry morning eight days later, Kerr and Sonia left Vera Cruz. With Tante Lily, they boarded a Spanish merchantman loaded with corn and tons of some kind of white, rocky ore. It was Tremont who delivered them to the dock in an ugly little carriage called a *volante* that he borrowed from their host of the past week, a gentleman who still used his Spanish title in spite of Republican ties.

This marquis, an elderly man, tall, thin and possessed of a luxuriant white beard he wore in a point at his chin, was apparently a friend of Tremont's with acquaintances among Washington's ambassadorial elite. He had also quickly become a conquest of Tante Lily's. Dressed impeccably, though with a quantity of gold lace on his waistcoat, he presented her and Sonia with bouquets of roses, verbena and oleander tied with yards of ribbon for their voyage, along with his profuse apologies that more of his friends and acquaintances had not come to bid them farewell.

Sonia was just as glad to be spared further speeches, salutations and protestations of the grand pleasure of their company. She only wanted to make for home, putting distance between her and the red-sand hills of Vera Cruz.

Their progress would not be swift. Fears of a blockade had slowed the arrival of the usual steam packets from American ports. Reluctant to stay kicking their heels in Vera Cruz for a moment longer than necessary, they had booked passage for Havana on the Spanish sailing vessel. Still, they should make port in two weeks, transfer to a steamer there in due time, and be at the mouth of the Mississippi in another week after that.

So they stood on the deck, waving to the marquis and Tremont, braving the sun for a last glimpse of the black-and-red walls of the Fort San Juan de Ulúa, the block-like houses behind the city walls, the church spires and great, flapping *zopilotes* that fought over carrion on the sand dunes rolling away from the incredible blue of the water. The lines holding the ship were cast off. They drifted away from the dock, were towed toward open water. Sails billowed above them then. These caught the wind with a resounding crack and they were away.

Tante Lily, standing at the railing next to Sonia, closed her eyes and breathed her thanks to a higher power while making the sign of the cross. When she opened them again, they were more luminous than usual. She turned to Sonia, but her tearful joy faded as she searched her face. "We will soon be home, where you can see your papa again and all your friends, *ma chère*. Are you not in ecstasies?"

"Of course," she agreed, summoning a smile. "I'm just a little tired, that's all."

"As well as a little sad, yes? It's always difficult to leave new friends and I'm sure you feel, as I do, that Monsieur Tremont is such a one. There was the voyage we shared from New Orleans, and then he has been so very kind since...since the business with Jean Pierre."

Those few words—how they brought it all back: the candlelit dining room where the smells of garlic, oil and caramelized sugar lingered, the two men facing each other with swords in hand, the terror and the rage. Sonia had wanted to kill Jean Pierre as she held the pocket-knife to his neck. The need had clawed at her, shaken her body from her head to her toes. She had, in that moment, understood something of the bloodlust that sometimes gripped men on the field of honor.

It was Kerr who had stepped close to put a calming hand on her arm and take the knife from her trembling hand.

What happened afterward was a blur. She hardly remembered being escorted from Jean Pierre's house or arriving at that of the marquis. The days since then seemed disjointed somehow. She had slept the clock around, and did the same the next night, and the next.

She still could not get enough rest. She had spoken to a few people in the days just past: Tremont, the marquis's daughter who was past fifty but looked no more than five-and-thirty, a number of townspeople who had called. Everyone had been so kind, so intent on banishing any unfavorable impression she might have gained of their fair city.

She could not remember exchanging more than a dozen words with Kerr.

He seemed to be avoiding her now. Alone at the prow of the ship, he faced the ocean instead of the land they were leaving behind. He looked well, dressed in a new frock coat, waistcoat and trousers made by the marquis's tailor at Tremont's behest, a gift in repayment for the mild concussion received at his orders. The gray broadcloth matched the depths of his eyes and made his shoulders look as broad as the ship's beam.

It also made him appear unapproachable, impossibly forbidding. He had been that way since it became clear they would be returning together to New Orleans. He fulfilled his duty as her escort, as he seemed to think it continued still, but not an iota more. Beyond the occasional discussion necessary to the position, they seldom spoke, were never alone. All personal contact was at an end.

They had made love for reasons that had little to do with desire and nothing to do with permanency. She had required an excuse to avoid marriage; he had wanted a pretext for a challenge. That neither had worked out as envisioned made no difference since the end was much the same. She had avoided being wed and Kerr had brought low the man who caused the death of his brother. What need was there to touch and hold, to kiss or to sleep in each other's arms?

Sonia clenched her hands into such tight fists that a seam split in her glove. She looked down, smoothing the gap in the leather, forcing her fingers to lie flat on the railing.

"I do wish Monsieur Tremont could have sailed with us," Tante Lily was saying. "I quite see that it will be best to transport his prisoner in an American vessel, of course. I only hope he isn't forced to wait in port for the invasion force he seems certain will come."

"No, indeed," Sonia said, following her aunt's train of thought with desperate concentration. How strange it seemed to think of Tremont as an agent of the United States government, or that the shipment of arms out of New Orleans could be important enough to warrant sending him to investigate the traffic in guns to Mexico. Now Jean Pierre was being held in Tremont's custody for the crime.

What would have happened to her, or to Kerr, if Tremont had not been on hand? She didn't care to think about it.

"You are not still holding a grudge for his abduction of you? He explained his reasons quite well, I felt. I should think you would be grateful it was he who took you and not another of Jean Pierre's hirelings. I shudder to think of the insult you might have suffered, or what injury might have been done to Monsieur Wallace."

"I doubt I would have been harmed. I was Jean Pierre's bride-to-be, after all." About Kerr, she was less certain. His death during the abduction would have been most convenient.

Alex Tremont had volunteered to remove her from the diligence, in part to make certain she was unharmed, but also because he had grown suspicious of Jean Pierre's intentions. He had taken Kerr's measure aboard the *Lime*

Rock, so he said, and was disinclined to allow him to be murdered out of hand. She and Kerr owed the American agent a great deal, when all was taken together.

"I never quite understood the business of the rifles," her aunt complained. "I realize Monsieur Rouillard was importing them into Mexico in partnership with Santa Ana's party. Still, Monsieur Tremont told us himself of their presence aboard the *Lime Rock* when we were hardly out of the Mississippi. Yes, and while Monsieur Wallace was there, as I recall. Did he really believe he might be involved?"

"Apparently so, until he came to know Kerr. Later, when he learned of the enmity between him and Jean Pierre, he knew it was quite impossible that they were working together. In any case, the arms were under the eye of Monsieur Tremont to serve as a trap for Jean Pierre. There was scant danger of them being used against American troops."

"Then the steamer was sunk by the Mexican man-of-war as it attempted to retrieve them. *Quel dommage*."

"Actually, the captain of the man-of-war had no idea they were aboard. His mission was to take the American commissioner traveling with us into custody, in part as a hostage, but also to discover what he knew of American plans in the event of war."

"So it was all a tragedy."

"That the arms sank with the *Lime Rock* was unfortunate, yes, since it removed Monsieur Tremont's excuse for meeting with Jean Pierre. I believe he called upon him to explain the loss, and so the results were the same."

"He was taken up with the other passengers when we were rescued," her aunt said, "but I never saw him questioned."

"He kept his identity concealed from Mexican authorities, he said. I believe the American commissioner may have aided him in that regard."

"Indeed. I've never seen such a to-do as that gentleman made when we reached port. He waved his official papers in everyone's face, demanding to be allowed to return to his country at once and threatening all manner of reprisal against the captain of the Mexican man-of-war for daring fire on civilians, yes, and for sinking a merchant vessel of U.S. registry as well."

"A good point."

"Yes." Tante Lily gave a theatrical shudder. "Let us hope they are more careful of those registered in Spain."

Sonia could only echo the sentiment.

Though they saw several ships on their first two days at sea, none appeared to take the slightest notice of them, much less prove hostile. They made good time, clipping along at five or six knots with a fair wind behind them. Supposing it held, they could expect to be in Havana in something just over a week's time.

It didn't hold.

The winds turned southeasterly, then died away altogether. The sails emptied and hung slack. They were becalmed.

There followed hours of hope when they made some little progress. These were succeeded by days when they were pushed off course and lost all they had gained.

After a week at sea, they could still sometimes catch sight of the peak of Citlaltépetl shining like silver as the sun struck its white snowcap, proof positive they had actually returned to Mexican waters.

The heat was trying, alleviated only somewhat by the cat's paws of wind that now and then rippled the water. Tempers grew short. Fights broke out among the seamen, and the men who gambled away the time in the gentlemen's sleeping cabin often came to blows.

The week at sea became two, and then leaned toward three. On the seventeenth day, the ship's cook, tired of complaints about the fare he put on the table, went temporarily mad and tried to cut off various body parts of his helper with a meat cleaver. On the eighteenth day, it was discovered that an importer of women's sundries from Paris was sleeping in the men's common room wearing nothing except a cream silk shawl with rose-red flowers and gold fringe. On the nineteenth day, Sonia woke with a queasy stomach and, counting back, realized it was highly possible she was going to have a baby.

Arriving in Havana ceased to be important. The greater the delay, the better, or so it seemed, since it meant more time to think before facing her father.

He would be livid. Never in this life would he understand the sequence of events that had led to this conclusion, much less his part in them. The reasons would not matter to him. He would only consider the scandal and how it was to be avoided.

Her papa would doubtless send her away again. She would be shipped forthwith to France or Italy, someplace with an accommodating convent where young women like her could have their babies and leave them with the nuns. Or else she would be married off to anyone who would have her.

As a future, neither course recommended itself to Sonia.

She considered telling Kerr. He had some right to know that he was to be a father, after all. It might make a difference in how he felt toward her.

Oh, but she had no wish to force the obligation upon him. That she had conceived was an accident of nature. There was no need for him to change his life or his future because of it.

Hers would be changed; it was inevitable. Yet what did it matter? After these past weeks, she would never be the same again.

Still, suppose the possibility was important to him? He was a man of deep emotions, stringent concern. Suppose he cared?

Back and forth in her mind she went, back and forth. When the winds finally turned and they sailed free, finally passing El Morro Castle and into the harbor at Havana, she was no closer to a decision.

Their luck changed in the Spanish city with its sleepy streets and mellow church bells. A steamer was leaving within twenty-four hours, and carried empty bunks. They barely had time to complete the formalities of landing and transfer their meager baggage before it would be time to board again.

Suddenly events moved with furious speed. The

Spanish officials stamped their papers, signed them with elegant scrawls, affixed a plethora of ribbons and gold seals and waved them on their way. They had a decent meal at an inn, slept a little and had their laundry done, then made their way back to the quay. The packet steamed out of the harbor and over a sunlit sea, making record time toward New Orleans.

Soon, too soon, the yellow-brown waters of the Mississippi River invaded the blue of the gulf and they were drawn up its mighty flow as if through a giant straw. The stunted oaks, shell mounds and endless sea of saw grass of the lower reaches gave way to moss-draped giants dressed in summer green. Plantation houses appeared amid fields of waving cane and shining cotton. Fishing shacks drifted past, giving way to flat-boats and warehouses until finally they rounded the great crescent that marked the city. And there were the endless ranks of steamers ready to sail, the ships at anchor, the bobbing dinghies, canoes and pirogues. There was the dear and dusty Place d'Armes and the beloved cathedral. There was home.

No one was on the dock to meet them. Her father did not know they were returning, much less when they would arrive. Time in Havana had been too short to write, since they had been certain to arrive before a letter. Sonia could have written from Vera Cruz in the days while they waited for a ship, but what could she say? To explain on paper was too difficult, too open to misunderstanding. All that was left, then, was to gather their belongings once more, her and Tante Lily, and descend the gangway. They might as well walk the short distance to the town house since they had so little to carry.

Sonia turned away from watching the steamer dock. Picking up her skirts, she moved back in the direction of the cabin where Tante Lily was packing.

"Wait."

Sonia halted, her throat tightening at the sound of that deep, rough voice. Her lips trembled into a polite smile of the kind she and Kerr had been exchanging for days as she made herself face him.

"Were you going to leave without a word, without even a polite goodbye?"

He leaned on the bulkhead with one shoulder, his hat in his hand and a small valise at his feet. The breeze off the river ruffled his hair into a wild mane and narrowed his eyes to silver gleams. He was far too attractive, and too dear, to be dismissed, and she didn't try.

"No, never." She stepped toward him, holding out her hand. "I am pleased to have this chance to thank you yet again, *monsieur*. You have been everything that is kind and generous on this journey, the perfect escort. I owe you more than I can ever repay. And you may be sure that I shall never...never forget you."

He took her hand, lifted it to his lips as he executed the graceful bow he had learned at some point during their venture together. "That sounds as if you expect never to see me again."

"Does it?" She had thought she probably never would, except perhaps from a distance. Abruptly, that seemed insupportable. Her ambivalence of the past several days fell away as if it had never been. Between one breath and the next, between her greeting and farewell, she knew what she must do. "I do apologize," she went on with scarcely a pause. "There is one last duty as my escort and protector that you may perform, if you will."

The straight line of his mouth lifted into a wry smile, one that brought the slashing dimple in his cheek to life. "Command me."

"Command me…"

She felt a little faint as her memory brought forth the last time he had said those words. Her face went hot, and she thought her very bones would melt. The answering heat in his gaze gave her hope, and courage. "I would be grateful if you would see me and my aunt to the town house."

He sobered. "I'll be—"

"This isn't a part of the job you undertook, I know," she went on before he could say more. "I'm sure you have other things to do, other things you're anxious to see about now that you're here."

"Truly, *mademoiselle…*"

"It isn't that I'm afraid to face Papa or to confess that I'm not married, or even—"

He released her hand, placed a finger to her lips. "I never intended anything else," he said when she fell silent. "Your father should have a report from me of just what happened in Vera Cruz."

"You meant to come."

"I would not leave you to face him alone."

"You feel responsible. I might have known."

He hesitated, then gave a determined nod and clapped his hat on his head. "It's time we put this behind us. I'll be at the top of the gangway when you're ready."

He meant to go on with his life once his part in the arrest of Jean Pierre was explained, once she was settled. She could hardly blame him. Still, she had one last chance left to make things right. Pray to *le bon Dieu* it was enough.

Twenty-Nine

Tante Lily's smile was roguish as she came toward him, as if she knew a secret but would not tell. Kerr gave her a bow and took the carpetbag she carried, but looked immediately to Sonia who walked a step or two behind her aunt.

He had been right earlier. She was pale again this morning, and her gown, admittedly not from the hands of the most fashionable modiste in the world, was looser than it had been when they left Vera Cruz. She had not been eating well, this he knew; little she had said or done in the past weeks had escaped his notice. Her skin was so translucent he could see the network of blue veins under it, and the shadows under her eyes matched the lavender ribbons that tied her bonnet.

Kerr frowned as he thrust her aunt's bag under his arm, picked up hers and his own valise in the other and followed her and her aunt down the gangway. She was not looking forward to the confrontation with her father, he was sure, but he hadn't thought she'd make herself sick worrying over it.

He should have been more attentive. She had seldom been out of his sight, but he had kept as far from her as possible and still be on the same ship. To be near made him ache to touch her, to touch her made him ache to have her, to feel that desperate need was to act upon it—and that wouldn't do. He had served his purpose for her in that manner. She needed nothing more from him. And he couldn't breathe the same air and be satisfied with less.

He'd thought it best that he keep his distance. Now he wasn't so sure. She still might have need of a protector.

At the foot of the gangway, he handed off the bags he carried to a pair of young black boys hanging around for that kind of custom, passing out a coin with each bag and directing them to the proper addresses. Giving an arm to each of the ladies, he headed toward the rue Royale.

It occurred to him, when halfway to the town house, that Monsieur Bonneval might not have returned from his trip upriver. Sufficient time had passed for the journey itself, but there was no way of knowing how long his business might have required. The question in Kerr's mind was whether the expedition might have some bearing on his association with Rouillard. If so, the gentleman needed to be made aware of certain facts. He also required instruction in the worth of his daughter and how she should be treated.

The carpetbags of the ladies arrived at the town house before them. Kerr flipped the boys who had brought them another coin, then followed Sonia and her aunt inside. The butler, called Eugene by Tante Lily as he grinned a welcome, mounted the stairs ahead of them with the bags while telling them over his shoulder that Monsieur Bonneval was in the salon. He left them at the door to that chamber, which stood open to the mild air of early summer.

Sonia's papa had heard them coming, it seemed. He was on his feet when they stepped through the door, a ponderous frown pleating the skin between his brows. Folding his news sheet with precision, he set it on the table beside his chair before coming toward them.

"What is this?" he asked in blank reproof as he exchanged bows with Kerr, kissed his sister-in-law on either cheek and performed the same perfunctory ritual for his daughter. "Please tell me you have not thrown away the expense of your wedding journey and your trousseau and shamed the man you were to marry. Explain to me at once why you are here instead of with Jean Pierre in Mexico."

Sonia turned white and swayed where she stood. Kerr, taking her arm, guided her to a settee and stationed himself behind its back. It was Tante Lily who rustled forward, answering as if the extraordinary questions had actually been civil. "You would not believe the adventures we have had, *monsieur!* What frights, what indescribable terrors. We have been shot at by a Mexican warship, shipwrecked—"

"Shipwrecked, *madame?*"

"But, yes. You are amazed, as who would not be, but I swear it's the truth." She walked to the bellpull beside the fireplace and gave it a tug. "I was myself taken prisoner aboard the Mexican man-of-war as well, and that is only the beginning. Let us have sherry and perhaps cake and savories to sustain us, and you shall hear all about it."

The recital took place much as Tante Lily outlined. She did most of the talking, applying to Sonia or to Kerr only on rare occasions as an aid to memory. An excellent job she did of it, too, sidestepping all mention of his and Sonia's separate escape from capture. That was, until she got to the part where the two of them arrived at Rouillard's place, and he was clapped in a makeshift cell.

"One moment, if you please," Bonneval said, raising his hand to call a halt, his gaze searching Kerr's face. "Why was this? What cause had you given for it?"

"None," Kerr answered, his voice a low growl.

"I find that difficult to believe. Monsieur Rouillard is not an unreasonable man."

Sonia's aunt drew breath, her eyes snapping with annoyance, but it was Sonia who replied.

"On the contrary, Papa, he is so unreasonable he thought he could get away with running guns to Mexico, also with abducting me and trying to have Kerr killed. You arranged my betrothal to a scoundrel, one who has been arrested for his crimes."

"Ridiculous. I will hear no further such insult on your lips. But there is something here I don't understand." He turned to Tante Lily. "Where was Monsieur Wallace that he did not arrive with you, *madame?* How could Rouillard have cause to put him in chains when he had never set eyes on him? What possible reason could he have for such action?"

"The answers to your questions are quite simple, Papa," Sonia answered in her stead. "Monsieur Wallace and I were not with Tante Lily. We were alone in the Mexican jungle for some little time, then again at the home of the Mexican lady who gave us shelter and then while traveling to Vera Cruz by diligence."

Her father reared back his head in shock. "*Mon Dieu.* Your fiancé sent you back to me because you had been compromised."

"Not at all. He was quite willing to marry me in spite of it."

"Then you will return to Mexico at once and become his wife. There is nothing else for it, nothing for you."

"Now there is where you're wrong," Kerr drawled. "Dead wrong."

"You will keep out of this, *monsieur.* You have caused quite enough trouble."

"More than you know, Papa. He is the father of the child I will have in something close to eight months."

Bonneval seemed to swell where he stood. Taking a quick step toward his daughter, he raised his hand.

Kerr moved with the deadly swiftness of a parry in a duel's heat. He caught Bonneval's arm, twisted it down and then up again behind his back. He could have broken it, might have if he had not realized, suddenly, what Sonia had said. Shoving Bonneval into a chair, he turned to face her.

She was going to have his child, yet she looked

thinner than when he had first seen her, first touched her by wiping black tears from her face. It didn't seem possible. Regardless, he wanted it to be true with a fierce longing that stunned him, left him naked and defenseless in his need.

"If she marries anyone," he said, feet spread and knotted fists at his sides, "it will be me."

Behind him, her father gave a harsh laugh though his features were pinched and gray. "Impossible. I'll have no *Kaintuck* for a son-in-law. I'll disinherit her and her bastard with her. No spawn of such a one will have a penny of what's mine."

"Keep it," Kerr said. "We won't need it."

Soft rose color rose in Sonia's face. Rising, she came to stand beside him, putting a hand on his arm as she turned with him to face her father.

"You are in no position to dictate terms, Papa," she said, her voice a little husky but steady. "The fate that came to Jean Pierre could also come to you. A gentleman we met on the *Lime Rock,* Monsieur Alexander Tremont, used his good offices to see to it that your name was not mentioned in connection with these contraband weapons imported by Jean Pierre. It was a matter of friendship, you see, his friendship with Kerr. But he knows, we all know, that you were closely involved."

"Nonsense," Bonneval croaked.

"I don't think so. Rouillard tried to talk his way out of the trouble he was in, you perceive. He told Tremont that you were closely involved, that you arranged to have the guns shipped from upriver while on these business trips of yours."

"It was an investment, no more," Bonneval said, grasping the arms of his chair, pressing back as if to get away from the accusations. "I had no idea what was being bought and sold at first. Then it was too late. Rouillard said, he threatened—"

"How it happened makes no difference," Sonia told him, her voice gaining strength as her father's bombast faded. "What matters is that it should stop. With war officially declared, the business could well become a hanging matter. And I don't believe my future husband would care to have that kind of scandal in his family."

The silence was instant and complete. Bonneval stared at his daughter. Kerr did the same while wild elation spiraled up inside him. She was valiant and intelligent, this woman of his, and she knew how to fight for what she wanted. He had no idea if what she needed was him or simply any man not Rouillard, but he intended to find out before either of them was a day older.

"Have it your way," her father said. He looked away from her, his face settling into lines that made him seem suddenly old. "Maybe you're right, maybe this is best. I was never happy sending you to Jean Pierre, but he came from good stock, and placed great value on having you as his wife." Papa Bonneval stopped, steadied his voice that had developed a quaver. "He hinted at ruin, you know, if I looked elsewhere for a husband."

"You were afraid of him."

Her father tried to grimace. "Rather, of what he could do. Once he was married to you, so I thought, our family name would be safe. I had no idea he would ever lift a hand to you. If I had, you would never have left New Orleans. I could not bring myself to watch you leave, even as it was."

"Oh, Papa," she whispered, and went to kneel before him, taking his hands in hers.

It was not the kind of thing a stranger should witness. Kerr stepped away and walked from the room.

He didn't go far, only to the far corner of the gallery. Putting his shoulder to the post there, he pulled a leaf from the wisteria vine that twined around it. He stood shredding it, dropping bits into an empty bird's nest just below the railing, as he watched the noonday shadows grow shorter in the courtyard below.

He knew to the second when Sonia left the salon at last and began to walk toward him. Turning, he watched her approach, the graceful glide of her walk, the rippling edges of her skirts, the way she smiled, the way she held her head—not with pride as he had once thought but with confidence. His body reacted in the way he'd grown used to, with sudden hardening and a drawing ache of yearning. But beneath it was something different, something richer and truer that approached reverence.

That he had held her in his arms and made love to her in all the myriad ways that a man with time on his hands could imagine was a miracle to him. He would never forget it as long as he could draw breath. That it might never happen again was a desperate darkness in his mind. But he could not allow her to sacrifice herself to his desire in this any more than he could have, finally, in Mexico.

Thirty

"Here you are," Sonia said as she neared Kerr. A little of her glad assurance faded as she surveyed the grim look on his face. "I was afraid you had gone."

"I wouldn't do that." Folding his arms over his chest, he put his back to the gallery post. "You made things up with your papa?"

"He seems all right now with whatever I do." She gave a small shake of her head. "He isn't a bad man or even an unreasonable one, really. It's only that he isn't used to thinking of how others may feel, and he turns stubborn when he knows he's in the wrong."

"A lot of us are like that," Kerr answered at his most laconic. "I waited because there are things that need to be said between us."

Hope, so very new inside her, faltered along with her smile. "Yes, I...I owe you an apology. I should have told you about the baby."

"You should," he agreed evenly.

"I was afraid you would feel responsible."

"And why not? I am responsible."

She looked down at her clasped hands. "You see? I knew how it would be."

"Some things a man has to own up to if he wants to call himself a man."

His voice had softened a fraction. It gave her the courage to at least try to explain. "But I didn't want you to feel caught by it like another shackle holding you. I still don't. Despite what you said to my father, you are not obligated to marry me."

"What if I want to be caught, if I can't wait to be obligated?"

She looked up, her eyes widening. "You really mean…"

He gave a hard nod, speaking with such precision every syllable seemed etched in stone. "More than anything on God's green earth, I want it. I want to hold and protect you all your days, Sonia Bonneval, to take you and our babe back to Kentucky with me and make a home there you'll never want to leave. I want to lie with you warm and safe in our bed while the rain falls on the roof and the winter winds howl. I want to stand with you on the porch while we watch our cotton bloom and our children grow as tall and strong as the mountains. I want—"

"You want to turn me into a *Kaintuck* woman," she said while tenuous joy unfurled inside her. His declaration was a tribute beyond price for such a man of few words.

"It's a fine thing to be, I promise. *Kaintuck* women are proud and free. They speak their minds and make people listen. They love hard and they love long, they latch on to what they want and never let go. They stand by their men and fight for what's right—and they teach their children to be just like them."

"They love?"

"Something desperate," he answered at once, "especially when they have a man who adores them from the topmost hair on their head to the smallest scar on their heel. I do adore you, Sonia, with every breath I take and every last beat of my heart."

She closed her eyes because not being able to see his face was the only way to say what she must. "Particularly since I'm going to have your child."

"You don't believe me. You think it's duty talking. I would have spoken during our days at sea, but thought you didn't need me, that there was no place for me in your life."

"You thought our agreement was at an end, and your position as my escort along with it."

"You could put it that way. Dear God, Sonia, to be near and not touch you was impossible, yet any hint of a tie between us on board ship would have been fodder for the gossips by the time we docked in New Orleans. The best thing I could do for you was to keep well away."

"So you may have thought," she said as she lifted her lashes, meeting his eyes with all the anguish she had felt during the long weeks at sea, "but you didn't ask me."

He opened his mouth as if he would demand to know how she would have answered, then closed it tightly again. Reaching into his frock-coat pocket, he drew out a parcel wrapped in ivory silk brocade. He stood for a moment, gazing down at it. Abruptly, he thrust it toward her.

"What is this?" she asked, taking it carefully in her hands.

"Open it." The words were gruff, determined.

She did so with care, folding back the silk wrapping, pulling the edges aside. When she was done, she held a confection of lace-edged white silk attached to carved ivory sticks and decorated with a silk tassel. A low sound, part sigh, part sob, left her throat.

"I took your fan while we were on the *Lime Rock*. You could call this a replacement, if you like."

She lifted her gaze to his, her eyes wet with unshed tears. "But it's a wedding fan."

"So the old gentleman said who sold it to me. It came all the way from Spain where it was made by the nuns. He said it would make a good beginning for a wedding basket, the *corbeille de noce* a man gives his bride in places like New Orleans. That's if I was so minded."

The strain in his voice, and the pain, reached her through the distress in her mind. She searched his face, seeing in it lines of sleeplessness that matched her own, also the ache of uncertainty.

She thought the love and compassion inside her would cause her heart to burst.

"Were you?" she whispered. "Were you so minded, that is?"

"I was. Then I remembered how one morning on deck I watched that fan of yours fluttering in the wind while I held it in my hands. Seemed it was trying to get away from me, just like you had been doing."

"You kept it safe regardless." The point was important, at least to her.

"Until I lost it when I stripped off my coat after the ship sank." He shook his head. "The thing is, you're still being held. It's not me that's trapped here."

"You think I'm trapped because I'm going to have a baby?" She lifted the fan from its silk wrappings before draping them over the nearby railing. Carefully, then, she spread the sticks so the strong yet delicate beauty of the lace was displayed. It was a lovely thing, but lovelier still was the thought behind it, and the implied vow.

Kerr Wallace did not take such things lightly. He never would. Nor would she.

"Aren't you? Your papa, your friends, your people will all expect you to marry. I'd be proud and honored to stand beside you, but don't know that you want me for a husband any more than you wanted Rouillard."

"Oh, Kerr," she said, her lips forming a tremulous smile. "We are all trapped in our fates. Whether they are mean and evil or good and joyous depends on the choices we make. Being truly trapped means never having a choice, or never making one. I have alternatives, really, I do. Hippolyte Ducolet would probably marry me if asked, and would be an amiable and undemanding husband. I could travel abroad a few years and return with a tale of being widowed. Or I could give birth at a French convent and allow the baby to be adopted. All these things would mean a return to boring respectability. I don't want that, I never did. I made my choice in a jungle temple in Mexico. Oh, yes, I gave you careful reasons, but never the one that mattered most. The truth is, I wanted you then and I want you now. I choose you as my husband, Kerr Wallace. Though I would like to return to New Orleans now and again to see my papa and Tante Lily, I want to live with you in Kentucky, to be with you for all the things you described. I want, so very much, to be a *Kaintuck*'s woman."

The gladness that rose in his face was like a shout. Still, his gray gaze remained shadowed, as if he was not entirely convinced. Stepping closer, he waded into her skirts, setting his hands at her waist to draw her against him. "You're sure?"

"Quite sure."

"Atrocious French accent and all?"

"I've grown quite fond of the way you speak, particularly when you say…" She whispered the words against his ear as she flowed against him, clasping the precious betrothal fan in one hand as she slid the other behind his head.

He groaned and pulled her closer, taking her mouth as if dying for the taste of her, the contact, the merging. She clung to him, sliding her arms around his neck and returning kiss for kiss, pressing against him as she had longed to for these many weeks, unable to get close enough. The pain of it was very nearly equal to the glory, even as it threatened to escalate beyond what might be respectable even for a newly engaged pair.

"God, Sonia," he whispered in entreaty as he released her lips, "when can we have the wedding?"

Drawing away a fraction, she swept her fan back and forth between them, cooling the searing flush that mantled her cheeks as well as the heat she could feel across the back of his neck. "Soon, *mon cher Kaintuck*," she murmured, her smile bright, the words glorious with promise. "Soon."

* * * * *

Be sure to watch for the next book in
the MASTERS AT ARMS *series,*
TRIUMPH IN ARMS
by Jennifer Blake.
Coming in February 2010.

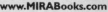

REQUEST YOUR FREE BOOKS!

2 FREE NOVELS
FROM THE ROMANCE/SUSPENSE
COLLECTION PLUS 2 FREE GIFTS!

YES! Please send me 2 FREE novels from the Romance/Suspense Collection and my 2 FREE gifts (gifts are worth about $10). After receiving them, if I don't wish to receive any more books, I can return the shipping statement marked "cancel." If I don't cancel, I will receive 4 brand-new novels every month and be billed just $5.49 per book in the U.S. or $5.99 per book in Canada, plus 25¢ shipping and handling per book plus applicable taxes, if any*. That's a savings of at least 20% off the cover price! I understand that accepting the 2 free books and gifts places me under no obligation to buy anything. I can always return a shipment and cancel at any time. Even if I never buy another book from the Reader Service, the two free books and gifts are mine to keep forever.

185 MDN EF5Y   385 MDN EF6C

Name _____ (PLEASE PRINT) _____

Address _____ Apt. # _____

City _____ State/Prov. _____ Zip/Postal Code _____

Signature (if under 18, a parent or guardian must sign) _____

Mail to **The Reader Service:**
IN U.S.A.: P.O. Box 1867, Buffalo, NY 14240-1867
IN CANADA: P.O. Box 609, Fort Erie, Ontario L2A 5X3

Not valid to current subscribers to the Romance Collection,
the Suspense Collection or the Romance/Suspense Collection.

Want to try two free books from another line?
Call 1-800-873-8635 or visit www.morefreebooks.com.

* Terms and prices subject to change without notice. N.Y. residents add applicable sales tax. Canadian residents will be charged applicable provincial taxes and GST. Offer not valid in Quebec. This offer is limited to one order per household. All orders subject to approval. Credit or debit balances in a customer's account(s) may be offset by any other outstanding balance owed by or to the customer. Please allow 4 to 6 weeks for delivery. Offer available while quantities last.

Your Privacy: Harlequin is committed to protecting your privacy. Our Privacy Policy is available online at www.eHarlequin.com or upon request from the Reader Service. From time to time we make our lists of customers available to reputable third parties who may have a product or service of interest to you. If you would prefer we not share your name and address, please check here. ☐

BOB08

JENNIFER BLAKE

32454 GUARDED HEART	___ $6.99 U.S.	___ $8.50 CAN.
32405 ROGUE'S SALUTE	___ $6.99 U.S.	___ $8.50 CAN.
32213 DAWN ENCOUNTER	___ $5.99 U.S.	___ $6.99 CAN.

(limited quantities available)

TOTAL AMOUNT	$ _____
POSTAGE & HANDLING	$ _____
($1.00 FOR 1 BOOK, 50¢ for each additional)	
APPLICABLE TAXES*	$ _____
TOTAL PAYABLE	$ _____

(check or money order—please do not send cash)

To order, complete this form and send it, along with a check or money order for the total above, payable to MIRA Books, to: **In the U.S.:** 3010 Walden Avenue, P.O. Box 9077, Buffalo, NY 14269-9077; **In Canada:** P.O. Box 636, Fort Erie, Ontario, L2A 5X3.

Name: _____
Address: _____ City: _____
State/Prov.: _____ Zip/Postal Code: _____
Account Number (if applicable): _____

075 CSAS

*New York residents remit applicable sales taxes.
*Canadian residents remit applicable GST and provincial taxes.

MIRA®

www.MIRABooks.com

MJB0209BL